$P_{re}$ ... wels

"David Hew... ... iters working today. Th... ... how good [he] is. Now, ... finds out."
—Steve Berry, bestselling author of *The Templar Legacy*

"**A really terrific series.**"
—Lee Child, #1 bestselling author of *Nothing to Lose*

## THE GARDEN OF EVIL

"A dark jewel of a thriller . . . A plot as serpentine—and suspense-filled—as the ancient Roman byways through which Costa stalks his prey."
—*Publishers Weekly* (starred review)

"Hewson's latest Nic Costa thriller opens with a shocker that will have series fans reeling. . . . Arturo Pérez-Reverte has long set the gold standard for mixing history, mystery, and modern life into literary stews of mouthwatering flavor and incredible subtlety, but it's time to agree that Hewson now shares that position—and is on the verge of claiming it outright."
—*Booklist* (starred review)

"*The Garden of Evil* is the sixth in the Costa series and is even more gripping than its predecessors. Hewson is a cunning storyteller and the opening is deceptively leisurely. . . . *The Garden of Evil* is impossible to put down."
—*Daily Express*

"Hewson sets his stories so firmly in place that it's possible to go from street to piazza to alley, and almost feel the stones of the walks or touch the stones of the ancient Roman bricks. *The Garden of Evil* is the best book so far in the Costa series, and that's saying a lot, but Hewson takes his plotting here a giant step further than in the usual cop/chase story." —*Toronto Globe & Mail*

"David Hewson is in top form with this novel, taking his readers on a gripping journey through the streets of the Eternal City." —*Choice Magazine*

"Captivating to the final page." —*Scotsman*

"It sizzles with grisly murders, well-drawn characters you will care about, dialogue to envy, and all in a story not to forget." —*Mystery News*

## THE SEVENTH SACRAMENT

"A sophisticated and original thriller that cements David Hewson's burgeoning reputation as one of crime writing's most exciting talents." —*Mystery & Thriller Club* magazine

"The interplay between Hewson's three cops—and between them and the especially rich supporting cast—lifts this novel far above the plot-driven *Da Vinci Code* and its many imitators. A superb mix of history, mystery, and humanity." —*Booklist*

"Every bit as convoluted and awe-inspiring as the Catacombs themselves." —*Mystery Lovers Bookshop News*

"Intricate . . . A mystery whose poignant resolution few readers will anticipate." —*Publishers Weekly*

"Brimming with realism, a touch of romance (which feels inevitable given the assortment of characters), a mystery to solve, and just a pinch of the macabre. It is always a pleasure to recommend David Hewson's series for the sheer joy of experiencing intelligent writing plus the added bonus of the picture-postcard visits to Italy."     —*Mystery News*

"Hewson delivers once again. His ability to combine seemingly innocuous facts and characters into a well-designed and -scripted story line ensures that readers are kept guessing until the end. Those who enjoy a good mystery should certainly consider this author. . . . Difficult to put down. One of the better reads of the summer."
                                                       —*Wichita Times-Record News*

"Rich and intricate . . . with results you won't see coming."
                                                       —*Sullivan County Democrat*

"Hewson spins a compelling tale that educates and entertains."                                       —*Richmond Times-Dispatch*

THE LIZARD'S BITE
#5 on the *Bookseller* (UK) Top 20 Fiction Heatseekers
List 2/9/07

"Told with dashing style, in atmospheric set pieces that capture the theatrical grandeur of Venice and the pockets of miserable squalor behind its splendid façade."
                                                       —*New York Times Book Review*

"This complex novel, a journey to hell and back, is leavened with food and humor and propelled by suspense and action. The atmospherics are extraordinary—Hewson does Venice every bit as well as Tony Hillerman does New Mexico. The ending is particularly satisfying, like watching a multistage finale to a spectacular fireworks display."      —*Boston Globe*

"Hewson takes the story well beyond its genre-bound premise, mixing Venetian ambience and the lore of glassmaking with a multifaceted examination of his characters' dark sides. A richly ambiguous finale only adds to the pleasure."
                                                            —*Booklist*

"Hewson's wonderfully complex and finely paced fourth crime novel . . . Hewson is particularly strong on characterization, revealing each personality subtly and naturally. . . . Newcomers as well as series fans will be enthralled."
                                    —*Publishers Weekly* (starred review)

"Hauntingly evocative . . . a suspenseful story with a surprising conclusion and characters the reader has come to treasure . . . Stylish, literate entertainment."
                                            —*Richmond Times-Dispatch*

### THE SACRED CUT

"Stunning . . . Hewson expertly blends historical material into the text. . . . All this historical detail gives the proceedings a tasty complexity comparable to Pérez-Reverte, but what really makes this novel work is the interplay between the trio of antiestablishment Roman cops. . . . A masterful mix of the high-concept historical thriller and the cynical contemporary Italian procedural."      —*Booklist* (starred review)

"A mesmerizing experience."　　　　—*Houston Chronicle*

"[With] stylish writing and his love of the city . . . Hewson serves up welcome snapshots of Italy much as Donna Leon does in her series set in Venice. . . ."　　　—*Washington Post*

"An intriguing blend of spy novel and serial-killer tale. Hewson's prose is top rate, his recurring characters even more interesting with each novel, his trademark twists as unexpected as always. *The Sacred Cut* is entertainment that challenges, fiction that's a cut above the ordinary."
　　　　　　　　　　　　　　—*Richmond Times-Dispatch*

### THE VILLA OF MYSTERIES

"A complex and satisfying mystery from a master plot maker."　　　　　　　　　　　　　—*Booklist*

"An atmospheric follow-up steeped in dark ritual."
　　　　　　　　　　　　　　—*Publishers Weekly*

"What happens in this titular place is so macabre and nasty it makes for a story you won't soon forget."
　　　　　　　　　　　　　—*Rocky Mountain News*

"Hewson writes a compellingly complex novel, one with numerous twists. Near the end, one surprises—and a second stuns. A haunting portrayal of evil—and damaged women. *The Villa of Mysteries* will leave readers eager for Costa's third adventure."　　　—*Richmond Times-Dispatch*

## A SEASON FOR THE DEAD
A Bill O'Reilly Book Club Selection

"A delicious and compelling view of the public art of Rome and the private intrigues of the Vatican." —*Library Journal*

"*A Season for the Dead*, like *The Da Vinci Code*, is a thriller that takes an unflattering look at the Catholic Church, but is better written and more sophisticated than Dan Brown's phenomenal bestseller. . . . The books differ, too, in that Hewson, far more than Brown or most thriller writers, has a serious concern for character. . . . Intelligent entertainment." —*Washington Post*

"Hewson's suspenseful, fascinating mystery has an appealing detective and many complex characters on both sides of the law. Twisting and turning through Italian history and art, Nic Costa's first case gives the serial murder mystery a new look." —*Dallas Morning News*

"Recurrent litanies of Roman street names and place names provide elegiac punctuation to a string of sadistically inventive murders and much collateral damage. That's pretty much all you need to know about an oft-grisly tale that never quite founders in its slough of lies." —*Los Angeles Times Book Review*

## LUCIFER'S SHADOW
A *Deadly Pleasures* Best Mystery/Crime Novel 2004

"Entertaining [and] fun." —*Kirkus Reviews*

"This intelligent and highly detailed thriller rivals Pérez-Reverte's *The Flanders Panal* in historical intricacy, complexity of motive, and multileveled storytelling. Masterfully plotted . . . Prepare for a devilish ride in which beauty masks wickedness, and righteousness is relative."

—*Booklist* (starred review)

"Good mysteries set in Venice are a growth industry . . . and David Hewson's new book is one of the best in recent memory. . . . Hewson has created a brave and fascinating double strand of linked plots, one set in 1773 and the other in the present. . . . Add horribly believable scenes of violence, enough sex to ensure the city's reputation for romance, as well as great gobbets of food and scenery both splendid and squalid, and you begin to see why *Lucifer's Shadow* is unputdownable."

—*Chicago Tribune*

# The Garden of Evil

## David Hewson

A Dell Book

THE GARDEN OF EVIL
A Dell Book

PUBLISHING HISTORY
Delacorte Press hardcover edition published August 2008
Dell mass market edition / March 2009

Published by
Bantam Dell
A Division of Random House, Inc.
New York, New York

This is a work of fiction. Names, characters, places, and incidents either are the product of the author's imagination or are used fictitiously. Any resemblance to actual persons, living or dead, events, or locales is entirely coincidental.

Library of Congress Catalog Card Number: 2007045762

ISBN 978-0-440-24298-7

Printed in the United States of America

www.bantamdell.com

OPM 10 9 8 7 6 5 4 3 2 1

# The Garden of Evil

# Part One
## The Little Death

One

# One

ALDO CAVIGLIA GLIMPSED HIS REFLECTION IN THE overhead mirror of the crowded 64 bus. He was not a vain man but, on the whole, he approved of what he saw. Caviglia had recently turned sixty. Four years earlier he had lost his wife. There had been a brief, lost period when drink took its toll, and with it his job in the ancient bakery in the Campo dei Fiori, just a few minutes' walk from the small apartment close to the Piazza Navona where they had lived for their entire married life. He had escaped the grip of the booze before it stole away his looks. The grief he still felt marked him only inwardly now.

Today he was wearing what he thought of as his winter Thursday uniform, a taupe woollen coat over a brown suit with a knife-edge crease running down the trousers. In his mind's eye he was the professional man he would have been in another, different life. A minor academic, a civil servant, an accountant perhaps. Someone happy with his lot, and that, at least, was no lie.

It was December the eighth, the Feast of the

Immaculate Conception. Christmas stood on the horizon, its presence finally beginning to make itself known beyond the tawdry displays that had been in store windows for weeks. Every good Catholic would attend mass. The Pope would venerate two famous statues of the Virgin, in the Piazza di Spagna and at Santa Maria Maggiore. Catholic or not, families would flock to the city streets, to shop, to eat, to gossip, to walk around and enjoy the season. In the vast racetrack space of the Piazza Navona, which followed the lines of the Imperial stadium that had preceded it, the stalls occupied almost every last square metre: toys for the children, panini of *porchetta* carved straight from the warm pig's carcass for the parents, and the Christmas witch, La Befana, everywhere, on stockings and pendants, decorations and candies, a half-hideous, half-friendly spectre primed to dispense gifts to the young at Epiphany.

Caviglia gripped the handrail as the bus lurched through the traffic past the stranded temple ruins of Largo di Torre Argentina, smiling at his memories. Theirs had been an uncomplicated, innocent marriage, perhaps because it had never been blessed by children. Even so, for Chiara's sake, he had left out a traditional offering for La Befana—a piece of broccoli, some sausage, and a glass of wine—every year of their marriage, right to the end, when her life was ebbing away like a winter tide retreating gently for the last time. He'd never had the money for expensive presents. Nor did it matter, then or now. The pictures that still remained in his head—of rituals; of simple, fond, shared acts—were more valuable than any lump of gold or silver could ever have been. When his wife was alive, they served as visible symbols of his love. Now that he was alone, the memory of their giving provided comfort during the cold, solitary nights of winter. In his own mind Christmas remained what it always was: a turning point for the year at which the days ceased to shorten, Rome paused to look at itself, feel modestly proud of what it saw, then await the inevitable arrival of spring and, with it, rebirth.

Even in the weather the city had endured of late—dark and terribly wet, with the Tiber at its highest in a quarter century, so brown and muddy and reckless it would have burst its banks without the modern flood defences—there was a spirit of quiet excitement everywhere, a communal recollection of a small, distant miracle that still bore some significance in an ephemeral world of mundane, fleeting greed. He saw this in the faces of the children spilling down the city streets and alleys, excited, trying to guess what the coming weeks would bring. He saw this in the eyes of their parents, too, remembering their youth, taking pleasure in passing some fragment of the wonder on to their own offspring in return. Nor was the weather uniformly vile. Occasionally the heavy, dark clouds would break and a lively winter sun would smile on the city. He'd seen it drift through the dusty windows of his apartment that morning, spilling a welcome golden light onto the ancient, smoke-stained cobblestones of the alley outside. It had made him feel at home, glad to be a Roman born and bred.

CAVIGLIA HAD LIVED IN THE CENTRO STORICO ALL HIS life and worshipped in the Church of San Luigi dei Francesi around the corner. His wife had adored the paintings there, the Caravaggios in particular, with their loving and lifelike depiction of Matthew, at his conversion, during his work, and finally at his death. One December eighth, twenty-five years ago it must have been, Caviglia had marked their visit by spending what little money he had from his baker's wages on a bouquet of bright red roses. Chiara had responded by choosing the most beautiful stem and pinning it into the strap of his floury overalls—he had come straight from work— then taking him in her arms in an embrace he could still recall for its strength and warmth and affection.

Ever since, even after she was gone, he had marked the day, first with roses, bought before breakfast from the small florist's store that stood close to the piazza, then a brief visit to the church, where he lit a single candle in his wife's memory. He no longer attended mass, though. It seemed unnecessary.

A SINGLE CARMINE STEM FROM TUSCANY SAT IN THE left lapel of his woollen coat, its supple, insistent perfume rising above the diesel odour and the people smell of the bus, reminding him of times past and how, in those last few weeks of her illness, his wife had ordered him, in a voice growing ever weaker, to mourn for a short time only, then start his own life afresh.

To the widowed Aldo Caviglia there was no finer time to be in Rome, even in the grey, persistent rain. The best parts of the year lay ahead, waiting in store for those who anticipated them. And in the careless crowds of Christmas, flush with money, there was always business to be done.

HE HAD AN ITINERARY IN MIND, THE ONE HE ALWAYS saved for the second Thursday in the month, since repetition was to be avoided. Having walked to Barberini for the exercise and taken a brief turn around the gallery, he had caught the 64 bus for the familiar journey through the city centre, following Vittorio Emanuele, then crossing the river by the Castel Sant'Angelo for the final leg towards St. Peter's. Once there, he would retrace his steps as necessary until his goal was reached.

Caviglia both loved and hated the 64. No route in Rome attracted more tourists, which made it a beacon for the lesser members of his recently acquired profession. Many were simply confused and lost. Aldo Caviglia, an impeccably dressed man in later middle age, who wore a perpetual and charming smile and spoke good English, was always there to help. He maintained in his head a compendious knowledge of the city of his birth. Should his memory fail him, he always kept in his pocket a copy of *Il Trovalinea,* the comprehensive city transport guide that covered every last tram and bus in Rome. He knew where to stay, where to eat. He knew, too, that it was wise to warn visitors of the underside of Roman life: the petty crooks and bag-snatchers, the hucksters working the tourist traps, and the scruffy pick-pockets who hung around the buses and the subway, the 64 in particular.

He gave them tips. He taught them the phrase *"Zingari! Attenzione!"* explaining that it meant "Beware! Gypsies!" Not, he hastened to add, that he shared the common assumption all gypsies were thieves. On occasion he would amuse his audience by demonstrating the private sign every Roman knew, holding his hands down by his side, rippling his fingers as if playing the piano. He had a fine, delicate touch, that of an artist, which he demonstrated proudly with this gesture. Before the needs of everyday life had forced him to find more mundane work, he had toyed with the idea of painting as a profession, since the galleries of his native city, the great Villa Borghese, the splendid if chaotic Barberini, and his favourite, the private mansion of the Doria Pamphilj dynasty, were places he still frequented with a continuing sense of wonder.

The visitors always laughed at his subtle, fluttering fingertips. It was such a small, secret signal, yet as soon as one saw it there could be no doubting its meaning: the bus or the carriage had just been joined by a known pick-pocket. *Look out.*

HE WAS CAREFUL TO KEEP RECORDS, MAINTAINED IN A private code on a piece of paper hidden at the bottom of his closet. On a normal working day, Aldo Caviglia would not return home until he had stolen a minimum of €400. His average—Caviglia was a man fond of precise accounts—had been €583 over the past four weeks. On occasion—tourists sometimes carried extraordinary amounts of cash—he had far exceeded his daily target, so much so that it had begun to trouble him. Caviglia chose his victims carefully. He never preyed on the poor or the elderly. When one miserable Russian's wallet alone yielded more than €2,000, Caviglia had decided upon a policy. All proceeds above his maximum of €650 would be donated anonymously—pushed in cash into a church collection box—to the sisters near the Pantheon who ran a charity for the city's homeless. He prided himself on the fact that he was not a greedy man. Furthermore, as a true Roman he never ceased to be shocked by how the city's population of destitute *barboni,* many young, many unable to speak much Italian, had grown in recent years. He would take no more than he needed. He would maintain a balance between his activities and his conscience, going out to steal one or two days each week, when necessary. For the rest of the time he would simply ride the trams and buses for the pleasure of being what, on the surface, he appeared: a genial Good Samaritan, always ready to help the stranded, confused foreigner.

THE BUS LURCHED AWAY FROM THE BUS STOP. THE TRAFfic *WAS* terrible, struggling through the holiday crowds at a walking pace. They had moved scarcely thirty metres along Vittorio Emanuele in the past five minutes. He stared at himself in the bus driver's mirror again. Was this the face of a guilty man? Caviglia brushed away the thought. In truth, if he wanted to, he could probably get a job in a bakery, now that he was sober. No one ever complained about his work. His late wife had thought him among the best bakers in Rome. There was a joke he now made to himself: *These fingers can make dough, these fingers can take dough.* It was a good one, he thought. He wished he could share it with someone.

*If I wanted to,* Caviglia emphasised to himself.

*You feel guilty,* said a quiet, inner voice, *for yourself and the life you are wasting. Not for what you've done.*

He glanced out of the grimy windows: solid lines of cars and buses and vans stood stationary in both directions. The sudden joy of the coming holiday vanished.

To his surprise, Aldo Caviglia felt a firm finger prod hard into his chest.

"I want the stop for the Vicolo del Divino Amore," said a woman hard up against his right side. She spoke in an accent Caviglia took to be French, with a confidence in her Italian which was, he felt, somewhat ill-judged.

He turned to look at her, aware that his customary smile was no longer present.

She was attractive, though extremely slender, and wore a precisely cut short white gabardine coat over a tube-like crayon-red leather skirt that stopped just above the knee. Perhaps thirty-five, she had short, very fiery red hair to match the skirt, acute grey eyes, and the kind of face one saw in advertisements for cosmetics: geometrically exact, entirely lacking in flaws, and, to Caviglia's taste, somewhat two-dimensional. She seemed both nervous and a little depressed. And also ill, perhaps, since on second consideration her skin was very pale indeed, almost the colour of her jacket, and her cheeks hollow.

She had a large fawn pigskin bag over her shoulder. It sported the very visible badge of one of the larger Milan fashion houses. Caviglia wondered why a beautiful woman, albeit one of daunting and somewhat miserable appearance, would want to advertise the wares of the Milanese clothes crooks and, by implication, her own sense of insecurity. The bag was genuine, though. Perhaps one thousand euros had been squandered on that modest piece of leather. The zip was halfway open, just enough to reveal a large collection of items—a scarf, a phone, some pens, and a very large, overstuffed wallet.

"I really need to find this place," she told him. "It's near the Palazzo Malaspina, I know. But I was never very good at directions. I've only been there at night. I . . ."

For a moment he feared she was about to burst into tears. Then he corrected himself. She was simply absorbed, in what he could not begin to imagine.

Caviglia smiled, then reached over her to press the bell. A cloud of rich, somewhat cloying perfume rose from her body. French, he thought again.

"The next stop, signora, if you are willing to walk. I will show you where to go. I have to get off myself in any case."

She nodded and said nothing. When the bus finally came to a halt, Caviglia put a protective arm around her and pushed through the milling mob to exit by the front doors, as a local would, in spite of the rules, saying loudly as he forced his way forward, "*Permesso. Permesso! PERMESSO!*"

He waited for her to alight from the bus, his hands behind his back. Out in the brief bright light of this December day, she seemed even more frail and thin.

"It's ten minutes on foot," Caviglia said. He pointed across the road. "In that direction. There are no buses. Perhaps I can find you a taxi."

"I can walk," she said instantly.

"Can you find your way to the Piazza Navona from here?"

She nodded and looked a little offended. "Of course!"

"Go to the end," he instructed. "Then turn right through the Piazza Agostino for the Via della Scrofa. Turn right again at the Piazza Firenze and you will find the Vicolo del Divino Amore on your left along the Via dei Prefetti."

"Thank you."

"You are entering an interesting part of my city. Many famous artists lived there. It was once part of the area called 'Ortaccio.'"

She looked puzzled. "My Italian is bad. I don't know that word."

Caviglia cursed his stupidity for mentioning this fact. Sometimes he spoke too much for his own good.

"It was an area set aside by the Popes for prostitutes. *Orto* may signify the Garden of Eden. *Ortaccio* signifies what came after our discovery of sin. The Garden of Humanity. Or the Garden of Wickedness or Evil. Or one and the same. But I am simply a . . . retired school-teacher. What would I know of such things?"

The merest of smiles slipped across her face. Though almost skeletally thin, she was exceptionally beautiful, Caviglia realised. It was simply that something—life, illness, or some inner turmoil—disguised this fact most of the time, stood between her true self and others like a semi-opaque screen, one held by her own pale, slim hands.

"You know a lot, I think," the Frenchwoman said. "You're a kind man." She stopped, smiled briefly again, and held out her hand. Caviglia shook it, delicately, since her fingers seemed so thin they might break under the slightest pressure. To his surprise her flesh was unexpectedly warm, almost as if something burned inside her, with the same heat signified by her fiery hair.

Then she took a deep breath, looked around—seeming to take an unnecessary pleasure in the smog-stained stones of a busy thoroughfare Caviglia regarded as one of the most uninteresting in Rome—and was gone, threading through the traffic with a disregard for her own safety he found almost heart-stopping.

He turned away before her darting white form, like an exclamation mark with a full stop made from flame, disappeared into one of the side roads leading to the Piazza Navona.

Business was business. Caviglia patted the right-hand side of his jacket pocket. The woman's fat wallet sat there, a wad of leather and paper and credit cards waiting to be stripped. Experience and his own intelligence told him the day's work was over. Nevertheless, he was a little disturbed by this encounter. There was something strange about this woman in white, and her urgent need to go the Vicolo del Divino Amore, a dark Roman alley that, to him, showed precious little trace of divine love, and probably never had.

# Two

ALDO CAVIGLIA STRODE TOWARDS THE CAMPO DEI Fiori and entered a small cafe located in one of the side roads leading to the Cancelleria, determined to count his gains, then dump the evidence. This particular hole in the wall was a place he'd always liked: too tiny and local to be of interest to tourists, and one that kept to the old tradition of maintaining a bowl of thick, sticky mixed sugar and coffee on the bar so that those in need of a faster, surer fix could top up their *caffè* as much as was needed.

All the same, Caviglia had added a shot of grappa to his cup, also, something he hadn't done for some months. This chill, strange winter day seemed to merit that, though it was still only twenty to eleven in the morning.

Within five minutes he was inside the tiny washroom, crammed up against the cistern, struggling, with trembling fingers, to extract what was of value from the bulging leather purse.

Caviglia never took credit cards. Partly because this would increase the risk but also, more important, out of simple propriety. He believed people should be robbed once and once only—by his nimble fingers and no others. That way the pain—and there would be pain, which might not merely be financial—would be limited to a few days or possibly a week. Nor would Caviglia look at the private, personal belongings which people carried with them in their daily lives. He had done this once, the first time he had been reduced to thieving on the buses to make ends meet. It had made him feel dirty and dishonourable. His criminality would always be limited to stealing money from those he judged could afford it, then passing on the excess to the kind and charitable nuns near the Pantheon. As a Catholic in thought if not in deed, he was unsure whether this was sufficient to guarantee him salvation, if such a thing existed. But it certainly helped him sleep at night.

Caviglia attempted to remind himself of these facts as he wrestled with the wallet in the extraordinarily narrow and confined space in which he found himself, increasingly aware that the large shot of grappa in his coffee cup had not been a good idea. Then the worst possible thing happened. The wallet folded in on itself under the pressure of his clumsy fingers, turned over, and spilled everything—notes, coins, credit cards, and what looked like a European driving licence—straight onto the grubby toilet floor.

He lowered himself onto the seat and felt like

weeping. Nothing could be left here. Every last item would have to be retrieved from the dark, grimy corners beneath the little sink, packed away again, and rushed to the nearest litter bin. If a single item belonging to the woman was found, he would surely be identified by the youth behind the bar. There had been two cases against him already, occasions when his concentration had lapsed and he had tried to ply his trade in the presence of an undercover officer. A third would mean jail and with it the loss of the little apartment the two of them had shared as a couple for more than thirty years. Everything that was of value to him might disappear if he left one stray item behind on the floor of this toilet in a tiny cafe built into little more than a cave behind the Campo dei Fiori.

With a sudden determination to put the situation right, he set about his work, recognising a growing inward conviction, one he had noticed but never acknowledged before: his time as a Roman street thief was coming to an end. Tomorrow, or perhaps the day after, he would be back walking round the bakeries, looking to return to the world of early-morning heat and dust, and the fragrant smell of rising bread.

After a minute he looked at what he'd collected; there was no alternative in the circumstances. The woman's wallet contained just under four hundred euros in cash and a few coins, several membership tickets for cinema and arts clubs, three credit cards, a passport-size photo of a handsome, though unsmiling, dark-haired young man with a close-cropped beard, and, to Caviglia's shock, a single condom in a shiny silver sheath. Her driving licence gave her name as Véronique Gillet and an address in the 3ème arrondissement in Paris. The same name was also on an identity card for the Louvre Museum. She was, it said, a senior curatorial assistant in the Départment des Peintures. The photograph was many years older than that on the driving licence, which showed a lovely young woman, perhaps in her student days, with shoulder-length lighter hair and a fuller, more contented face. She had an almost palpable air of happiness about her. It made his heart ache.

*And you're sick,* Caviglia thought immediately, feeling a stiff, cold weight of self-loathing begin to form in his stomach.

Something else had fallen out of the wallet, too, a small pink plastic box, one that had puzzled him at first, and now, to his despair and mortification, was beginning to make sense.

He reached beneath the foot pedal for the water tap on the basin and retrieved it. The front had the universal emblem for medicine, a symbol Caviglia had come to know and recognise during his wife's illness. The caduceus, a kindly doctor had called it. Two serpents writhing round a winged staff. With a deepening sense of foreboding, he opened the lid. Inside was a collection of transparent foils containing tiny red pills, almost the colour of her hair. A date and a time were written beneath each tablet. He peered at them. The next was to be taken at eleven-thirty, just forty minutes away. And the next after that at three o'clock, then again four hours later. Whatever ailment the woman suffered from required, it seemed from the medication, six doses a day, at very exact intervals.

A small card sat next to the foils. He took it out and read there, in a very precise female hand, written in French, English, German, and simple Italian, *This medication is very important to me. If you find it, please call me on the number below, at any time. Even if I am unable to collect it, I will at least know I need to find some more. I will, naturally, be grateful.*

Aldo Caviglia leaned back on the flimsy plastic toilet seat and felt stinging tears—of rage and shame and pity—begin to burn in his eyes. The woman's face hung suspended in his memory, pale and damaged and in need. All because an idle old man would rather steal wallets on the 64 bus than go out and earn an honest living.

He scooped up what he could of her belongings, gathered them into his pockets, and stormed out of the cafe without pausing to utter a customary farewell. He had no phone but he knew where she was. Caviglia strode across Vittorio Emanuele without stopping, holding his arms outstretched, like a cross, like a figure in one of those church paintings he admired so much, utterly oblivious to the discordant chorus of angry horns and the stares of the astonished locals watching from the pavement.

# Three

O MORE THAN SEVEN MINUTES LATER—HE checked on his watch—he was in the Vicolo del Divino Amore, wondering how he could track her down. It was like many a city *vicolo*: narrow, dark, hostile to the outside world. Behind some of these plain doors and stone façades might lie entire mansions, busy offices, veterinary clinics, or private clubs for visiting foreigners seeking female company. This was, he reminded himself, Ortaccio. But Rome's whores were no longer confined to a specific quarter on the orders of the Pope. Like all criminals, like Aldo Caviglia himself, the prostitutes roamed freely, on the streets, in apartments and houses scattered throughout the city.

He strode along the dark, narrow alley, avoiding the badly parked scooters, scanning for a pencil-thin Titian-haired figure in a white gabardine coat. There was no one in the Vicolo del Divino Amore. Just dead grey buildings and the small church he half knew, locked, without a light inside, and, opposite, a long wall of plastic sheeting and scaffolding. A vague memory pricked Caviglia's imagination. The construction men were probably labouring to repair some distant part of the great Palazzo Malaspina, which sprawled through this part of the city, a vast monstrosity of Renaissance brick that was one of the last private palaces still in original hands in Rome.

This told him nothing. Without concern for the consequences, Caviglia dashed the length of the *vicolo,* then, when he reached the Piazza Borghese without seeing a thing, entered the nearest cafe, ordered a single *macchiato* out of politeness, and commandeered the house phone. He fed a couple of coins into the machine and dialled the number she had given on the card, waiting as it ran through some invisible ethereal network he could not begin to imagine, from Rome to Paris and back again, finally delivering a ring tone after a good half-minute. All the while he fought to perfect his story, how he would explain what he had "found" in the street and had immediately decided to follow her in order to return it.

But it was pointless. The ring tone went on and on. Nothing more. No message. No voice at the other end. He glanced out the window, hoping her business was done and she might have gone on to the bright open space of the square behind the palace of the family that had once been known as the Borgias. She could be anywhere. If the pills were so important, she should surely have left some answering service on her phone.

Except, Caviglia reminded himself, she was ill. Sick people, as he knew only too well, lacked logic sometimes.

Towards the end they lacked any concept of care for themselves at all.

"Signora..." he said to the woman behind the counter, then described the Frenchwoman in detail, thinking, as he did, of the way she was dressed, which was not casual, but careful, the kind of clothes a woman would wear for a business appointment. Or a date.

Nothing happens quickly in Roman cafes. The formidable middle-aged figure behind the counter discussed the possibilities with her husband, who was making panini for the lunchtime rush, with an elderly pensioner loitering over a cappuccino, then a workman in grubby blue overalls at the end of the bar, and finally three women gossiping over cakes. Caviglia listened, feeling miserable. No one had seen a flame-haired pencil-slim woman in a pale coat and scarlet skirt.

"Why was your friend here?" the woman asked. "We don't see many tourists...."

He thought of the identity card. "She's in the art business. I think she had an appointment perhaps. Is there a dealer nearby? Or a painter?"

The woman laughed. "You've missed the painters by four hundred years. They all lived here once, you know. Caravaggio had a place..."

"Where?" he asked immediately, for no good reason.

"It was a long time ago. Who knows?"

The old man at the end of the bar raised a skinny finger. "There *is* a studio, though," he said.

"What are you talking about, Enzo?" she barked at

him. "*We* can barely afford to live here anymore. How could some painter manage the rent?"

"I don't know. But he does. Opposite the church. The green door before all that damned . . ." He stopped and stared at the workman at this point. ". . . noisy building work down there."

The man in the blue overalls finished his coffee and laughed. "If Franco Malaspina's offering money, do you think I should turn him down? How often does *that* happen?"

The pensioner tapped the side of his nose, ignoring the question. "I've seen artist types going in there. Brushes. A canvas. That I-am-so-much-smarter-than-you look all those arty-farty queers have." He drew in a long, asthmatic breath to make one final point. "They wear black all winter *and* summer long too."

"Green door," Caviglia repeated, and was out into the street.


SURE ENOUGH, OPPOSITE THE CHURCH WAS A FLIMSY wooden entrance the colour of cemetery grass, not to a house or office, but to an alley, no more than two metres wide, running alongside what he took to be some rear extension to the Palazzo Malaspina. The door was unlocked. He walked through. The sunlight deserted him. It was cold and damp in this stone and brick slit cut between an ancient mansion and some nondescript building that could have been anything: a home, an office, or simply some cheap storage place for the busy city centre half a kilometre away.

There was a single obstacle at the end: a bright, shiny metal security door, the kind used to protect warehouses and places worth looting. Not expecting anything, his head in a whirl, knowing he was running short of options and ever more desperate to return the wallet and the drugs, Caviglia strode purposefully forward and tugged on the handle.

To his surprise, it slid easily on silent runners, disappearing behind the wall to the right. Inside was darkness, a sea of black so unmarked by any visible feature it surely betokened a space of some size. He blinked, walked in, and groped around both sides of the wall, hunting for a light switch, finding nothing. After a moment his eyes began to adjust. In the distance to the right he could just make out a slender line of yellow light, the kind of illumination that might fall beneath a distant door leading off to one side.

Aldo Caviglia felt for the woman's belongings in his pocket, seeking, with no good reason, some kind of reassurance from them. Then he edged gingerly forward into the gloom, hands in front in order to detect any high obstacle, hoping his feet wouldn't encounter anything low and hidden on the floor.

He was, he judged, halfway to the door when he heard her. The voice—high, pained, stretched by such an agony he could not begin to imagine what caused it—drifted through the damp, fusty air of the black space before him, pulsing with an exact and heart-rending rhythm, not that of a breath, but a blow of some kind, a persistent, continuous attack which drew from her a long, harrowing cry as if she were being tortured.

Wild, formless fears rose in Caviglia's head. He pressed on, more determined than ever, stumbling over stray bricks, feeling the right-hand wall to keep himself upright, watching the diagonal slant of light grow larger with each tentative, trembling step. There was a smell to the place, too, organic, sweet, and a little rotten.

Her repetitive, rasping sighs increased, in pitch and rhythm and volume. Through the wordless stream of anguish and stress there began to ring a single comprehensible word, spoken in French, the first consonant soft and breathy, the final silent, sounds so unlike the Italian.

"Jésus . . . Jésus . . . Jésus . . ."

He reached the stripe of yellow, unable to guess what might lie beyond. Some young thug bent upon rape? A vengeful lover turned violent? Madness in a dark and narrow urban street, unseen, unheard by passersby, for whom this was simply another ordinary day?

Without thinking, Aldo Caviglia found himself shouting, too, not knowing what he said, anxious, above all, to drown out the sound of her voice in his brain, since it disturbed him greatly, in ways he could not fully comprehend.

"*Stop, stop, STOP!*" he screamed, throwing open the door, entering the room, glad that he had finally found a word to which he could pin some logical thread of thought.

It was bright in there. An artist's studio, as the pensioner in the cafe had said. An array of easels stood around a room that resembled a dusty, jumbled-up warehouse in which pots of paint had exploded in all directions and with extraordinary force. Colours ran everywhere: blues and blacks, reds and yellows, in golden streaks and white, white puddles, spattering the high brick walls, the floors, and even the dusty, pale ceiling. Rays of winter daylight fell through the single long, grimy window.

Caviglia had to force himself to see through the bright, insane confusion there in order to work out what was happening, where the Frenchwoman, in her distress, might be. The moment he had entered, her screaming had ceased, instantly, in a way that was, he hoped, linked with his arrival, not some other dread event.

Finally, the sea of disparate, swirling pigment ceased to churn in front of his eyes and he saw her. Saw *them*.

They lay like a single conjoined beast in front of a large, brilliant canvas which served as a backdrop for their exertions, and was so bright, so full of some strange simulacrum of life, that he was unable, at that moment, to understand what he was seeing.

# Four

Véronique Gillet was stretched out naked, a thin pale skeleton of a figure on a dark red velvet chaise longue drawn up beneath the painting, which itself seemed to feature some similar, though more bulky, nude form. Her head rested on the single raised arm of the sofa's head, lolling, inanimate. Her legs were loosely entwined around the torso of a standing man who wore a creased and bloodied red shirt and was positioned in front of her waist, still moving forward at the hip with a dying, measured motion Caviglia now recognised as the cadence of her diminishing sighs.

The man's expression was crazed, that of an animal fixed on its prey, mindless, intent on one thing only.

Her face was turned towards Caviglia and the door, not out of some deliberate intent, he thought, but simply because that was the way her head had fallen. The eyes of Véronique Gillet were no longer the vivid, attentive grey of an exotic feline. They were dead and glassy. Her bright red hair was matted with sweat, so much that it clung tightly to her skull. Her attacker's hand held a knife tight to her throat, where it had drawn a dark red line, lazy and curving, out from her collarbone towards the base of her neck.

Caviglia ran forward, yelling, screaming, shouting as loudly as he could in the hope that someone in the street beyond would hear and come to his aid. Still, he was unable to concentrate on the point where his attention ought to lie—the man, the animal, the murderer— because his mind would not leave two incandescent burning points of visual focus in front of him.

He tripped on something, a can of paint perhaps, and stumbled to the hard floor, cracking the side of his skull hard on the ancient flagstones. The sweet stench of decay seemed to be everywhere, rising in his nostrils, filling his head with nonsense.

In these moments strange thoughts are born. He recalled what the woman in the cafe had said about the artists who had lived in this neighbourhood. Among them Caravaggio, who had painted so many vivid depictions of life and death in Rome: Saint Peter on the cross in Santa Maria del Popolo; David with the dangling head of Goliath in the Villa Borghese, where Caviglia would direct tourists looking for some peace in the city on a sweltering summer day. And the martyrdom of Saint Matthew, in his own church of San Luigi dei Francesi, no more than a few minutes' walk from where he now scrabbled on a dusty, paint-strewn floor, trying to make sense of the nightmare that had risen from the dark Roman gutter to despoil this lustrous festival of the Immaculate Conception, when no one should have thoughts for anything but life and the world, children and the future, the coming shift of the season with its subtle, eternal metamorphosis from dark to light.

He blinked and when he opened his eyes again they were fixed, unfailingly, on the painting, unable to look anywhere else. What he saw made him catch his breath. This was, in some cryptic, unknowable way, the very scene he'd just witnessed. The woman there, naked, surrounded by figures who attended to her in ways which were both loving yet inimical, too, was gasping, through lips that were full and rosy and fleshy, brimming over with life.

The picture possessed a frightful beauty, one which burned so brightly that, once witnessed, it could never be unseen.

Something real intervened in his view. The figure— Véronique Gillet's lover or murderer or both—had disentangled himself from her torso. He now stood above Aldo Caviglia. The bloody knife was in his hand, something the old disgraced baker understood fully, without needing to look.

There was no point in fleeing the inevitable. He set his gaze on the canvas, marvelling at the full figure there, painted with such care and beauty and exactitude, it was surely the work of a master. Her flesh seemed to pulse with warmth and blood, even on the razor's edge of an ecstatic epiphany so real, so violent, it might take away the last, precious vestige of life itself.

"Be quick," Aldo Caviglia murmured, and, against all instinct in the presence of such savage wonder, screwed his eyes tightly shut, waiting, one last taut breath held close inside.

# Part Two
# The Vicolo del Divino Amore

# One

GIANNI PERONI DIDN'T FIT IN A BUNNY SUIT. HE wandered round the overcrowded storeroom looking faintly obscene, the white plastic overall clinging tightly to his large frame, its colour almost the same shade as his face. He was angry, too, and willing to make this plain to anyone who came in proximity, from Inspector Leo Falcone on down.

It was now mid-afternoon, two hours since the Questura got the call about suspicious cries coming from the address in the Vicolo del Divino Amore. A routine visit by a uniformed officer had rapidly escalated into a full-blown murder inquiry, with Inspector Falcone deputed to lead the team. It was, Nic Costa felt, a little like old times. Teresa Lupo and her chief morgue monkey, Silvio Di Capua, were poring over two bodies, both the apparent victims of violent attacks. Scene-of-crime officers were starting to pick their way around a room that looked like a forensic team's nightmare: spatters of wild colour, and blood and dirt and dust, were everywhere—on the floor, on the walls, on the grubby tables and chairs. It seemed much like an artist's studio. There were easels and used pots of paint, some commercial household brands, some artistic. There was also what appeared to be a substantial canvas some way behind the two corpses on the floor, now outlined by white chalk and tended by Teresa and her team of acolytes. Costa knew that he would have to see that before he left, but for now he would leave it as it was, hidden under a green velvet coverlet so large it draped down both back and front, obscuring it from view entirely.

Some things had changed, though.

"Sovrintendente."

Falcone's voice echoed clear and commanding in the cold empty space. Costa daydreamed. He'd spoken to Emily on the journey over. She was in a class at the architectural school in the Piazza Borghese, no more than two minutes' walk away. Costa had mentioned his destination, though not the purpose. From the warm, inquisitive tone of her voice, he knew what she'd do: walk down into the narrow, dark lane and try to take a look for herself. Emily still yearned to be in law enforcement, even though her architectural career seemed about to blossom, thanks to an internship with one of the city's largest partnerships.

"*Sovrintendente,*" Falcone repeated, more loudly. The old inspector was now almost fully recovered from a recent gunshot wound. He had a slight limp, nothing more. Inside the Questura, Falcone was once more, if not the top dog, a substantial intellectual force, the officer to whom the awkward cases were assigned. He was also a man at peace with himself again, apparently happily alone after a short, odd romantic entanglement. And, like Peroni and Teresa, utterly delighted to have attended the brief civil marriage ceremony at which Costa and Emily Deacon had become man and wife three months ago to this day.

The senior officer leaned over and whispered into Costa's ear, "Nic!"

"I'm sorry," Costa found himself stuttering. It had been a remarkable year. The tragedy of a child lost in a miscarriage, a wedding, and then, returning to the Questura the previous Monday, discovering his promotion had come through while he and Emily were on a too-brief weekend break in Sicily. "Sir," he added.

"And so you should be," Falcone complained. "Your honeymoon is over, Officer. Pay attention, please."

While he spoke, Falcone was watching Gianni Peroni fulminate by the side of the two bodies, spitting complaints in the direction of anyone within earshot. The inspector was wondering perhaps what the big man, once an inspector himself, thought of his partner's rise through the ranks. It was certainly a subject that had occupied Costa's thoughts since he returned to work, and one he had to discuss with Peroni, soon.

"What would you do in my shoes?" Falcone asked, eyes sparking with interest, hand on his trim silver beard.

"Seal the room and keep it sealed," Costa answered instantly.

Falcone nodded. "Why?" he asked.

"It's going to take days before forensic manage to sweep this place properly. It's a mess. We'll need to bring in experts, and if that's to mean anything we must make sure there is no unnecessary disturbance. Also . . ."

He glanced at the manpower crammed into the cramped and jumbled space around them. There were thirteen people there, including two photographers and three civilians from the media department, two of them trainees, who were preparing what to say to the press and TV. Only seven people were serving police officers. This seemed to be the way of things lately. The investigative process was becoming muddied, mired in procedure, dictated more by lawyers than the need for the swift, clear discovery of facts and culpability.

"I think we need to keep the numbers down as much as possible. There's a lot of material in here. I know everyone's careful. But all the same . . ."

The inspector grimaced. "We do these things by rote these days, Sovrintendente. The first act, always, is to pick up the manual and read what it says. You're right . . ."

Having little patience with politeness, the inspector brusquely ordered the media team to get out and watched them slink towards the door, casting mute and furious glances in their wake. Then he folded his long arms and glanced towards the two corpses in front of him, a thoughtful finger momentarily stroking his silver goatee, a familiar expression of wry amusement in his angular, tanned face.

"On the other hand," he added with nonchalant ease, "it would appear to be a relatively straightforward matter."

A man of late middle age, wearing a smart suit and an expression frozen halfway between horror and simple mute fury, lay curled on his side, clutching his stomach, gripping himself in the taut, terrified agony of a vicious death. The black wooden shaft of what Costa suspected would turn out to be a large kitchen knife protruded from beneath his rib cage, staining his white shirt with a ragged patch of dark, congealing blood. Next to him was the naked corpse of a much younger woman, so thin her rib cage was showing.

The contrast between the two was marked. The woman's face, which had a still, bloodless beauty that transcended life, was almost peaceful. She lay on her back, legs slightly raised and akimbo, in a position that could, possibly, have been post-coital. She had short fiery red hair, which was disarrayed, as if by some kind of violence, and somewhat greasy, maybe from sweat. There was a wound in her throat, perhaps a hand's span long and probably from a knife, logically the same one that killed the man. The cut ran down towards her breastbone, though it was not deep, it seemed to Costa, since there was much less blood than appeared on the shirt of the other victim. Her pale grey eyes, like those of her apparent attacker, were wide open, though much more distended, as if through some kind of medical condition. They stared fixedly at the ceiling in an unwavering gaze.

Her lips were a cold shade of blue, starting to resemble the same dull tone he could see in her dead eyes.

"He didn't do it," Peroni insisted.

"He?" Falcone asked.

"*He*," the big man responded, stabbing a fat finger in the air. "Aldo Caviglia. I arrested him once for stealing on the buses. I've warned him twice too. He's a petty thief. A sad, confused little guy. He steals..." Peroni looked pale. He was never happy around death. "He *stole* wallets for a living, for God's sake. The last time I caught him he promised he'd stop."

Costa noticed something about the dead man's appearance: a bulge in his jacket. He knelt down beside Teresa Lupo, receiving a warning glance from the pathologist as he did so.

"Touch nothing without my permission," the pathologist warned.

"The pocket?"

Teresa looked, saw what he was getting at, then reached into the man's jacket and withdrew, in her gloved fingers, a woman's expensive leather wallet.

Peroni swore.

"Sometimes people lie, Gianni," Teresa told him. "It's shocking, I know. But at least..."

She was sifting through the contents and dropping each item one by one into an evidence bag.

"...He's given you some ID for her."

Teresa straightened up and showed them the card. The three police officers read it.

"French," she said. "Might have known."

"Why?" Falcone asked immediately.

"You really don't notice much about women, do you, Leo? Alive or dead. She's wearing mascara, so beautifully applied I can't quite believe it. She still has perfect makeup, despite all that's happened here. The only other thing she has on are a couple of diamond earrings too beautiful for most of us to contemplate. Also . . ."

The pathologist nodded towards some large white bags beneath the paint-stained window.

"She was wearing a winter outfit that must have cost a fortune. And the shoes. In this weather. This was not someone out for a day's sightseeing, I can tell you that. She was dressed up for something. A business meeting. A date."

"Were the clothes torn?" Costa asked.

"Not in the slightest," Teresa said. "They were folded up nice and neatly, the way you do before you go to bed." She glanced again at the card. "Perhaps she was doing business on behalf of the Louvre."

Falcone coughed into his fist.

"Sorry, sorry," she added. "That's your job, isn't it?"

"Very much so," Falcone agreed. "Did they have sex?"

Teresa dropped the card in the evidence bag, passed it to Di Capua, and frowned down at the dead Caviglia on the floor.

"These two? No. I am guessing here. I'll tell you more later, once we have them back in the morgue. But some sneaking feminine intuition tells me that couples who expire post-copulation rarely do so with one partner naked and the other fully dressed and looking like he's going to an interview with his bank manager. Even his zip's done up, Leo. Think it through for yourself."

"She *is* naked," Costa pointed out.

"I said 'they' didn't do it. She did. And rough sex, too, though not necessarily rape. There's minimal bruising. Unprotected, though. I'll have your DNA sample ready first thing in the morning. A good dinner says it isn't that of our light-fingered friend here. Nor," she added quickly, "do I think she killed him. It's just meant to look that way, and not well orchestrated either. Someone was in a hurry. Look at the details. She's on the floor. And there's a perfectly good chaise longue over there. Why would they get down to it here? We would also have to assume that she killed him first, then expired herself. Remarkable in itself, and even more so if she then managed to lie down flat, quite unclothed, on a cold stone floor, all ready for the grave. No—"

Falcone held up a lean, tanned hand, demanding silence. "Enough," he said quietly. "Leave us something to do. Please. Clearly we are meant to believe something here."

"Aldo Caviglia couldn't hurt a fly," Peroni insisted. "Why would someone pick on a poor old soul like him?"

"That's what we're supposed to find out," Costa said automatically, and was shocked that it sounded like an admonition.

"Thank you," Peroni said quietly. "Sir."

"Blue lips," Costa murmured, ignoring him.

Teresa was staring at the dead woman's face, interested,

but worried also, it seemed to Costa, by the distance there had to be between a *sovrintendente* and an *agente* who was more than twenty years his senior.

"Quite," she said. "Do you notice the smell?"

"I thought this whole place smelled bad," Costa said. "Drains."

She grimaced, as if she'd missed something important. "It does stink, you're right. But she has a particular smell. A little like sweaty socks, in case you're too polite to say."

"Is it unusual?" he asked.

"Not around any cops I know," she answered. "But on a woman like this?"

Watched by Falcone, Costa knelt down and leaned over the corpse. The smell was obvious: direct and pungent.

"It takes an hour or so to degrade that much," Teresa remarked.

"What does?" Falcone demanded.

"Amyl nitrate."

"A sex drug?" Costa asked, astonished.

"Hold on there," the pathologist cautioned. "Amyl nitrate is a very useful pharmaceutical in the right circumstances." She was staring directly at Costa, challenging him to think. "It's relief for angina. And emergency revival in heart cases."

"Blue lips," he said again.

"Quite." She was grinning. "No wonder you promoted him, Leo."

Falcone sighed. "So this woman died of a heart attack. During sex? And the drug was there either for stimulation or to revive her?"

"I am merely a pathologist," Teresa replied. She held out a hand. Peroni took it and helped her to her feet. "If I'm to help you with the rest, I need to get these two out of here and safe and warm to my lair. We have everything we're going to get *in situ*. Silvio can stay behind and supervise the rest. I'll need her medical history from Paris. You don't mind if we handle that?"

"No," the inspector said, nodding. "Just the medical side. You agree?"

"Of course," she concurred, smiling pleasantly.

"I told you Caviglia didn't do it!" Peroni pointed out.

She smiled and patted his arm. "So you did. Good for you."

"He stole her wallet, though," Falcone added. "He came here for some reason. He saw something . . ."

The room had gone quiet. The other officers who'd been working alongside the forensic team waited, except for the pair who seemed to be lifting some loose masonry close to the rotting iron window.

"Perhaps he saw this," Costa suggested. He walked over to the large easel behind the corpses and, very carefully, removed the green velvet drape, exposing the canvas.

Not a word was uttered for a good half a minute. Not a breath even, it seemed.

"Perhaps he did," Teresa whispered, breaking the silence.

\*    \*    \*

NO ONE COULD TAKE THEIR EYES OFF THE PAINTING. even the presence of two corpses, one clearly murdered, the other dead through strange and suspicious circumstances, did nothing to distract their attention from the canvas at that moment.

Falcone walked over to join Costa, his gaze fixed on the shining naked form, three-quarters life-size, in front of them.

"I need to know who owns this property," the inspector ordered. "I want Caviglia checked with the rape unit just in case. Sovrintendente?"

Costa was lost in the swirl of the painted flesh, the extraordinary expression on the subject's face, and the entire artfulness of the work, with its stylistic flourishes, the names of which came back to him from the lost years when he'd spent most of his endless, empty free time in the city's art galleries. *Sfumato, chiaroscuro, tenebrismo* . . .

"*Sovrintendente!*" Falcone repeated, unamused this time.

"We need to find an art specialist," Costa replied eventually, finally able to turn his attention away from the painting. "And good security."

"This is a murder scene," Falcone snapped. "Of course we need good security."

"I'm not an expert. But this is either a genuine and unknown Caravaggio, or an excellent attempt to forge one. Either way, I think . . ."

Falcone glowered at the canvas. Since Costa had

unveiled it, there hadn't been a moment's activity in the room.

"The painting can wait," the inspector grumbled, then strode over to the easel and roughly dragged the green velvet drape back across the frame and the tantalising figure of the woman.

"Sir?"

It was one of the pair who had been working by the window. The cop looked shocked and a little pale. The three men went over to look.

The uniformed officers had laid out what they'd found. It was a collection of photographs. Costa picked up a couple of them.

"These didn't get printed in any lab," he said. "This is cheap, thin paper. The kind you use at home on a printer."

Peroni leaned over his shoulder. "No lab is going to develop those, now, are they?" he observed.

"Where did you find them?" Falcone asked.

"There was a loose flagstone beneath the window," one of the officers replied. "We just looked. These are just a few. There must be fifty or more in there."

"Keep looking," Falcone ordered, then took the photos and spread them out on a dusty chair.

Costa stared at the images on the flimsy homemade prints. It was clear that they had been taken in this very room. There was the same stone floor. In places he could see splashes of paint, and even a pot and a brush. In one photograph there was the corner of the green drape used for the canvas they'd uncovered too.

There was the link. Every photo portrayed the head and torso of a naked woman. Most of them looked foreign. Some were black, with the overblown hair and excessive makeup of the African hookers who worked the suburbs.

It was impossible to judge the expressions on their faces. It could have been rapture, sexual or spiritual. Or pain in the final moments of life.

He turned to Peroni.

"Do you know any of them, Gianni?" Costa asked.

"What the hell is that supposed to mean?" Peroni roared.

Costa cursed his own stupidity. The big man had once been one of the most effective officers working the illicit sex scene in Rome. His career had collapsed because once—just once—he'd slept with a vice girl himself.

"I'm sorry. I phrased that very badly. You worked vice for many years, and very well indeed," Costa explained patiently. "I think these women look like hookers. But if you thought so, too, it would mean a lot more."

Peroni sighed, then shrugged apologetically. "They look like hookers." He glanced back at the corpse of the Frenchwoman, now surrounded by attendants making the body bag ready. "She doesn't, though. She . . ."

Peroni stared at the photos again. Then he picked one up in his gloved hand.

It was a muscular black woman with a head of long hair, artificially straightened and glossy. She seemed to be trying very hard to look as if she were in the throes of ecstasy. All the women in the photographs did.

"I've booked her," Peroni said. "Nigerian. Quite a nice kid." He stared out of the grimy window for a moment. Then he spoke again. "She's on the missing persons list. Has been for a few weeks. I saw it on the board. I recognised . . ."

Falcone was cursing under his breath again, and this time Costa was sure there was something specific behind his reaction.

Then, before he could ask, there was a brief pained scream from the team raising the flagstones. Costa looked at the men. They were standing back from the area on which they'd been working. The blood had drained from their faces. One of them looked ready to throw up.

Falcone was there first, even with the limp. He took one look at what was emerging from beneath the damp, algaed stone.

"Doctor," he said, just loudly enough to bring Teresa Lupo to his side. Costa and Peroni moved forward to look. Then the big man swore and walked away.

Something wrapped tightly in semitransparent plastic, like a gigantic artificial cocoon, was emerging from the grey, damp earth beneath the solid floor of the studio. Costa glanced at it and started to walk, rapidly, around the room. There were several areas where the grey flagstones appeared to have been moved recently, sometimes hidden by paint pots, sometimes by empty easels or furniture.

When he got back to Falcone, Teresa Lupo was hovering over the discovery with a scalpel in her hand.

"I don't think this will be pretty, I'm afraid," she said firmly. "Those of a delicate nature should leave now."

Costa stayed and watched. He and Falcone were the only police officers who did. The face beneath the plastic was grey and dirty and, in spite of the substantial period that must have passed since she was killed, undoubtedly that of the Nigerian woman Peroni had recognised. The stench that rose the moment Teresa made the incision would, he thought, live with him for a long time.

"I don't think she's alone," Costa said, catching Falcone's eye, realising, to his dismay, that the old inspector did not, for some reason, appear to be surprised. "We have to—"

There was a sound from outside. Not in the alley, somewhere else. Costa glanced behind the painting. There was a dusty door there, beyond an ancient dining table covered in paint stains, half hidden behind some old sackcloth drapes. It was ajar.

"He's still here," Costa muttered, then leapt the table and headed for whatever lay beyond, out in the cold grey day.

# Two

$\mathcal{I}$T WAS A COURTYARD OF A KIND, A MESSY PLACE OF junk: old wooden cases, discarded furniture, a couple of tall metal filing cabinets rusting to nothing on the green cobblestones. A man could easily hide here. A single narrow corridor, dank with moss and decay, led off from the far corner, inwards, through the heart of whatever greater building—the Palazzo Malaspina, Costa's memory wanted to tell him—sprawled across this hidden enclave of the city, then, he assumed, onto the street. And freedom.

Falcone was barking orders into his radio, demanding immediate action from the officers outside in the *vicolo*. Costa wanted to tell him this narrow malodorous alley didn't run that way. It burrowed deep into the labyrinthine palace itself. Stumbling out into the grey daylight of the yard, he could hear the crush of bodies behind him, Peroni's voice in the lead, above the tense chatter of men working themselves into the state of mind that went with a pursuit.

Costa stopped and took his bearings, thinking. Why would a murderer wait so close to the scene?

Some did. Some couldn't resist it.

One of the officers who'd found the buried corpse appeared at his side. With the automatic instinct that seemed to come with the job for some, he'd taken out his gun and was now holding it in front, uncertainly, wavering between the high filing cabinets, an obvious place for someone to hide, and a pile of old furniture near the wall.

Costa pushed down the barrel of the weapon. "No guns," he insisted. "It could just be a kid."

And that was a stupid thing to say, he thought. Kids wouldn't mess around places like this. It was all too dark and dank and scary, particularly if you peeked in the windows and saw what was going on inside, beneath the placid gaze of that naked woman on the canvas.

The grimy yard was at least ten metres on each side, and half of it crammed with junk, some of it looking as if it had been thrown there years ago. The surrounding building rose six storeys high, past grimy barred windows, a line of scarred black brick leading to the leaden December sky, filled, at that moment, by a flock of swirling starlings.

Costa looked up. He didn't see a single face at any of the rain-streaked panes of near-opaque glass in the storeys above. Then he stared down the long narrow corridor leading to God knew what. It was empty, and towards the end turned into a tunnel, a pool of darkness formed by the overhanging building above. A tiny square of dim daylight was just visible at the end. There wasn't time for a man to escape them so quickly, surely. Nor could he have got there without making a sound.

"Assume he's here," he told the officer quietly. "We'll go through the junk piece by piece until we find something or he moves. Assume—"

There was a voice. Peroni was bellowing. Behind a rotting wooden desk, its metal legs like skeletal limbs made of rust, was the shadow of a figure, crouching, only the shoulders, torso, and legs visible.

Something struck Costa the moment he saw it. The man wasn't trembling. He was as still and calm as a statue.

"YOU HAVE TO COME OUT OF THERE," COSTA SAID calmly, walking forward, signalling to the officer with the revolver to keep it trained down towards the stones just in case.

"Sovrintendente!" Falcone yelled.

Costa ignored him and continued walking forward. "You need to come out now, sir." He spoke in a voice he hoped was low on threat but brooked no argument. "This is a crime scene and we have to talk to you."

The figure was no more than three or four strides away. He didn't move.

"Start moving!" Peroni bellowed.

Costa glanced back at the men behind him. Falcone was silent now. It wasn't like the old inspector.

"Out!" Peroni roared, and that did it. The long dark form—the intruder was dressed in dark khaki, some kind of military-style top and trousers, with black boots tied tight around the ankle, just like a soldier—was starting to move.

"Stand by the wall," Costa ordered. "Hands above you. This is just a routine matter. Just a . . ."

He didn't go on. The figure had worked its way free, with an agile athleticism that gave Costa pause for thought. He still couldn't see a face. Just a long, lithe body, muscular and fit, at ease in the anonymous military clothing.

"Dammit!" Falcone shouted, pushing his way through the crowd of officers jamming the free space in the courtyard. "This is my investigation, Costa. You do what I tell you."

"Sir . . ." he said, and watched the figure in khaki emerge from behind the rotting carcass of a mattress, pink and grey stripes hanging down in ragged tatters from the burst mouldy body.

The man wore a black full-face gas mask with a glass eye shield that revealed nothing at all. He had a repeating shotgun in his right hand, held tight with a professional deliberation, and, in his left, some kind of canister that was already beginning to smoke at the handle.

"Weapons!" Falcone cried.

Costa wasn't really listening. Sometimes these things

came too late. The smoking canister was already spinning in their direction, turning in the air, releasing a curling line of pale fumes that carried before it the noxious smell Costa knew from the last riot he'd had the privilege to attend.

The thing burst with a soft explosion, and a dense white cloud instantly enveloped them. Coughing, eyes streaming, he instinctively stumbled clear, down towards where he expected the exit corridor to be, eyes tight shut, a handkerchief clutched across his mouth and nose.

Gasping for clean air, aware of the curses and screeches of the men behind him, trapped in the noxious fumes, Costa was sure of one thing: Falcone would haul him over the coals for the way he had handled this particular encounter. Perhaps with good cause.

Then, as he half knelt, half fell against the grubby courtyard wall, something brushed his shoulder.

He looked up. The khaki figure was standing there, still in his mask, which hid, Costa guessed, a broad, self-satisfied smile.

The shotgun was pointed directly into Costa's face, the barrel no more than a hand's length away.

Costa coughed, tried to look the man in the eye, and said, "You're under arrest."

Then he watched, feeling a little baffled and not, for a single moment, frightened.

Nothing happened. Costa looked again. Somehow the fabric of his would-be killer's military gloves had gotten tangled in the gap between the trigger and the metal guard, preventing the firing of the weapon through nothing more than a shred of fabric and luck. It was a small and temporary thing to keep a man alive, but Costa wasn't much minded to think on it. Instead, he kicked out hard with his right leg and hit the gunman painfully on the shin. The shotgun tilted up towards the sky and fired, with an explosive screech that rebounded round the black brick and sprayed hot pellets through the air. A soft lead rain dappled the ground around Costa.

Then the gas returned, and this time it was in his eyes, stinging like wounds from a million crazed bees, sending tears streaming down his cheeks, bile surging in his throat.

Costa swore. Behind him men were screaming. He rolled out of the drifting smoke haze and saw the brown-clad figure disappearing down the corridor, into the dark pool of shadow, towards the grey patch of light at the end.

With an aching reluctance, he lurched down the slippery cobblestones, coughing, choking, realising there was no one from the team behind in much of a state to help him.

The memory of the shotgun barrel poking in his face burned as badly as the tear gas. He took one more look down the alley. Whoever it was had got a good head start on them all.

Costa watched as the military form emerged from the

shadows and fell into the bright light at the distant wall, then stopped, turned, ripped off the gas mask, hitched the shotgun up to his shoulder, and stared back at him.

He wore a black military hood beneath, the kind the antiterrorist people wore, tight black cotton with two tiny slits for eyeholes. It was too far to take a worthwhile shot from this distance. The man was, surely, making some kind of point.

Costa watched as the hood contorted around the mouth, the lips closed, then formed a perfect O, and those distant hands closed round the trigger.

Somehow he could hear the single word the figure was mouthing, even though that was impossible.

*Boom,* the man said, and then laughed.

What happened next came so naturally Costa didn't even have to think about it. He ripped the service pistol out of his shoulder holster, took some vague aim down the brick corridor ahead, and let loose four rounds in rapid succession.

The figure in khaki had fallen back against the wall, twitching and shrieking in a way that Costa, against his own instincts, found satisfying.

But it wasn't a wound. It was shock and fear and some kind of outrage that he should be a target in the first place. The man hauled himself to his feet and dashed a vicious glance back down the alley before he stumbled to the right and out of sight. But at least the brief moment of fear Costa had instilled in him re-dressed the balance a little.

Without waiting to see what condition the others were in, he dashed towards the brick tunnel ahead, lurching like a sick man, holding the weapon loose and impotent by his side, dimly aware he had only a couple of rounds left in it now, against a furious, murderous individual with a repeating shotgun who was surely about to try to bury himself inside the heart of Rome on a busy holiday afternoon.

There was no time to radio for assistance. He wasn't sure he had the voice to make the call anyway. All Costa could do was run, and, with the old skills he still retained from his marathon days, he found that rhythm almost instantly.

When he emerged from the cold black overhang of the building at the end of the passageway, he blinked at the sunlight, and the location. He was now just round the corner from the Piazza Borghese. As he squinted his stinging eyes against the sudden sun, he saw a khaki figure limping towards the square.

Inside his jacket his phone was ringing. He recognised the special tone. It was Emily calling. She'd have to wait.

# Three

CHE RAIN HAD LEFT THE COBBLESTONES OF THE piazza Borghese greasy and black. This was one of the few open spaces between the Corso and the river. Every day hundreds came here to park, strewing vehicles everywhere: cars and vans, motorbikes and scooters. Students from the nearby colleges were gathered in one corner, arms full of books and work folders, laughing, getting ready for lunch. Costa couldn't see anyone of interest, no athletic, brown-clad figure with a shotgun anywhere. Just a few shoppers and office workers walking the damp pavement.

Costa scanned the square, wondering where a fugitive might run in this part of Rome. There were so many places. South towards the Pantheon and the Piazza Navona was a labyrinth of alleys that could hide a hundred fleeing killers. West lay the bridge over the river, the Ponte Cavour, and escape into the plain business streets beyond the Palace of Justice. And both north and east . . .

street after street of shops, apartment blocks, and anonymous offices. He didn't know where to begin.

Backup would arrive soon. The officers from the studio, Gianni Peroni, a furious Falcone.

Costa took one last good look around him and sighed. Then the phone rang again. That familiar tone again. This time he answered it.

"May I take it you're hunting for a gentleman wearing a Rambo outfit, a very suspicious-looking expression, and trying, rather poorly, to hide the fact he's got a rifle or something on his person?" she asked.

Once an FBI agent, always an FBI agent.

"Just tell me where," Costa ordered his wife quietly, grimly.

"I've followed him to the Mausoleum of Augustus. I could be wrong but I think he may be headed down into it. Good place to hide, among all those bums."

Costa knew the monument, though not well. Roman emperors got mixed deals when it came to their heritage. Hadrian's mausoleum turned into the Castel Sant'Angelo. Augustus, one of the most powerful emperors Rome had ever known, came off much worse. Over the centuries, his burial site had been everything from a pleasure garden to an opera house. Now, after Mussolini laid waste to it in preparation for his own tomb, one he never came to occupy, it was a sad wreck of stone set in its own rough green moat of grass, half hidden between the 1930s Fascist offices set behind the Corso and the high embankment by the Tiber. The scrubby city grass was a favourite sleeping place for local tramps. The interior was a warren of dank, crumbling tunnels. It was so unsafe the public had been barred years ago.

"Thanks," he told Emily. "Now go get a coffee. Somewhere a long way from here."

He didn't wait for an answer. He started running north, towards the river. There was construction work everywhere. The authorities were creating a new home for the Ara Pacis, the Altar of Peace, one of the great legacies of Augustus, and a sight that had been withheld from Rome and the world for too long. But for now the area was a mess of cranes and closed roads, angry traffic and baffled pedestrians wondering where the pavement had gone.

He rounded a vast hoarding advertising the new Ara Pacis building and found himself facing the southern side of the mausoleum, with its locked entrance and steps leading down to the interior. It looked more dismal and decrepit than he remembered: a rotting circle of once golden stone falling into stumps at the summit, crowned by grass and weeds and ragged shrubbery. A couple of tourists hovered near the padlocked gate, wondering whether to take photos. Beyond the railing, Costa could see a bunch of itinerants huddled around the familiar objects that went with homeless life in the city: bottles of wine, mounds of old clothing, and a vast collection of supermarket bags bulging with belongings.

Then, as he was about to dial in for assistance, his

eyes came upon something worryingly familiar: a blonde woman in a long black winter coat. Emily was beyond the railings, just inside the mausoleum grounds. Costa briefly closed his eyes and murmured, "Wonderful."

His wife was sitting on the wall of a weed-riddled flower bed just the other side of the tourists, trying to look like a visitor who'd plucked up the courage to vault the fence. And, to his eyes, doing a very bad job of it. She was too animated, too interested, to be genuinely absorbed by the miserable sight in front of her. As he was realising this, she turned, caught sight of him, nodded down towards the green ditch in front of her, and mouthed a single word: *Here*.

At that moment a vast lorry bearing construction equipment roared in front of him and stopped with a sudden deliberation that meant, Costa knew instantly, it wasn't moving any farther. He dashed round the rear, a long way, heart thudding, found the temporary barrier for the works by the very side of the Ara Pacis, taking out his gun again, reminding himself there were now just two shots in the magazine, and probably no time to hope to reload as he ran.

When he rounded the timber hoardings, the tourists were still there. Emily was gone. His breathing halted for a moment. The police phone shook in his pocket. He took it out with trembling hands. It was Falcone.

"Where *are* you?" demanded the inspector.

"Augustus's mausoleum. He's inside. There are people around. We need to approach this carefully."

"That goes without saying," Falcone answered abruptly, and the line went dead.

"Indeed it does . . ." Costa murmured to himself.

He walked over to the tourists and told them to go somewhere else. They gaped at his face and his weapon, then fled. After that he climbed over the railings and scanned the area. The tramps were getting interested. One of them wandered over and demanded money. Costa brushed him aside. He came back.

"There's a woman here. And a man in brown. Where?" Costa asked.

One of the seated figures, huddled in an ancient black overcoat, nodded round the corner, past some green and dingy buttress that looked ready to collapse.

"Thanks," Costa said, nodding, and walked on, knowing, somehow, exactly what he'd see.

All the same, his heart froze the moment he found them.

They were no more than twenty metres away. The figure in khaki had met her—lured her?—into some dark dead end up against the deepest part of the moat, a place with no easy exit. He had his arm round Emily's neck. She was struggling as he dragged her backwards. The gun dangled over her chest, its dull barrel pressing against the black fabric of her coat. He was dragging on the hood as he fought to restrain her.

Costa let his weapon fall to his side, walked forward, and tried to count his options. A thought occurred to him.

*Emily knows you now.*

\*    \*    \*

THE KHAKI FIGURE DRAGGED EMILY ALL THE WAY TO the mausoleum's stone wall. There was nowhere else to go. Costa walked forward until he was no more than five paces from them. His wife's face was livid with rage. She never responded lightly to violence. The shotgun had been hard at her throat for at least part of their journey into this dark, shadowy alcove in the masonry. She looked mad and ready to act. The figure in khaki had no idea the woman in his grasp was a trained law enforcement officer, a woman who'd learned how to deal with hostage situations, skilled in self-defence, one who possessed, in all probability, more knowledge and experience in dealing with this kind of problem than Costa himself.

"Half the police in Rome will be here any minute." Costa said it quietly. "So how bad do you want this to be?"

"I really don't mind."

The voice behind the black hood was interesting. Cultured. Haughty. Local.

"Everyone minds in jail," Costa said. "Ten years or twenty. It's a big difference."

The figure laughed and Costa got the feeling, again, that this was someone outside the normal criminal mould.

"I'm not going to jail," the man responded, without a trace of doubt in his voice. "Not ever."

The gun was still tight across Emily's chest. There

was fury in her eyes, and a part of it, Nic knew, was aimed in his direction for taking this gentle, firm approach, for not trying to nail everything down with force and unbending iron will. Officers possessed different styles, Costa suddenly realised. This hoodlum had his wife, and a shotgun at her throat. All the training in the world meant nothing, sometimes, out in the cold light of day.

"Please..." Costa said, and held out his empty left hand in a gesture of pleading.

"Don't beg, Nic," Emily spat at him. "You *never* beg. It's the worst thing. You can do. The *worst*..."

He should have expected it. In one swift movement, Emily lifted her right leg and twisted it behind her, raking the man's shin with her sharp, hard heel. Then she arced her elbow back and jabbed it fiercely into his left shoulder, finding the most tender patch there as she fought free.

Costa took one step forward, raised the pistol in his right hand, and aimed it straight at the black hood, straight into those dark unseeable eyes.

Emily had hurt him. The man was crying with pain from the vicious scrape to his leg, hugging the shotgun to himself the way a child clung onto a toy.

"Let go of the gun," Costa said softly, "or I will, I swear, shoot you."

He stole a glance at his wife. Emily was to his right, just a step away, not close enough for the man to seize her again, not with the gun trained on him.

"Emily," Costa said firmly. "You don't belong here. Go back to the entrance. Now. Everybody will be here in a moment."

He could feel the heat in her gaze. This wasn't the way she thought things ought to be done.

"I'm fine. There's nobody else here, Nic. Can't you see?"

The man wasn't whining anymore. He was watching the two of them from behind the hood, his head cocked slightly to one side, listening, taking this all in. Taking in the fact they were more than mere acquaintances. Costa was certain of that.

He hadn't moved the shotgun an inch. It still lay in his arms like some evil infant. Then he mumbled something.

"What?" Costa asked.

"Pretty white girl," the man in brown said.

He laughed, and it was more like a giggle.

He leaned forward, looking conspiratorial.

"You *know* her."

"The gun," Costa emphasised.

The hood nodded.

Slowly, he held it out with both hands, one on the barrel, one on the stock, parallel to his body. He didn't do anything else.

"Drop the damned gun!" Costa yelled, and found his own weapon stiff in his outstretched hand.

What came next was a shrug. A gesture so Roman Costa had seen it a million times. When a street seller didn't have the change. When an errant motorist got caught for speeding. On all those small occasions when a tiny tear appeared in the fabric of an ordered life, and everyone—the culprit, the victim, the witness—just wished above all else they could pretend it had never happened, had never been seen.

"Pretty white girl," the hooded figure murmured again, in a different voice, one lower, one more serious, a voice that made Costa feel a chill run down his backbone.

He could see it now. The gun was horizontal in his hands, of no threat to anyone ahead, apparently unusable. But the thumb of the man's right hand—a thumb enclosed in the black cotton of a soldier's glove—was hooked through the trigger piece, ready, poised.

And the barrel had a certain, intent direction.

"Em—" Costa whispered, and was immediately aware that something—some bellowing, inhuman roar—wiped out the final syllables of her name.

# Part Three
## Funeral Rites

# One

$\mathcal{A}$ BRILLIANT WINTER'S DAY, SUNLIGHT STREAMING through the bedroom windows of the farmhouse, pigeons cooing noisily on the roof, the buzzing drone of a distant jet turning for Ciampino.

Costa woke and in that shifting, formless space between dream and reality was briefly disoriented as he struggled towards consciousness. From downstairs he could hear a soft, familiar feminine voice calling his name.

Still half asleep, he dragged himself to the door and walked to the head of the stairs.

"Nic," she said, "it's time. You have to get dressed. There are people here."

Pepe, the small terrier that had accompanied his youth, now approaching sixteen and refusing to accept his frailty, sat at Bea Savarino's feet, quiet and calm, staring at him placidly from the foot of the stairs. Bea wore black, just as she had for his father's funeral, after all those long months of nursing him through the final stages of his illness. On the low table next to her sat a pile of unopened Christmas cards, most still with two names at the top of the address.

"Of course," he said.

A person did not disappear easily. Emily was dead. It didn't mean that every trace of her being, her sharp, keen personality, had departed the house. Bea had patiently, subtly taken her clothes to the charity shop during the ten days since the shooting, had cleaned the house, reorganised it so that his life did not fall apart any more than was necessary. There was an excuse, naturally. Her own apartment in Trastevere was undergoing some work, which made it convenient for her to stay at the farmhouse again, with Nic's permission, which he gave willingly, not quite thinking or understanding much at the time, for a simple and obvious reason: inside he felt dead, utterly detached from anything that happened around him.

In his work he'd told so many bereaved relatives that it was impossible for their loved ones to be given speedy funerals because they were the victims of crime. He'd said, always, he understood their grief. Now he really did, and it wasn't what he'd expected at all. Had Teresa Lupo not intervened with a clear-cut statement that she would not, under any circumstances, permit Emily's body to lie in the police mortuary any longer, since there were no evidentiary or scientific grounds for its retention, his agony would be continuing, as it would have for most civilians. Instead, for him, came a fixed point in the calendar, a date on which the remains of his wife of a few, too-short months would make one final journey, then disappear behind a pair of velvet crematorium curtains. After which her physical presence would be gone forever, leaving a chasm in his own existence which seemed to grow with each passing hour, not diminish.

It was the week before Christmas and he was a widower before he'd turned thirty. Costa hadn't wept yet. He'd still to find the key to that particular secret. It had eluded him from the moment he recovered consciousness after the figure in khaki clubbed him to the ground during those few, agonising seconds by the Mausoleum of Augustus, a sequence of events that continued to replay themselves inside his head with a cruel, vivid authenticity when he least expected it.

That, and the possibilities. What if she'd taken his advice and gone for a coffee, against, he knew, all her innate instincts? Or what if he'd shot the bastard straightaway when there was the slightest hesitation? As these images revolved in his brain, endlessly, never resting, her death seemed to swim in what-ifs and alternative endings. One more prominent than the other, and he could hear the words uttered from his own throat; as if he'd had time to say them directly to that figure with the black hood and the unseeable eyes: *Shoot me instead. Take my life because it's so much less worthy, so unimportant next to hers, which is bright and smart and leading to something she has yet to imagine for herself.*

And that was the harshest thought of all. Because

inside it lay something Emily Deacon——he'd never really thought of her with the married name——would not have tolerated for an instant. Self-pity. Defeat. The tantalising, appealing black pit of gloom into which it was so easy to descend, a place he knew already, a dark haven that beckoned him, in a bottle, in a wallowing morass of despair.. Which was why the white lie about the apartment in Trastevere was invented, why his father's former caregiver——and perhaps onetime lover——moved in so quickly to try to save him.

"NIC!" THE FAMILIAR FEMALE VOICE SAID AGAIN, WITH that half-scolding tone he'd come to know so well.

Bea walked upstairs carrying the black suit from the cleaners, a white shirt ironed so perfectly it seemed new, and a dark tie she must have bought for the occasion.

He took them and said thank you.

Bea, pretty Bea, the stiff-backed, elegant woman he'd loved, in a way, as a child, stood in front of him, her eyes full of concern. She had a tan from a winter holiday in South Africa. The customary gold necklace hung around her neck. There were wrinkles on the tanned skin now as she approached sixty, though she looked as beautiful as ever in an expensive dark funeral dress and shoes.

"You must come," she said, and put a firm, warm hand to his cheek.

"I will, I promise," he replied obediently.

She had something on her mind and was reluctant to come out with it.

He stared at her, waiting.

"For pity's sake, Nic, let a little of this grief go," she pleaded. "God gave us tears for a reason."

It was a strange thing for a lapsed communist, even one as middle-class as Bea, to say.

"I didn't think you believed in God," he observed.

"I don't know what I believe in anymore, Nic. Do you?"

# Two

$f$OUR HOURS LATER THEY WERE BACK, MEANDERING around the table of food Bea had prepared, chattering in the idle, restless, uncomfortable way that happened after funerals. People he knew. Strangers from America, who were distant with him, for good reason. This was the first time they'd met Emily's Italian police-officer husband. It would be the last too.

Teresa Lupo had hardly spoken a word. She was in the kitchen, a disconsolate, untidy figure seated on a chair at the table, not eating or drinking, Peroni holding her hand, watching the tears pouring down her cheeks. The pathologist had been fine in the crematorium. It was the farmhouse, the place the four of them had spent so many hours, that got to her. Teresa worked with death, was comfortable with its presence in the surroundings where it belonged. In a house, one that had so briefly been Emily's home, everything was different.

Costa walked over from the living room, placed a hand on her shoulder, saw the way she wasn't able to meet his eyes, then received a knowing nod from Peroni. There came a time when there were no more words of consolation left, for any of them. This was that time. Emily was gone. He'd spent eleven days in some curious limbo where bureaucracy—formal identifications and death certificates—mixed with the ludicrous long hours dealing with funeral directors. And, in between, when he found the opportunity, trying and failing to convince Falcone to let him return from compassionate leave to work on the case.

Instead, the inspector had insisted he stay away, placing a car at the end of the drive to keep the determined army of curious media out and, Costa knew, him in. Emily had told him what the newspapers were like. A photogenic death always meant headlines. She'd been proved right, and the lurid facts of the case had only served to feed the media frenzy. The beautiful wife of a Roman police officer was dead, murdered in front of his eyes by a killer who'd fled a crime scene where, it later transpired, several other women, one of them an upper-class French art historian, had died. The story contained all the elements the media loved: attractive women, vicious crimes of a sexual nature, and an apparent inability on the part of the police to locate a single potential suspect, in spite of a huge, and national, hunt.

Costa had ordered every important newspaper, had watched most of the daily news bulletins, and had followed the case on the Web, the way Emily had showed him. Two things continued to nag at him. It was impossible, surely, to believe the police had not come across a single lead in a case so rich with forensic evidence. And no one ever mentioned the painting, the image of which had yet to be entirely displaced by the shocking memories of what came after.

He waited until people began drifting away. Leo Falcone had arrived with Raffaella Arcangelo; the two seemed so friendly that Costa wondered if that romance had returned. A sudden death altered the landscape. Falcone was a man who enjoyed his own company, but had found something else during the time Raffaella had cared for him the previous year. Now that he was fit and active in the Questura, he had no need for her physical support. But emotionally ... Costa wondered, as he watched Falcone slyly remove himself from the dwindling crowd, find the back door, then disappear into the garden.

He excused himself from the kindly American cousin who stood next to him, running out of words, and followed Falcone outside. There had been a time when the inspector would have been smoking one of his foul-smelling cigarettes. That habit had disappeared. He was seated by the decrepit wooden table that looked out over the bowed, blackened vines, a place where Nic and Emily had entertained all four of them—Falcone and Raffaella, Teresa and Peroni—often the previous summer.

Costa took a seat next to his boss and stared at the land. Everything—the house, the garden, the fields—

seemed larger somehow. Emily's absence magnified the world and its emptiness.

FALCONE CAST A QUICK LOOK BACK THROUGH THE french windows, into the lounge.

"I'd smoke if I could get away with it. Women..."

Costa briefly closed his eyes and stifled his astonishment—which should not, he knew, have been so great—at the man's lack of tact.

"You and Raffaella... I don't want to pry, Leo."

"Oh." Falcone kicked at some pebbles on the ground. Sometimes he was alarmingly childlike. "That's back on. I called her." He turned to look at Costa, as if asking for some kind of reassurance. "I needed to, Nic. Not just to make arrangements for today. I wanted to see her. Everything seemed so cold otherwise. It wasn't that I felt alone, you understand."

Costa made some sympathetic sound.

"God..." Falcone shook his head with a sudden bitter fury. "I miss Emily. I miss that bright mind. And talking to her. She didn't think the way we do. I could listen to her throwing an idea around for hours. It's all so... futile."

He turned to Costa and made his next point with that familiar long index finger. "Had that architect's career not worked out, I would have got her into the police, you know." He sighed. "Lord knows we need officers who see things differently. Particularly today."

76 ・ David Hewson

"Leo . . ." Costa said, a little testily.

"What?"

"Is this your version of sympathy? Do you behave this way at all funerals?"

"Most funerals I avoid!" Falcone replied, hurt. "What do you mean?"

"I mean, you're saying what I'm supposed to say. And I'm listening to what you're supposed to listen to."

"Oh." The old man nodded. Perhaps there was a vestige of comprehension there. "*That* kind of sympathy."

Falcone reached over and patted Costa's knee. His avian face had a winter tan, the silver goatee was newly trimmed, and his eyes were full of intelligence, understanding, and a firm, unbending friendship.

"You surely know how I feel, Nic. How we all feel. Do I really have to spell it out? I'm not a man for wasted words. I never have been. If you need me, you know where I am. The same goes for Gianni and Teresa, though I imagine they've told you that ten times over, because that's their way."

They hadn't, in fact. Costa understood why. In some strange way the four of them were so close that they had no need of these spoken reassurances. Those were reserved for outsiders.

"So?" Falcone asked.

"So what?"

"So when would you like to come back to work?"

"I'll be back the instant you want me."

"Good. There's an attachment coming up in Sicily

just after Christmas. It would be an excellent opportunity under any circumstances. People-smuggling. Rome needs some expertise there."

"Sicily." Costa groaned.

"Sicily," the inspector agreed.

Costa waited, searching for the words.

"This is what friends are for, Leo. I have never exercised that friendship until now. I want this case. Emily's murder. You have to give it to me."

A swarm of dark crows danced on the horizon, near the distant circular outline of the tomb of a long-dead Imperial matron, Cecilia Metella. Falcone watched them for several long seconds, then said, "I can't do that. I find it grossly unfair of you to exert personal pressure in this way. Compassionate leave could stretch to a month or more if you want it."

"I'd be even crazier after a month. This is enough. Besides, I have every right . . ."

The crows lost their importance. Falcone turned to him, a flash of anger in his face.

"You have no rights whatsoever, other than those of any other bereaved civilian. Don't be so ridiculous. An officer investigating his own wife's death? What do you think the media would make of that? Or those clowns on the seventh floor?"

"It's an investigation into several murders. I would leave my own feelings to one side."

"Who do you hope to fool with that argument? Me? Or yourself?"

Costa didn't have a good answer, only pretexts, and now, faced with Falcone's stubbornness, he knew they wouldn't work.

"I have to do something."

Falcone shook his bald head. It gleamed under the low winter sun.

Costa sought the words. These thoughts had dogged him ever since her death. They wouldn't go away. "I can't bury her, Leo. Not properly. Unless . . ." He sighed. "I need to work. Otherwise everything just keeps going round and round in my head."

Falcone shrugged. "Then work in Sicily."

"I have to do something *here*."

"I hate personal issues," Falcone grumbled. "You feel responsible. It's understandable. Anyone would. It's the way we're made. It will pass."

"No," Costa murmured. "It won't. Not on its own."

"And what if you fail?" the older man asked severely. "What will that do to you?"

"I won't fail." That thought had really never occurred to him.

Falcone sniffed, took a sly look back at the house again, slipped a small cigar out of his pocket, then lit it. "You have no idea what you're asking. We are more than a week into this investigation, yet I have nothing . . ." He scowled. Some thought, some irritant, affected him at that moment. " . . . nothing concrete to show for all the work we've done. Frankly, several aspects baffle me more every time I look at them. With you gone and

Peroni drooping around the place like a dog that's lost its best friend...we're not in top form, to be honest. They're already whispering upstairs that perhaps we should hand over everything to the Carabinieri. If I could do this, Nic, do you honestly believe I'd turn you down?"

"You can find a way," Costa insisted. "You always do."

Falcone was up on his feet, with an easy swiftness that showed the injuries that had troubled him since the shooting in Venice were now in the past. Falcone could do it. His standing in the Questura was high again. He could do anything he liked, if he wanted.

And now he was angry. The heat suffused his walnut cheeks.

"Dammit!" he barked, just loud enough for a few faces at the window to turn in their direction. "What kind of occasion is this to start throwing professional demands at me?"

"It's my murdered wife's funeral, sir," Costa replied with a flat, cold disdain.

# Three

$\mathcal{H}$ALF-RECOGNISED FACES, PEOPLE HE HADN'T SEEN for years. Funerals always brought them out, and Costa had never been good with names. They were almost all gone within thirty minutes, leaving Bea clearing away the plates and glasses and Costa talking to a somewhat embarrassed Raffaella Arcangelo alone in a chair in the dining room, stroking the ancient, half-slumbering dog.

"You'll have to go and speak to him, Nic," she said. "It's freezing cold out there, he doesn't have a jacket, and he won't come in of his own accord."

"It's like dealing with a child," he complained.

She nodded. "I have very little experience with children but I must admit it does sound very similar. All the same . . ."

Costa stormed outside, bracing for another argument. Falcone was back at the decrepit wooden table, puffing on another cigar, blowing the smoke out towards the dead, hunched vines waiting for spring and a reawakening.

He watched Costa sit down, then said, "You'd have to work over Christmas."

"That," Costa replied, exasperated, "is hardly an obstacle."

Falcone nodded. "I hate Christmas too."

The last few people were drifting outside, Raffaella among them. They couldn't, Nic knew, leave without saying goodbye. This had to be brought to an end.

"What am I supposed to *do*, Leo?"

The shrewd old eyes flashed at him again. There was an unmistakable expression of self-doubt in them, something Costa had rarely seen in his boss. Falcone reached into his jacket pocket. He withdrew a copious set of keys and removed two from the ring.

"These are for my old apartment in the *centro storico*, in Governo Vecchio. You know it?"

Costa had never been invited there. The place predated Raffaella and the apartment she had shared with Falcone. But he knew the location, just a stone's throw from the Piazza Navona.

"I had been planning to move back there now that I can walk properly," Falcone went on. "But Raffaella prefers Monti. Here."

He handed Costa the keys.

"I have a home," he protested, waving a hand at the house.

"Bea can look after it. In three days' time I want you to pack your bags. Expect to be gone a week or more.

And"—the finger jabbed at him—"don't tell a soul where you're going."

This was interesting, Costa thought.

"Teresa is due to deliver some kind of news to me then," Falcone continued, before Costa could ask a single question. "The woman never hurries, naturally. You have a reason to be at that meeting. Take it. We are due at that damned studio for her theatricals. Afterwards you will return to compassionate leave. In my apartment. I will explain later."

He looked lost for a moment, staring at the grey horizon as if seeking answers. "Finding a criminal is only half the challenge," he added cryptically. "Don't make me regret this, Nic."

Costa didn't have time to answer. A voice drifted from the door. It was Raffaella. Falcone dipped the cigar down below his waist and flicked it into the vineyard with a long, agile finger.

"You have some identification for these dead African women?" Costa asked in a quiet voice.

"What do you think?" Falcone grumbled. "If a man wishes to commit a crime, best commit it against the underclass. These women's families are too scared to complain. Or . . ." He didn't wish to go on.

"Someone has to be able to ID them, Leo."

"You'd think . . ." the inspector replied with a sour, pinched smile. "Fake names. Fake identities. These are illegal immigrants desperate to stay out of our way. Even when we do find them . . ." He shrugged.

"There must be—" Costa insisted.

"Nic. Please. Enough. I have two officers in Nigeria at this very moment, following up the only real lead we have. It could take months of work, even if people there are willing to speak to us, and they won't be. Do not equate your absence in all this with a lack of effort on our part. Nothing could be further from the truth."

Costa shook his head. "I never meant it that way," he murmured. "I just don't understand—"

"None of us understands. Perhaps Teresa will shed a little light on matters when we meet. But there's something else you must do first. That painting we found in the studio. You must either tell me it's important or let me forget about it altogether. An art expert attached to the Barberini is due to start looking at it shortly. I will make some calls, arrange an appointment for you. I happen to have made this expert's acquaintance before. She comes highly recommended. The woman's name is Agata Graziano. The gallery has a laboratory close to the Piazza Borghese. She's the best apparently. And there's one more thing . . ."

He elaborated no more and simply gazed at the still-smouldering cigar on the cold winter earth. Then he said: "I want whoever did this, Nic. Just as much as you."

Part Four

The Barberini's Expert

# One

$\mathcal{I}$T WAS RAINING WHEN HE DROVE OUT OF THE FARM-
house three days later, leaving Bea performing some unnecessary cleaning, and issuing persistent queries about
where he was going and why. Costa had no sensible answers. He had a suitcase full enough for a week away, as
Falcone had demanded. He felt glad to be out of the place,
too, to be moving. Inactivity didn't suit him, and perhaps
the inspector understood that only too well. The previous
night he'd barely slept for thinking about the case, and
Falcone's strangely gloomy assessment of what had been
achieved so far. It was highly unusual for the old inspector
to be so pessimistic at such a relatively early point in an investigation.

The city was choked with holiday traffic. The narrow
lanes, now full of specialist shops selling antiques and furniture and clothes, were cloaked in skeins of Christmas
lights twinkling over the crowds. It took ten minutes to
find somewhere to park near the Piazza Borghese, even
with police ID on the vehicle.

Costa's opinion of the painting at the crime scene had not altered since the black day of December 8. In truth, for him, little had changed since the moment Emily had been snatched from life. It was as if his world had ceased to move, and in this sense of stasis the only certainty that remained was what he'd realised about the canvas he had first seen in the studio in the Vicolo del Divino Amore. Either it really was an unknown Caravaggio or somehow they had come across an extraordinary fake. There had been plenty of copyists over the years, both genuine artists working in Caravaggio's style by way of tribute and con men trying to hoodwink naive buyers into thinking they had discovered some new masterpiece. At home, alone, desperate to think of something other than those last moments by the mausoleum, Costa had taken out his old art books, delved deep into the images and the histories there, welcoming the respite he could take from the thoughts that haunted him. The dark, violent genius who was Caravaggio had lived in Rome for just fourteen years, from 1592 until 1606, when he fled under sentence of death for murder. Every genuine homage that Costa could find had made it plain through some reference, stylistic or by way of subject, that it came from the brush of another. Every fake was, by dint of the original's extraordinary technical skill, modest in reach, an attempt to convince the potential buyer that it came from Caravaggio's early period in Rome, when he was open to quick, cheap private commissions, though even then only on his own terms and for subjects of which he approved.

As Nic remembered it, the canvas from the Vicolo del Divino Amore seemed to fit neither of these templates. That painting was bold, extraordinarily ambitious, and far more substantial than an ordinary collection piece thrown up on some brief commission in order to pay a pressing bill. It stood more than two metres wide and half as high, housed in a plain gilt frame that had faded to the dark sheen of old gold. Even with the briefest of glances, Costa had been able to detect telltale signs of the painter's individual style. Seen from an angle to the side, close to where the body of Véronique Gillet lay on the grey flagstones, still and deathly pale, he had been able to make out the faintest of incisions, preparatory guide-lines cut with a stylus or sharp pen, similar to those etched into plaster by fresco painters, a technique no other artist of the time was known to use on canvas.

The *sfumato*—a gradation from dark to light so subtle that it was impossible to discern the blend of an outline or border—appeared exquisite. Taken as a whole, the abiding style of the piece went beyond mere *chiaroscuro,* the histrionic balance of light and shade first developed by da Vinci. During his brief life, Caravaggio had taken da Vinci's model and emboldened the drama with a fierce, almost brutal approach in which the core figures were set apart from the background and the characters around them by a bright, unforgiving light, like a ray of pure shining spirit. The effect was to heighten the emotional tension of the scene to a degree hitherto unseen in the work of any artist. There was a technical term for the style Caravaggio had pioneered, *tenebrismo,* from the Latin *tenebrae,* for shadows, and it was this that made paintings like the conversion of Saint Paul and the final moments of Peter on the cross so electrifying, so timeless.

HE FOUND HIS VIVID RECOLLECTIONS OF THOSE CANvases racing through his head as he followed the directions Falcone had given him for the laboratory of the Galleria Barberini. When he got there, he realised it could have been no more than half a kilometre from the studio in the Vicolo del Divino Amore itself, though the distance was deceptive, since a straight line would run principally through hard Renaissance brick and stone, unseen halls and buildings hidden behind high, smogstained windows.

Both the laboratory and the studio appeared to be part of the black lumbering mass that was the Palazzo Malaspina, an ugly façade for what was reputedly one of the finest remaining private palaces still in original hands. No one set foot inside the palazzo itself without an invitation. But it was no great surprise, Costa decided, that areas of the vast edifice were rented to outsiders. Shops, apartments, offices, and even a few restaurants seemed to find shelter in the area covered by its sprawling wings.

The small, almost invisible sign for the Barberini's outpost was in a side alley off the relatively busy Via della Scrofa. He rang the bell and waited for only thirty seconds. A guard in the blue civilian uniform of one of the large private security companies opened the door. He had a belt full of equipment and a holster with a handgun poking prominently out of the top. There were valuable paintings here, Costa reminded himself. One perhaps more valuable than anyone else appreciated.

Before he could say a word, a short slender figure in a plain billowing black dress emerged from behind the guard's bulky frame.

"I'll deal with this, Paolo," she declared, in a tone that sent the man scuttling back to his post next to the door without another word.

The woman was perhaps thirty, dark-skinned, with a pert, inquisitive face, narrow and pleasant rather than attractive, with gleaming brown eyes beneath a high and intellectual forehead. A large silver crucifix hung on a chain around her neck. A black garment which Costa thought might be called a scapular was draped around her slight shoulders. She seemed somewhat anxious. Her full head of black shiny hair hung in disorganised tresses, kept untidily together by pins. In her left hand she held a couple of creased and clearly old plastic grocery bags bulging with papers and notes and photographs, as if they were some kind of replacement for a briefcase.

It took a moment for Costa to understand. "I'm

sorry, Sister," he apologized. "I'm looking for the Barberini laboratory. I have an appointment."

She reached into one of the plastic bags, took out a very green apple, bit into it greedily, and, mouth full, asked, "You are Nic?"

He nodded.

"Come in. You don't look like you do in the pictures in the papers," she replied, turning, then marching down the long corridor with a swift, deliberate gait, her heavy leather shoes clattering on the wooden floor.

He followed, hurrying to keep up. "You read the papers?" he asked, surprised.

She turned and laughed. "Of course I read the papers! What am I? A monk?"

They walked into a brightly lit chamber at the end. It was like entering an operating theatre. The painting sat on a bright new modern easel beneath a set of soft, insistent lighting that exposed every portion of it. Costa stared and felt his breath catch. The canvas radiated light and life and an extraordinary, magnetic power.

The nun sat down and finished her apple in four bites. Then she placed the core back in one of the grocery bags, took out a wrinkled paper handkerchief, and patted her lips. Costa had little experience in dealing with the city's religious community. There was rarely any need.

"I've an appointment with Signora Agata Graziano," he explained. "Will she be long?"

She folded her slender arms and stared at him. "Are you a detective?"

He shuffled on his feet, stealing glances at the painting. "Rumour has it," he muttered.

"Then tell me what you make of this. You have an appointment with a woman. You come here. I am a woman. You see me." Her skinny arms opened wide, a look of theatrical disbelief spread across her dark face. "And . . . ?"

Costa blinked. "I never thought you'd be a nun."

"I'm not. Sit down, please."

He took the chair next to her.

The woman's alert, dusky face took on the patient, if slightly exasperated, expression of a teacher dealing with a slow pupil. "I am a sister, not a nun. I took simple vows, not solemn ones. It's complicated. I won't trouble you with this."

"I'm sorry, Sister."

"Agata, please. When I am here, I am here as an academic. When I am at home, you can call me 'Sister.' Except you are not allowed in my home. So the point is moot."

"I consider myself both enlightened and chastised."

She laughed. "Oh . . . a *sarcastic* detective. I like that. Convents lack sarcasm. Throw it at me as much as you like. Now, your first question."

"Is it genuine?" he asked, gesturing at the painting.

She rolled her large brown eyes and threw back her head. Then, to Costa's amazement, something akin to a curse, albeit a very mild one by Roman standards, escaped her lips.

"Nic, Nic, Nic," Agata Graziano complained. "When I walk outside my convent, I'm a historian first and a lover of art second. I don't make rash judgments. I need to ask some scientific people in here to examine paint and canvas samples. To take X-rays and consult with others of their ilk. Also, I need to look further at what records we have from that time."

The painting was so near he could almost touch it. Costa was enjoying the ability to see it up close again, under decent light. Nothing there changed his original opinion.

"The records won't tell you much," he suggested.

She stared at him, another teacher-like look, this time of exaggerated surprise, and said, "What?"

"If this is a private commission of Caravaggio's, the chances are there won't be a mention of it anywhere," Costa replied. "From what I've read, the only reliable records are for his church works. It makes sense. Those paintings had to be paid for with public money. That had to be accounted for. When he was employed by individuals, he might have had nothing more than a letter. Perhaps not even that."

"I was under the impression art was the responsibility of the Carabinieri," she observed.

"I was under the impression the Barberini employed its own people."

She delivered up a jocular scowl, one that said *touché.*
Then nothing else.

"Why *are* you here?" he asked.

"Because they believe I happen to be the best person for
the job. Their usual suspects are in New York, supervising
some coming show at the Metropolitan Museum. My luck.
And"——she emphasised this point with a sharp look at the
painting——"they are correct. There are a few things I don't
know about our mutual friend Michelangelo Merisi da
Caravaggio. But they are just a few, and on those no one else
is any the wiser either. There. Immodesty masquerading as
frankness. I have one more thing to confess."

She hesitated. "And you?" she asked.

"I'm just interested. That's all," Costa answered.

"I meant about something to confess."

He didn't know what to say.

Agata Graziano screwed up her eyes with a sudden
embarrassment so real Costa wondered what to do.

"Oh, I'm sorry. I read the papers. I'm an idiot. I apologise."

"For what?"

"For treating you like this. You lost your wife and
here I am making jokes."

Costa wanted to utter something about the way the
earth kept turning regardless of individual tragedies.
Instead, he said, "I came back to work because I wanted
to. I'll deal with what that brings."

"A brave idea," she observed. "But a wise one? What

do I know? I'm just an academic who thought this was purely business when clearly it isn't."

"This is business," he emphasised.

"If you insist. I am not very good at sympathy, I'm afraid."

"There's no need to be. You don't know me."

"Is that relevant?" she wondered. "In any case I am saddened by your cruel loss. I cannot begin to imagine how it must feel." She paused, a little uncertain of herself. "Can we consider that done with now?"

"Please. There's one other reason to think you won't find a record," he said quickly, wishing to change the topic.

"That being?"

"Paintings like this weren't for public viewing. They were commissioned for some special room in the house. To be seen only by a wife or a lover, or a male friend one wanted to impress."

He stopped, wondering whether he was blushing. Years ago he had read widely about this type of work in an effort to understand how much of Caravaggio's output, and that of his peers, might have been lost. The depressing answer was: a lot. The famous canvases of naked young boys—works that, some believed incorrectly, had led the artist to be accused of being a homosexual—fell precisely into this category. They were daring, at the very edge of acceptability in a city where sexual crimes could carry heavy penalties and sodomy itself was deemed worthy of a death sentence. Such paintings only survived because they had entered large and well-maintained collections early in the seventeenth century. Lesser, or more obscure, works were often destroyed or reused by later artists for their own purposes. Countless examples from private collections of the period, by Caravaggio and his contemporaries, had been lost forever, recorded, if at all, only in the private correspondence and diaries of those who had been lucky enough to see them. Costa was unsure how to elaborate on these delicate matters with a woman who called herself a sister.

"So you think it might be genuine?" he asked again.

"Persistence," she answered. "You are a detective after all. I have a confession. When your inspector called, I was able to obtain a dispensation from my normal duties in the convent. Most of them, anyway, for a few days. So I have a little spare time on my hands, which I spent yesterday examining this painting, then this morning looking at what archival material I could lay my hands on easily. They kept very good records in the sixteenth and seventeenth centuries, by the way. You should be grateful. The Uffizi owns a letter from a contemporary of Caravaggio's, the poet Giambattista Marino, which may refer to a canvas very like this one. In 1599 Marino writes that he saw a painting of Caravaggio's which was so consummate in execution, and so reckless in subject, he doubted anyone dare show it, even to those closest to him. Least of all the man who commissioned it, who was a cardinal in the Church."

"Then how come this Marino character got to see it?"

"Where's your imagination?" She seemed a little disappointed by his question. "Marino was a poet. He lived in Ortaccio, just as Caravaggio did. They probably got drunk together all the time."

"Ortaccio," he replied. So much was coming back from the days when he spent every waking hour with a book about Caravaggio and his world. "The cardinal was Del Monte?"

She clapped her small brown hands in delight. The noise rang around the empty room, loud and happy.

"Bravo! I think you are a well-informed detective." She was idly fidgeting with the crucifix on her chest as they spoke and seemed, to Costa, utterly without guile, without a single layer of self-awareness sitting between her and the world.

"I read in the paper that your father was a communist," she remarked. "I imagined you would know nothing of a churchman such as Del Monte."

He felt a little disturbed by the degree of interest she had taken in him since Falcone had, presumably, called her the previous day to ask for assistance.

"Communism is a kind of faith too," he replied.

"The wrong one. But I imagine a misplaced faith is better than none at all. What do you think?"

"I think Del Monte was no ordinary churchman," Costa answered. "He had arcane tastes. He was a cardinal, a favourite of the Pope. But he also dabbled in alchemy and obscure science. There were rumours of homosexuality and licentiousness."

"It was Rome!" she cried. "There are always rumours, just like now."

"I agree. It was a bohemian court at the time. Galileo was one of his hangers-on while Caravaggio was there. A work such as this would not be out of place, though one can see why it was not on general show."

She nodded, watching him with those gleaming eyes. "Even a sister knows the sexual content of this painting would be a little rich for the time," she agreed. "Perhaps for these times too. There is one more thing we know from Marino's letter. He writes that Caravaggio 'took Carracci's whore and turned her into a goddess.' Any idea what that means?"

"None," Costa replied, baffled.

She beamed. "Well, I'm pleased *I* can tell *you* something new."

Agata Graziano led him across the room to a computer screen on a nearby desk, then sat down and began typing. Almost instantly a painting appeared on the screen, one similar to the canvas in the room, but paler, cruder. It was clear from the style and execution that the artist was not Caravaggio.

"You can see this in the Uffizi today when they feel like showing it. Just a few years later, dear old Annibale was painting the ceilings in the Palazzo Farnese and declaring himself the most pious creature in Rome. And here you have him depicting..." She stared at him frankly. "...what, exactly, do you think?"

Costa was still trying to grasp the implications of the canvas on the computer screen. It was like the Caravaggio, but unlike it.

"Pornography?" she asked bluntly, when he remained silent.

"If it was pornography, I doubt it would be hanging in the Uffizi."

"Pornography masquerading as art, then," she observed. "Which would be worse, since therein lies hypocrisy."

"I really don't know," Costa said, and meant it.

"Tell me what you *see*, Nic," she insisted. "Spare me no details."

Her skin was so dark he wondered whether he truly saw a blush there.

The computer told him the plain facts. The painting by Annibale Carracci was known as *Venus with a Satyr and Cupids*. It depicted the goddess half reclining on a rich velvet bed, her back half turned to the viewer, a crumpled sheet discreetly covering her midriff, then winding round her torso until her right hand gripped it, in a gesture, perhaps, of fading bliss. A dark-skinned Dionysian satyr leered in front of her, bearing a bowl overflowing with grapes. Behind her head a small cupid played, gazing out of the frame of the canvas. Another small figure was depicted at the bottom left of the scene, and it was this that lent the work its curious, half-obscene nature. The creature's face was positioned by the thigh of the goddess, as if it had recently been close to her, and, in a gesture of astonishing frankness, a small, stiff, muscular tongue protruded lasciviously from its mouth. Its eyes were wild and rolling. While the body of the goddess seemed to hint at intimacy—in the stiffened muscles of her abdomen and the arched position of her legs—her face was placid, almost detached. It was as if the expression Carracci wished to paint on her had been transferred, instead, to the cupid between her thighs in some final failing of courage.

Costa said this all out loud, keeping his eyes firmly on the canvas.

"Good," Agata complimented him. "But let's leave the inferior. What do you think of this?"

She gestured at the canvas on the modern easel. Costa took a step towards it, trying to force himself to think carefully, logically.

An art teacher at school had once told him, "Always begin with the name." The title of a work was not some simple label. It described both its direction and ambitions, and its origins too. So he dragged his attention away from the canvas itself and looked at a small golden plate in the middle of the lower horizontal arm of the frame. It bore the same words as the Carracci, this time written in carved, archaic capitals: VENUS WITH A SATYR AND CUPIDS.

This painting was like its inferior relative in some respects, perhaps even inspired by it, since the canvas in the Uffizi was dated circa 1588, when Caravaggio was fifteen and merely an apprentice. But in execution it was entirely different. This work was more adventurous, more competently delivered, and infinitely more erotic, too, though in a subtle, almost sinister way. The artist had produced nothing explicit. Instead he placed the onus of interpretation entirely upon the viewer. An innocent might see this as some strange classical idyll, a mythical female beauty surrounded by her admirers. But a more mature—more carnal—interpretation was hidden inside the exquisite strokes of the artist's brush. Caravaggio had played this trick often enough, daring the beholder to imagine what deeds and actions were taking place just out of view or obscured behind some foreground object. Never had the master done it with such elusive wit and cunning skill.

There were clear references to another Caravaggio work Costa knew only too well, and had often visited in the sprawling palace of the Doria Pamphilj in the Piazza del Collegio Romano, perhaps a ten-minute walk away. The model for this Venus was surely the same as the beautiful red-haired woman in *The Rest on the Flight from Egypt*. But she was not slumbering with the infant Jesus in her arms, unknowingly listening to a lustrous angel playing the violin to sheet music held by a grizzled Joseph. Here she was entirely naked, back half turned to the viewer, as in Carracci's work, recumbent on some scarlet sofa, and attended again by two cupids and a more dominant leering satyr, central to the composition behind the woman. Like Joseph in the painting in the Doria Pamphilj, this larger male figure had in his hands a piece of music, single notes this time, distinct on the stave, with impenetrable lyrics in Latin beneath. The cherub in the sky to the right held a jug from which some pale liquid fell slowly, carelessly, into a silver goblet in his left hand, poured, one imagined, for the goddess. The second cherub, in the left-hand corner, lay lazily on one elbow, mouth open, singing from the satyr's notation, and with a tongue that protruded only slightly, not with the rigid, suggestive vigour of Carracci's satyr, though once again it seemed to carry some reference to the earlier work, with its fleshy, almost obscene grotesqueness. The creature carried a perfect golden apple in its right hand. In the background were more trees, some bearing fruit, and a scene reminiscent of a classical Renaissance garden, a subject Caravaggio had never, to Costa's recollection, depicted in any other work.

Costa examined the satyr's face closely and felt, for a moment, dizzy with a sense of revelation. The bearded individual there, inquisitive, prurient, unable to draw himself away from the scene though a part of him found it disturbing, was uncannily similar to the several self-portraits Caravaggio had inserted in everything from the famous martyrdom of Saint Matthew in Luigi dei Francesi to the late, spectacular beheading of John the Baptist in Malta. At that moment Costa felt he was staring into the very features of the stricken, violent genius who had died on the beach at Port'Ercole in 1610, a hundred kilometres from Rome, on a futile final journey home spurred by a papal pardon for the murder of an enemy in a street four years before.

"It has to be authentic," he murmured.

"Then what is it?" Agata demanded. "Caravaggio would never stoop to making copies, even when he was starving."

Costa saw her point. The central figure in the painting—he recalled now the name of the volatile Ortaccio whore, Fillide Melandroni, used by Caravaggio as a model for biblical and mythical characters—was quite unlike the Venus in Carracci's version, remote, distanced, controlled, almost detached from the scene. On the canvas before them, Venus had been transformed by a knowing adult imagination. Alive, engaged, ecstatic, she ceased to be an unreal mythical goddess at play in paradise. She became a living woman, one in a familiar state for those able to recognise it. The canvas was innocent—until seen by someone who was not.

Even so, it seemed distant from the grim and seedy serial murder into which he had unwittingly led Emily, with such terrible results.

"I don't know exactly," he murmured. "Do you?"

Her small, round mouth screwed up into a childlike grimace. "I told you," she replied. "I'm thinking. Slowly. There's no other way. How can I call you?"

She took a small notebook out of the nearest plastic bag and stared at him. Costa once more had the feeling that he was a schoolboy in the presence of the brightest and sternest teacher. The encounter was over, he realised, with some relief. In truth it wasn't a meeting at all. It was a test, an interrogation so subtle he had scarcely perceived it.

Wondering how well he had done, Costa circled the cell phone number on his card and passed it over.

"Just use this for the time being. You won't find me in the Questura." He had to ask. "And you?"

The throaty musical sound of her laughter echoed around the room once more.

"I've taken vows of common and personal poverty and that includes business cards. I have no phone of my own, mobile or otherwise. You may pass on a message through the convent. Here."

He watched her scribble something on a sheet of paper and rip it from the pad.

"But if you should need me once this present dispensation is over, do not call between 5:45 a.m., when I rise, and 9 a.m., when I finish breakfast. Or lunchtime. Or after 4:30. If I decide to go out, it will be later."

"You can do that?" he asked automatically. "Go out?"

There was, finally, something akin to sympathy in her half-pretty, half-plain face, the face, he realised, and admonished himself for the thought, of a shopgirl or waitress, a million young working-class women with lives that had somehow escaped this curious individual in the cheap black dress, a member of some religious order whose name he hadn't thought to ask.

"Occasionally," she answered, still laughing. "There. That's something else we share in common along with poor Michelangelo Merisi da Caravaggio. You see me in my prison. And I see you in yours."

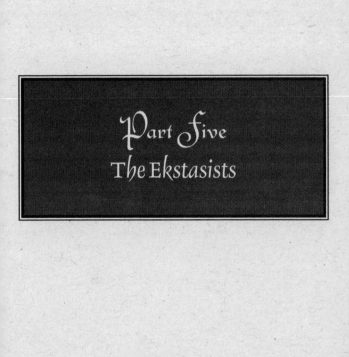

# Part Five
# The Ekstasists

# One

$\mathcal{I}$T WAS A SHORT WALK FROM THE STUDIO TO THE Vicolo del Divino Amore, a brief journey blighted by memories of that final pursuit of the figure in the black hood, with the shotgun hidden beneath his khaki jacket. Snatches of that last dark day assaulted him with a cruel swiftness that had in no way diminished with time. The conversation with Agata Graziano, which was both amusing and, when it fell to the subject of the painting, a little disturbing, had proved a distracting interlude. But Emily still lay there always in his imagination, waiting. In spite of her sheltered background, Agata had seen through him from the outset. This was not entirely business. This was personal. It would be impossible to feel quiescent about the end of his life together with Emily until a resolution was reached.

The section of the street outside the studio's green door was still cordoned off, with three bored-looking uniformed officers stationed outside. In front of them stood a small crowd of the curious: men and women in winter coats, looking disappointed to discover that the scene of the most infamous crime to have occurred in the city in years appeared so mundane from the outside. Costa could see at least two press photographers he knew and ducked through the huddle of bodies hastily in order to avoid them. There was, he thought, precious little in the narrow alley for the prurient. Short of more discoveries, the Vicolo del Divino Amore would surely soon return to some kind of normality.

He showed his pass and went in, preparing himself for Teresa Lupo's performance. She usually had a theatrical touch to her revelations. Even so, she must have asked them back to this place for a reason. The studio was not as he remembered it, resembling more an archaeological dig than a crime scene. Forensic officers were still busily working there. They had set out a secure walk-through area, outlined by tape, across the worn flagstones. Beyond the yellow markers a small unit of specialists in identical white bunny suits—the same now worn by Falcone's team—were bent over an array of careful excavations in the floor, each marked out by more tape, some carrying spades and pickaxes, others with evidence and body bags and scientific equipment.

Teresa herself stepped out from behind the barriers the moment Costa walked in, followed by her assistant, Silvio Di Capua. Falcone led the way, followed by Peroni, Costa, and, a little behind everyone else, a woman officer, Inspector Susanna Placidi, who was introduced as the head of the sexual crimes unit. Accompanying her was the last person Costa expected to see: Rosa Prabakaran, the young Indian detective who had been attacked and injured during an investigation the previous spring. After which, Costa had come to believe, she had disappeared from the Questura altogether.

The smell still lingered, pervasive and disgusting, a cloying foul stink.

Teresa Lupo glanced at him with a sad, sideways look, then said to them all, in a calm, formal manner, "Thank you for coming. I asked you here so that you might appreciate a little of the magnitude of the task ahead of us. We are not one-tenth of the way into it. What I will tell you today are simply a few initial findings. I hope for much more in the way of answers, but I can't give you any timescale about when or how they will come. This place defies conventional analysis in many ways. It was, I think, a real art studio once. It was also . . . something else." She glanced round the cold interior. "Something I don't quite understand yet."

"So long as we have a start," Falcone observed impassively. "Some facts, please?" He eyed the excavations.

"Facts," Teresa grumbled, and cast her round, glassy eyes over the excavations in the stone floor "They were all women, all black. All battered to death, from what I can determine. Nor are they all accounted for. There is female DNA here that doesn't match that of any of the victims. Blood mainly, which means either these women got killed and taken somewhere else, or they escaped or were allowed to leave for some reason. The most recent corpse dates from less than a month ago. The oldest, maybe twelve or fourteen weeks. Beyond that…we have a wealth of potential forensic material, but nothing that is linked to any existing criminal records, or …" Here, she allowed herself a somewhat caustic glance at Susanna Placidi. "…anyone fresh to try them out against."

Costa was beginning to appreciate Falcone's despair. "Wouldn't it have been obvious there were corpses here?" he asked. "Surely someone would have noticed? The smell…"

Falcone intervened, as he'd promised. "Sovrintendente Costa is here out of courtesy," the inspector announced. "We all share in his grief, though none of us can conceive of its depth, of course. I asked him to attend this one meeting so that he could appreciate that fact, and see how hard we are working to find those responsible for these crimes, and for the murder of his wife. After which he will return to compassionate leave."

"Thank you," Costa muttered, embarrassed. "The smell…" he insisted.

"Normally you'd be right, Nic," Teresa replied, and seemed relieved that the conversation had moved on to practical matters. "But our friend—or friends, more likely—had a plan. A little scientific or industrial knowledge, too. You recall how the first victim we found looked?"

Costa thought it would be a long time before he forgot. The corpse had seemed to emerge from some kind of semi-transparent plastic cocoon.

"The bodies were stored in some way?" he asked.

"Out back the killer had a machine," Teresa explained. "It's exactly the same kind of device they use in industrial locations or packing plants. Anywhere you need to shrink-wrap something so that it's airtight. It wasn't going to keep that way forever. But it did a damned good job in the time they had."

"He's clever. He had everything covered in advance," Susanna Placidi added. She was a neurotic-looking individual in civilian clothes—an ugly tweed wool jacket and a heavy green skirt—with a broad, miserable pale face that looked as if some unseen disappointment lurked around every corner.

"We found a stolen van around the corner," Rosa Prabakaran added. "Not a large one. Just big enough for a corpse. There was a very expensive bouquet of lilies in it. And a coffin. Plain wood."

"It was for the Frenchwoman," Teresa said immediately. "What other reason would there be?"

"The French Embassy is more than anxious for news," Falcone said. "What am I supposed to tell them?"

"What about Aldo Caviglia's family?" Rosa snapped. "Don't they feel the same way? Do you need to be white and middle-class to get attention around here?"

Peroni whistled and looked at the ceiling. Teresa gave the young woman detective a filthy look.

"Everyone gets dealt with around here," she said patiently. "Caviglia was murdered. Until you people find the man who did it, there's not much more to say. But the Frenchwoman's different. Silvio?"

Di Capua shuffled over, a short stocky figure in his bunny suit, bald-headed, with a circlet of long, lank hair dangling over the collar of his top. He carried a set of papers and a very small laptop computer.

Teresa took some of the documents from her colleague and glanced at them. "You can tell the French Embassy she died of natural causes. If it's any comfort, I don't imagine we will be using those words about anyone else who's expired hereabouts. The French won't argue. I spoke to her doctor in Paris. He's amazed she lived as long as she did, and frankly so am I. Congenital, incurable heart disease. Plus she had full-blown AIDS, which was unresponsive to any of the extremely expensive private treatments she'd been receiving for the past nine months. They kept away the big day for a while but not for much longer. She saw her physician the week before she died. He told her it was a matter of weeks. Perhaps a month at the most."

"We've been through this before," Peroni objected. "She still had a knife wound."

"A scratch," Di Capua said, and called up on the computer a set of colour photographs of the dead woman's neck and face, then her pale, skeletal torso. They all crowded round to stare at the images there, frozen moments from a death that had taken place just a few steps from where they now stood. Even Peroni looked for a short while before he turned away in disgust. Costa could scarcely believe what he was seeing. Perhaps time or the light in the studio had played tricks. Perhaps the curious painting had disturbed his powers of observation, amplifying everything—the light, the atmosphere, his own imagination. When he'd first seen the body of Véronique Gillet on the old grimy floor, he'd been convinced she, like Aldo Caviglia, was the victim of some savage, unthinking act of violence. In truth, the knife mark barely cut through her white, flawless skin. Now the thin, straight line of dried blood looked more like an unfortunate accident with a rosebush than a meeting with a sharp, deadly weapon.

"She died of heart failure when he attacked her?" Peroni suggested, coming back into the conversation, pointedly not looking at the photos. "It's still murder, isn't it?"

"Oh, poor sweet innocent," Teresa said with a sigh. "Take a deep breath. It's time for me to shatter a few illusions about our pretty little curator from the Louvre. As I told you when we first arrived here, Ms. Gillet had intercourse shortly before she died. And no, I don't think it was rape. There's nothing to indicate that. No bruising, no marks on her body. No skin underneath her fingernails. This was consensual. Sex on the sofa, in front of that creepy painting. With a knife to add a little spice to the occasion."

Peroni looked out over the stinking holes in the flagstones to the dusty window. It had started to rain: faint grey streaks coming down in a soft slanting veil onto the smoke-stained stones of the *centro storico*.

Susanna Placidi glowered at the two pathologists. "How the hell can you know that?"

"Evidence," Di Capua said simply. "Here. Here and here."

He pointed to the photos. Elsewhere on Véronique Gillet's body, on the upper arms, on the smooth plateau of her stomach, and beneath her breasts, there were healed cut marks and a network of shallow but visible scars from some earlier encounter.

Teresa Lupo went through them, one by one, indicating each with a pencil.

"These are indicative of some form of self-inflicted wound, or ones cut by a . . . partner, I imagine that's what we'd have to call it. Human beings are imaginative creatures sometimes. If you want specialist insight into sado-masochistic sexual practices, I can put you in touch with some people who might be able to help."

"They could be just . . . *cuts*," Placidi objected.

Falcone sighed. "No. They are not simply cuts. One perhaps. Two. But . . ."

Costa forced himself to examine the photos carefully. In places, the light scars crisscrossed one another, like a sculptor's hatch marks on some plaster statuette. And something else, too, it occurred to him, and the thought turned his stomach.

"There are too many," he said. "Also . . . I don't know if there's a connection, but Caravaggio made this kind of mark in many of his paintings. His incisions are one way people identify his work."

He looked hard at the photographs. The small, straight cuts on the woman's flesh, mostly healed, but a few still red and recent, were horribly similar. He tried to remember where they were on the canvas they had found: on the naked goddess's upper arms and thighs. Just as with Véronique Gillet.

"The painting—" Costa went on.

"Is a subject for another conversation, and another officer," Falcone interrupted, and gave him a quick, dark glance. This was not, it seemed, an appropriate moment.

"I know nothing about art," Teresa Lupo declared. "But I can tell you one thing. She came here to die. Or, more precisely, to make sure that when she died, it happened here, which would suggest to me that she knew this place, knew the people, and certainly knew what went on." Her bloodless face, expressive in spite of her plain, flat features, flitted to each of them in turn. "But what do I know? You're the police. You work it out."

"And the man?" Falcone asked.

"Six stab wounds to the chest, three of them deep enough to be fatal on their own," Teresa replied immediately, and watched Di Capua take out a folder of large colour photographs, ones no one much wanted to look at. Blood and gore spattered Aldo Caviglia's white, still-well-ironed shirt. "This is extreme violence I would attribute to a man. Women tend to give up around the third blow or go on a lot longer than this. A couple went into the heart."

"Aldo was not the kind of man to get involved in nonsense like this," Peroni protested. "Creepy sex. It's ridiculous . . ."

"You don't know that, Gianni," Costa observed. "How many times did you meet him?"

"Three? Four? How many does it take? He wasn't that type. Or a voyeur or something. Listen . . . I've talked to his neighbours. To his sister. She lives out in Ostia. She works in a bakery. Like he used to." The big man didn't like the obvious doubt on their faces. "Also, I spoke to the woman in the cafe down the street. She said someone who sounds like Aldo came in, white to the gills, desperate to find some skinny, red-haired Frenchwoman. He was *trying* to find her. He had her wallet. OK. It's obvious how that came about. Perhaps . . ." Peroni struggled to find some explanation. "Perhaps he just changed his mind and wanted to give it back."

"Pickpockets do *that* all the time," Rosa suggested sarcastically.

"He was not that kind of man," Peroni said, almost stuttering with anger.

To Costa's astonishment, Rosa Prabakaran reached out, put her hand on Peroni's arm, and said, "I believe you, Gianni. Caviglia was a good guy. He just couldn't keep his hands to himself, but that's not exactly a unique problem in Rome, is it?"

"You're in the wrong job," Peroni replied immediately,

pointing a fat finger in the younger officer's face. "You have something personal going on here. I'm sorry about that, Rosa, not that I imagine it helps. But you should *not* be on a case of this nature. It's just plain . . . wrong."

The forensic people were starting to look uncomfortable. So was Teresa Lupo. Her people liked to work without disruptions.

"Why is it wrong?" Rosa asked him, taking her hand away, almost smiling. "There are plenty of officers on this force who've been robbed sometime, or beaten up in the street. Does that mean they can't arrest a thief or a thug? Is innocence of a crime now a prerequisite for being able to investigate it?"

"That's just clever talk," Peroni snapped. "Everyone here knows what I mean."

The room was silent. Then Leo Falcone folded his arms, looked at Peroni, and said, "We do. And in normal circumstances you would be absolutely right. But these circumstances are anything but, I'm afraid."

"You bet this isn't normal," Teresa agreed. "*Normally* I'm fighting to find material to work with. We're positively dripping in the stuff here. I've got blood and semen. DNA aplenty. Silvio? Fetch, boy . . ."

Di Capua went to the rear door, where a pile of transparent plastic evidence bags had grown waist high. He came back with a swift selection. They looked at what lay inside.

"We haven't had time to take it all away yet," Teresa continued. "We've been too busy digging. There are whips. Flails. Knives. Masks. Some leather items that are a little beyond my imagination. We have a wealth of physical evidence here the likes of which I have never seen in my entire career. We could nail the bastards who killed these women with one-tenth of this evidence. Just point us at a suspect and we'll tell you yes or no in the blink of an eye. This is the mother lode of all crime scenes. All we need from you is someone to test it against."

The room was again silent.

"*Well?*" Teresa asked again, somewhat more loudly.

"Let's take this outside," Falcone murmured.

# Two

$\mathcal{I}$T WAS FREEZING COLD IN THE CONTROL VAN parked at the head of the street, by the Piazza Borghese. The interior stank of stale tobacco smoke. The smoke came from a large middle-aged man in a brown overcoat who sat on one of the metal chairs in the van, awaiting their arrival. He introduced himself as Grimaldi from the legal department, then lit another cigarette.

Peroni was the last to sit down at the plain metal table in the centre of the cabin. He took a long, frank look at Falcone, who wasn't meeting his gaze, then at Susanna Placidi, who'd placed a large notebook computer in front of her and was now staring at the screen, tapping the keyboard with a frantic, uncomfortable nervousness.

"Shouldn't we have a few more people in on this conversation?" Peroni asked. "Six people murdered. The press going crazy. Is this really just down to us?"

"What you're about to learn is strictly down to us," Falcone replied, and cast the woman inspector a savage look. "Tell them."

Placidi stopped typing and said, "We know who they are."

The utter lack of enthusiasm and conviction with which she spoke made Costa's heart sink.

"You know who killed my wife?" he asked quietly.

"We think we can narrow it down to one of four men," Placidi replied, staring hard at the computer screen.

"And they're just walking around out there?" Peroni asked, instantly furious, with Teresa beginning to make equally incensed noises by his side.

"For the time being," Falcone replied, and nodded at Rosa Prabakaran.

Without a word she reached over, took the computer from the uncomplaining Placidi, and began hitting the keys. She found what she wanted, then turned the screen round for them all to see.

It was a photo taken at the Caravaggio exhibition Costa had worked the previous winter, organising security. In it, four men stood in front of the grey, sensual figure of *The Sick Bacchus,* which had been temporarily moved from the Villa Borghese for the event. This, too, was a self-portrait, a younger Caravaggio than that seen in the religious paintings and the *Venus* now undergoing scrutiny under the expert eye of Agata Graziano. Dissolute, saturnine, clutching a bunch of old grapes the same hue as his sallow skin, staring at the viewer, like a whore displaying her wares showing a naked shoulder; despite this, the only focus of hope and light in the entire canvas.

The men in front of the painting looked equally debauched. One, vaguely familiar, seemed more than a little drunk. He stood on the left of the line, with his arm around the shoulders of the man next to him in a tight proprietorial fashion. The other two stood slightly apart, looking like friends in the process of turning into enemies for some reason.

"They call themselves the Ekstasists."

Costa couldn't take his eyes off them. He gazed at the blank, cruel masculine faces on the screen, trying to imagine what each would look like inside a black military hood.

"Him," Costa said eventually, indicating the one on the far left, the man with his arm around the shoulders of his companion.

The two women officers exchanged glances and said nothing.

Grimaldi, the lawyer, finally shuffled his chair up to the table and took some interest.

"The man wore a mask," he pointed out. "How can you be sure?"

"I'm not. I'm guessing. You can still bring him in on that."

Grimaldi sighed and said, "Ah. Guesses."

"He has the same build," Costa insisted. "The same stiff posture. As if he used to be a soldier. This—"

"This," Grimaldi cut in, "is Count Franco Malaspina. Who was a soldier once, an officer during military service, for which he was decorated several times. He is also one of the richest and most powerful individuals in Rome, a patron of the arts and of charity, an eligible bachelor, a face from the social magazines, a fine man, or so a casual scan of the press cuttings might have one think." Grimaldi hesitated and cast his sharp dark eyes at each of them.

Costa knew the name. As far as he was aware, Malaspina continued to own the vast private palace which bore his family name, which sprawled through Ortaccio, embracing both the Vicolo del Divino Amore and the Barberini's studio. He'd surely seen the man's picture in the newspapers. Could it be simple chance recognition that made him point the finger of blame?

"I'm sorry," he said. "Perhaps I was just remembering the wrong thing."

"Perhaps," Grimaldi agreed. "All the same, let me tell you a little about Franco Malaspina."


THE LAWYER DIDN'T EVEN NEED TO REFER TO NOTES. He simply spoke from memory as Costa stared at the photo on Rosa's screen, an image of a tall, athletic twenty-eight-year-old merchant banker with an eponymous family palace in Rome, homes in Milan and New York, and, said Grimaldi, enough files in the Questura to fill an entire lifetime for most criminals, every last one still open. Malaspina was heir to a fortune that had been built up by his clan over more than three centuries, one that began with the bankrolling of a Pope. He was a true

Roman aristocrat of a dying breed, and came from a family with unusual antecedents. Unlike most of the city's nobility, the Malaspinas had embraced the era of Mussolini, seeing in the dictator opportunity, and not the coarse, proletarian Fascism most other ancient families detected and instantly despised. His grandfather had served as a minister for Il Duce. His own father had been a rabble-rouser on the fringes of right-wing politics, and consequently had been loathed in Rome, a city that was temperamentally left-leaning, until his death in a plane crash five years ago.

Costa had no recollection of Franco Malaspina being involved in machinations around the parties that formed the continuing, argumentative coalitions at the heart of the Italian state; only the vague memory that he was a notorious player in the money world, one who sailed so close to the wind that the financial authorities had investigated him more than once. Not that these probes had resulted in any form of action, which meant that Malaspina was either innocent or so deeply powerful no one dared yet take him on. There were good reasons for caution. Men of his sort liked to build up fortunes before turning to the Senate and Parliament to lay wider, deeper foundations for their power.

Rosa identified the others in the photograph; all the men were strangers to Costa, though two names were familiar. Giorgio Castagna was the son of the head of a notorious porn empire, a Roman playboy rarely out of the showbiz magazines. Emilio Buccafusca was the owner of an art gallery that specialised in some of the more controversial areas of sculpture and painting. He had frequently clashed with the law over the public display of work that bordered on the extreme. The previous winter his gallery had provoked public outrage for exhibiting several "death sculptures" by a Scandinavian artist supposedly consisting of genuine human body parts encased in clear plastic.

After a field day in the media, a worried Questura *commissario* had dispatched Teresa Lupo to the gallery to investigate. She'd denounced the organs as demonstrably animal in origin, probably from slaughtered pigs. Buccafusca had laughed out loud at the time; now he didn't seem in the mood. Both men appeared somewhat inconsequential next to the aristocratic Malaspina, though they were all of similar stature, dressed in black, Castagna and Buccafusca with similar pinched and bitter faces.

There were more photographs, too, from other arts events. Malaspina's expression—self-satisfied, confident, powerful—was constant throughout. In the early photos the others looked much the same way. Something had happened over the previous few months to change that. There, Costa knew, Falcone would see his opportunity.

The fourth figure, a man completely unknown to Costa, usually skulked close to the background, and seemed somewhat out of place in such company. He was short, sandy-haired, and chubby, about thirty, with a florid, slack face and an expression that veered, in these photos, from boredom to a visible, subservient fear.

"Being an avid reader of junk magazines," Teresa Lupo said, staring at the same image, "I feel I've met most of this Eurotrash already. But who's fat boy?"

"Nino Tomassoni," Rosa Prabakaran answered. "He's the only one here who doesn't have much money, as far as we can figure out. He's an assistant curator at the Villa Borghese."

*Tomassoni*. The name sparked a memory for Costa, one he couldn't place.

"The man is probably on the periphery of all this," Placidi added. "Perhaps he's barely involved at all."

Falcone scowled at her. It was exactly this kind of imprecision in detail that he despised in an officer.

"His name is on the list," Falcone pointed out. "If that means nothing, it means nothing for the rest of them."

"The list?" Peroni wondered. "You're accusing these men of some pretty nasty stuff. They are people who like to wear nice suits. And all you have against them is a list?"

Placidi sighed, then pulled a sheaf of printed papers out of the folder in front of her and stacked them on the table. "They're more . . . messages really," she said. "We got another this morning."

"You did?" Falcone was clearly unaware of this latest missive and displeased by that fact.

"It arrived just before I left for this meeting," she

answered with a sudden burst of temper. "I can't be held responsible for keeping everyone informed about every damned thing. This is the same as the others. An untraceable email from a fake address. Nothing the computer people can work with."

She placed the sheet of paper on the table in front of them, not looking at the words. It was a standard office printout.

*Placidi, you cow. What ARE you morons doing? Do I have to spell it out? The Ekstasists. Castagna. Buccafusca. Malaspina. And that stupid helpless bastard Tomassoni. Are they paying you scum enough to let them get away with this? Does it turn you on or something? Can you sleep at night?*
*PS: Whatever you think THIS IS NOT FINISHED!!!*

"That's it?" Costa asked. "That's your case?"

"No!" It was Rosa Prabakaran, angry. "That's not it. We have messages just like this one detailing a string of vicious attacks on black prostitutes, throughout the city, covering a period of almost four months. Where and when and how. We've tracked down some of the victims. The poor women are so terrified they won't tell us a thing. And now"—she nodded back down the alley, towards the studio—"we know why. Those women are the ones who survived."

"Let me get this straight," Peroni cut in. "You have a string of sexual attacks? And not one of these women will sign a witness statement?"

"I had one," Rosa answered. "She described everything. The men. Four of them. What they did." She paused. "They took turns. The point..." She stopped again, embarrassed. "They wanted to see her in the throes of an orgasm. Not faked, the way hookers do. The real thing."

Costa thought about the photographs they had found in the studio: shots of women in the throes of either agony or ecstasy.

"And if they didn't get what they wanted?" he asked quietly.

"Then things turned violent. Very violent. These people weren't paying for sex. Not in the way we know it. They wanted to see something on the faces of these women. They wanted to know they put it there, and capture the moment somehow." She paused. This was difficult. "The one woman who would talk to us said the men had a camera. That they filmed everything. Her cries most of all. When they felt she was faking...they beat her."

"All hookers fake it," Peroni pointed out with vehemence. "What kind of lunatics would do something like that? What do they expect?"

Costa looked at his friend. Peroni had spent years in vice. In that time, he must have seen some dreadful cases. The expression of shock and distaste on his battered face now told Costa he'd never heard of anything quite like this.

"Obviously they don't know hookers," Costa suggested.

"They've known plenty of late," Rosa continued. "These are sick bastards. Clever bastards too. I thought I had that girl. Two days later, she walked out of the hospital and vanished. Maybe back home with money. Maybe dead. There's no way of telling."

Falcone couldn't take his eyes off Susanna Placidi. Costa knew why. A witness in a case like that should never have been allowed to flee, whatever the circumstances.

"Who do you think the messages are from?" Teresa asked.

The two female officers glanced at each other. The lawyer, Grimaldi, was silent, staring at the photos on the screen.

"We don't know," Placidi admitted. "Probably someone we don't know about. Someone on the periphery who thinks it's gone too far. Or Tomassoni..."

"It sounds like a woman, don't you think?" Teresa asked. "Listen to the words: 'Placidi, you cow!' I've been called a bitch a million times by some jerk male. But never a cow. They don't talk to you like that."

"A woman, then!" Placidi screamed back. "How the hell am I supposed to know?"

Teresa leaned over, impatient, close to anger. "I said it *sounds* like a woman. Perhaps it's meant to. In which case they are clearly overestimating our abilities somewhat. What does it matter? We've got DNA. We've got forensic coming out of our ears from that mucky room of theirs. Just go and arrest them and leave the rest to me."

Falcone sat back, folded his arms, and waited for Placidi to respond. Grimaldi had adopted precisely the same position.

"We've tried to arrest them," the woman inspector admitted. "We've been to the lawyers more than once. The trouble is . . ." She scattered the emails over the table. "This is all we have. The women won't talk. We can't . . . The evidence we have is all so vague."

Her miserable eyes fell to the table again.

Teresa turned her attention to Falcone. "Leo, give me an hour with these creeps and a bag of cotton swabs and I'll put them in a cell before bedtime. There's a bunch of dead bodies here and they're itching to talk."

He looked at her, then shook his bald, aquiline head.

"Why not?" asked Peroni.

Falcone picked up the sheets of messages on the table. "Inspector Placidi told you. These are all we have," he said. "If they are what they appear, they clearly come from someone inside the group, someone who's apparently frightened about what his friends are doing. Someone whose name does not appear on these lists, though I wouldn't wish to rule that out."

"So what?" Costa wondered.

"So alternatively they may be some kind of practical joke," Falcone went on. "Tomassoni apart, these men are often in the public eye. Publicity attracts cranks. We all know that. They could be innocent."

Susanna Placidi banged the table with her fists. "They are not innocent, Leo! These sons of bitches are laughing at us."

"She's right," Rosa said quietly, confidently. "Taunting us is part of their fun, I swear."

"That's hardly going to get anyone in court, is it?" Falcone observed severely. "A look in their eye. A policewoman's instinct."

"Whoever wrote these emails knows the places!" Rosa screeched. "They know the victims, unless you think these women have been making it up and putting themselves in hospital too."

"I am aware of all this," the old inspector replied coldly. "I don't think for one moment that these are crank messages. From the point of view of Malaspina and his friends, though . . ."

"It's a good defence," Costa agreed. "They do attract cranks."

Falcone nodded, grateful for his support. "Furthermore——"

"No!" It was Teresa Lupo, livid. "I do not wish to hear any more of this. I've told you we have the evidence. You've told me you have the suspects. Bring these jerks in and leave it to me."

She watched their faces. No one spoke until Grimaldi, the lawyer, took a deep breath, then said, "If only it were that easy."

"I am here to tell you a simple truth," he went on. "Inspector Placidi and her team have attempted to do this very thing and failed. Unknown to me or anyone in my department, they arrested all four men named in these messages, without sufficient evidence or adequate preparation. Then they threw these anonymous, unconfirmed allegations at them in the absence of the slightest evidential corroboration, and ..."

Placidi's face was reddening.

"And now we have to live with the consequences, which are damaging in the extreme," Grimaldi concluded.

"I had to do something!" Placidi objected. "I had to take the risk. The women wouldn't talk when it happened, and two weeks later they had disappeared. We had nothing *but* these emails. Did you expect me to sit on my hands until some smart-ass from elsewhere came up with something better?"

Falcone cast a fleeting sideways look in her direction, one Costa had seen in the past. He wondered if Placidi understood how dangerous was the ground beneath her.

"These are intelligent, important, well-connected men," he pointed out. "Did it not occur to you that perhaps that was part of their enjoyment too? Feeling untouchable, beyond the pathetic efforts of the law?"

She said nothing.

"These men were never going to throw their hands up in the air and offer you a confession, Susanna. Had you thought about it for one moment, you would surely have known that."

"There were women getting raped!" Placidi pressed.

"It now transpires there were women getting murdered," Grimaldi declared. "Which is all the more reason to do your job properly. Instead, you offended some extremely influential people."

Teresa Lupo's eyes started to dilate with a sudden, growing fury.

"You also forewarned them of the police investigation," Falcone continued, "without sufficient evidence even to substantiate a temporary arrest. They now understand fully what we will look for in the way of concrete evidence. They can prepare for that eventuality."

Placidi was close to tears. "I didn't know . . ."

Falcone looked at the rest of them and then Grimaldi. "You'd best tell them," he suggested.

The lawyer took out a notebook from his jacket and consulted it. "Two weeks ago, after being approached by Inspector Placidi's team, a team of lawyers representing all four of these men went before a magistrate, *in camera*," he said. "We had insufficient notice. Malaspina knows the legal system. He winds it round his little finger. He has the advantage of being extraordinarily rich and in league with some important figures in the organised crime world too. It is a deadly combination."

"And?" Teresa demanded.

"By the time we were able to assemble a competent team, he was already challenging the legal rules through which we may and may not demand any physical evidence, both fingerprints and DNA specimens, from people who refuse to give them willingly."

The pathologist's large face turned a shade paler. "Rules? *Rules?* We know what the rules are. Either they give us a sample willingly or I get a piece of paper and force it out of them."

It was that straightforward. All Costa needed if any subject refused a DNA sample was the approval of a senior officer in the Questura to take one by force if necessary. Most suspects ceased to resist once they realised they'd be compelled to provide a sample within a matter of minutes.

Grimaldi's scowl was that of a man denied something he dearly craved. "Thanks to Malaspina's lawyers, and our own incompetence, the rules have changed," he told them. "From now on we may obtain physical material against the will of a suspect only on the basis of a judicial order. So if they object strongly enough, we have to go before a magistrate, where we must make our case. We are, in a nutshell, screwed."

The pathologist let loose a stream of Roman epithets.

Grimaldi waited for her to draw breath, then continued. "The standard routine you have all grown accustomed to using in these situations is now out of the question should any suspect refuse. Unless you can find sufficient firm and incontrovertible evidence to put to a magistrate." Grimaldi picked up the papers, then dropped them on the table. "Which, having spent the last hour going through what you have here, I must say you do not possess."

Teresa's mouth hung open in astonishment. "You mean I can pick up any amount of beautiful physical evidence I like and we can't match it to a suspect unless he or she deigns to *cooperate*? These people are criminals, for God's sake! Why should they do us any favours?"

"They won't," the lawyer agreed. "Unless they know they're innocent. We're trying to appeal the ruling, but to be honest . . ." He frowned. ". . . the question of human rights is rather fashionable at the moment."

"What the hell about the rights of these women?" Teresa demanded.

Grimaldi's eyes widened with despair. "Why are you arguing with me? It is useless. This is now the law. I wish it were otherwise, but . . ."

"I could always arrange for one of these nice gentlemen to bleed on me a little," Peroni suggested. "Or steal one of his coffee cups."

The lawyer shook his head. "Anything gathered by subterfuge will not only be inadmissible but may well damage our chances of a successful prosecution should we be able to gather sufficient evidence by other means. This is a general observation, by the way, one we must now apply to every case from this point forward, not simply to these four charming gentlemen who call themselves the Ekstasists."

A bitter, almost despondent look appeared on Falcone's lean face. "Welcome to modern policing," he said. "What Grimaldi has explained to you will be standard practice in all cases from this point on until we can successfully challenge it. Other officers are having this change in policy explained to them privately over the next few days, though not the reasons for it. We would like to keep those to ourselves." He grimaced. "At least for a little while."

Teresa Lupo glowered at the female inspector across the table. "*You* did this? Your cack-handed blundering has put the onus on *us* to prove bastards like these need to show us they're innocent? That's half our working practices dumped straight out the window. Just because you barged in there without doing your homework first."

"No!" Susanna Placidi screeched back at her. She pointed at the photos on the screen. "I did my best. Malaspina is responsible for this. That man—"

"Not good enough," the pathologist yelled. "You're incompetent, Placidi. This is—"

"Ladies. *Ladies!*"

Grimaldi had a loud and commanding voice. It silenced them, for a little while at least.

Costa waited for the temperature to fall a little, then said, "In that case, you'd better start looking for some proof."

"Where?" Susanna Placidi demanded.

Grimaldi stared at Falcone and raised an interested eyebrow.

"That," the inspector announced, "is something you no longer need worry about." He shook his head, stared at the desk, then at her. "This case...appalls me, Placidi. We have lost a dear friend. There are women who have been attacked—and worse—in this city of ours, while it was your responsibility to protect them. Your laxness and incompetence have cost innocent people their lives. You have damaged our ability to unravel the dreadful mess you have left behind. And all you can say is...you did your best. If that was the case, your best was sorely lacking. You can go home now. This case no longer concerns you." He reached over and dragged the computer to his side of the table. "Nor any in the future, if I can help it. Breathe one word to a soul about what we have discussed here and I will, I swear, drag you in front of a disciplinary tribunal and finish what's left of your career for good."

Grimaldi took an envelope out of his pocket and placed it in front of her. "These are formal suspension papers, Inspector. I will confirm the notice was properly delivered."

Placidi was speechless, red with rage, her eyes brimming with tears.

"I will give you a lift home, signora," Grimaldi offered.

"I have a driver and a car!"

"Not anymore," the lawyer replied.

# Three

$f$ALCONE WAITED FOR THEM TO LEAVE, THEN HE got up and checked the door. There was no one else in earshot.

"This is my city," he told them. "*Our* city. It's got its problems, God knows. But I always thought a woman could walk safely on these streets. Any woman. Black or white. Legal or illegal. I don't care. I will *not* allow that to change. Not under any circumstances. Whatever the cost."

It was Peroni who broke the silence. He was laughing, just for a moment, and with precious little mirth.

Falcone's grey eyebrows rose. "Well?"

"I love it when the word 'cost' comes into your conversation, Leo," Peroni observed pleasantly. "It always suggests life is about to turn interesting."

Falcone ignored the taunt. He looked relaxed. Determined, too. Costa knew this mood. It meant someone was about to wander outside the usual rules.

"Look at us." Falcone smiled, opening his hands in a

wide, expansive gesture. "Two careers in autumn. Two careers in spring. And the best criminal pathologist in Italy."

"No praise, please," Teresa protested. "You know how uncomfortable that makes me."

"It's true! What better time for you to test your skills?" Then, more grimly, "What better time for *us*?"

His eyes drifted to the computer screen. The image of Franco Malaspina was caught there, frozen by some paparazzo's camera. The millionaire had frizzy dark hair and the features of a Sicilian, an angular, handsome face almost North African in its dusky hue. His bleak black eyes glittered back at the photographer, staring at the lens intently, full of the easy willful arrogance of a certain kind of Roman aristocrat.

"This man thinks he and his friends are unassailable," Falcone said. "I have close to one hundred officers in the Questura on this case, two in Africa seeking earlier victims as potential witnesses, and I have put out every appeal I can think of to our friends in the Carabinieri. This is not a time for internecine rivalries and they know it. These are the kinds of crimes none of us ever expected to see in Rome, and we must do all in our power to bring these men to face justice. Yet . . ." He wrestled his slender hands together in frustration. "I cannot tell any of them the names we have here. If I did that, these four men would know. Their lawyers would return to court again, screaming harassment of the innocent. Tame politicians would be dragged out of their beds to hear their complaints. We all know how these things work. We would lose what little we have, perhaps forever. There is an army of officers, good men and women, who will do everything they can to find some conventional—some might say old-fashioned—evidence that might break this case. Yet they must work in the dark, since I daren't share with them a word of the information you have heard here. They will fail, with dignity and professionalism, but it will be failure all the same."

"Leo—" Costa began.

"No," the inspector protested. "Hear me out. Unless they have left some obvious and stupid form of identification in this hellhole of theirs, Inspector Placidi's incompetence means these four have every right to feel untouchable." He glanced at Teresa Lupo. "Am I mistaken, Doctor?"

"I told you, Leo. We are swimming in forensic. In proof."

"What? A business card? A letter? A driving licence?"

"*Proof!*"

"By which you mean scientific proof. DNA and prints. The two primary pillars of our investigative process today. You heard Grimaldi. They are useless. Proof means nothing if I can't take it before a judge. They have us gagged and bound, don't you see? Without some miracle I cannot foresee, the only ones who can establish their guilt are these men themselves. All our conventional means of attack are worthless. I can do . . . nothing."

He placed his long forefinger on the photograph of Franco Malaspina and stared at Costa. "And I want them, this creature most of all. He is not some Renaissance prince who can flaunt himself on these streets regardless of the law."

Falcone glanced at his watch. "At twelve-thirty the four of you will meet in the Piazza Navona, outside the Brazilian Embassy. I will arrange for lunch to be brought round to my apartment at one." He glanced at Costa and Peroni in turn. "The place has only two bedrooms, I'm afraid, so you two can fight over the sofa between yourselves."

"I'm staying in your apartment?" Rosa Prabakaran asked, astonished.

"Until further notice," Falcone declared.

Teresa Lupo's arms flailed in the air in protest. "And I'm supposed to walk out of the biggest murder case we've had in years and throw in my lot with some private underhand snooping of yours?"

"If there is one thing I have learned about you in recent times," Falcone replied, "it is that you will do what you feel like regardless of anything I say. I invite you along to listen and then decide. Given that no one, not God himself, seems privy to either your working methods or your diary, I doubt you will have much difficulty being engaged simultaneously in both your conventional work and a task that is a little... different, and something else besides for all I know."

Teresa was momentarily speechless, then muttered, "Was that a compliment or not?"

"I will not rest until these bastards are in jail, and neither will you," Falcone continued, ignoring her question. "I have gone through what passes as Placidi's investigation log on this case. There is a strand of evidence no one here knows about, an odd, possibly worthless thread. Susanna Placidi certainly thought so. Which was why she buried it at the bottom of the pile."

The grey eyes travelled over them all and fell on Rosa Prabakaran.

"We have an appointment with a statue," Falcone said cryptically. "After that you are on your own."

# Part Six
## Incriminating Verses

# One

*S*TATUES CAN'T TALK," PERONI INSISTED.

The five of them—Costa, Rosa, Teresa, Peroni, and Falcone—stood in the tiny open space known as the Piazza Pasquino, named for the battered three-quarters statue of a man with no arms and an unrecognisable face turned as if to look towards some vanished companion. Falcone had arrived on time, then marched them there immediately. They were in a busy narrow street which fed off the sprawling Piazza Navona. The rain had halted for a while.

"This statue can," Falcone replied. "Unfortunately, the only police officer who had the wit to listen was Agente Prabakaran."

Smiling at that, Rosa walked forward. She pointed to the worn, stained stone on which the statue known as Pasquino stood, and explained, "The antiracist people told me. They found it first."

The base of Pasquino was covered with posters, hastily pasted there, most in frantic, badly written script, though a few were printouts from a computer and even had simple photographs and cartoons on them.

Costa remembered this place from his schooldays. Pasquino had been plastered in anonymous messages for centuries. In recent times most were antigovernment, posted there by left-wing or anarchist groups, or ordinary citizens who wanted to vent their anger without revealing their identity. He couldn't recollect ever seeing any racist material. Racism was rare in Rome. The sight of Pasquino jogged another memory, though Rosa got there first.

"There are other statues that used to serve the same function," she said. "They placed messages on those too."

"Later," Falcone interrupted, and ushered them down into the narrow medieval street of the Governo Vecchio. His apartment was a hundred metres or so along from Pasquino's piazza, on the first floor, next to an upmarket shop selling expensive fountain pens and mechanical pencils. The place was huge and beautifully furnished. Falcone was clearly proud of it, judging by the brief, modest tour he insisted upon—out of the practical consideration, naturally, that they would now be closeted there for some time. There was an elegant living room decorated in plain, modern taste, two bedrooms, a well-equipped kitchen with a small balcony, and a line of healthy potted plants glistening after the morning's rain. The apartment was spotless, with the smell of recent cleaning. He had prepared for this moment. There was also a box full of smart clothes, sent by Bea from the farmhouse, which Falcone passed over without a word of explanation.

The inspector beckoned them to the table, opened the briefcase he'd brought, and took some photos out of a folder.

"More statues," he said, and glanced at Prabakaran. "Agente?"

She pointed to the representation of a muscular man built into a brick wall. He wore a beret and was holding a barrel over a drinking fountain. Water still trickled from the cask, though the statue looked centuries old. "This is Il Facchino. The Porter. It's in a side street off the Corso, near the Piazza del Collegio Romano. And this . . ." She removed another photo from Falcone's folder: a weather-worn full-length statue of a Roman noble in robes, standing on a plinth against a grime-stained marble wall.

"I recognise that," Peroni said instantly. "It's in Vittorio Emanuele, next to the church, Sant'Andrea della Valle. I chased off some classy whores doing business there years ago. It's also"——the big man glanced at each of them, to make sure they would be impressed—— "the scene of the first act of *Tosca*."

Teresa blinked. "You know opera?"

"One of the hookers told me. I said they were classy. I didn't hear any statue talking, though."

"He's known as Abate Luigi," Rosa continued, ignoring the distraction. "Pasquino still talks today. I thought even you might have noticed, Gianni. The statue's always covered in cryptic slogans. Usually, if you can understand them, ones that insult the same few people in the government."

"I know it!" Peroni insisted. "What the hell has this got to do with us?"

Costa intervened. "The talking statues were a way of making a point that could have got you into trouble if your name was attached to it. Perhaps a political point. Perhaps just ratting on a neighbour." A memory troubled him; it came with a mental picture of Emily, lovely in a shirt and jeans by the side of the gleaming lagoon, that lost summer eighteen months before. "In Venice they used to do it privately, by posting unsigned letters through those lions' mouths I once showed you. In Rome, we prefer something a little more public. But these days only on Pasquino. You say there were messages on the other statues?"

"Exactly," Falcone said, and removed a large envelope from his case and spread the contents on the table: sheet after sheet of words, jumbled together in the random yet semi-logical way a madman might have worked. He glowered at the messages and pointed at a set of enlargements of the head of each of them. "Placidi didn't even look closely enough to see this."

Magnified, it was clear there was a crest on the top of each, an ancient coat of arms of some kind. When he caught the direction of Costa's gaze, Falcone threw a photographic blowup of the emblem onto the table.

Three dragon-like creatures were depicted there, limbs writhing, talons clutching at the screaming torso of a female figure entangled in their scaly embrace. The beasts possessed vicious, grinning features, half human, half beast. The expression on the woman's face might have been pleasure or pain, rapture or the final rictus of terror.

A title ran above the chilling emblem in contorted medieval script: *The Ekstasists*.

THE VERSES WEREN'T WRITTEN BUT FORMED FROM words and letters cut out of the headlines of newspapers and magazines, then pasted together to form cryptic poems.

Rosa began to sort them into three separate piles, then read out one from the first.

"*You baboon whores, beware the bad thorn's
  prick.
It's blood he lusts for, not the thing between
  your legs.*"

"Malaspina," Costa said. "The bad thorn."

She nodded. "This was stuck on Pasquino the morning after a hooker was left for dead near the Spanish Steps. Right next to another talking statue they call the Baboon."

"That's a hell of a stretch, Rosa," Teresa complained.

"So everyone told me. But there's a pattern once you see it. The messages each make some cryptic reference to one of their unpleasant little club. We've a total of thirteen: four each for Castagna and Buccafusca, five for Malaspina. Here's another one."

She picked out a sheet from the second pile.

> "Run quick, poor Simonetta!
> The mountain chestnut spills its spiny seeds
>    regardless.
> And snakes are deaf to your black cries."

"The chestnut being Castagna?" Peroni asked, knowing the answer.

"That one was left on Il Facchino *before* the event," Rosa explained. "The following day a black woman was raped, then beaten with a wooden club in the Via dei Serpenti in the Monti district, close to the Forum. We couldn't possibly have understood the reference to snakes and mountains beforehand, of course. These guys are not stupid. They're not trying to lead us to them. It's some kind of a joke. A tease."

"Who the hell is 'Simonetta'?" Teresa demanded.

"You'd know if you moved in art and history circles," Rosa replied, looking at Costa.

So many memories were coming back to him at that moment, from his single days when much of his free time was spent in art galleries, staring at the works on the walls, trying to understand what he saw there and link it to his native city's past. And, too, from the delightful time he'd spent working security for the exhibition in the Palazzo Ruspoli, when he and Emily had finally decided to marry. An entire room there had been devoted to the Medici dynasty.

"Modern academics believe that the first Duke of Florence, Alessandro de' Medici, had a black slave for a mother," Costa said. "It was kept secret as much as possible, of course. But there were so many reports it's generally thought to be true. The woman's name was supposedly Simonetta."

"The Medicis were black?" Peroni asked, amazed.

Rosa smiled. "A little. Millions of people are, you know. Where's the surprise? White Italians have been screwing us for centuries. Simonetta, incidentally, didn't come from Florence. She was from near here. Lazio. Collevecchio. Thirty minutes up the A1. It's a little too chichi for coloured people these days. But the prostitute they attacked worked the motorways. She was picked up from the Flaminia service station by three men she swore she couldn't identify. Flaminia is the nearest service point to Collevecchio, which means . . ."

She left it there.

Teresa, astonished, asked, "You really think these bastards would go to those lengths to make some kind of obscure point? Why, for God's sake?"

Falcone didn't let the policewoman answer.

"To see how long it would take us to figure out what they were doing. Rosa's right. This is a game, a test. The kick they get out of taunting us is as much a part of their pleasure as the crime itself."

He stabbed a long finger at another message. This time Costa read it.

> *"The mouth of darkness truly bites.*
> *Unlike the mouth of truth.*
> *Ask dirty sweet Laeticia."*

" 'The mouth of darkness' is presumably a play on the name Buccafusca," Falcone said. "This one was pinned to Abate Luigi the day after an Angolan illegal immigrant, Laeticia Candido, landed in hospital. The staff—not the victim—called the Questura. She'd been found unconscious near the Bocca della Verità. The mouth of darkness and the mouth of truth." He appeared stiff with visible outrage.

"The woman had bite marks on her breasts and other parts of her torso. The bites removed substantial amounts of flesh. She will be scarred for life. The only thing she would say about her attackers was that they carried a camera and filmed her throughout."

Peroni gazed at the pages on the table and let loose a long, pained sigh.

"When Susanna Placidi's people asked for a statement," Falcone continued, "Laeticia Candido wouldn't even file a complaint. If it weren't for the message, we wouldn't know there was a connection at all, which is one more reason why they send us these things. Now she's gone. Home probably. I have the Angolan police looking and some of our officers on the way to help. I am not hopeful."

Costa had a sudden picture in his head: the Bocca della Verità, where lines of happy tourists queued patiently to place a hand into the gap of an Imperial-era water-culvert cover, believing a spoken lie might snap it off, just as Gregory Peck promised Audrey Hepburn in *Roman Holiday*. This was central Rome, out in the open, next to the busy Lungotevere, an area where street safety had never been an issue.

"How the hell can this happen, Leo?" Teresa asked, outraged. "Why didn't someone pick it up?"

He frowned. "Susanna Placidi didn't have the experience, the imagination, or the learning. Or the witnesses. We believe those women who survived the attacks were paid off, as was Laeticia Candido. We don't have a single signed statement, one we could use in court. As far as we know, most victims have returned home, doubtless carrying the kind of money they wouldn't pick up working the streets. Or they're dead in that hellhole in the Vicolo del Divino Amore. What does that leave us? A few anonymous emails mentioning this odd and inexplicable term, 'the Ekstasists,' and some vile street graffiti that seemed unconnected until Rosa here put two and two together. Meanwhile, Placidi ignored everything of use and simply marched in on those grinning aristocrats, thinking they'd hold out their hands the moment they saw a badge."

"Why did she do that?" Costa asked. "She must have had evidence."

He caught the dark thunder in Rosa Prabakaran's face.

"It was a routine follow-up. We had Malaspina's licence plate caught on CCTV. Nothing more. We were just going through the routine and . . ."

They waited. She shook her head.

"You need to meet him to understand. He laughed at us. It was subtle. He didn't say an incriminating word. He didn't need to. I was there, with Placidi, and both of us knew immediately it was him. He *wanted* us to know. It was what he planned. And . . ." She raised her slender shoulders in a gesture of frustration. "Then Placidi did what Malaspina wanted of us all along, I guess. Brought in everyone, demanded DNA, warrants, the lot. We had nothing except a licence number and a smirk on that stuck-up face. It was impossible. Unbelievable. Malaspina and his cronies walked free because we lacked the evidence, and we never even tried to lay these messages at their door."

"It's not unbelievable at all." Falcone reached for the photograph of the man, drawing a finger over his fine, dark features. "It's the sequence of events he had in place for the moment we came for him."

Rosa said something caustic under her breath.

"I know, I know," Falcone said with a pained sigh. "You tried to tell Placidi. But this is a highly unusual case, and we are temperamentally inclined to struggle with anything that lies outside the norm. Would I have made the same mistake if you'd come to me? I'd certainly have wanted some answers. The rape unit doesn't have that stretch of the imagination. It's about rape. And this"—his eyes drifted to the window—"is about a lot more than that somehow." He stared at the messages. "The Ekstasists. Why would wealthy, powerful young men wish to capture some wretched street prostitute reaching a moment of rapture? Educated men like these?"

"'Educated'?" Rosa asked, visibly inflamed by the word.

"Educated," the inspector repeated. "Listen to the words. *Listen.* They think they're writing a kind of poetry. They believe they're taking part in some kind of performance, one that's not quite real, maybe. I don't know. These people aren't born criminals . . ."

"You wouldn't say that if you saw some of the women they left raped and bleeding in the road," Rosa spat back at him. "And they were the lucky ones."

"These men are not *ordinary* criminals," Falcone insisted. "Which means we cannot hope to apprehend them using ordinary means. If we treat them the way they want us to, then we will surely fail once more. Teresa will ensure her people rake over every last stone and speck of dust in that dreadful place to find some link with these men beyond the prints and DNA we can't use for the moment. I have officers on two continents trying to find someone who will put their names in a statement."

He stared at them in turn, to emphasise the point he was about to make. "But if we put them under formal surveillance with what little we have, they can and will go back to their lawyers. They will take us to court for harassment, and they will win. I do not intend to let that happen."

Teresa Lupo pulled the set of photos in front of her and put a finger on Franco Malaspina's swarthy, smug face. "You think you know what's going on here, Leo. It's time to share."

He sighed, then shook his head. "I know very little. This is guesswork, and guesswork alone. I can't broach it in the Questura. You all know the politics of the department at the moment. We have a new commissario, the man who turned up from Milan last week. I have scarcely discussed this case with him yet. That's the way things are. Management comes before crime. Do not expect me to fight a battle I can't hope to win."

"What are you thinking?" Teresa persisted.

He took a deep breath. "I think this is some kind of strange brotherhood, a rite of passage with its roots in these men's mutual affection for art, since that is the only thing they have in common apart from breeding. I believe Véronique Gillet was a part of it, an active member who came here to die in that place, at the hands of one, perhaps more, of these men, willingly. The unexpected arrival of Aldo Caviglia changed all that. They now no longer have this killing room of theirs or the painting which may have had some special significance. So what do they do?"

"They give up," Costa said without hesitation. "They go back to being rich, ambitious private citizens, who keep quiet company with their criminal friends but do nothing wrong in public, not a thing. And then..."

It was so obvious and so simple. None of this happened through need or some conventional criminal urge. If Falcone was right—and he usually was—the entire deadly interlude was just a game, a bloody prank. Once the risk became too real, the men went back to leading apparently blameless lives, smug and safe inside their remembrance of the evil they had achieved, and their certain understanding that their guilt was known to the authorities too. Their lawyers killed what past suspicion might damage them. The police struggled to find a single new act with which to pursue the case.

"That would be my guess," Falcone agreed. "So in the circumstances we can only tread water, or be... a little creative."

They were silent. There was a look in Falcone's eyes Costa now knew well. This was the moment the case went beyond the usual. This was why they were here.

Falcone walked over to the long modern sideboard and came back with a new laptop. He placed it on the desk and turned it on. Very quickly three photographs appeared on the screen: live video, fed from cameras that must have been high up on a wall overlooking the street.

The lenses were focused on three figures everyone in

the room knew by now: Pasquino, Il Facchino, and Abate Luigi, three grubby stone statues, damp, malformed shapes in the winter rain. Falcone pressed more keys. The screen was instantly covered in row after row of tiny video images, from all the CCTV cameras in all the familiar places every *centro storico* cop had come to know from past investigations.

"Obsessive men respond to obsessive acts. Count Franco Malaspina isn't the only one who can write messages," Falcone murmured, and threw on the table a sheaf of pages, each bearing the small obscure crest of the Ekstasists at its head. Each was also covered in the large spidery writing that Costa recognised as Falcone's own.

# Two

$\mathcal{C}$HREE HOURS LATER COSTA WALKED IN SILENCE with Leo Falcone to the Palazzo Doria Pamphilj, wearing the suit, white shirt, and tie that had been brought from home, thinking about what he'd heard. Teresa had returned to the Questura to continue the difficult—perhaps hopeless—hunt for some clue in the wealth of material she was retrieving from the Vicolo del Divino Amore. Peroni and Rosa were mastering the surveillance system which Falcone had somehow inveigled from some acquaintances in the security services. It was sophisticated, quite unlike anything Costa had seen in use by the state police. Falcone must have pulled some important strings. In addition to the existing surveillance network, each of the talking statues was covered by three cameras, all capable of night sight. Every second, the computer logged a video frame from each. Whenever anyone approached a statue close enough to post a message on it, the monitoring system kicked in and generated an audible alert. That way whoever was on duty could be in constant touch with what was happening in the different locations without having to keep his or her eyes glued to the screen. It was better than standing out in a doorway in the miserable winter weather.

There was plenty of other work besides. Falcone had retrieved every last document in existence on the three suspects, from newspaper clippings to private internal reports held by the police and security service archives. The public information was depressingly predictable. Apart from a few traffic incidents, the newspapers had no evidence to suggest that Franco Malaspina, Giorgio Castagna, and Emilio Buccafusca were anything other than the rich, privileged individuals they purported to be on the surface. In private, however, Malaspina—and he alone—had been the subject of no fewer than five investigations by the police, the Carabinieri, and the Direzione Investigativa Antimafia. Each had ended in failure after intense legal threats and sudden silences among potential witnesses. Malaspina was a man who knew how to work with the system. In some ways he seemed to believe he owned it.

In the Piazza del Collegio Romano, Falcone stopped. This was where they would part: the inspector back to the Questura; Costa to meet Agata Graziano, at the inspector's request, in the gallery set in the sprawling private palace that lurked behind the busy shopping street of the Corso.

"Are you OK with what I'm doing?" Falcone asked Costa. "Be frank."

"I'm OK."

"You're involved. You probably feel that's not enough. But this may be a long game, Nic. We need to improvise. We have to shake them out of their lair. Inside their rich men's homes, locked up with their lawyers . . . they're untouchable. If we can get them into the street, they're on our ground. There we might bring them down."

AFTER THEY LEFT THE APARTMENT, FALCONE AND Costa had walked round to two of the statues, Pasquino and Abate Luigi, and, when there was a gap in the passing pedestrians, posted the scrawled message, with the Ekstasists' copied insignia on the top.

It was Falcone's wording, an adaptation of some doggerel from Dante in a book from the inspector's own shelves.

> *Behold the solstice, brothers!*
> *With it the shadows shorten,*
> *On chestnut, thorn, and darkening mouth.*
> *Now the light of truth falls on love, divine and*
>    *profane.*
> *Now you lose your Venus forever.*

It was an obscure message for obscure criminals, one Falcone had to explain to Gianni Peroni. The big cop remained sceptical. The winter solstice was three days away. From that point on, the days lengthened, and the noon shadows began to abbreviate. The message for the Ekstasists, all three principals spelled out by name, was, the inspector hoped, cryptic but couched in their own kind of language: what had happened in the Vicolo del Divino Amore would soon be revealed. Furthermore, the painting, seemingly the talisman for their acts, was out of their hands, and would remain so.

"These are arrogant men," Falcone had observed after the last message was posted. "Arrogant men. And, in the case of some, I suspect, scared. With luck this will prompt a response. Someone may panic. Perhaps even put up a reply of their own."

"You think they'd take the risk?"

The inspector frowned. "Risk is a part of the thrill. Or so it seems to me. Why else do they keep taunting us? It's like a bullfight. The closer they are to the horns, the more they feel alive. They will want to respond in some way. I'm sure of that. They like those talking statues because they're public and that feeds their own vanity. No ordinary criminal would advertise his work that way. This scum thinks they're special. Perhaps if we give them a little of their own treatment in return . . ."

He glanced at Costa with a mournful expression. "There was nothing you could do about Emily, you know."

"How can you be certain of that?" Costa answered with a swift, unintentional brusqueness. "You weren't there."

"I know because I know you," Falcone replied

instantly. "If something was capable of being achieved, you would have achieved it, Nic. Not that any of this will help in the present circumstances. It's only natural you blame yourself. I just hope that with time you can find some way to release your grief." He frowned. "I speak for us all, Nic. You have friends. We care for you. We're concerned that you must let this grief out from inside."

"I'll mourn when I'm ready," Costa said simply. "When I have the time."

"Don't count on the time," Falcone replied.

"Meaning?"

"Meaning Malaspina is a man with many friends. People like that come up with tricks you'd never dream of, not in a million years."

Money and position mattered in Rome, and always would. Falcone could not pass up any opportunity, or the chance to create one. Costa appreciated that.

"Why am I meeting Agata Graziano again?" Costa asked. "Is she allowed out whenever she pleases?"

"Not at all. She has a temporary dispensation," Falcone replied. "Didn't she tell you? Also, she's a sister, not a nun. It's different. Agata Graziano is a remarkable woman. I know that for a very good reason."

Costa waited. Falcone had given something away, uncharacteristically, and now regretted it.

"Do I find out?" Costa asked.

"I suppose I'll have to tell you now," Falcone sighed, something like a blush staining his cheeks. "Though I do not wish this broadcast at large. A little over twenty years ago my marriage was collapsing, through my own stupid fault. It became clear to me I would never become a father. I wasn't the only one," Falcone hurried on. "It was a kind of tradition among a few of us in the same position. A little charity on the side sometimes made it easier to get through the day. So in that sense my generosity was selfish. Just as it is for Franco Malaspina."

"I never imagined."

"Quite. I suppose you never imagined people knew about your habit of giving money to beggars every day, too."

"That stopped," Costa admitted with a little shame.

"You got married. You found someone you loved. You were looking to start a family of your own. It was only natural. I..." Falcone laughed at his own embarrassment. "They said I had to sponsor a particular girl in the convent orphanage. They chose her for me, naturally. As luck would have it, they chose Agata Graziano, though I'm still not sure she ever really was a child. I first met Agata when she was nine years old and she was just as serious and awkward and curious about everything as she is now."

So that was the connection. "Did she have to become a nun? Because she was in the convent orphanage?"

"Sister! She belongs to a different order."

"Sorry. Sister."

"No," Falcone replied with obvious care. "She could have done anything she wanted. In a sense she did, with university and her studies. I observed in silence from the sidelines, visiting her only three or four times a year. Taking her on trips occasionally. Watching her grow, which was wondrous, but no more so than for any other child, I imagine. I knew she was remarkable from an early age. Then . . . I imagine everyone thinks that." His sharp eyes glanced at Costa. "In twenty years I haven't heard her express the slightest desire to leave that convent and I never once questioned her decision. Agata has enough difficult ideas rattling around that intelligent head of hers without you adding to them."

"I'm sure you're right."

"I am. Remember that. If anyone can get to the bottom of that painting of yours, it's Agata. Why do you think I asked for her in the first place? Always use someone you know if you can, Nic. Remember that when everything gets more complicated in the years to come. Make the most of Agata's knowledge. And . . ." A brief expression of doubt passed across Falcone's face. "Take care of her. I fear she's not as resilient as she believes. I must go now. Really . . ."

Costa was thinking of the clothes Falcone had sent for from the farmhouse, insisting he wear them for the evening. They were the best he had.

"Why am I getting dressed up like this to go to a gallery, Leo?" he asked.

The inspector coughed into his fist. "Didn't I mention that?"

"No."

"Ah. After the gallery there is an event. The Barberini's staff party. I thought you might enjoy it."

Costa's mind went blank. "A party? You want me to go to a party?"

"It's not just a party. It's in the Palazzo Malaspina. You will be there as a civilian. A guest. No one can complain of harassment. It's just a little idea I had . . ."

Costa nodded, beginning to understand. "He will be there. Malaspina."

"I expect so," Falcone admitted. "Oh . . ." He half turned as he strode away. "Have fun, won't you?" he ordered, and was gone.

# Part Seven
## The Song of Solomon

# One

*H*E FOUND HER IN THE SALETTA DEL SEICENTO, exactly where he expected: in front of the central painting on the long wall, Caravaggio's sumptuous depiction of *The Rest on the Flight into Egypt,* with its elderly Joseph holding the music for an ethereally beautiful angel, who bowed a violin to a slumbering Virgin and Child. Agata Graziano was accompanied by a slender man with bright golden hair and a face not unlike that of the divine being with the violin, though somewhat older and a little careworn. Both he and Agata were, however, intent on studying the painting to the work's left: another Caravaggio, this time the slumbering penitent Mary Magdalene.

She turned to smile at him as he arrived.

"Riddles," she remarked. "Nothing but riddles. Do you recognise the woman here?"

"Fillide Melandroni," Costa said promptly.

"Exactly. One of the busiest ladies of her time, and here she is, the model for both the Magdalene and the Virgin herself. And"—a flicker of puzzlement crossed

Agata's dark eyes—"the woman in our own mysterious canvas. Do you wonder Caravaggio wound up being run out of Rome? Even if he'd never murdered that man in the street."

Her gaze fell on the slumbering Magdalene, a portrait so exquisitely human in its portrayal of both physical and spiritual exhaustion that its subtle, intense power made Costa's mind reel whenever he saw it.

"Here's another thing," she pointed out. "You see what she's wearing? These are the clothes of a Roman prostitute. An Ortaccio whore. This is what Fillide looked like when she went about her business." That glimmer of self-doubt flickered across her face again. "Not that I'm much qualified to offer you an opinion there. Caravaggio would have produced these about the same time, working no more than a five-minute walk from where we stand. You can see it in the colours, the people, the style. The life, more than anything. This was perhaps 1596. Michelangelo Merisi was still young, undamaged by the harsh reality of everyday Rome. He had just entered the household of Del Monte, painting by day, listening to philosophers and alchemists in the evening. And Lord knows what else . . ."

She glanced at him. "Still, that's not my territory either, is it? Here's something else." Her hand pointed to the scroll of music held by the elderly Joseph, listening, in wonder, to the angel's violin. "Music. *Real* music. Alexander?"

The man standing beside her looked at Costa and

smiled. Then he began to sing, a slow wordless melody detailed in a perfect alto voice, halfway between a choirboy and a diva.

When he stopped, he grinned at Costa's discomfort. "Don't worry, we won't get thrown out. This is one of my party tricks. Alexander Fairgood. I run music events here from time to time."

"Ah," Costa replied, understanding. He walked forward and examined the sheet of music in the raddled Joseph's worn and elderly hands. "I always thought it was just . . . notes."

"That's what riddles are for," Agata pointed out. "Making you think. Tell him, Alex."

He was American but spoke Italian in the easy, fluent way foreigners did after a few years in the city. "This is what's known as a Marian motet. A form of medieval religious music dedicated to the Virgin Mary. This particular piece is an extract from a work by an obscure Flemish composer, Noël Bauldewijn. The words are from the Song of Songs, 7:6 to 7:12. I have this from memory, in Latin or Greek, Hebrew or English. Lord knows I've sung it enough."

His clear, firm voice rang throughout the chamber and the corridors beyond once more, timeless and in perfect, controlled pitch, now declaiming a set of rich and sonorous verses precisely, word by word.

The man's voice had an ethereal clarity that stilled every other sound in the gallery. Costa didn't understand a word.

"It's Latin," Fairgood announced, looking a little testy. "No problem. I'm used to translating it for Romans. The price is you get it in English. It sounds more alluring that way. Can you manage?"

"I'm fine with English," Costa said, knowing somehow he didn't have to ask this question of Agata.

> "Come, my beloved, let us go forth into the
>     field; let us lodge in the villages.
> Let us get up early to the vineyards; let us see if
>     the vine flourish, whether the tender grape
>     appear, and the pomegranates bud forth:
>     there will I give thee my loves."

Fairgood grinned. "That was the King James Version. Pretty racy for an old Protestant Scot, don't you think?"

"It's a love poem?" Costa asked. "An *erotic* love poem?"

"It's the Song of Songs!" the American replied, astonished by Costa's ignorance. "*The* erotic love poem. And this other thing you gave me to look up . . . Not that I know why, though I might guess." He glanced at Agata, hoping for clarification.

"When I can tell you, I will tell you, Alex," she said sweetly.

"I should hope so," the American grumbled. "It's the same piece of music but with a different verse set to it. One Bauldewijn never put there in the original."

He took a slip of paper out of his pocket and, this time, spoke the words in his relaxed Italian.

> *"His left hand is under my head, and his right*
>    *hand doth embrace me.*
> *I charge you, O ye daughters of Jerusalem, by*
>    *the roes,*
> *and by the hinds of the field, that ye stir not*
>    *up, nor*
> *awake my love, till he please."*

Alexander Fairgood stared hard at the canvas in front of them, a wan smile on his handsome face.

"You know," he said softly, "I always used to think this was the most sensual thing I'd ever seen in my life. The way that half-naked angel has his feathered wings turned towards you, making you ache to stroke them." He indicated the lazy, knowing eye of the donkey behind the grizzled head of Joseph, its gaze taking in everything. "I always wondered what would happen if Mary woke and discovered this vision there, next to the old man who wasn't even the father of her child."

"I've told you a million times," Agata said patiently. "The subject—or at least *one* subject, because there are many here—is the same as the Song of Songs. Does love stem from spirituality or from sexuality? Will one beget the other? And where, in the balance, lies the love of God?"

He eyed her, his expression coy, teasing. "It's sex

wrapped up as religion, Agata. If you spent more time out of that chaste little nunnery of yours, you'd know it."

"I *am* spending more time out of it, in case you hadn't noticed," she retorted. "Thanks to a dispensation."

"Temporary only, then," he murmured with a frown. "What a pity."

"Thank you, Alex," she said, and glanced at the door.

"Oh," he said. "I have overstayed my welcome."

She folded her small arms and said nothing.

The American took one last look at the painting in front of them. Like the work in the Vicolo del Divino Amore, it seemed to pulse with a vibrant life of its own, though one softer and more gentle.

"I never tire of coming here," Fairgood told them. "Particularly in such interesting company. But this other painting I heard about . . ."

His voice was transformed in an instant into a disembodied plainchant that sent a shiver down Costa's spine.

"*His left hand is under my head, and his right hand doth embrace me,*'" Alexander Fairgood sang, then stopped, clearly delighting in the resonance of his own voice as it echoed through the Palazzo Doria Pamphilj's labyrinthine galleries.

"IT'S REAL," SHE SAID, IN A LOW, EXCITED VOICE WHEN the musician was gone. She gripped Costa's arm, her fingers tight on the cloth of his coat. "I knew it the moment they first brought me to it. But that was instinct. This is fact. See here for yourself. This is the same model. Fillide. The music has the same antecedents. The style, the artistry, the feeling of the thing . . . I can sense Caravaggio in the paint, for pity's sake. Can't you?"

"Yes," he answered quietly, and felt a pang of concern.

"And yet . . ." She breathed deeply, unhappy with her own bemusement. "What does it mean? Why a subject he never broached before or after? He must have understood how wonderful it was. Why stop *there*?"

The same questions kept nagging at him.

"He produced our painting while he was in the employ of Del Monte?"

She nodded energetically. "I think so, but towards the end. If you look closely, you can detect the man's age, his moods, his growing anger and depression in the strokes of the brush. In the early years, when Caravaggio produced canvases like these he was as happy as he would ever be. This was before the churches began to hire him, before the gloom and the fear we see beginning to rise in the Contarelli Chapel and the Matthew cycle. Before death and decay began to infect his mind. He lived with Del Monte, with those poets and magicians and alchemists, their whores and their boyfriends, and somehow, somewhere along the way, a patron—perhaps Del Monte himself—came along and showed him that inferior Carracci, put some money in his pocket, and said . . . what?"

"Be better and more daring," Costa replied immediately.

"More daring?" she echoed, astonished. "He was trying to out-paint even himself. He was trying to put on canvas something—some moment, human, divine, diabolic, I don't know—except that it had never been painted before. And when it's finished...nothing. Except for that brief mention in the journal of Giambattista Marino, it may well have never existed. From the moment of its creation that painting's been some kind of secret. Who's kept it? Why has it never been displayed, discovered, sold? Where has it been? In Rome, surely. But where?"

Some unfathomable inner knowledge threw an idea into his head at that moment. "In the hands of someone, some family that never needed the money," Costa suggested. "Or the public acclaim of owning it."

Agata Graziano scowled. "That's guesswork. Besides, what rich family would own a painting like this and *not* show it? Those people delight in letting the rest of us know how fortunate they are."

"I'm a police officer," Costa replied, shrugging. "Sometimes guesswork is all I have."

"Then I pity you." She took his hand, turned the wrist, and glanced at his watch. Timepieces, it seemed, were another possession Sister Agata Graziano avoided. "I can't stay here any longer. My head will burst."

And yet, in spite of herself, Agata found herself turning again to the wall, this time to the smaller canvas of the Magdalene: Fillide Melandroni, asleep, slumped, dressed in the rich costume of a late-sixteenth-century Ortaccio whore.

"Do you ever hear their voices?" she asked softly.

Costa knew instantly what she meant. "When I look at the paintings, of course," he answered honestly. "That's Caravaggio. These aren't idealised human beings. They're the people he met every day, and when we see them we realise they're the same as those we meet, too, people just like you and me. They're not history. They're *us*."

"They *are* us," she agreed, and there was some grim note of self-reproach in her voice. "Still. I know where they lived and where they died. I walk the same pavements, pass the same buildings, stay awake at night over the same fears and doubts."

Her attention never left the canvas on the wall for a moment: Fillide Melandroni, long dead, sleeping, gripped by a deep, exhausted fatigue that verged on mortality itself.

"Sometimes," Agata said slowly, "I imagine I see a man in the street, a dark-haired man, with that incomplete beard and a sad, shocked face. He is staring at me from the other side of the road, not seeing the traffic, not noticing anything except the faces and the pain and the same bright, damaged humanity he saw there too." She gripped his arm more firmly. "We inhabit their world, Nic. They inhabit ours. Why else would a man want to paint, except to live forever?"

Her dark glittering eyes studied him before returning

briefly to the painting of the sleeping Fillide. "And...
Alexander said it. He would kill to see a painting like
that. Someone has. People have died. The reason you
wish to talk to me is that you believe I can tell you why."

"I hope so," he replied.

"Will that help you, Nic? You?"

There was no similarity whatsoever between Emily,
his lost wife, and this eccentric woman whose life was so
distant from anything he could imagine that she might
have come from the moon. Nothing except their mutual
insistence on one subject alone: the truth was there to be
faced, however terrible it might turn out to be.

"I don't know, but I hope so," he answered, and found
himself following the line of her gaze, straight to the
slumbering female figure on the canvas on the wall.

Something caught his attention on the face of the
Magdalene, a detail he had never seen before. He blinked,
then looked again. At first it appeared to be a flaw, a rip
in the canvas, exposing some tiny bright white element
beneath the paint. Then, as Agata noticed what he was
seeing, he moved closer, so close it seemed improper, yet
he was propelled by her insistent arm.

Nic Costa had lost count of how many times he'd
walked through the doors of the Doria Pamphilj, how
many hours he'd spent in its glorious corridors, over-
whelmed by the beauty of its collection, and the open,
everyday way in which it was displayed, as if in a home,
not a museum. He had never before seen this minuscule
speck on the cheek of the sleeping woman. Agata Graziano

had taught him something: how to look. Now he felt transfixed by the revelation, so small and yet so large: a single element, infinitely human, depicted with the rudimentary perfection of an unconscious genius.

A single glassy tear was caught, frozen in a discrete moment of time on the cheek of the slumbering Fillide Melandroni. As she slept, in the guise of the once-fallen Magdalene after the Crucifixion, aware of the tragedy that had newly entered the world, a part of her, her soul perhaps, wept. The sight of this infinitesimal secret ripped at his heart, dragging out its own dark tragedy from the depths, as it was meant to.

"You're learning," Agata whispered, casting him a glance that seemed to contain some distant, studied admiration.

# Two

*T*HEY WALKED THROUGH THE CENTRO STORICO, Agata pointing out the streets he thought he knew well, now realising how mistaken he had been. She understood them so much better, and in so many different dimensions: where the painters they both revered had lived and fought and died. It was like a lesson from the freest and frankest of university professors. Agata talked of the society—rich, violent, hedonistic, and yet, in a sense, deeply religious, even moralistic—that had first nurtured Caravaggio, then, as his behaviour worsened, began to reject him, finally delivering the death sentence for the killing that dispatched him into exile. As she spoke, Costa realised there was something he had never really sought before: the spirit behind the brush, the burning creative animus that had driven one lone rebel, with little in the way of formal education or tuition, to redress the focus of painting and seek the divine in the mundane, the thieves and prostitutes, the criminals and the vagabonds, who walked the streets of Rome.

It was all, she said, a question of *disegno,* which, for the painters of Caravaggio's generation, meant not simply "design" but, as one of his contemporaries put it, "*il segno di Dio in noi,*" the sign of God in us.

"Do you see the sign of God anywhere today?" she asked.

"No," he replied, and shrugged. "Sorry. Do you?"

"Everywhere! You must learn to look properly. I will deal with this lapse."

They strode past the grand home of Caravaggio's onetime patron, Agata speculating about the behaviour of the eccentric Archbishop Del Monte and his bizarre household in what was now the genteel home of the Senate, guarded by innumerable uniformed Carabinieri. Then they made their way across the busy Christmas traffic bickering to fight its way through the perennial jam at the Piazza delle Cinque Lune as she talked passionately about the past in the present, daring him to sense its nearness. No more than three minutes away, towards the Corso, stood the Piazza di San Lorenzo in Lucina, the place where Caravaggio fell into the deadly street fight that led to his exile from Rome. The same distance towards the river, beyond the Via della Scrofa, which led towards the Vicolo del Divino Amore, lay the Tor di Nona, the tower where some of his fellow ruffians had been imprisoned after the desperate knife battle, perhaps with the wounded Caravaggio among them, until, with the aid of some of his aristocratic admirers, the painter was able to flee the executioner.

"They are here, Nic," she insisted. "*He* is here. You simply have to look and listen. Come."

They turned the corner into the small cobbled piazza. The early Renaissance façade of the Church of Sant'Agostino stood above them, its pale travertine, visibly plundered from the Colosseum some five hundred years before, now luminescent in the orange streetlights. He followed her up the long, broad flight of stone stairs, through into the vast echoing nave. Instinctively, he turned to his left, towards the painting he'd seen countless times, and knew would see afresh through her eyes.

"No," she said, and took his elbow, guiding him away. "I didn't bring you here for that."

*The Madonna of Loreto,* an exquisite Caravaggio Virgin with the infant Jesus in her arms, the holy pair framed in the doorway of a simple stone house, staring down at two grimy pilgrims, stood in the gloom at the edge of his vision, like a sombre, glowing beacon.

"If he worshipped," Agata said, "and I believe he did, he worshipped here. They all came to this place. The artists and the poets. And worse. This was an altar for the fallen. They had need of it most of all. Where would the Church be without sinners?"

She turned to face the entrance and he did the same, seeing the sculpture there, a pale study of two figures illuminated by a sea of candles.

"This was the whores' church, too," Agata Graziano told him. "The seat of worship for what was once Ortaccio. The mistress of Cesare Borgia is buried here. So were some of the most famous prostitutes of Rome, not by the Muro Torto, where the law dictated. You won't find their tombs here anymore, though. All gone, out of a sense of..." She frowned. "...decorum. I'm just a humble sister with a fondness for art. I know no more of your world than I wish to. But this puzzles me. That men should want a thing so badly, and then feel filled with shame when they achieve it. Fillide felt no shame. Why should she? Look, Nic, look closely..."

He'd never spent much time on the figures there at all, though a dim memory told him that they had some special significance for the ordinary women of Rome. Sometimes, when visiting the Caravaggio, he'd seen them slip up to the larger statue, the Madonna, almost furtively, place an offering in the box, light a candle, cross themselves. Then, with one last sideways glance, step gently forward and touch the silver slipper that protected the Virgin's foot.

He stared at the placid, beautiful woman carved from stone, seated majestically beneath the half-shell cupola of the alcove, with the child standing, one leg on her lap, one on her throne. How could he have been so blind? Above her hair, lit by the forest of blazing candles in the niche, rose a starry halo. Around her chest, tight beneath her breasts, ran a silver garland. The child was magnificent, rising to face the world, a bright, brave metal robe girding his waist. Wreathed in light, surrounded by flowers and mementos, messages and photographs of children, so many of them, she was beyond Christian iconography, timeless, like Venus displaying the infant Cupid, a prize, a miracle in her arms.

"What do women pray for when they come here? When they touch her feet like that?" he asked.

"Again, you are asking the wrong person. This is the Madonna del Parto, the Madonna of motherhood, of birth. It's a belief that predates my faith. That through womanhood comes the fecundity of mankind. So I imagine they pray for the child they are bearing or hope to." She hesitated. "Even a woman like Fillide, perhaps, though a Christian sensibility gave her generation the notion, the stain, of sin too."

He thought of the painting hidden in the studio, its message lurking beneath so many surface deceptions. And he remembered Emily and the child they had lost. There were no prayers to ease that pain, no candles and flowers, or the worn, comforting touch of a statue's silver foot shining in the gloomy belly of an ancient church marooned in its own quiet piazza, a few steps from the choking bustle of modern Rome.

"When they came here," Agata asked, speaking in a loud, firm voice, the way the priest did at Emily's funeral, when all else whispered, "what do you think they saw? Del Monte and Caravaggio. Galileo and Fillide Melandroni. What did they seek?"

"*Disegno*," Nic replied simply.

The design of God in us.

He was unable to avoid her fixed, interested stare.

"You are a good pupil, Nic Costa," Agata Graziano

declared with a sudden serious turn. "I only wish I were a better teacher."

He began to object.

"No," she interjected. "A good teacher would have some answers."

"I could ask an easier question," he suggested. There was a moment's hesitation before he found the courage to say it. "Who are you? Where did you come from?"

All sense of amusement departed her face. This dark, austere, yet pretty woman, hugging herself tightly in the long black coat of the nun she was not, looked back at him, suddenly uncertain of herself.

"What interest is this of yours?" she responded.

"I'm curious. It's part of the job. Most of the job, to be honest with you."

"Well, there is nothing to know. I was one abandoned child among many. They thought my mother was a woman of the kind..." She looked around the church. "...who would once have dreamed she might enter a place like this, and doubtless would never have been pretty enough or rich enough. My father was a seaman. He was African, I think. From Ethiopia. That is all I know and all I wish to know. The sisters took me in, raised me, and then, when they saw something worth cultivating, set me on this present course through the simple medium of education. My story is wholly unexceptional, for which I am grateful." A shadow of doubt crossed her face. "Now, for a day or two, I am something else. One of you. Thanks to your inspector."

"Another of Leo's gifts."

She looked a little cross. "He told you?"

Costa was aware that he had done something wrong. "Just the basics."

"Why on earth would he do that?" she asked, not expecting an answer. "In another man I would have said it came from misplaced pride. But not him. Never. How odd."

She pointed a short, commanding finger at his chest. "What Leo did was charity, and charity is best performed in silence. I am grateful for it, and wish to hear no more."

She gazed at the statue: the bright, gleaming Madonna, an older goddess, too, perhaps, with the magical child in her arms. There was something there, Nic thought, something that was beyond even Agata Graziano.

"We are done with the dead," she declared, and set off for the door. "For the time being anyway."

Costa hesitated, staring at the statue, thinking of Emily. Thinking of what it might be like to be in the same room as the man who had taken her life so casually.

Leo Falcone demanded a high and difficult price of everyone he knew. Costa wondered, for a moment, whether he could pay it, whether he could enter a room with the men he knew to be the Ekstasists and act as if nothing were wrong.

"Nic?" Agata asked from the door. "Are you coming or not?"

He had never said this to Falcone, but the suit the inspector had ordered to be brought from the farmhouse was the one Costa had worn for their wedding.

"I'm coming," he answered.

# Part Eight
## The Palazzo Malaspina

# One

$\mathcal{T}$HIRTY MINUTES LATER THEY STOOD ON THE steps of the Palazzo Malaspina. The entrance dominated much of the narrow seventeenth-century street that led, in a few short minutes, to the Mausoleum of Augustus, a place Costa had yet to find the courage to revisit. The Vicolo del Divino Amore was even closer around the corner, as was the Barberini's small external studio, where the canvas of Venus with her satyrs now resided. Everything about this case, it seemed to Costa, was contained in the small, secretive warren of dark, dingy alleys here, the labyrinth that was once Ortaccio.

They stopped at the foot of the curving stone staircase. A heraldic decoration ran the length of each side: a stone shield half a metre high, divided into two halves, one stippled, one plain. A bare angular tree in the centre with three short horizontal branches on the left and two on the right. From each emerged sharp spines, top and bottom of the branches. *Mala spina*. The bad thorn.

Agata Graziano looked at him, a shadow of guilt in her charming face.

"I lied a little, Nic," she confessed. "This isn't simply the Barberini's Christmas party. We're sharing it with one of the private galleries too. It's about money, of course. We can't afford it on our own anymore."

He thought of Falcone and realised he should have expected this.

"Let me guess. The Buccafusca Gallery."

"Yes," she replied, impressed. "You're quite the detective. How did you know?"

"Falcone told me. After a fashion."

"Ah. He is an . . . interesting man. He likes you. I can see that."

"Interesting," Costa agreed.

"I merely wish you to know that some of the things you see here will be Buccafusca's," she added. "Not ours."

"I can't wait," Costa replied, and then followed her through the front doors into a grand marbled reception area set beneath an alcove with a carved scalloped half shell many times the size of that over the Madonna del Parto. He watched the private security men, who seemed to know Agata Graziano, nod gravely and take off their caps before ushering the pair of them into a square, echoing hall of pillars and shining stone façades, an extravagant lobby more in keeping with that of an embassy than a private home. A palace like this was, for Costa, a rare blank sheet. The home of the Malaspina dynasty— now occupied, as far as he knew, by its sole surviving member—was a sprawling complex that covered a vast area of this part of Rome, and never opened its doors to the public, not even for a day.

The place was a wonder; the crowds would have flocked there. Smaller mansions, such as the Palazzo Altemps, had been acquired by the state and turned into grand museums, former aristocratic homes that were as much exhibits themselves as the rich and varied collections they held. The Malaspina clan had escaped such a fate. They maintained their secret hidden lives behind the soot-blackened walls of a city fortress that was dark and forbidding from the outside and full of light and beauty within.

Beyond the entrance was a vast cobbled courtyard, with a large statue of Cupid stretching his bow at its centre. On all sides rose three floors, the first two open to the elements, with an arched colonnade on the ground, and a balustrade balcony on the second. Lights blazed from every level, silhouetting a sea of bodies talking animatedly, members of a society to which Costa knew he would never belong. He felt hopelessly out of place, and perhaps she saw that, because Agata Graziano took his arm for one brief moment, and said, "Don't worry. I'll look after you if you look after me."

"Agreed," he murmured, and then they pushed their way through the first ground-floor hall, where a noisy throng of people gossiped. The Buccafusca Gallery insignia, a black mouth, open in greed or ecstasy, it was unclear which, appeared everywhere; all the objects surrounding them appeared modern and ugly.

"*Salut*," Agata declared, grabbing two glasses, orange juice for her, *prosecco* for him, as a scantily clad waitress fought her way past. "I may join you in that before long."

He cast his eyes around the room: bright, shiny people, beautiful, fixed on each other, looking as if they owned the world.

"So this is how the upper classes live," he observed. "I always wondered what I was missing. Perhaps . . ."

He could see them now, across the room, and the sight of them blended with the images in his head: of Rosa Prabakaran's photographs, and that dreadful experience close by a long-dead emperor's tomb, just a short walk away from where they now stood in this strange, artificial party.

Looking at the four—Malaspina, Buccafusca, Castagna, and the stocky, uncomfortable Nino Tomassoni by their side—he realised that any of the taller men could, in theory, have been the hooded figure. But there was something about Malaspina—the commanding, stiff stance, the smug assumption of superiority—that convinced Costa he was the man, could only be the man.

"Are you comfortable with the aristocracy?" Agata Graziano asked, watching him.

"I don't have much experience," he admitted.

"Well," she said, shrugging, and beginning to fight her way through the sea of silk-clad bodies with a jabbing elbow and a forceful determination, "let's start."

# Two

CHRISTMAS," FRANCO MALASPINA DECLARED, "THE
same thing every year. A party for the Barberini. A line
of cheques to be written. Everyone presumes on my
charity, Sister Agata. Why did I do this? Tell me. Please."

Agata laughed. It was a deliberate taunt, cheerfully
delivered, though Costa felt the atmosphere was not as
cordial as Malaspina pretended. The three men by his
side had shambled away when they approached. The trio
seemed unhappy, uncomfortable, as if they had been
bickering, stopping only because of the arrival of company.

Malaspina possessed the kind of too-perfect
Mediterranean tan that seemed to be *de rigueur* for a certain kind of young Roman aristocrat. His craggy face,
marked by a prominent Roman nose, was intelligent but
disengaged, as if everything around him was of no great
significance. Buccafusca and Castagna were of similar
build but less striking in appearance, with the dark hair
and pale, serious faces of bankers or bureaucrats, and a

manner that was diffident in the extreme. Tomassoni, short, overweight, and sweating visibly under the hot lights, looked as if he didn't belong in the place and couldn't wait to get out. All three of them had now reassembled a few metres away, close to another strange modern sculpture, talking quietly, furtively, among themselves.

"You do this because you are a good man at heart, in spite of all your pretences, Franco," Agata replied happily. "One day you'll be married and have children of your own. Then you'll think differently. Then you'll remember Christmas as it was when you were a child."

Malaspina looked her up and down. "I spent Christmas with servants," he complained. "It's not the same. Besides, of course I'm a good man. Don't you read the papers? I can show you the accounts if you like." He hesitated, staring now at Costa. "So why have you brought a policeman to interrogate me?"

"I'm not here to interrogate anyone," Costa replied politely. "Sister Agata and I were working together. She merely suggested I come along. If this offends you . . ."

"Why should it offend me?"

"Some people are not fond of us . . ."

"Not me!" Malaspina raised a glass. "To law and order. But *order* most of all. You'll drink to that, won't you?"

Costa sipped his *prosecco,* unable to take his eyes off the man. Franco Malaspina was not what he expected. In flesh, close up, he seemed amiable, larger than life, and yet ill at ease, with them and with himself, both forthright and subtly reticent. Costa had, he was forced to admit, no idea what to make of him. The voice didn't ring a bell. The physique, the posture . . . these could have matched many in Rome.

"Of course, Agata," Malaspina continued, "if I marry, I should marry you. Imagine the publicity. I finally find the last worthwhile virgin left in Rome."

She said nothing.

Malaspina looked at Costa and tapped the side of his nose. "Agata is a fan of Dante, as are we all, though for different reasons. She sees herself as Beatrice. Beautiful, chaste, alluring. And dead."

He laughed at his own joke. No one else did.

"You are too intelligent to make such a foolish comparison," Agata objected. "You know Dante as well as any of us. He loved Beatrice, and she died. Through that he discovered there was a greater love than the physical. A spiritual love."

Costa caught his breath. Something in Agata's words had produced a moment of bleakness in Franco Malaspina's eyes. It was only there for a second, but it was unmistakable, and also unreadable. Anger? Sadness? Grief?

"You sound like the Pope," the man groaned. "This is Christmas. Even for a pagan like me, it's not a time to talk of death."

Agata nodded in agreement. "I'm meant to sound like the Holy Father, aren't I?"

"No. It's a waste, Agata. A beautiful woman. Someone

with feelings. I know you have them. You know too. We're all human, the same little animals with the same desires and fears. What's the problem?"

He stared into her eyes.

"Be like the rest of us, bold now and chaste afterwards," Malaspina murmured, watching her draw back to stand closer to Costa. "Who's to know? Is that all your god is? Just a spy in the bedroom?"

"Franco does this to me all the time," she told Costa, half serious, half joking. "It's one of his tricks."

"Tricks," he answered softly. "You bring a policeman into my palace and accuse *me* of tricks." Franco Malaspina gazed at Costa, still and confident of himself. His teeth were unnaturally perfect. His eyes, bright, unafraid, glittering, held him. "Why are you here?" he asked.

"I told you," Costa insisted. "I was invited to a party. Nothing more. If it's a problem ..."

The man took a deep breath, as if disappointed by the mild reply. "You're the one whose wife died. I saw it somewhere. In the paper, I believe. They took pictures of you at the funeral. How does that feel?"

"Franco!" Agata intervened. "Don't be so rude."

"But I'm curious," he protested. "He has no need to answer. Not if it offends him."

"I'm not offended," Costa cut in. "How does what feel exactly?"

"Being followed by scum like those reporters. Nosy

bastards, invading your life. When you've done nothing wrong. I've had them too."

"Not like this," Costa replied sourly.

"No." And the man had changed again. He seemed genuinely upset. Almost penitent. "It was wrong of me to presume in that way. I'm sorry. To lose the woman you love . . . I should never have asked. It was rude of me. Here . . ."

Malaspina's right hand, the one Costa believed, when he entered that room, had taken the life of Emily, was extended now. "Shake, please," Malaspina said. "Accept my apologies and my condolences. It's the fate of everyone to be bereaved one day." That strange, lost expression crossed his face once more. "I am merely fortunate never to have lost anyone who mattered to me. An absentee father scarcely counts."

"Thank you," Costa said, and took his hand. Malaspina had an extraordinary grip, strong and insistent. And then it was gone, and the aristocrat stood rocking on his heels, seemingly embarrassed by his own actions.

"You know a little of Caravaggio, then, do you?" he asked, as if it were small talk.

"A little," Costa confessed.

"Only the art, I imagine. Not the man. The life. What made him."

Costa agreed.

"Only the art."

"'*Nec spe, nec metu,*'" Malaspina said quietly.

Costa shook his head. Agata came to his aid.

"Oh, not that rot again, Franco. 'Without hope or fear.' It was the motto of a certain kind of Roman individual in those times." She glanced across the room, at Buccafusca and Castagna, or so it seemed to Costa, then turned back to Malaspina.

"So you've read Domenico Mora, Franco?" she asked him. "Or do you just spout what the others tell you?"

"I read," he answered immediately, stung by the question. "We all do."

"You've lost me," Costa confessed.

"They have a certain little club, Nic," she explained. "Men without girlfriends often do, I believe. They think it's their duty to behave like stuck-up pigs when they feel like it because that is what a true Roman gentleman does, and has done for five centuries or so—"

"A knight offends fearlessly," Malaspina interrupted, sounding as if he were quoting something. "For therein, and only therein, lies true distinction." Then he smiled, as if it were all a joke. "But only in the right circumstances. Most of the time I'm an absolute angel."

Agata Graziano looked at him the way a teacher would regard a stupid child.

"So was Caravaggio. Yet he spent the last four years of his life fleeing a murder charge and squandering his talent," she observed mildly. "Violence in the name of honour. What did it get him?"

"We're still talking about him, aren't we?" Then, with no warning, he turned to Costa and asked, "Are you part of this investigation into the death of Véronique Gillet and those prostitutes?"

"I'm not part of any investigation," Costa said simply. "I thought I'd made that clear. Tonight . . ." He raised his glass again. ". . . I'm merely happy to drink your wine. Why?"

"Because I knew her, of course," Malaspina responded. "We all did."

"Poor Véronique," Agata added. "I met her once or twice, only briefly. This is a small world. Not that she said very much. I never did understand why she visited Rome so often, to be frank. The Louvre never bought anything or lent much in return either."

"The French stole what they wanted two centuries ago," Malaspina muttered. "What happened?"

"I have no idea," Costa answered with a shrug. "As I said, that is not my case."

Agata shook her head. "She was murdered, surely? What other explanation is there?"

Malaspina sighed, then said, "Véronique was a very sick woman. She didn't have long to live. She told me so. Perhaps she was no innocent party, Officer. Have you thought of that?"

"I've thought of nothing."

That answer displeased his host. "Then offer an opinion. You do have one, don't you?"

"An opinion?" Costa drained the glass and handed it to the passing waitress, refusing another. "From what little I know, I would guess she was involved somehow. But

I doubt one woman could achieve such a succession of deaths on her own. Someone must have helped her. Perhaps even instigated what went on." He glanced at Agata, wondering whether to say what he wanted, then reminding himself that sometimes duty came before tact. "She had sex shortly before she died."

"Well, that's a comforting thought, anyway," Malaspina said. "Tell me. Is that painting genuine, do you think?"

"You've seen it?" Costa asked.

Malaspina laughed. "Of course I've seen it!" he responded. "The money I give to the Barberini . . . If they didn't call me in to get a private view of something like that, I'd want to know why." He enjoyed Agata's discomfort. "Oh dear. You feel some misplaced sense of ownership towards the thing. That's a pity."

He leaned down to peer into her pert face. "It's called 'privilege' for a reason, dearest. So . . . is it genuine?"

"The painting is part of a serious investigation, sir. While this is none of my business, I would suggest that is not a question one should address publicly. For reasons of—"

"I'll address it," Agata interrupted. "Professionally I will not be able to say this for many weeks. All the obvious signs are there. We had some results for the pigment tests and the canvas this afternoon. They date to the late sixteenth or early seventeenth century. The X-rays show it is a virgin work, with nothing of any import underneath except some preliminary sketches. All the trademarks . . . the incisions, the stylistic peculiarities we asso-ciate with the artist. More than that"——she smiled at Costa openly, with some affection——"when I stand near a Caravaggio, I feel something. A little faint, a little excited, and more than a little scared. Don't you agree, Nic?"

He nodded. "Exactly."

"And I don't?" Malaspina asked angrily. There was heat in his cheeks now. The transformation was immedi-ate and astonishing. "You think I am somehow less per-ceptive than the two of you?"

"I have no idea, Franco," she replied sweetly. "Your true feelings about anything are entirely unknown to me. When I see evidence of them, I shall judge."

"Best be nice to me, Agata." Malaspina nodded at the room around him. "That way you can hope to come and see it here if I happen to be feeling generous. This will be one Caravaggio the hoi polloi won't sully. The Palazzo Malaspina is not the Doria Pamphilj. You'll have to beg to get in."

Both of them stared at him mutely for a moment. It was if a different man were now talking to them.

"What do you mean?" she asked eventually. "The painting is in the custody of the Barberini. No one's mentioned it may be moved elsewhere."

"They will. Soon too. Didn't I tell you? I'm amazed the police haven't found out yet. The hovel where they found it belongs to us. The Malaspina estate has been unchanged for three centuries. We never sold off one square metre. I own so much around here I find it tedious to keep track of it all. There's even a whole precinct near the Piazza Borghese we picked up from a Pope somewhere along the way. Gambling debts or a woman, one or the other. What's new?"

"Ownership of the studio in the Vicolo del Divino Amore scarcely makes the painting yours," Costa pointed out.

"No? Talk to my lawyers." His sharp black eyes held Costa. The man was laughing at them now. "If this painting isn't mine, then whose is it? In the absence of proven title, ownership falls to the landlord. I checked with the idle little agent we employ to look after these matters. The place hasn't been rented out for years. As far as that idiot knew, it was empty, which rather begs the question why he wasn't seeking to rent it. If no one else can claim it, the thing is mine."

"That may be the law," Costa agreed. "But possession—"

"You are not listening to me," Malaspina barked, now animated for the first time since Costa had been introduced to him. "Lawyers. The more you have, the more you gain. Now that I know Agata's opinion, I will stake my claim tomorrow. Let's see if anyone dares come to court to dispute it. I doubt it will be a long wait. You should be grateful for that, shouldn't you? One less thing for you to worry about."

"I wouldn't expect any early judgments," Costa replied, scanning the room, wondering what the others were doing.

"It's mine!" Malaspina's voice had risen to a shriek.

Costa stared at him. "That painting is not yours, sir. Not yet, if ever. It is evidence in a murder case in which several women have died through extreme violence. Possibly crucial evidence. That we shall see."

"Lawyers!" Malaspina yelled. Agata took a step back. Costa stood his ground. "I will drown you in lawyers. I will send them to your home. I will have them throwing stones at your windows when you lie in bed alone at night. The painting is mine."

"One day, possibly," Costa acknowledged. "But not now. And not soon. Whatever case you may have for title, we are the police and we have ultimate claim when it comes to matters of physical evidence." The thought came from nowhere and it pleased him to say it. "That which we have in our possession already, to hand." He paused, for effect. "Identifiable and tagged."

"You—"

"As long as this murder investigation stays current," Costa interrupted, "that painting will remain in police custody, secure and out of sight of everyone. Once we can put someone in jail for these terrible crimes"—he smiled at Malaspina—"perhaps you can see it then."

The man swore and with a sudden, strong flick of his wrist sent the contents of his glass flying into Costa's face.

"You do not know with whom you are playing, little man," he spat viciously.

Costa took out a handkerchief and, with no visible

sign of anger, wiped the drink from his face. "I think I'm beginning to get an idea," he observed calmly.

He looked into Malaspina's eyes and wondered what he saw there. A kind of fury, surely. But an irrational desperation bordering on fear and despair, too. This man did not simply desire the painting they had under lock and key in the Barberini studio. He craved it, like an addict longing for his fix.

# Three

OH DEAR," AGATA GROANED AFTER MALASPINA HAD stormed off. "We've upset a sponsor. I must say, he's more touchy than usual tonight. He didn't like you being here, Nic." She peered at him. "I think something upset him, don't you?"

"Who knows? Is his behaviour always this erratic?"

She thought about the question. "Sometimes. Franco doesn't much like anyone, I think. Himself most of all. There's a sadness about him I don't understand. You know, one time he actually made some reference to the colour of my skin. As if his is much different. All this wealth. What more could a man ask? And yet..." The smile disappeared. "You see the world of art from the outside and think it is nothing but beauty and intellectual rigour. Those things do exist. But so do ugliness and jealousy, obsession and some bitter rivalries. We're living, breathing people, too, and while I try to avoid all that as much as I can, it is not entirely possible. In order to work, one must be strong enough to face down these problems. Véronique Gillet . . ." She hesitated.

"What about her?"

"She seemed a very strange, very sad woman. She frightened me a little. There was something *so* compulsive about her, about the way she needed to be with *them* all the time. She was very strong and determined about something, I don't know what. And lost too."

Her dark head of unruly hair had nodded in the direction of Malaspina and his acquaintances, then she gazed straight into Costa's face.

"I'm not a worldly woman, but I must say this. Somehow, I would not be surprised had Véronique been part of Franco's pathetic little band of hooligans."

She stiffened inside her shapeless black dress and began to toy with the crucifix around her neck.

"Do you know what they do?" he asked.

Very quickly, with the acuity he was beginning to expect, she was suspicious.

"No. Why should I? I do hope you and Leo aren't playing me for a fool. I promised to try to help you get to the bottom of that painting. Nothing more."

"Nothing more," Costa agreed.

She still didn't look convinced. "Franco and those idiot friends of his are simply late-developing teenagers, playing a stupid game. Véronique was different. Darker, somehow. I promise you. I've known Franco for five years or more. He's variously infuriating or charming, depending on his mood. He gives generously to the

Barberini every year, and other charities, too, I believe. That's the man. He is an aristocrat. He feels he can behave as he wishes. You live with it or . . ."

The strains of a string quartet began to drift through from an adjoining corridor. They were playing some kind of odd, atonal jazz. For Malaspina, Costa thought, nothing could be quite how one supposed.

Her glass was empty. He picked up a fresh one from a passing waitress. She took it from him, smiled, then exchanged the orange juice for *prosecco* from the tray.

". . . or you will never enter his world."

"What kind of game?"

"A secret one. I don't know. Women. Drink. A bit of upper-class football hooliganism perhaps, since I believe this is fashionable among the aristocracy once more. When he comes into the studio, Franco always talks a little about what he's been up to. I think it's part of his pleasure. Seeing how far he can go with a humble little thing from the Church like me. It doesn't work. I'm not ignorant."

Her eyes were bright and intelligent. "How can I hope to do the work I do and be blind to human frailty? Or evil? I meant it about the Mora book. All these ridiculous notions of virtue through violence. This is nothing new. Men like Malaspina and the rest have been behaving this way in Rome for centuries. Millennia even. For some it's almost a duty."

The expression on his face must have betrayed him.

"You've never heard of Domenico Mora, have you?" she asked.

"Should I?"

She grinned. "If you want to know a certain kind of male, you should. Domenico Mora was a Bolognese soldier. He wrote a book called *Il Cavaliere.* It was a response to a treatise on courtesy, *Il Gentilhuomo,* by Girolamo Muzio. Mora, being a soldier, took a different view. His thesis was that the true gentleman was beholden to no one, and best served his position by letting that be known at every possible occasion. By confrontation, violence, rudeness, and arrogance."

"Towards women too?"

"Women weren't important in Mora's world, except for the obvious purpose. What mattered was one's status. Mora said that the source of the pleasure one acquires in insolence towards others is the feeling that, in the injury you inflict, you claim an exceptional superiority over them. For the likes of Caravaggio and all those other young blades, this was a way of life. Arguments, duels, death even." She hesitated, thinking of something. "The remarkable thing about Michelangelo Merisi is that, when it was over, he went home and painted such exquisite scenes of beauty that I must forgive him his excesses, as did the Pope in the end, though too late. Some other, greater idea still nagged away at the man. *Disegno.* It was in him, he knew it, and I think that caused him pain. He would have been far happier without it. He would never have painted a worthwhile canvas either, of course."

There was sudden, raucous laughter from the far side of the room: Malaspina swaggering through the crowd, glass held high, dark face contorted with some brief manic pleasure. Costa could just catch sight of Nino Tomassoni at the edge of the crowd. He was staring at the other man with an expression of fear mingled with hate.

"It doesn't make them happy," Costa said.

"Is unhappiness a rarity? Caravaggio must have been the most miserable man in Rome, yet he had glimpses of heaven too. Franco and his thuggish friends will see the light, Nic. Today they toy with those ridiculous ideas. In five years' time they'll have wives, be fathering children, and getting apoplectic about the wayward state of society. It's a passing phase. That's all."

More laughter, this time from some of the women, in their bright, expensive evening dresses, listening to Malaspina tell a crude joke at the top of his voice, so that everyone might hear.

"I can't imagine being married," Agata continued quietly. "It seems such a . . . loss of identity. We spend so much time trying to find out who we are. Then we throw it away on a whim."

Agata Graziano looked at Costa, something unfamiliar—indecision, perhaps even fear—in her face. "I need to be presumptuous, Nic. Before you turn red in the face and refuse to answer, you should know this: I am not asking out of idle curiosity. The question pertains directly to this strange painting you and Leo brought me. Well?"

He wondered if there was anything, any part of the human experience, this woman didn't want to understand, even if she refused—through fear, reluctance, or some inner conviction—to be a part of it herself.

"Ask away," Costa replied.

"Which came first when you met your wife? The spiritual side? Or the physical?"

The words were so unexpected he burst out laughing, freely, with a sudden, involuntary rush of emotion he hadn't known since Emily died.

"I have no idea."

"Then think about it. Please."

"I can't. It's not a conscious decision, one before the other. Love is..." He was blushing, and he knew it. "...unplanned. Perhaps a little of both, I imagine."

It was a good and interesting question and he wished, with all his heart, she hadn't asked it, because the thought would, he now knew, nag him forever.

"The two seemed...inseparable. I don't know how you'd divide one from the other."

Her sharp eyes sparkled, watching him. "If it's not conscious, where does it come from?"

"Atheists fall in love too," he replied, understanding where she was going.

"Which proves nothing. A blind man cannot see you or me. Does that mean we don't exist? So tell me. What comes first?"

He shook his head, exasperated. "You can't ask that

question. I can't answer it. Nothing's quite that straight-forward."

He tried to think of an explanation, one that might make sense to him and to this inquisitive, quick-witted woman from a different life.

"Something happens," he told her. "You only see it afterwards, I think."

"Something happens? Specifics."

"A moment. A word. A look. A thought . . . a recollection. The memory of a gesture. The way someone picks up a cup of coffee or laughs at a terrible joke. A smile. A frown. It . . ." Nic Costa sighed and opened his hands, lost for something else to say. "I'm sorry."

"Why?" she asked. "You gave me my answer." Agata Graziano glanced nervously at her feet, then asked, "Does it also happen at that moment, Nic? The one depicted in the painting? Is that when you truly know?"

"No," he said immediately.

"You're blushing very profusely," she pointed out.

"What do you expect? This is not a conversation . . . not the kind of thing you talk about. With anyone. Least of all . . ."

But the Ekstasists wanted to capture that intense, private instant for themselves. That was why they raped and murdered on the streets of Rome. They needed to understand something. So, though she was reluctant to admit it, did Agata Graziano.

"You mean least of all someone like me?" she replied.

"I would have thought I'm the obvious person. Someone who's utterly disinterested in the matter."

"All I can tell you is the truth as I see it."

She shook her head, cross suddenly, and with herself this time. Her dark hair glittered under the lights of the bright chandeliers.

"This infuriating painting is designed to drive me mad. It's a game, a joke, a riddle, like Franco and his stupid gang. Why did he never paint anything like it again? Not because he couldn't. And what on earth does it really mean? Caravaggio was not Annibale Carracci. He wouldn't paint pornography for anyone who came along bearing a full purse."

An abrupt flash of displeasure crossed her face, and it was directed at him.

"It would all have been so much easier if you could have answered yes to that last question."

"Why?"

"Because then it would have had some personal dimension? The discovery of God in some small, intimate physical moment. But it's not. It's more than that. Or less. Oh . . ." A modest curse escaped her lips. "I blame this on you. And Leo Falcone. And now . . ." She took hold of his wrist again, turned it, and checked the watch there. "It's late and I'm in trouble. That hasn't happened in months. I'm none the wiser, too, which is worse. Men!"

He liked her anger. It made her more vulnerable somehow.

"I'm sorry if your carriage has turned back into a pumpkin."

"Unlike Cinderella, I have no need of a carriage. Or fairy stories. Furthermore, my sisters adore me, which is why they are so indulgent. Therefore your analogy is quite poorly chosen."

"I'm a lot wiser," he replied. "I know we have a painting that appears to depict a woman, no ordinary woman, some kind of goddess, in the moment of ecstasy. That she is surrounded by men, one of whom is singing a refrain from an erotic poem, the Song of Songs. I knew none of that this morning. All I knew was"—it came out before he could halt the words—"that somehow, in some strange way, this has to do with Emily's death. That perhaps, if I appreciated how, I would understand that better also."

She folded her arms and gazed at him. "You will never give up, will you?"

"Not until I know," he replied without a moment's hesitation.

"Know what, exactly? A name? An identity?"

"More than that. I want to understand what caused this. I want to see the instant this darkness appeared, from nowhere"—this thought depressed him, even as he uttered it—"to infect us."

"That is an interesting quest." She said it quietly, nodding to herself, thinking.

Then she grasped his wrist and checked the watch again. "We have time for one more viewing," she insisted.

"There's only so much trouble a sister can get herself into in a single night."

"We're going back to the studio?"

"Exactly."

"Why?"

"Because you are a genius."

"I am?" he asked, bewildered.

"I believe so. Let's put this conundrum to bed once and for all, I hope. Are you with me?"

She knew there could only be one answer. Costa tried not to look back as they left, remembering Falcone's words. It was important not to give these men any more excuses to run to their lawyers. Even so, he wondered whether they would be watching, Malaspina and Buccafusca, Castagna and the short, insignificant man he knew to be Tomassoni, a name that continued to stir some distant memory he could not yet place.

But they were nowhere to be seen and that was strange. This was Franco Malaspina's home. In a sense, it was his party. Yet Costa had the distinct feeling that the man had left, with his fellow Ekstasists, venturing together out into the dark Roman night.

Part Nine

Revelations

# One

$\mathcal{G}$IANNI PERONI DIDN'T NEED A MACHINE TO TELL him something was wrong. He'd stayed glued to the screen most of that evening while Rosa went through some personal documents on Malaspina and his circle sent round by Falcone. Teresa Lupo was now in the kitchen making dinner, grumpy at the lack of progress in the studio in the Vicolo del Divino Amore. Nothing had advanced during the day; her team was still awash in physical evidence, but lacked a single item that could directly link the crimes there to any one individual.

"Stop being some grubby Peeping Tom," Teresa ordered, and returned to the table with three plates brimming with gnocchi covered in tomato sauce and cheese. "You can't stay watching that thing all night. Besides, Leo told you ... it would bleep if anyone came near the statues."

"I can bleep for myself," Peroni objected, and took a big forkful without looking, a good portion of which went straight down the front of his white shirt.

"Sorry," he murmured, then put a fat finger on the computer screen. When he took it away they could just make out the image of a figure, shadowy and unidentifiable under the streetlights.

"Him," he said simply.

It was a man in a dark coat, collar up, face indistinguishable in the night. That was the problem with CCTV, the police system, and these special cameras Falcone had organised. They were surveillance devices, not identification systems. There wasn't enough detail for Peroni to see what the man really looked like.

The two women abandoned their food and came to sit on either side of him.

"What about him?" Teresa asked.

"Listen to someone who knows how to read these streets of ours. I have spent a lifetime watching Romans walk around this city and I know when something's amiss. It's a freezing cold night in December. Spitting with icy rain. No sane person stays outside in that weather. Except him."

"Has he done anything, Gianni?" Rosa asked.

"No..." the big man replied, in that deliberately childish way he used when he was trying to argue. "That's the point."

Teresa grabbed a forkful of food, most of which made it to her mouth, then said, still eating, "So he's just standing there. Where is this?"

"Abate Luigi," Peroni replied immediately. "The first act of *Tosca*. Remember?"

"If you continue to throw opera at me like that I'll take you to one of the damned things."

He turned to stare at her. "This is work," Peroni objected.

"He's a man in the street," Rosa said. "Just standing there."

"It's not a street," he insisted. "It's a dead end that doesn't go anywhere. And yes, he's just standing there, though I swear he keeps looking at the statue too."

He took some more food, then said, "He wants to see it, but he daren't. Leo said our email would flush these bastards out, looking to see what we were saying about them. For all they know, there's a different message on every damned statue. This is one of Malaspina's bunch. Maybe the man himself. I'm telling you. I can feel it."

Teresa slapped him cheerfully around the head. "It's a man in the street who's probably waiting for one of those high-class hookers of yours. Get real. And remember, Leo said just to look and see where he went. Nothing else."

"Nothing else?" Peroni answered, aghast. "Look at the picture on this stupid thing. It's night. There's no moon. We can't identify him. As long as we're sitting here we're useless. Maybe"—he flicked a finger at the screen—"we could try and see where he went using all these other cameras Leo's got us wired up to. But I don't believe it. This is just some idiotic pile of plastic crap. It doesn't catch criminals for us. It can't pick up the phone and scream for backup. It's . . ."

He stopped, displeased with himself, wishing he felt confident enough to think he was off duty and able to open a beer.

"We all want to do something, Gianni," Teresa said, then, to Rosa's embarrassment, she took his battered face in her hands and planted a noisy kiss on his lips.

"I *will* do something," he insisted. "Watch me."

Teresa pounced with another theatrical kiss. When it was over, Rosa groaned, took her eyes off the screen, and said, "Not now. Our friend's leaving."

Peroni swore.

"Did he do anything?" Rosa asked.

"Not that I saw. . . ."

"Then what—"

"I was just imagining," he interrupted, feeling as miserable and dejected as he had on the day of Emily Deacon's funeral. One pressing thought continued to nag Peroni: if he felt this way, what emotions still ran through Nic Costa's sensitive soul? "You eat. I'll watch."

"Food . . ." Teresa shoved the plate in front of him.

He pushed it away and muttered, "Later."

Gianni Peroni wasn't much of a one for instinct alone, least of all that gained through the artificial medium of a nighttime surveillance camera watching some ancient statue in a tiny, grubby piazza by the side of a church off one of Rome's busiest streets. Nevertheless, he found he didn't much care for a beer anymore, not even when the man with the upturned collar walked right out of sight of the camera, heading north, back towards the Piazza Navona. There was another camera there, part of Falcone's covert surveillance scheme that was also hooked into the *centro storico*'s CCTV system through an arrangement made outside the Questura's normal channels.

That was the way things were, and the way they would remain until these men were brought to book.

He was happy with the idea. Simply uncomfortable with pursuing it in the cosy remote warmth of Leo Falcone's apartment, with a plate of good gnocchi going cold by his side.

"North," Peroni said, knowing that this would take the figure in the dark towards the most visible of those statues, Pasquino, which stood at the very end of the street in which they were now located, perhaps no more than a minute away on foot if he ran as quickly as he could manage.

He keyed through the cameras along the way and saw nothing. There were so many back alleys, so many cobbled channels through this part of the city. This was the Rome of the Renaissance, not a place built for stinking modern traffic or the eager lens of some video camera perched in a private corner, its grey monocular eye fixed permanently on the shifting, ceaseless world below.

This remote, soulless form of policing was stupid. What's more, it could become an obsession, and was, he thought, for Nic already, which only made things worse.

"Eat . . ." Peroni muttered, and took a big forkful.

Then he turned the camera to Pasquino, not expecting

to see a thing except a few midweek diners wandering through the drizzle, debating where to eat.

The fork stopped a finger's width from his mouth. Tomato and garlic, gnocchi and cheese, dripped onto the computer keyboard in a steady thick rain.

"Gianni," Teresa said uneasily.

"He's there. Look. It's him."

There must have been hordes of men wandering the street that night with their collars turned up, their faces hidden from the rain.

"You don't know..." she began, then he snatched some of the photos from across the table and laid them out over the keys.

"Tall, well built, young...:" Peroni murmured. "It could be any of them. If only he'd move into the light so we could see his face."

"It could be any number of people," Teresa objected.

They watched the figure in the wet raincoat wander towards the statue at the end of the road, against the wall of the cut-through to the Piazza Navona. Falcone's taunting poem had been there four or five hours now. The email boasting about it had gone out around the same time. It was a crazy idea, Peroni thought. Any sane criminal would never have risen to the bait. But Falcone understood these men somehow, understood that this was all some kind of tournament, a challenge, a deadly diversion the enjoyment of which depended, surely, on the degree of risk.

The man in the gleaming coat walked steadily towards the statue of Pasquino, a two-thousand-year-old torso damp in the rain, strewn with messages, one of them very recent.

"Do it," Peroni muttered. "Do something. Anything."

The man in the coat walked past the statue and the posters, his head scarcely turned there. Nothing happened. Nothing.

"Shit," Teresa grumbled. "Are you going to eat your food or not?"

He refused to take his eyes off the screen. Something was going on. The figure had turned back, as if unable to stop himself. He was now over the low iron railings that protected the statue from nothing but badly parked traffic.

The three of them watched. With his back to the camera, the man took something out of his pocket and, in a series of crazed, violent movements, scraped at the paper on the stone, casting anxious sideways glances around him.

"Show your face," Peroni snarled. "Show your face. *Show your damn face . . .*"

There was one last stab at the stone, and a scattering of paper tumbling down to the rain-soaked pavement.

Peroni was fighting to get inside his coat before anyone could say a word. By the time he'd got it around his big frame, Rosa was ready to leave too.

It wasn't the kind of thing he did normally. But at that moment it seemed appropriate. Gianni Peroni retrieved his service pistol from its leather holster, slammed out the magazine, checked it was full, and slammed it back.

"Wonderful," Teresa moaned. "What am I supposed to tell Leo if he calls?"

"Watch the screen." He grabbed the earpiece of his mobile phone and stuffed it into place. "Try to see if you can make out where he's going now."

"And Leo?" she asked again.

Rosa was at the door.

"We go to Navona," Peroni ordered. "When we're there, we decide."

He kissed her quickly on the cheek. There wasn't time to register the concern, and the fear, in her eyes.

"Tell Leo this time the bastard doesn't get to run away so easily."

# Two

$C$HE NIGHT WAS COLD. THERE WERE NO LIGHTS IN any of the adjoining buildings. The Barberini's outpost was set in an external block of the Palazzo Malaspina so distant from the main building he couldn't even hear the sound of the music he knew must be there, and the voices too: men and women looking forward to the Christmas holidays and a break from work, a time for family. There was, as far as he could see, no one else in the entire block except the armed guard from the private security firm, the same man who had let him in to the building that morning, and now did so with a cheery, unsurprised enthusiasm.

"Sister Agata," the man chided her, "you work too hard. You and your friend disturb my sleep."

"Go back to it," she said quietly. "But don't snore."

Then, silent, she led him ahead, still carrying the two overfilled grocery bags full of papers and reference material that she had left with a puzzled checkroom attendant at the Palazzo Malaspina when they'd arrived.

They walked into the long, dark corridor that ran past closed offices to the room with the painting. Costa felt detached at that moment, full of random thoughts and emotions, about the case and what had happened, about himself and his loss. Had Malaspina and his group really left the palace? He had no idea, and that realisation in itself felt awkwardly distant somehow, making him appreciate he had not yet found his way back into thinking like a police officer. Emily's death still stood in the way, and he had no idea how long that obstacle would remain, or whether, in truth, he wished for its removal.

There were many places Malaspina and his friends could have disappeared to in that bright, sprawling palace. But if Falcone had done his job, they now had something on their mind. An anonymous email designed to taunt them, one that, thanks to his own encounter with Malaspina, just might lead them to break cover. And then there was Costa's presence in the man's very private home. Could both have explained Malaspina's tense and aggressive demeanour?

It was possible, he knew. It was also possible that Malaspina was talking to his lawyer already, trying to stir up some new harassment accusation. Costa had done his best to avoid that possibility. The way Falcone had engineered their meeting meant that there would be no formal instructions on hand in the Questura to support any such charge. Nevertheless . . .

A part of him was already beginning to wonder how he might feel if these men succeeded in escaping responsibility for their acts. Like every active police officer, he recognised the pulse, the temperature, of an investigation. The telltale signs were there. The presence of Grimaldi the lawyer, with his sour face that said "This is going wrong already." The constant concern in Falcone's eyes, the way the inspector was willing to work outside the rules, not caring about any personal professional risk to himself and those he was using . . . All of these indicators told Costa that failure was by no means a remote possibility. If the Ekstasists simply sat back and did nothing remotely illegal again, there might be precious little chance of apprehending them.

Nor, some small inner voice whispered, would anyone else die, or be snatched from some squalid street assignation and taken to a dark, dismal corner of the city and subjected to a brutal ordeal, simply for the gratification of a bunch of playboys and their hangers-on. That would be a kind of result, and he retained sufficient detachment, even at that moment, to ask himself the all-important question: how much was he seeking justice, and how much vengeance?

What was it Bea had said the day of the funeral? *For pity's sake, Nic, let a little of this grief go*. He hadn't wept, not truly, not yet. The taut dark tangle of loss and anger remained locked inside him. In the company of Teresa and Peroni—Falcone too—up to a point, it was easy to pretend it wasn't there, until they started subtly introducing the subject into the conversation. Talking to Agata Graziano, a woman of the Church, quite unlike any he'd ever met, that inner act of delusion was possible too. But the knot remained, begging for release, like some bitter black tumour inside, waiting to be excised.

Then Agata reached the door of her room, the focus of her tight, enclosed universe of intellect, and turned on the light. Costa found himself dazzled once more by the painting, which, under the glare of the harsh artificial bulbs, seemed to shine with a force and power that burned even more brightly than they had during the day.

She walked over to the computer and called up a familiar painting on the screen: a stricken man on the ground, an executioner standing over him, clutching a knife.

"What can you tell me about this?" she demanded, returning, so easily, to the role of teacher.

"*The Beheading of Saint John the Baptist*, Valletta, Malta. Caravaggio painted it while he was in exile from Rome, trying to be a knight and failing."

She looked unimpressed. "In order to become an apprentice knight of the Order of Saint John, he would have had to swear an oath that went something like 'Receive the yoke of the Lord, for it is sweet and light. We promise you no delicacies, only bread and water, and a modest habit of no price.' Bit of a comedown after the Palazzo Madama and Del Monte's bohemian crowd. No wonder the poor boy didn't stick it. You're giving me history, Nic. Facts, for pity's sake. I can get those from a book. I want more. I want *insight*."

He felt tired. He didn't want to go on. He needed

sleep, needed a break from this world that Agata had dragged him into. It possessed too many uncomfortable dimensions. It was the universe that Caravaggio had spun around himself, and it was too real, too full of flesh and blood and suffering.

Nevertheless, the memories were there. He'd spent so much of his life, before the arrival of Emily, in the company of this man. It was impossible to break that bond now.

Costa sighed and pointed at the stricken Baptist, dying on the grimy stone of the prison cell, his executioner about to finish the act with a short knife drawn from behind his back.

"He signed it," Costa said wearily. "It's the only painting he ever put his name to. It's in the blood that flows from the saint's neck."

"Really?" she asked. "You've been to Malta? You've seen his name there?"

"I can't go everywhere there's a Caravaggio painting, Agata. Can't this wait until the morning?"

"No." She frowned. "I've never been to Malta. They won't let that painting travel. It's the only one of his important works I've never seen. One day perhaps. But now. Look!"

She hammered at the computer keys and zoomed in on the focal point, the dying man, and then, more closely, the pool of gore running in a thick lifelike flow from his neck.

"Use your eyes, Nic, not secondhand knowledge.

There is no name. He didn't sign this painting. You picked that up from a book, like everyone else. Paintings are to be seen, not read. What Caravaggio writes in the saint's blood is *f. michel*. Which, depending on your viewpoint, means *frater* Michelangelo—to denote his joy at becoming this trainee knight. Or, perhaps, *fecit*, to denote his authorship of the painting. I know which I believe. Three months later he was expelled from the order, from Malta entirely, 'thrust forth like a rotten and fetid limb,' they said in the judgment, which they delivered to him in front of this selfsame masterpiece. There's gratitude."

He shook his head. "I give up. I am tired. I am stupid. I do not see the connection."

She dragged him back to the luminous canvas that dominated the room.

Costa stood in front of the naked red-haired woman, who seemed so close she was real, her pale, fleshy back towards him, her mouth open, legs tantalisingly apart, sigh frozen in time, watched by the leering satyr with Caravaggio's own face, holding music that clearly came from the same brush as that in the Doria Pamphilj earlier in the day.

"You will stand there until you see something," Agata ordered. "Concentrate your attention on the area beneath this lady's torso, please. I offer that advice out of more than mere decorum. Now I must fetch something."

With that, she left the room.

He closed his eyes, trying to concentrate, then focused on the painting. The nude female form swam in front of his eyes. It was the most seductive, the most dreamlike, of compositions, from her perfect, satiated body to the lascivious satyr and the two cherubs—*putti,* common symbols in religious Renaissance painting, though here they had a more earthly and lewd aspect, each fixed on the woman's orgasmic cry. One sang from the left-hand corner. The second perched in a perfect blue sky, carelessly pouring some ambrosial fluid from a silver jug, the thin white stream spilling into the goblet below, then—he could see this now he had learned to stand close—running over the edges, down to a hidden point behind and beyond the central figure's fulsome torso.

It was hard to concentrate on the area she had indicated. This part of the canvas contained nothing: no object, no intriguing swirl of pigment, no depth or the slightest attempt to create it. What he saw, beneath the gentle curve of the nude's ample thighs, was a patch of vermilion velvet, lacking the sheen and texture of the remaining fabric around her, the coverlet on which she lay.

He stared and he thought. When Agata came back, carrying something he didn't dare look at, Costa said, "This isn't right."

"Go on," she urged.

"You told me it had been X-rayed. That it was impossible it had been under-painted and over-painted."

She was doing something with her hands, down at her waist. He still lacked the courage to look.

"For a policeman you are remarkably imprecise at times. What I said was that it was clear this had not been painted over another work."

"Perhaps it's been restored."

She shook her head. "There isn't the slightest sign of any general restoration. My guess is this canvas has been in storage for years. Centuries perhaps. Even when it was on display it would have stood behind a curtain, which would have blocked out any daylight, were people stupid enough to position it near a window. It's never needed restoring. What you see, for the most part, is what Caravaggio painted a little over four hundred years ago."

*For the most part.*

"Here," he said immediately, and pointed to the plain flat patch of paint. "I thought it had to be restoration. It lacks anything. Depth or substance, interest or any deliberate withdrawal of interest, which is what I'd expect of an area of the canvas that he didn't feel was of great importance."

She said nothing, simply gazed up at him with that pert dark face, smiling.

"I could have painted that," Costa said. "And I can't paint."

"You can learn, though," she replied, grinning.

Finally, he looked at what she was doing. He found it hard to believe.

"What's that?" he asked, knowing the answer. "What are you doing?"

"This is white base and ammonia," Agata said, dipping the small, strong brush she held in her right hand deep into a tin pot of pale paste that had a distinctive and pungent smell.

She moved in closer to the surface of the canvas, her eyes focused on the area beneath the flaring swell of the nude's thigh.

"What does it look like I'm doing? I'm removing some paint."

# Three

PERONI RAN TOWARDS PASQUINO, FEELING HIS AGE-ing legs complain beneath him. He wasn't fast enough anymore. By the time he made it to the battered statue, now with newly shredded scraps of paper scattered over the litter at its base, there was no sign of their man in the steady winter rain, no dark figure hurrying through the vast, nearly deserted stadium of the Piazza Navona.

Rosa, keeping up easily with his pace, gave him a sideways look, one he recognised because Costa did it a lot these days too. It said: *I'm younger than you, and quicker. This is my call.*

"Teresa," he barked at the neck mike of the phone, "did you see where he went?"

He still wasn't happy about Rosa being on the case. The girl was inexperienced. She was angry at the way her insight into the investigation had been ignored by her boss, Susanna Placidi. More than anything, in Peroni's view, she was still marked by the grim Bramante affair that previous spring, a dark, brutal investigation in which the young agente had been attacked by a man who had played the police with the same cruel skill the Ekstasists now appeared to possess, and the same relish too.

"*What am I?*" the voice in his ear snapped back. "*Surveillance now? Of course I didn't see. These cameras aren't everywhere.*"

"Look north," Rosa suggested. "He wouldn't have gone into Navona if he wanted to head in any other direction. He'd have been doubling back on himself."

She'd keyed herself in to the conference call. Peroni should have expected that. All the young ones were so bright when it came to playing with toys. So were Malaspina and his men. But toys didn't protect you forever, no matter which side you were on.

"*I'm looking,*" Teresa answered. "*This would all be so much easier if we could call in for support.*"

"We can't!" Peroni yelled. "You know it."

The line went quiet for a moment.

"*I know, I know it. I was just saying. I don't want you racing round Rome on foot, pretending you're a teenager. You're old, you're unfit, and you're overweight.*"

"It's pissing with rain, I am looking for a murder suspect, and I have no idea what to do next," he snapped back. "I am so honoured to receive your personal views on my physical state at a moment such as this."

He was gasping for breath, too, and his heart was pounding like some crazy drum. She was right, and he wished there were some way he could hide that fact.

"*Well?*" the pathologist asked.

Rosa could probably outrun even Costa, he thought. Nic was a long-distance man, built for endurance, not speed.

"Find him, and Rosa can go ahead."

He looked at the young woman in the cheap black coat. If he'd been back on vice, he'd have been wondering why exactly she was out on the street on a night like this, flitting through the trickle of late-night shoppers and revellers brave enough to dodge the rain. She was listening to every word, eyes gleaming with anticipation.

"You do nothing without my permission," he ordered, jabbing a finger in the air to make the point.

"Sir," she said, with a quick salute.

Peroni heard a familiar sigh of relief in his earpiece.

*"There,"* Teresa declared. *"That was so easy. I picked him up a moment ago. At least I think it's him. If it is, he did go north. He's not running. He's walking nice and slowly. I imagine he thinks he's passing for one more idiot getting wet out shopping for the night."*

"Where?" Peroni yelled.

*"Going right past that funny old church, Sant'Agostino. You know, if I were a betting person—and I am—I'd say he's headed back to where this all began. The Vicolo del Divino Amore. Or thereabouts. What did Nic call it?"*

"Ortaccio," Peroni murmured, remembering. Then he watched Rosa Prabakaran set up a steady, speedy pace north, out past Bernini's floodlit fountain of the rivers, picking up speed to put a distance between them he'd find hard to close.

There were still a few stalls left out from the Christmas fair. Men were putting away sodden cloth dolls of La Befana, the witch, dragging in sticks of sugar candy from the wet, covering up the stalls of Nativity scenes as they were buffeted by the choppy winter wind. He looked up and saw the moon caught between a scudding line of heavy black clouds. A spiral of swirling shapes, starlings he guessed, wheeled through the air. It was Christmas in Rome, cold and wet and pregnant with some kind of meaning, even for a failed Catholic like him.

There were times, lately, when Gianni Peroni wished he could remember how to pray. Not the actions or the words. Simply the ability to reconnect with the sense he'd once possessed as a child that there was some link, some bright live fuse, that ran from him to something else, something kind and warm and eternal. Meaningful and yet beyond comprehension, which made it all the more comforting for the solitary, insular child he had been.

After one quick curse at the rain, he began to follow, heart pumping, head searching for solutions.

# Four

$\mathcal{I}$T WAS LIKE WATCHING A SURGEON AT WORK. AGATA
Graziano pulled over an intense white lamp and bent
down to the base of the canvas, applying the paste in
small squares, one at a time, with a compact paintbrush,
then removing it quickly with another solution that
smelled of white spirit.

. She worked slowly, patiently, with a hand so steady
Costa couldn't imagine how such precision was possible.

And as she laboured, something began to emerge
from beneath the pigment that had been dashed on,
then revarnished, to hide it.

He lost track of time. She sent him for some water,
for her, not the process. When he came back, he looked
at this woman. He'd not met Agata Graziano before that
day, yet now he felt he knew her, in part at least. There
was an expression in her eyes—excitement, trepidation,
perhaps a little fear—that he connected with, and that
connected the two of them too. This painting contained
something she needed to know, had to know, with the

same relentless hunger he felt. There was a shared desperation between them, and he wondered what pain on her part had placed it there.

"I can't work with you hovering over my shoulder," she said after a while.

Beads of sweat stood on her brow, like lines of tiny clear pearls. She wore a taut, serene expression of absolute concentration. When she finally beckoned him over, he looked at his watch. She had been working on the canvas for no more than twenty-five minutes. It had seemed like hours. What he saw when he came to her side was something new and entirely unexpected. Agata had not simply uncovered a signature. She had found something else, something that took a moment to make its identity clear, because nothing he had seen, in any work of that period, by any artist, bore the slightest resemblance to what had been painted there by the artist in the original version.

It was the size of a child's hand, a pool of white, milky liquid, the same colour as the stream that fell from the cherub's jug and spilled over the lip of the silver goblet set by the nude's pale thighs. The feature sat with the same sticky intensity he had seen in the puddle of gore flowing from the dying Baptist's neck. The trickles that ran from it formed letters in the same flowing, erratic hand as on the canvas in the co-cathedral in Valetta: the writing of Caravaggio himself.

"What is it, Nic?" she asked, her voice trembling. "That substance. I need you to tell me."

"It could be.... milk. I don't know. I've never seen anything like it."

"This was a private painting. It was kept behind a curtain. Perhaps in a master's bedroom. Perhaps in the palace of Del Monte, where Lord knows what occurred. Milk?"

He understood the question—and the answer. Agata had told him earlier that day what kind of trick the artist was playing here, putting flesh on the ideas that had been forming in his own head. This canvas was challenging the viewer to make his or her interpretation of what it portrayed, daring the beholder to transform a scene that was, at first glance, almost innocent into something else, something that became illicit, secret, intensely intimate, but only through the presence of a living human being to provide the final catalyst.

"It's the aftermath of sex," Costa said. "In Malta he wrote in warm blood. Here, he wrote in..." He stared at the leering satyr's face, Caravaggio's face. "He wrote in a simulacrum of his own semen."

She took his arm. Costa bent down to read the words as she spoke them aloud: *fra. michel l'ekstasista.*

"Brother—there can be no doubt about that here—Michelangelo Merisi, the Ekstasist, a made-up word," Agata said. "This is impossible! It makes even less sense than before. What is an Ekstasist, for pity's sake?"

He couldn't speak. He didn't have the courage to tell her.

She threw the damp and now misshapen paintbrush

onto the stone floor and swore once more. Then she placed her small fists together and, eyes closed, looked up at the ceiling.

"Why does this elude me? Why?"

This close there was something else he noticed, and he knew why Agata had missed it. All that interested her was the canvas. Everything else was irrelevant. He remembered his old teacher's words again. *Always look at the title.*

Costa walked over to the table where she kept her tools and implements. He found a small chisel and returned with it to the canvas.

"What on earth do you think you're doing?" she demanded.

He placed the chisel beneath the nameplate. There was the smallest of gaps there.

"If we're going to take this thing apart, we might as well do it properly. When you made me stand here staring at that part of the painting, I noticed something else. This isn't right either."

He forced the chisel blade beneath the plate, twisted, and forced away the wood there.

Agata came to join him, looking, staring, entranced.

"Oh my God . . ." she whispered.

# Five

THIS WASN'T HER KIND OF WORK. TERESA LUPO found it hard keeping her attention on ten or more tiny video screens at one time, each showing the same kinds of figures, people in dark winter coats, struggling through rain that was starting to turn sleety and driving. The man—if it still was him—had continued to head north, through the labyrinth of Renaissance alleys that had turned into the shopping streets and the offices of modern Rome.

It was getting ridiculous. Rosa was racing these black streets in vain. Peroni was breathless, trying to keep up with her. Even if Teresa could have picked up the phone and brought in support, she doubted they'd have much chance of tracking down a lone figure, in a dark coat, face unseen, on a night like this.

Then, to her astonishment, she saw him. *Him*. It was the centre screen on the monitor. He was stopping to take cash from an ATM machine in the Via della Scrofa, his black frame captured perfectly by the surveillance camera situated to keep an eye on the location. She watched. The machine coughed up. Lots and lots of notes that went straight into his coat pockets. Not the kind of amount you'd take out for a night on the town. He had a scarf up tight around his face. She couldn't see who he was. But this was the same man, Teresa knew. It had to be: the stance, the clothes, the shifty way he kept his head down . . . Instantly, she was on the line to Rosa, sending her in the right direction, with Peroni, breathing heavily down the phone line, some way behind.

Then, as she heard Peroni's rasping, loud voice bellow something she couldn't hear, the landline handset on the table rang. She knew she ought to ignore it. But this being Leo Falcone's apartment, the man had to have one of those newfangled phones with a little panel on the top that told you the number of the person calling, and the name if you'd put it into the address book.

It was flashing at her now and it said: *Questura—Falcone.*

Typical. He even keyed in his own office phone number.

"*What?*" she yelled when she picked it up.

There was a pause. Falcone never liked shouting unless it came from him.

"I was merely calling in to enquire about progress."

"We have him, Leo," she yelled back. "He came along and tried to scrape that stupid poster of yours off the statue."

"You saw him? Who he was?"

"No! Do you ever look at these little toys of yours before you give them to other people to play with? You can't see people's faces very well. Particularly when they've got their collars turned up. Have you seen the weather out there?"

The brief silence that followed was so typical of the man she wanted to scream. Leo Falcone had many talents, and one of them was the unerring ability to hear something in your own voice you desperately didn't want him to detect.

"I told you to try to identify him, either visually or by tracing where he went," he said. "Nothing more. Well?"

"Peroni's going crazy, Leo. Emily died, remember?" she screeched. "We can't all just bottle up our emotions like you. . . ."

It was uncalled for, unfair, and, quite simply, cruel. Falcone felt the loss as much as anyone. Perhaps his inability to show that made it worse. She would never know.

"I'm sorry——" she began.

"Where is he?" the calm, distanced voice interrupted. "Where's Peroni? And Prabakaran?"

She rattled off the street names in an instant. Then the phone went dead without another word.

"You're welcome," Teresa murmured, and stuffed the mobile headset back on. It took a moment before she realised both Rosa and Peroni were screaming for directions over the crackly line.

"He's leaving a cash machine in the Via della Scrofa,

still going north," she said without thinking. "Towards the Palazzo Malaspina. Anywhere in that area. Also, I suspect Leo's on his way, too, so be careful."

Peroni said something quite unlike him. He sounded old, she thought. Old and thoroughly pissed off with the job. And that wasn't just because of Emily or the mess that had followed.

"Be careful," she murmured again, to no one, and then went quiet. "He's taken some money. A lot of money."

A thought came to her: it was only intuition, but it had seemed, for a moment, as if this were a strange, foreign act. A man taking out cash from a street machine, something he didn't do often. Then putting all that money straight into the pockets of his coat, not a wallet.

"I think it's Franco Malaspina," she said quietly. "Or someone else who isn't in the habit of keeping a lot of cash about his person. The rich are like that, aren't they?"

The figure in black had stopped under a streetlight. She watched as he paused, took out a pack of cigarettes from his jacket, and lit one. It made a small white point of light on the monochrome screen. He seemed so calm, so certain of himself. For a second the light of a passing vehicle caught his face. With a flash of her fingers, she stopped the video, rewound a couple of frames, and froze the picture. It might be Malaspina. There wasn't enough in the way of detail to tell one way or another.

No more traffic came along to help. The roads were empty. It was getting late.

The figure stood back from the rain-filled gutter as a dark and shiny new van drove up. It stopped by the side of him. A man got out. He wore a hooded anorak, the top close around his head. Unrecognisable in their similar clothes, the two of them exchanged words.

She watched what happened next and felt her mind go numb.

The second man went to the rear of the van, took out something the length of a child's arm, and began to examine it under the streetlight. He passed it to his colleague. Quickly, with the swift, professional skill she'd expect of a soldier or a cop who'd spent too long in weapons training, the first man in black bent back into the open van and removed a stack of cartridges, loaded several into the repeating magazine, then tucked the sawn-off shotgun beneath his coat before slamming the door shut.

Then the two of them got back in the van and began to drive away. North. Towards the Palazzo Malaspina. Towards Ortaccio.

"Gianni!" she yelled into the neck mike. "For Christ's sake! Peroni!"

Her voice rang around Leo Falcone's empty dining room. Nothing came back from the phone but static.

# Six

$\mathcal{H}$E COULD FEEL HIS HEART POUNDING AGAINST his ribs, his breath coming in short, painful gasps. Peroni was running along some dark, nameless alley leading off the Via della Scrofa, seeing Rosa's short, dark frame ahead, steadily adding to the distance between them.

"Leo?" he barked into the neck mike. "*Leo?*"

The walls were high around him: five or six storeys of apartments set over stores that were full of Christmas gifts, lights dimly twinkling over jewellery and paintings, upmarket clothes and furniture, all the pricey individual glitter that took place at ground level, in public, in this part of the city.

Even so, he found himself yelling out loud, looking like a madman to anyone watching, screaming into the blackness, at nothing but his neck mike, "For Christ's sake, man. There are two bastards with shotguns wandering out here. Forget the rules. Call in backup."

There was no reply. Teresa had already told him Falcone had left the Questura for the scene. Was he bringing support? The sight of two armed men wandering through Rome at night was certainly good reason to do so. But if they were from the Ekstasists... Peroni knew enough about the labyrinthine workings of the Italian legal system to understand why Falcone might have reservations. With good lawyers and bottomless pockets, it might be easy to get away with a simple fine for possession of a weapon in a public place, and bury forever the prospects of a conviction for Emily and the dead of the Vicolo del Divino Amore.

A good minute before, Rosa had turned a corner, heading left, straight into the web of ancient twisting lanes that led towards the place where those women had been dug out of the cold grey Roman earth, retrieved from the rubble of centuries, wrapped in plastic like still, dark grubs trapped inside a tight cocoon.

He listened to the lilting sound of another female voice, excited, breathless over the open communications line, chanting the names of streets so old, so obscure, he'd never really understood what they meant.

Gasping for breath, cursing his age, Peroni leaned against a wall that was damp from the rain and black with grime and soot.

"Wait for me," he panted.

"*How long?*" she demanded.

"Tell me where. It's the studio, isn't it?"

"*No,*" Rosa said anxiously. "*I thought so too. But they turned away from that one block away. They're going around the back of the Palazzo Malaspina. Towards the Piazza*

Borghese. Maybe . . ." She hesitated. "*Are we sure these are the right people?*" she asked. "*This looks like a robbery or something.*"

It was Teresa who answered. Peroni felt remarkably grateful for the simple sound of her voice.

"*It's them,*" she said simply over the line. "*Leo? For God's sake, are you there?*"

*Silence.*

"Wait for me," Peroni ordered, and began to run again, his legs leaden from the effort, his body soaked in a cold and clammy sweat.

# Seven

COSTA STARED AT THE TITLE HE'D UNCOVERED with the chisel. Agata had let go of his arm now. She was crouched down, examining the words with a magnifying glass she had retrieved from the set of tools on the table behind.

The letters appeared carved in an archaic script that was similar to those on the title plate that had been used to cover them, though these were more elegant, more individual. It occurred to him that the two had, perhaps, been contemporaneous, the second placed over the other shortly after the painting was completed, as if to hide it from view, perhaps in a hurry.

The words read: *Evathia in Ekstasis*.

"It means nothing to me," he confessed.

"It means everything," she murmured, and he could hear the trepidation in her voice.

She lifted the glass so that he could see the words more closely. As he did so he realised they weren't carved at all. That was simply a trick of the artist. They were painted onto the wood in a style designed to imitate the cut and gouge of a chisel. There were scratch marks there, too, fine lines, just as there were on the painting.

"He painted the title?" he asked. "Caravaggio? Why would he do that? Surely it was beneath him?"

"He did it for the best reason of all. No one else would. No one else dared."

Costa stepped back and had to fight to turn his attention away from the canvas. The woman there, her mouth half open in that eternal sigh, seemed so lifelike he felt that he would touch warm flesh if he were rash enough to reach out and place a single finger on her pale, perfect skin.

"This was a private painting," he said. "For a man's bedroom. Kept behind a curtain. I still don't understand why he'd have to put a name on it himself. And why that would need to be covered up so quickly."

She'd gone back and retrieved the glass of water he'd fetched for her, and was now sipping it, eyes sharp and thoughtful, shaded a little with fear.

"*Evathia* is the Greek for 'Eve.' *Evathia in Ekstasis* means 'Eve in Ecstasy.' This isn't Venus at all, though there is a tradition in some quarters to associate the two of them. Remember the Madonna del Parto? Mary with Jesus on her lap. Or Venus with Cupid. It's hard to tell the difference sometimes. They're both associated with the spring, with birth and fecundity."

"So?" he asked.

"So imagine, Nic. Imagine that the owner of this

painting realised how dangerous it was, even hidden behind a curtain. To protect himself he had the artist put a new name on it and afterwards, unless you knew the secret, your perspective was changed. The painting was tamed. We were tamed. Not him, surely. Or . . ." Her eyes never left him. ". . . those who came after and knew what this really was, those who owned it in the years that followed. When someone outside the secret is allowed to see the canvas, we see the new name, not the real one. We behold the beautiful satiated woman and the apple and assume this is Venus with the fruit Paris gave her. Not something else, the elemental gift Eve plucked from the tree. We see this bearded, lascivious figure and assume he is some kind of satyr. But where are the horns? Where are the goat's legs? This isn't a satyr at all. This is . . ." Her eyes lost their focus. She was thinking, and deeply shocked by what that revealed. ". . . blasphemy. And pornography."

His head whirled with images, other canvases, other works by Caravaggio, as his mind fought to find some comparison with what he saw now, so close he felt he could sense Michelangelo Merisi's presence alive in the room.

"We're meant to witness what only God saw before, Adam and Eve at their first coupling," Agata murmured, almost to herself. " 'And Adam knew Eve his wife.' Genesis 4:1, directly after their expulsion from the Garden of Eden. The Lord said, 'Behold, the man is become as one of us, to know good and evil.' Full of that

knowledge, they make love, and the world loses its innocence. Seven verses later Cain kills Abel. Lust and evil
with all their consequences are set loose on humanity.
Caravaggio paints the very instant the world turned,
when, with that single sigh of ecstasy, Pandora's Box is
opened, and everything we now think of as good and bad
comes flying out, never to be confined again."

It was cold in the studio, and deathly quiet. She
glanced at Costa, guilt and fear etched in her dark features.

"This is the moment of the Fall. The instant no one
ever dared depict before because it was too intimate, too
shocking," she murmured. "Caravaggio seeks to be both
sacred and profane at the same time, and to engage us in
his guilt for doing so, since this canvas only becomes
each of those things because of our presence here, our
shared part in that original sin."

She shook her head, then glared at him. "Why did
Leo Falcone give me this? Why me?"

If she was right—and it seemed impossible to think
otherwise—this surely was the worst sight with which to
confront a woman like Agata Graziano. It was something
a sister of the cloth was never supposed to face.
Perhaps—and he realised this was a thought that had
been dogging him since they first met—it stirred
doubts, about herself, her calling, even her religion, that
had been swimming around that intelligent head for
years.

She deserved the truth, he thought.

"Because Franco Malaspina's gang of thugs call themselves the Ekstasists," Costa said quietly, feeling sick with guilt. "Because we need to stop them."

Her hair flew furiously around her shaking head.

"What? *What?*"

"I'm sorry, Agata. We never knew."

"This dispensation is done with," she spat back at him, livid, her eyes bright with rage. "Take me back to my convent. None of this concerns me now."

Her arms gripped her small frame tightly. Costa didn't know what to say or do to comfort this woman. He could only guess at the whirling conflict occurring inside her at that instant. And yet . . . she couldn't take her eyes off the canvas.

"I'll drive you," he said. "Please . . ."

Then there was an unexpected sound, one that made them both start with shock. His phone had sprung to life, shrieking in his jacket pocket with a harsh, electronic tone that was out of place in the studio, an unwelcome intruder from another world.

Costa took it out and tried to listen.

Something got in the way. It was the growing noise of voices, angry voices, shouting, bellowing, from outside the door, down the long dark corridor where the security guard in the blue suit had been gently dozing, a revolver at his waist.

As they listened, too taken aback to speak, the roar of a weapon rent the air. Costa felt seized by a sudden spasm of cold dread. He recognised the precise timbre of that sound. He had heard it once before, in the muddy grass at the foot of the Mausoleum of Augustus, the moment Emily had been ripped from the living.

Agata was walking towards the door, furious.

He raced to intervene, grabbed her roughly around the waist, and stopped her forcefully. Two small brown fists beat on his chest. Agata Graziano's tearstained eyes stared at him in rage and fear.

He was an off-duty cop, chasing the ghost of an idea, with nothing in the way of official police backing. That meant many things. But at that moment, more than anything, it meant he didn't have a gun.

"We need somewhere to hide," Costa said, scanning the room.

A second explosion burst down the corridor, echoing off the thick stone walls of this distant, half-forgotten outpost of the Palazzo Malaspina. Afterwards the air was filled with the rank dry smell of spent ammunition, and the sound of a man in agony.

# Eight

*T*HERE WERE TOO MANY DARK STREETS, TOO MANY disturbing possibilities running through Leo Falcone's head. He'd heard Peroni's bellowed call over the open voice link. Then he'd issued a single order before sending his Lancia screaming hard across the black, slippery cobblestones of this tangled quarter of the *centro storico.*

The two men weren't heading for the Vicolo del Divino Amore but for Agata's laboratory. That could only mean one thing. They wanted the painting.

He had pushed his luck to the limits, setting up a private, possibly illegal, covert operation with the sole aim of placing unauthorised surveillance on Malaspina and his accomplices. He could put up with the heat from that if he had a conviction, certain and guaranteed, lying down the line. If there was the slightest doubt, the tiniest crack through which these most slippery of men might wriggle, then he would be lost. They would escape once more, for good in all probability. His career would be over, alongside that of Peroni and possibly Costa and

Rosa Prabakaran too. He had no great concern about his own fate; he surely did not wish to share it with others. However loudly Peroni yelled, Falcone was determined he would not call in for assistance until he was certain it was both necessary and would result in success.

The long, sleek car sped along the Via della Scrofa, now just a minute, perhaps two, away from the half-hidden lane where the Barberini's outpost lay.

There was one other cop in the vicinity, too, Falcone remembered, at the party in the palace nearby. He was reluctant to involve him, given the history. But they were shorthanded. They needed help.

He barked Costa's name into the voice-operated phone. A single word was all he needed.

"Nic?"

Waiting for an answer, he wondered what it had been like to spend an evening with the pretty and charming Sister Agata Graziano in Franco Malaspina's extravagant palace, one of the few grand mansions in Rome Leo Falcone had never visited in his entire career. Costa deserved some time in pleasant company, a few hours to take his mind off the pain Falcone knew would be there, and would remain, until this case was closed.

It took an unconscionable number of rings for an answer to come. Falcone listened to the snatched, breathless conversation and heard, with a growing dread, the line go silent halfway through.

"Where are you?" he barked. "Where *are* you?"

His head alive and confused with myriad possibilities,

he spun the vehicle sharply round to perform a U-turn in the Piazza Borghese, knocking over the stand of a newspaper vendor packing up his stock for the night. Sheets of Christmas wrapping paper flew into the air.

He fought to get the vehicle under control, and finally managed to manoeuvre it hard and fast the wrong way down the narrow alley that led to the studio.

Braking sharply, he brought the Lancia to a halt a few metres short of the entrance to the Barberini's office. Falcone flew from the vehicle, took out his handgun, and held it high and ready. To his relief, two familiar figures were coming up the alley from the south, one fast and young, the second older, out of condition, and struggling.

There was a van parked there, badly, blocking the street entirely. Its back door was open. The interior was empty.

A menacing smell reached him from the door: spent ammunition. Somewhere, beyond the light in the open doorway, he heard the sound of a man's weak cries and, more distant, angry, violent shouting.

He was still considering this when the two of them arrived, almost together. Peroni's face was pale and troubled; his breath came in snatched gasps.

"Sir . . ." Rosa Prabakaran began.

The big man pushed her to one side. "We need to get in there," he urged, then somehow found the strength to drag out a weapon and hold it low by his side. "Now, for God's sake. Nic's there. You left the line open, you old fool. We all heard it."

Falcone wondered, not for the first time, about these lapses. They seemed to happen with increasing frequency; everyone was getting older.

"I did," he said, and nodded, remembering now. Conference calls on the private system they'd used stayed there until they were closed. That was doubtless what sent Peroni racing here, too fast for his own good.

Falcone looked at the weapon in Rosa Prabakaran's hand. It was obvious the young cop had never used a gun in anger before. The pistol trembled in her fingers.

"Stay behind me," he ordered. "Do what I say always."

He made the call he knew was inevitable now, and wondered how long it would take for them to respond. On a quiet, wet night before Christmas, the Questura was scarcely at its most alert, even when an inspector demanded urgent assistance at a shooting incident. The most recent statistics had shown that it took between ten and twenty minutes for uniformed cars to arrive at incidents outside the centre of the city, where the tourists were. No one would be patrolling these dead, silent streets as a matter of course. This was his to deal with, no one else's.

Inspector Leo Falcone entered the dim light of the Barberini outpost's door with a steady, determined stride, and became aware, the moment he crossed the threshold, of the distinct and pervasive stink of human blood.

# Nine

CHERE WAS A STOREROOM. IT TOOK ALL HIS strength to drag her there, as she kicked and fought, his hand over her mouth, his arms tight around the rough fabric of her black dress. The door was ajar. Costa levered it open with his foot, grabbed her more tightly, and dragged the two of them through into the darkness.

She struggled all the way, wrestling in his arms. They fell against the shelves. Cans of paint tumbled to the floor, old easels, dusty, unused for years.

"Nic!" she screeched.

He pulled the door shut, then, in the meagre light that fell from the cracks above and below, he pushed her to the end of the small, enclosed chamber and held her close. In the gloom her eyes glittered with emotion.

"They have weapons," he said simply. "They kill people. We keep quiet. We wait."

She stared at him and withdrew from his grip, standing back against the shelves he could just make out in the stripes of yellow illumination from the room beyond.

They contained the junk of ages: fusty books, small canvases wrapped in sackcloth, and palette after palette of long-dried paint.

"Why did you bring me into this?" she whispered with obvious bitterness. "What did I do?"

He glanced at the door. "You knew enough to unlock the painting," he answered immediately. Then, before she could say another word, he placed his finger to his lips.

They were there, outside, moving swiftly, arguing. Angry voices. Two. And a further sound too: a man in pain, howling, pleading for help. The security guard surely, from along the entrance corridor.

One voice, more than the other, seemed familiar from the Barberini's party that evening. Franco Malaspina. Agata surely thought so too. She listened in shock and covered her mouth with her small, dark hand.

The noise of them grew louder. It was obvious what they wanted. The painting. The canvas was large, perhaps manageable by one man, but much easier for two. They were talking about how to remove it, what to cover it with, how to proceed.

And they were different: one confident, masterly, the second scared, fearful.

Finally, the other, weaker one spoke up.

"You shot him," he moaned in a high-pitched, almost feminine whimper. "You *shot him*. For God's sake."

"What do you think we brought these things for?" the second voice snapped.

"He's alive!"

There was a pause. Costa watched Agata. She seemed ready to break.

The bolder intruder spoke. "I'll deal with that on the way out. Don't squawk. You can wash the blood off later. Now help me move it. We don't have time . . ."

Agata's eyes went glassy. She stumbled. Her elbow caught something—a box file, covered in dust—teetering on the edge of the shelf. As it balanced in the darkness, she reached for it, caught thin air, her flailing fingers sending more old and grubby objects tumbling noisily to the floor, a telltale cacophony of sound announcing their presence.

The room beyond became silent.

Then a voice, the one he thought he knew, said loudly and full of confidence, "I wondered why the lights were on. Careless . . ."

# Ten

$\mathcal{I}$T WAS MORE THAN A YEAR SINCE LEO FALCONE HAD fired a weapon, and that was on the firing range, on the routine duty he regarded as an administrative chore. Inspectors didn't shoot people. If he could help it, none of these officers did either. That was not why the police existed.

He tried to remember what he knew about how to enter a building safely. It wasn't a lot. So he clung to the walls of the entrance corridor, with its ancient, smoky ochre walls. The plaster was peeling from the damp beneath the old stone of the palace in which the corridor lay like an afterthought, tucked into the hem of a sprawling pile of dark masonry that sat, unvisited and unknown, in this strange and, for Falcone, increasingly inimical part of the city.

Right arm out perpendicular to his body to ensure Peroni and Rosa stayed behind, Falcone took a series of rapid strides, hard against the wall, seeing nothing, hearing voices ahead. A bright light indicated the studio where he had first approached Agata Graziano and asked for help, a decision he now regretted deeply. There were no more shots, though. That gave him some satisfaction. Then he moved forward again, gun held high, ready and visible, and beckoned the two figures behind him to dash safely into the alcove on the right, where Falcone dimly recalled the presence of a middle-aged security guard.

Rosa went first, squeezing behind his beckoning hand. Falcone stared down the corridor and briefly turned to nod at Peroni to wait. Then they looked at one another, a familiar expression of shared dismay in each man's eyes. Rosa had let out a sudden, high-pitched shriek. Falcone turned, spat something low and vicious in her direction, hoping it would shut her up, and crossed the corridor.

There was a figure in uniform on the floor, brutally wounded, sitting upright against the wall clutching his bloodied stomach with both hands, a look of intense fear in eyes that were fast fading towards unconsciousness.

Falcone listened to him say something that might have been "Help me."

"There are people on the way," the inspector said, and, feeling a rising tide of fury enter his head, stormed back into the corridor with a firm intent, weapon in front of him, not knowing whether the female agente and Gianni Peroni, his only support at that moment, were following on behind.

# Eleven

$\mathcal{C}$OSTA TOOK A DEEP BREATH, THEN STEPPED IN front of Agata and looked around him, seeking something, anything, that might count as a weapon. He was still searching when the old wooden door that separated them from the studio exploded in a roar of heat and flame. The shotgun blast came straight through it, just a metre or so from where he stood hoping to protect her. A thin scattering cloud of lead shot fell around them, ricocheting off the high walls, peppering their heads and shoulders with tiny searing balls of fire.

Agata was screaming. Something caught Costa in the eye: dust or a shard of wood. He was aware of the barrel of the weapon crashing through what remained of the door and a figure there, following it: all in black, with the familiar hood.

He had the weapon crooked in his arms. The eyes behind the slits stared at them, dark and malevolent. The man was fumbling in his jacket for more shells, which he casually stuffed into the maw of the gun as if he were on some idle weekend game shoot.

The entry didn't take more than a moment, too little time for Costa to attack.

Instead he held his arms wide open, fingers grasping into the darkness, a gesture that meant nothing.

"You don't need the woman," he said firmly. "Take me if you like. But not her. She has no idea what this is about. She has no idea who you are."

Without realising it, he'd backed all the way to the end of the storeroom. She was trapped behind him, trembling, crouched against the wall.

The long, deadly shape of the weapon rose, loaded now.

"That bitch always had a sport in the blood," the figure said, in a low, dead voice, half recognisable, half lacking any human feeling at all.

He brought the gun up easily, with the kind of familiarity a hunter used, as if it were second nature.

This was all a question of timing, Costa thought, something it was impossible to know. He wasn't even sure what his hand had found on the shelf, only that it was hard and heavy and easy to grip.

As the gun moved towards horizontal, he took tight hold of the metal handle and swung it in front of him with as much force as he could muster. The can of ancient paint flew off the shelf, towards the shape in black, who had moved forward sufficiently to be silhouetted against the bright studio lights behind. It crashed into his face, the lid bursting open as it met the woollen hood.

A flow of pigment the colour of ancient blood flooded over the black fabric. The can crashed to the ground. A cry came from behind the covered mouth. It was something, Costa thought. It was . . .

. . . nothing.

Before he could attack again, the man took a step back, wiped the paint from his face with one elbow, and stood there, madder than ever, the weapon swiftly back between his hands.

Costa threw something else from the shelf, something not so heavy or awkward. It bounced off the wall, just catching the barrel of the gun as it exploded.

Fire and heat and a terrible, deafening noise filled the air. Something took hold of his left shoulder and flung him backwards with agonising force. Feeling giddy, and aware of a growing, burning pain racing through his body, he tumbled into Agata, whose slender arms managed, almost, to break his fall to the hard ground.

*One more time,* he thought, knowing what was happening now without needing to look. That was all. The man with the gun was getting closer, intent on finishing this for good.

Costa turned, ignoring the searing, spreading ache from his shoulder, and threw himself forward. He caught the barrel, placed his right hand, palm down, over the two gaping holes there, and forced it up towards the ceiling, waiting for the moment when the agony would begin again as the shells tore through his flesh and perhaps gave them a few more brief moments of survival.

# Twelve

$f$ALCONE SAW A TALL, MUSCULAR FIGURE DRESSED in black, hooded, struggling with the painting, weapon on the floor. He barked the first words that came into his head, in a voice that was loud and forceful and brooked no argument. The man raised his arms over his head and started to talk, in a falsetto babble riddled with fear.

"Shut up!" Falcone yelled, then ordered Rosa to keep her gun on him.

Something was happening at the far end of the room, in an annexe that lay beyond the canvas and the bright, piercing lights that stood above it.

Peroni came to his side, weapon raised.

"How well can you shoot, Leo?" he asked.

He didn't dare answer, and instead watched in despair as three figures tumbled through the door, the first all in black, too, with a shotgun held in the air by Costa's struggling arm as the young officer, his left shoulder covered in blood, his coat ripped by pellets, pushed the intruder out into the light.

Agata Graziano was fighting just as hard, kicking and punching and screaming at the faceless attacker.

It seemed to take an interminable time for Falcone and Peroni to join them, with Rosa continuing to cover the second man, on the inspector's orders. One armed individual was enough to deal with. These situations deteriorated into chaos so easily. As Falcone raised his pistol towards the head of the first angry figure wrapped so tightly into the mêlée of bodies in front of him, he realised this was not a solution that would work at all. They couldn't fire because they couldn't safely distinguish one from the other in the sea of flailing arms, the tight grip of bodies, they'd become.

For a second, no more, there was an opportunity. Costa was down, hard on the floor, his legs kicked from beneath him by the taller, stronger shape in black, but able, along the way, to drag the long grey profile of the shotgun's barrel with him, finally hauling the whole weapon from the grasp of those powerful dark arms as he did so.

Falcone made a mistake at that moment, and knew it in an instant. He looked at Costa, and had to stop himself asking the obvious. *Are you all right?*

By the time he'd dragged his attention back to where it mattered, everything had changed.

The man in black had Agata Graziano tight in his arms, terrified and furious. The barrel of a small handgun was hard against her temple, pressing into her olive-coloured skin, making a clear and painful indentation. The second intruder glanced at Rosa Prabakaran, then, without any protest on her part, limped over to the store-room doorway and stood there by the man in black's side, silent, submissive.

Falcone kept his own weapon directed straight ahead, towards the one who mattered.

"You will let her go," he said simply.

It was the best he had and he knew immediately how weak it sounded. Something happened then that made him feel old and stupid and out of his depth.

In a room with four police officers, three of them armed, one of them wounded, though not badly, it appeared to Falcone, this masked and murderous creature laughed, easily, without fear. As if none of this touched him, or ever would.

He dragged Agata Graziano closer to his chest, holding her like a shield, in a tight, avaricious grip. With his free arm around her throat, he turned the weapon in his right hand abruptly to one side, ninety degrees, away from the threat ahead.

Before Falcone could say another word, the man pumped two shells into the skull of the hooded figure next to him.

Agata Graziano struggled helplessly, eyes white with terror, feet almost off the ground in the power of his grip. Costa, who had been slyly working his way across the stone slabs in the direction of the man's legs, stopped on the instant. The small black revolver's barrel was back at the terrified woman's temple.

"If the painting isn't outside in thirty seconds," said the voice behind the hood, a calm, male voice, controlled, patrician, "I will blow these bright brains straight out of her skull."

# Thirteen

IT WAS RAINING. THERE WERE STILL NO POLICE
cars. Just Falcone's Lancia and, a little way along the narrow alley, beneath a single streetlight, the van, with its
rear doors open.

Falcone and Peroni had the canvas in their arms and
followed the hooded man, who was dragging Agata
roughly, the gun never leaving her forehead. Rosa, on
Falcone's instructions, followed behind.

There was nothing any of them could do. Agata was a
hostage, held by a man with no desire for negotiation.
Costa clutched his aching shoulder, feeling the lead shot
biting into his flesh, the blood from the wound making
his clothes stick to his skin. Unseen by the figure in
black, he'd picked up a weapon, snatching the gun left
on the floor by the dead intruder. It felt useless in his left
hand, the only good one, and there wasn't a sound from
anywhere, not a siren, not a tire squeal in the night.

"I prefer the car," the voice behind the black wool
mask said, and his arm tightened around Agata's neck,

holding her so hard that her face was taut under the pressure. "Keys."

Falcone took one hand off the painting and removed them from his pocket, holding them out in the cold night air.

"You," the man barked at Rosa.

"I'll do this," Costa said, then, ignoring the pain, tucked the gun back into his waistband beneath his jacket before stepping in front of the young agente to take the keys from Falcone, keeping his eyes on the man and Agata all the time.

"In the ignition," the voice behind the hood ordered. "Engine running."

Costa opened the driver's door, sat briefly in the seat, brought the potent engine of the Lancia to life, and got out.

A large delivery truck had come to a halt at the top of the alley, blocking that exit. There was only one way out, past the abandoned van the intruders had brought. The exit route was narrow. Not easy. As he walked away from the vehicle, Costa stopped, stared into Agata's eyes, hoping she might understand. There was, perhaps, one final chance.

Falcone lifted the rear hatch and, with Peroni's aid, manoeuvred the canvas into the interior as Costa stood his ground, no more than a metre from the masked man and Agata, now still and tense in his tight grip.

"I can go in her place," he said again, not moving.

"You're not so much fun."

Costa raised his bloodied right arm and pointed at the face behind the mask. "If there is so much as a scratch or a bruise on this woman when next I see her, I will kill you myself."

There were words he didn't catch. Then the man in black pushed Agata through the driver's side, ordering her to climb into the passenger seat, holding the gun to her head all the time, scanning the four cops by the vehicle constantly, waiting for any kind of movement. There was not, Costa knew, a single opening. It was well done. Finally, when she was in the seat, he let himself fall deftly into the car, working his feet into the pedals, taking the wheel with his free left hand.

The door closed. Costa heard the electronic locks slam shut. He wondered how many times Agata had been inside a vehicle in her entire life. She lived in the centre of Rome. She was, in her own eyes, a working woman, one who took buses and the metro, not expensive cabs and cars.

He doubted she had the first clue how to open a door held shut by central locking, even if she knew where to find the switch.

The hooded head hung out of the open window for a few seconds.

"Follow me and she dies," he said in a firm, low voice which betrayed not the slightest degree of trepidation.

# Fourteen

COSTA TURNED AND WALKED AWAY, LIMPING A LIT-
tle, conscious of the blood flowing from his shoulder, intent on moving towards the abandoned van. As he did
so, he surreptitiously removed the weapon from his belt,
letting it hang loose in his left hand. Before the Lancia
could begin to move, he was squeezing through the narrow gap between the van and the stone wall, barely wide
enough for one person, a slender space in the darkness
into which he could disappear. On the other side . . . he
was praying the gunman hadn't worked this out yet. He
guessed there was room—just—for Falcone's car. But
only if it negotiated the gap carefully, in first gear, and
with some manoeuvring.

The high-powered car's eager cylinders roared with
sudden life. Its tires squealed on the cold, damp cobblestones of the lane. The shining vehicle reversed. From
his position in the pool of black by the van, Costa saw
what he expected. The driver had been focused on more
important matters than the traffic. When he looked

behind, he saw the truck at the head of the lane blocking the obvious exit. There was only one way out: past the van. Past *him*.

The Lancia edged forward, towards the space on the far side. Costa waited, moving farther forward behind the open rear door, heart pumping, trying to summon what strength he still had.

He was aware that there was a second or two during which he might act, nothing more.

From the far side of the vehicle came the teeth-jagging racket of metal screeching against metal as Falcone's prized possession began to squeeze into the narrow gap between the van and the far wall. He heard the wheels squealing over the stones as the driver locked and turned them, trying to negotiate a corner that was near impossible.

Gradually, the gleaming hood began to emerge, and Costa knew he had one slim chance, the moment when the passenger door would be briefly free before the body of the vehicle cleared the obstacle and they would be gone, flying into the night, to a place and a fate he could only guess at.

The Lancia lurched forward, almost free. He could hear the powerful engine growling with anticipation.

"This I will not allow," Costa muttered to himself, then judged the timing instinctively, seeking the precise instant he saw the full length of the passenger door by his side before extending his wounded arm, screaming as he did so, "Down! Down! *Down!*"

He saw her face frightened but alert through the glass and that single exchanged glance was enough. She was ready. She was quick. He watched her wayward head of hair dive towards her lap, then turned the weapon in his good hand towards the dark figure at the wheel, placing a single shot through the very top of the side window, praying it would hit home.

There was a bellow of gunfire and the shattering of glass. Splintered shards jumped up into his face, sharp and stinging. He thrust his good hand through the window, then, with the shaft of the pistol, raked at the break there to make it larger, dashing the weapon round and round, screaming words he couldn't hear or understand. It was enough to get his bloodied right fist through and find the lock. Except she was there already, before him. The passenger door of Leo Falcone's police car swung open, took him in the chest, sent him reeling backwards, as a body flew out, into his flailing arms.

"Nic!" she yelled.

"Behind me!"

The others were squeezing their way through the narrow crack by the side of the van. There wasn't enough room for them to gather. He couldn't get the picture of that sawn-off shotgun out of his mind either. He had failed Emily this way once. Twice . . . It was unthinkable.

"*Behind me!*" he bellowed, and felt her slim body squeeze past his aching, screaming shoulder, to some place that might count as safety.

The Lancia revved angrily. The figure behind the wheel was alive, and furious.

But not stupid enough to engage in a battle that was lost.

Costa managed to loose off one more shot with his weak left hand. By then the car was forcing its way out into the open alley, unmindful of the damage caused by stone and metal. Once free, it found a sudden and violent life. Tires spinning wildly on the black shining stones, it careered off the far wall and leapt out into the open space. He watched, the gun loose in his hand, his fingers too cramped, too pained to think of another shot, as the vehicle disappeared in a wild, torque-driven arc, disappearing into the warren of streets he had come to think of once more as Ortaccio, a web of twisting ancient passageways that could lead almost anywhere in the city.

Costa leaned back on the door of their truck and closed his eyes.

He felt weak and stupid, almost paralysed by the aftershock and the wound to his shoulder. But more than anything, he felt elated. This time the man in the hood, with his deadly shotgun, had failed.

"You're hurt," she said, sounding cross, as if it were his fault somehow. "Where are the doctors? Leo? Where are the doctors?"

"Coming," Falcone said.

When he opened his eyes again, the inspector stood next to her, bending down to look at his shoulder.

"He'll live," the inspector added. "Now, Agata—"

"'He'll live'! *'He'll live'!*" she roared. "What kind of thing is that to say?"

"I'll live," Costa broke in, and stared at her, still only half able to believe she had possessed the speed and the wit to take the minute possibility he had created.

"Agata . . . Did you recognise him?"

She stopped, and glanced at both of them. "Recognise?"

"Was it Franco Malaspina?" he asked, and noticed a sudden, disappointed intake of breath on Falcone's part when he heard those words.

"How do I know, Nic? I never saw his face."

"The man knew you," he pointed out.

"He did," she agreed. "Still . . . All I heard was that muffled voice through the mask. Perhaps. I don't know."

Her bright eyes gazed at him through the steady rain, asking a question she didn't want answered. Why he needed this so much. Half suspecting, he knew, the answer.

"We know it's Franco," he said quietly, not caring what Falcone thought anymore. "I told you. *They* are the Ekstasists, Malaspina and the rest. They killed those women in the Vicolo del Divino Amore. My wife. We *know*. The man's so rich and powerful and clever, we can't prove a damned thing. Not without a start. Not without some small concrete piece of evidence. Something that will force his hand." He knew it was the wrong thing to say. Provocation. Leading a witness on. He didn't care anymore. "A simple, positive identification would do that."

Falcone was staring at his shoes. Peroni and Rosa were walking around the other side of the van towards them. Costa knew where they must have been. Inside. A place that seemed, briefly, almost irrelevant at that moment.

"Is this true, Leo?" she asked. "That you suspected Franco all along? You involved me in this, knowing what manner of man he is?"

Falcone held out his arms, pleading. "I was desperate, Agata. We all were. I'm sorry. If I had thought for one moment..."

"Is it true?"

Falcone's eyes were back on his feet. "This is not the way we do these things," he said in a low, despairing voice. "There are procedures and rules about evidence. Placing ideas in a witness's head...If I were to use you as a witness, there would be the issue of protection. He is a dangerous man." He hesitated, reluctant to continue. "More dangerous than you can begin to know. I don't want to hear any more of this. I won't."

She didn't wait long.

"It was Franco Malaspina," she said. "I am sure of it. I know his voice well. I heard him speak my name. There. Use it. I will say this in court. Use my testimony, Leo!"

The inspector shook his head and sighed. "Don't go down this road. There's no turning back."

"I will say this to you. Or to anyone else in Rome who wishes to hear."

Falcone took out his radio and put out a call for the immediate arrest of Malaspina, Buccafusca, Castagna, and Tomassoni, with all caution to be taken when approaching men who might be armed and dangerous.

"A doctor too," Agata Graziano insisted. "For Nic. And those men inside."

Peroni coughed into his big fist. "Those men inside are beyond doctors," he said. "I think you can cross Emilio Buccafusca off that list too. Judging by the wallet on the corpse in there, he's out of this already."

A distant siren broke the silence of the night. From somewhere in the direction of the Mausoleum of Augustus, a blue light flashed down the alley, like some mutant Christmas decoration newly escaped from the tree.

Part Ten
The New Commissario

# One

WITHIN FIFTEEN MINUTES THE ENTIRE AREA around the Barberini studio was flooded with a tangle of police vehicles and officers stretching as far back as the Piazza Borghese. A city-wide alert had been issued for Falcone's stolen vehicle, so far without results. Costa had been seen by the duty medical officer and dispatched, with Agata insistently by his side, to the hospital for treatment for his wounded shoulder. Scene-of-crime were preparing to seal off the studio and start work on the body of Emilio Buccafusca, under the supervision of Teresa Lupo, who had found her own way to the scene, and taken control of her team without a single order from anyone. There was an excess of activity and resources, one suspect dead, one missing, both with clear links to the earlier cases in the Vicolo del Divino Amore.

Falcone should have felt happier than he did. It was Franco Malaspina behind the mask. He was sure of that. But Agata's identification under pressure from Costa was so vague, and came about from crude prompting.

Even in a mess like this, with evidence available everywhere, a rich, powerful Roman aristocrat would retain some friends, and—possibly—sufficient influence to disrupt the momentum of the case at the very point at which it appeared to be about to break.

There were still too many unknowns, and one of them was striding through the rain towards him at that moment, a tall skinny figure about his own build, but with a full head of wavy black hair damp from the weather, not that the man cared much. Falcone had spent little time with Vincenzo Esposito since the man arrived from Milan to take up the position of commissario in the Questura. He had no idea what to make of him, and nor had anyone else, since he was utterly unlike any of the officers—all Roman, all risen through the local ranks—who had preceded him. A few years short of Falcone's own age, quietly spoken, sharply intelligent, and—to the dismay of active officers—keenly interested in the minutiae of the investigative process, Esposito was a mystery to those he commanded, and seemed happy to keep it that way.

Falcone had looked through newspaper cuttings after his appointment. There was nothing there except an illustrious though quiet career, one that had included busting a clan of the 'Ndrangheta crime organisation while working in Reggio di Calabria, and bringing about the successful prosecution of several state officials for bribery in connection with public-works contracts in his native city. These were the actions of an ambitious officer. One, Falcone hoped, who had limited time for authority when a little leeway was called for. It was possible he would find himself suspended, alongside those he had inveigled into the illicit surveillance operation against the Ekstasists, once the dust of this night had cleared. It was also possible he could talk his way out of things, for a while anyway.

Only the morning before, he had met Esposito in a corridor in the Questura, between a conference with the primary team working on the bodies in the Vicolo del Divino Amore and the visit to his own apartment to brief Peroni, Costa, Teresa Lupo, and Rosa Prabakaran. There had been a brief exchange of words—the kind of sentiments that officers expressed in the middle of difficult cases.

And Falcone had let something slip, quite deliberately, knowing that Esposito was aware of the interest in Malaspina, and the difficulties that caused.

The man had listened and said simply, "The rich are with us always, too. Sadly."

After which he had excused himself, then, with a backwards glance, headed off down the corridor to one of the endless management meetings that always reminded Falcone why he didn't want to be a commissario.

Esposito didn't look displeased at being dragged out of bed. He seemed energised, interested, even a little amused.

"You do spring surprises on me," the man observed cheerfully. "I've just been chatting with that young

Indian officer of yours. I thought we had one investigation. Now it transpires we had two."

"I had intended, sir—"

"No need," the commissario interrupted. "I don't expect to be told everything. Unless it's absolutely necessary." He stomped his feet and clapped his hands together. It was an act. The night wasn't that cold. "Well. Is it?"

"I don't believe so at the moment."

"Good. No one has seen your car. Don't you find that odd?"

"Very," Falcone grumbled. There had been a single sighting of the vehicle, on the Lungotevere by the new museum for the Ara Pacis. The police car which made the identification was blocked behind another vehicle on a red light in a side street. By the time it reached the main road, the stolen car was nowhere to be seen.

"Unless it's in that damned palace round the corner, eh?"

"It's big enough," Falcone admitted. "That would seem rash, surely. An underground car park would be the obvious place. If he was a criminal, I would suggest he might have easy access to some truck used for car theft. Someone could simply drive up a ramp and it's out of sight."

Esposito seemed amused by this idea. "*If* he's a criminal? I read the file. These animals have murdered at least seven women and attacked God knows how many more, just to get their dirty pictures . . ."

"I'm not sure it's quite as simple as that."

"I am. Malaspina murdered the wife of one of our own officers. And one of his brothers-in-arms tonight, in front of you. *If.*"

"I meant if he were a career criminal. Part of some organisation."

"A criminal's a criminal," the commissario noted cryptically. "So your suspect is gone. And that painting he loves too."

"I will find this man," Falcone insisted.

"I should hope so. And this young officer of yours? Costa? Is he badly hurt?"

"They will be picking shot out of his shoulder for a few hours. It won't be pleasant. It won't be fatal either. He is a very . . . persistent individual. Rather too much for his own good sometimes."

"So I'd heard. Then he should rest. He never took sufficient compassionate leave in the first place."

"I know."

Esposito watched him keenly. "You have ideas, *Ispettore?*"

"A few. For later. They are insufficiently developed."

"And now? Think about this. It's important. Are you sure it was Franco Malaspina? Absolutely? We can't play fast and loose with a man like that. One more screwup and he's probably free for good."

"We have a positive identification from Sister Agata Graziano, a woman of the Church."

Falcone was aware of the hesitation in his own voice. So was Esposito.

"Of a hooded man who said very little indeed, from what Prabakaran tells me," the commissario observed.

"It will put no one behind bars. But perhaps it will unlock enough doors for us to find the evidence that will. Though I hope to have something better before long."

Esposito looked at the sea of bodies and vehicles around him, the forensic team climbing into their white bunny suits, the organised mayhem that followed any major crime incident, a necessary flow of procedures and bureaucracy set down so firmly on paper that every senior officer knew it now by heart. He didn't seem much interested.

"I'd be a damned sight happier if we simply picked up this creature behind the wheel of your car," he complained. "That would make everything so simple, which is doubtless why it won't happen. Do we really need all these men and women earning expensive overtime at this hour of the night?"

"Those who are not involved in the crime scene are waiting, sir."

"For some magistrate who's been dragged out of bed to give you carte blanche to charge through the Palazzo Malaspina?"

"Good God, no," Falcone answered, aghast. "That's what he'd expect. If Malaspina's there, it means he's fixed some alibi already. If not . . . it's irrelevant. His lawyers have us wrapped in cotton wool. We can't apply for a warrant without notifying them first, and that would extend any hearing until the daylight hours at the earliest."

The commissario beamed. For the first time in a while, Leo Falcone felt quite cheered. Something told him he wouldn't necessarily be fired. Yet.

"So?" Esposito wondered.

"So I have applied for warrants to enter the homes of Giorgio Castagna and Nino Tomassoni. Castagna lives in the Via Metastasio, two minutes to the south from here. Tomassoni has a house in the Piazza San Lorenzo in Lucina. It's just as close."

Esposito looked pleased. "I know Rome. No need for directions. We could walk there. But we won't, of course. I want this done properly."

"Sir . . ."

"In fact . . ."

He put a gloved finger to his lips, thinking. Vincenzo Esposito had a pale, softly contoured, and elongated face, that of one of the Piemontese peasant farmers Falcone used to see as a child when he was on holiday in the mountains, or in the bloodless, idealised paintings so popular in the north. It was difficult to imagine the man in the flush of anger or engagement.

"You take Tomassoni," he ordered. "I shall visit Castagna. With Agente Peroni by my side. Is that agreeable to you?"

"Well . . . as you wish," Falcone replied, a little staggered by the directness of this intervention. "Peroni?"

"An interesting man. I have read his file. I have read all your files."

Falcone said not a word.

"I like this city of yours," Esposito declared. "Now, may we go and arrest some criminals, do you think?"

# Two

*HEIR DESTINATION WAS IN ANOTHER DARK,*
narrow alley in a part of Rome that Gianni Peroni was
beginning to dislike. He felt tired and worried. He was
concerned, too, about this new commissario who seemed
so friendly and had picked him out by name, even going
so far as to pat him on the shoulder as they rode to the
address that was registered for Giorgio Castagna.

Commissario Esposito took one look at the dingy
street and the shiny door, that of a single house, not the
apartments one would normally expect.

There were ten other men with them, one of them a
sovrintendente, Alfieri, who was less than pleased to discover Esposito didn't appear to regard him as his most
senior officer around.

"Why are you an agente?" the commissario asked idly
as they looked at the door from down the lane, thinking
of their mode of entrance.

"Because the people in charge at the time got sentimental," Peroni replied immediately. "I should have

been fired. I was an inspector. They found me in a cathouse when it got raided. My life was a little... strange at the time."

Esposito said nothing.

"Why are you asking this?" Peroni demanded. "Since you clearly know it already if you've read the papers."

"Sometimes it's better to hear things than read them. Don't you agree?"

"Of course..."

"And also because..." Esposito shrugged. "I have to make a decision when the dust has settled. Do I throw the book at you all for running this little show outside the rules? Or..."

The commissario looked at Alfieri, who was shuffling on his big feet and standing in front of some muscular agente Peroni didn't know, one who was passing a large, nasty-looking implement from hand to hand, somewhat impatiently.

"We are talking, Officer," he pointed out. "A private conversation."

"S-sir," the man stuttered, "we have someone here who has done the new entry course."

Esposito raised an eyebrow at the large metallic implement in the hulking agente's grip.

"No more mallets, eh? Isn't progress wonderful?" He turned to Peroni. "What would you advise?"

"Nic and Rosa had nothing to do with this. He's still in mourning. She was just obeying orders."

"I meant what would you do here?"

It was obvious. Anyone who'd worked Rome for a couple of decades would have known the answer from the outset. But the new generation, men like Alfieri, were formed by the courses they went on, not by what they saw about them on the street.

"The house is terraced," Peroni pointed out. "I know this area well enough to understand there is no rear exit. It simply backs onto whatever lies behind. They didn't build passageways out the back in those days."

"So?" Esposito asked.

"If it was me, I'd ring the doorbell," he answered.

Esposito nodded across the street and ordered, "Do it."

Grumbling low curses, aware he was exhausted and his temper on a short fuse, Peroni wandered down the alley, stood in front of the house, and looked at the bell and the upright letter box built into the centre of the old wooden door.

He pressed the buzzer, then popped a fat finger through the letter box and lowered his head down to its level as best he could, trying to peer through. To his surprise there was a light burning brightly on the other side.

After that he went back across the street and looked at Alfieri.

"I'd use your toy instead."

"Sir!" the man answered, with a burst of bitter sarcasm.

But he went eagerly all the same, ordering the heavily

built young agente in front of him, taking obvious satisfaction as the metal ram began to work on the door.

Peroni stayed with Esposito, who wasn't moving.

"That was decisive of you," the commissario noted.

"It was indeed. Were you listening? When I said all
that about Nic and Rosa not really being a part of Leo's
little freelance venture? One's still in mourning, the
other's still green."

Esposito stared at him, puzzled. "I always listen,
Agente."

The metal toy was starting to do its work. The ancient wooden door, which might have sat there for a century or more for all Peroni knew, was trembling on its
strong hinges like a tree falling under the axe of some relentless, vindictive forester. Dust—clouds of it—was
starting to hang around the entrance as the frame began
to come away from the plaster and brickwork that held it
in place.

"There's no rush," Peroni said, putting a hand on this
odd new commissario's arm as they crossed the street,
successfully slowing their progress.

"Why?" Esposito asked immediately.

They were nearly through and Peroni was beginning
to feel guilty. He could see what would happen. The
heavy planked wood would fall backwards, as if there
were a hinge on its base, straight down onto the stone
floor he suspected must lie behind.

The two of them were no more than a couple of
strides away when it finally began to go. Esposito was free

of him, walking quickly towards the action. Some bosses always had to be there first, Peroni reminded himself.

It came loose with a whip-like crack. Peroni watched it go over, trying to calculate, as best he could, the effect it might have on what he believed he had seen through the letter box.

Gravity wasn't his fault. Nor the overenthusiasm of a bunch of officers newly returned from a course on how to smash their way into private homes.

"Why?" Esposito turned to ask again as he marched to join the others.

Peroni stopped. The massive wooden slab tumbled backwards. Plumes of plaster and brick dust rose from around its frame as the old and once solid structure that held it in place collapsed under the blows it had received from Alfieri's strongman. Whatever lay behind the door . . .

This wasn't a conversation Esposito had allowed to develop.

Led by the commissario in his black raincoat, the team pushed into the brightly lit space that now appeared before them, making the grunt-like noises of enthusiasm men tended to produce on occasions like this.

It didn't last long. Someone—Alfieri, Peroni suspected—screamed. Then the entire pack of them retreated in haste, waving their hands in distress that, on the part of a couple—though not Vincenzo Esposito—appeared to border on horror.

A pair of naked legs—a man's, and he was pretty sure

of the identity—flapped down onto them, pivoting from some unseen point above, pushing gently against their faces and hands. The body had been given some brief renewed life by the force of the door as it came off its hinges and fell backwards, piling into the corpse somewhere above the knee.

Peroni walked forward, cocked his head through the doorway, looked up, and saw what he'd expected all along, ever since he got a glimpse of those white, dead legs through the narrow slit of the letter box. The pale, misshapen naked body of a man was suspended there, hanging from a noose which appeared to be thrown across an ancient black beam that ran, open and horizontal, across the entrance space at the first floor.

"Because of that," he said.

# Three

$\mathcal{F}$ALCONE KNEW THE PIAZZA DI SAN LORENZO IN Lucina well. It was a small, very old cobbled square by the side of the Palazzo Ruspoli in the bustling shopping street of the Corso, with a porticoed church that looked more like an Imperial temple than a home for Catholics, and a handful of houses that must have gone back centuries.

It was an expensive location for a lowly official of a state art institution. As he stood with his men at the edge of the cobbled square, their flashing lights reflecting on the damp stone, the racket of their engines bringing activity to the windows of the surrounding apartments, Falcone found himself thinking, not for the first time, of Costa's insistence that the key to this case somehow lay in the past. A past that might, perhaps, be unreachable through any conventional means. More and more, Falcone felt himself to be a player in a drama that was taking place in another era, another century altogether,

one in which he lacked sufficient understanding to follow the rules, or even begin to comprehend them.

This had to change. They owed that to all those dead
women, Emily included. Yet for all the progress he felt
sure they ought to make over the next few hours, Falcone
felt unsure of himself. Out of caution, he had placed a
call to the Palazzo Malaspina, enquiring whether the
count was at home, only to be told that he had left the
palace after the party for "private business" and had yet
to return. Even without Agata's questionable identification, this was sufficient to make it possible for
Malaspina to have been at the scene in the Barberini studio. Still, it was too soon, Falcone felt, to exert any pressure on the man. If it was him behind the black,
all-covering hood, he was surely closeted with his
lawyers now, concocting some alibi. Or else he had fled
the city altogether.

In the absence of usable physical evidence, could one
man possess sufficient money and influence to bury his
direct involvement in several bizarre murders forever?
This question had nagged Falcone ever since he became
aware of Malaspina's background. He loathed to think
that it could be true. Yet he knew enough of the ways of
those who lived at the summit of society to understand
that they did, from time to time, abide by rules and
mores which would never be allowed to the masses living
further down the ladder. Bribery, corruption, casual acquaintance with criminals . . . These failings occurred in
all walks of life, in business, in local and national govern-

ment, and, on occasion, in the law enforcement agencies too. Could they extend to turning a blind eye to the vicious deaths of a series of unfortunate women?

Only in the minds of a privileged few, such as Franco Malaspina and those he had assembled around him. Men like Nino Tomassoni, who was now, perhaps, in bed in his home, an ancient building, decrepit and untouched by recent paint, just a few short metres from the neon lights of the Corso, with its ribbon of stores, some with the Christmas lights still winking, even in the dead of night.

What was it Susanna Placidi had said? Tomassoni was the weak one, perhaps the original source of the emails themselves, a peripheral player at the very edges of this drama. If so, he was there for a reason, and it was one Falcone felt determined to discover.

He turned to look at the team he had assembled: four armed men, one with the necessary equipment for taking down the door to the house should that be needed.

"Follow me," he ordered, then walked directly to Nino Tomassoni's front entrance, put his thumb on the bell push, and held it there. After ten seconds, no more, he nodded at the entry man to begin taking down the door.

There was no time for niceties. Besides, Tomassoni, if Susanna Placidi had got just one thing right, was a small man who might possibly be cowed by a show of force.

"When you're in," Falcone commanded the men

around him, "I want you to make the noise from hell. I'll deal with the neighbours."

That seemed to go down well. He watched the door fly off its hinges in a cloud of dust.

"Everyone goes inside," he ordered. "The man may be armed and accompanied."

He was the first to step through the cloud of dust that followed the final hammer blow. And the first to come to a halt, too, amazed by what lay beyond the threshold.

When the grey cloud cleared from the forced entry, he found himself faced with a scene that seemed to come from a different century. The interior of Nino Tomassoni's home—the residence, Falcone already knew from intelligence, of a solitary man unknown to his neighbours, one who had inherited his expensive central address from parents who had emigrated to the United States years ago—was like nothing he had expected, more a film or theatre set than a home fit for the twenty-first century.

Though it was now past three in the morning, gaslights flickered inside glass bulbs down each of the long walls of the narrow entrance room, casting a faint orange glow over the interior. Paintings in gold frames hung alongside them. On each side stood a pair of ornate carved gilt chairs, worn antiques with tattered red velvet seats and backs, and a shaky aspect that probably made them unfit for use. The floor was dusty stone, unswept for ages. From somewhere came a dank smell, the kind Falcone associated with the ill-kempt homes of solitary, impoverished bachelors, places that reeked of rotting food, stale air, and solitary habits.

"This is creepy," someone said from behind him. "Like a museum or something."

That was right, Falcone thought. Just like a museum, and the idea gave him some encouragement, though he was not quite sure why.

"Room by room, floor by floor," he ordered quietly. "I do not understand the layout of this place. It's . . ."

*From another time.*

The words just slipped into his head.

"I want someone to take a look at the back to see if there's some way out there, and that way blocked if it exists. I want—"

His phone rang. It was Vincenzo Esposito. He sounded shocked, a little out of sorts, which was probably a rare experience for the man.

Falcone listened, absorbing the news. Esposito would remain at Castagna's home for the rest of the night, and he had ordered a permanent guard for Agata Graziano to be sent to the hospital in San Giovanni where she had gone with Costa.

"Don't lose any more witnesses," the new commissario ordered, his voice low and grim over the phone.

"No, sir," Falcone replied, and cut the call.

THE HOUSE HAD THREE FLOORS AND NO REAR ENtrance, simply a blank wall, without windows on any level. The gaslights seemed to be intermittent. In other areas, weak yellow bulbs, usually hanging from the ceiling by a single wire, without a fitting or shade, provided the illumination. There were no carpets and little in the way of furniture; no sign of a human presence.

Many riddles continued to nag him about the nature of the Ekstasists. The studio in the Vicolo del Divino Amore was just one of them. It was, Falcone felt sure, a place they used only occasionally, *in extremis,* when their games moved beyond some norm that was simply decadent and into a realm that was more dangerous, doubtless more tantalising. They were an organisation, one that needed a home. Malaspina was too intelligent and circumspect to allow it to be inside his own palace. Buccafusca and Castagna were well-known men in the city, too, likely to arouse comment and suspicion if their illicit activities took place on premises with which the public were familiar—an art gallery, or the porn studios out near Anagnina where Castagna's father based his grubby empire. So Nino Tomassoni, a quiet, insignificant minor bureaucrat in the gallery of the Villa Borghese, who lived a solitary life in a house a short walk away from everywhere in what was once Ortaccio, offered a solution of a kind.

The ground floor was occupied by nothing more than storage space crammed with junk: old furniture, discarded boxes of papers and magazines, many pornographic, and several bags of household rubbish. On the second they found one large bedroom, with a dishevelled double bed and sheets that looked as if they hadn't been washed in weeks, and a smaller room with a single mattress and no sign of recent use. The floor above contained a small study, with a computer that was still on when Falcone touched the keyboard, open at an email application. He called for one of the younger officers to come forward and start using the thing.

"Can you see what's been sent from this recently?" Falcone asked.

The man flailed at the grubby keyboard.

"There are four months of old messages, in and out," the agente replied after a couple of seconds.

"Good. Call in the forensic computer people. Tell them to take it away for analysis. But . . ." He stopped the man before he left the grimy seat at the table on which the machine sat. "First tell me if there are any messages to Susanna Placidi here."

The keyboard clattered again. Several emails came up on the screen. They were familiar. Falcone smiled and patted the officer on the shoulder.

"Progress," he said. "Now, there's a word we haven't heard in a while. Let's take a look at the next floor."

He led the way up the narrow, steep stairs and was aware, from some hidden sense, that this place was different, in a way that made him take out his weapon instinctively and hold it in front of him in the darkness.

The door was open, the entire floor beyond a space without so much as a stick of furniture from what he could see. A single skylight stood off-centre in the pitched, low roof. Through it a wan stream of weak moonlight fell, revealing nothing but bare worn planks in the centre of the room.

Falcone felt for a light switch. It took some time for him to realise there was none. But there was the smell of gas, faint yet discernible, and as his eyes adjusted they found the shapes of the same glass bulbs he had seen on the ground floor. He had no idea how to turn on gas-lights, and no desire to find out.

He took a flashlight from one of the officers behind him and cast it around the pool of darkness that lay impenetrable in front of them. There were shapes, familiar ones. And from somewhere, he thought, the sound of faint movement, of someone disturbed by their presence.

"Fetch more light," Falcone ordered in a loud, confident voice.

Two officers ran downstairs, out to the vans for gear.

Falcone strode into the centre of the room, dashing the beam of the flashlight everywhere, taking in what it revealed.

He should, perhaps, have expected this. In front of him lay an array of paintings, canvas upon canvas, each stored leaning against the next, protected by some kind of cloth covering, stacked in a fashion that was half professional, half amateur.

The corner of one piece of cloth was incomplete. Falcone lifted it and ran the beam across what lay beneath. He saw pale flesh, naked women, bodies wrapped up in one another. And a kind of style and poise that spoke of skill and artistry.

"What is it, sir?" the officer who had worked at the computer asked.

"Fetch me more light and we'll see."

Falcone still recalled well the time he had spent working alongside the Carabinieri art unit in Verona, with the pleasant major there, Luca Zecchini, who would spend hours showing him the vast register of missing artworks which every officer on the unit would be required to inspect from time to time. The size and richness of it amazed him, and the fact that there was a market for works which could never, in normal conditions, be shown to a single living soul because of their fame.

The brighter floods arrived. He ordered the sea of searing brightness they created to be turned towards the piles of paintings, then walked around them, throwing off the covers, hearing the low buzz of excitement grow behind him.

"I know that," someone said after a while.

"It's one version of *The Scream* by Munch," Falcone explained. "I believe it's been missing from Cöpenhagen since 2004. This..." He stared at another work, a smaller, older canvas. "...looks like Poussin, I believe."

There were pictures here he thought he recognised from Zecchini's register, works perhaps by Renoir, Cézanne, Picasso, and a host of earlier artists beyond his knowledge, unless they were all very good fakes.

He moved towards the farthest corner, an area where

not the slightest mote of moonlight fell, and one which was still in shadow from some large canvas under wraps covering the entire diagonal of the space there.

"What we have here, gentlemen," Falcone went on, "is a storeroom for stolen works of art, one that seems to have been sitting beneath our noses, in the centre of Rome, for years."

Falcone stopped and kept a firm grip on his gun. "It would be fitting," he added, "if we could match up these objects with their so-called owner, don't you think?"

In one quick movement he threw aside the sackcloth over the painting and stepped behind the frame. The man was there on the floor cowering, hands around his knees, head deep in his thighs, not saying a word.

Nino Tomassoni was wearing a grubby pair of striped pyjamas and stank of sweat and fear.

"This is a fine collection," Falcone said drily. "Would you care to tell us where it came from?"

The figure on the floor began rocking back and forth like a child.

"I asked a question," Falcone added.

The man mumbled something.

"Excuse me?"

"He will k-k-kill me . . ." the crouching man stuttered.

The expression in his bulbous eyes was more fear than insanity. Falcone wondered how long Tomassoni had been hiding here, and how he had come to know the events of the night. There was so much to ask, so many ways in which this strange little man could provide the means by which they might find a way, finally, into the depths of the Palazzo Malaspina and close the door on its owner forever.

"No one will kill you, Nino," he said calmly. "Not if we look after you. But all these paintings . . ."

Falcone cast his eyes around the room. This was a miraculous find in itself. He could scarcely wait to call Vincenzo Esposito to tell him the news.

"I fear this looks very bad."

Out of interest, he lifted the sackcloth on a small canvas to his left and found himself staring at a jumble of geometric shapes and human limbs that seemed to him, perhaps erroneously, reminiscent of Miró.

"Did he bring the painting here?" he asked.

The man said nothing and stayed on the floor, holding his knees, mute and resentful.

"The Caravaggio?" Falcone persisted. "After he stole it from the studio tonight, and killed your friend Buccafusca along the way, did he bring it here? If so, may I see it?"

"That animal was not my friend," the figure on the floor muttered, still rocking.

"This is your decision," Falcone observed with a shrug. "We will find out in any case. I was merely offering you an opportunity to demonstrate your willingness to cooperate. Without it . . ."

Tomassoni stabbed an accusing finger at him from

the floor. "The Caravaggio was mine! Ours. It always has been. Since the very beginning."

This was beyond Falcone. "I do not understand."

"No! You don't! It's *ours!*" He glanced around the shrouded canvases mournfully. "It's the only one that is. And now I don't even have it. Now . . ."

He stopped. Falcone smiled. It was an answer of sorts. These interviews always began with a small, seemingly insignificant moment of acquiescence. It would suffice.

"Perhaps you would like to get dressed," he suggested. "This is going to be a long day. I think pyjamas are not the best idea. You should bring some of your other things too. Whatever you want from this home of yours. I believe you will be in custody for a while. Safe and secure, I promise that."

The man shuffled to his feet. He was short and overweight, perhaps thirty-five. Not Malaspina's class or kind. Nino Tomassoni must have offered something different, something particular, for him to have moved in those circles.

"And thank you for those messages," Falcone added. "The emails you sent to my colleague. They will work in your favour. As to the postings on the statues . . ."

He didn't like the look on Tomassoni's face. It was vicious and full of spite.

"What about them?" the man asked.

"Were they your work too?"

"For all the good it did me," he replied. "I'll get my things."

Falcone bent down and retrieved the object he had noticed on the floor from the start. It was a specialist radio, and when he turned it on it was easy to see the unit was tuned to a police frequency. It wasn't hard to understand how Tomassoni had worked out what had happened that evening. Buccafusca's death had been broadcast on the network. The threat to himself must have been obvious after that.

"This is illegal too," the inspector noted. "I hope I shall have reason to ignore it."

The little man swore again and shuffled through the mill of bodies, then hurried downstairs a floor and walked into the bedroom, closing the door behind him.

He got there so quickly Falcone was several steps behind, and fuming at the way the officers on the landing simply let him through.

"Rossi," he yelled at the man closest to the door, "what the hell do you think you're doing letting a suspect slam a door in your face like that? Get in there and watch him."

He knew what had happened the moment he heard the noise: a loud, repetitive rattle that seemed to shake the very fabric of the ancient, fragile building in which they stood.

"Get down!" Falcone yelled, and pushed the nearest man he could find to the floor, watching the rest of them follow, terrified. A storm of dislodged plaster began to descend on them. The ancient wallpaper rippled beneath the deafening force of gunfire.

The nearest officer to the door got a foot to it, then retreated back behind the wall. Falcone could see—just—what was happening beyond the threshold, and imagine in his mind's eye how this came about.

He had left the vehicles outside unattended, needing every man he had. Now someone was standing on one of them, possibly the Jeep that was directly beneath the window, and letting loose with some kind of repeating weapon—a machine gun or pistol—directly through the glass, straight into the dancing, shaking body of Nino Tomassoni.

Flailing across the floor, intent on avoiding the hail of shells that was pouring into the building, Falcone rolled towards the staircase, found it, then, followed by two other men who had the same idea, half fell, half stumbled down the steps to the ground floor. Clinging to the damp wall, he made his way towards the entrance and the collapsed door they had brought down earlier.

"Behind me," Falcone ordered, and watched the shining cobbles and the dim streetlights, gun in hand, wondering what this might be worth against the man outside.

The noise had stopped. By the time he felt the cold night air drifting in through the empty space at the front, another sound had replaced it: an engine at full rev, squealing across cobbles.

"Damn you," Falcone swore.

He threw himself out into the street, men yelling at his back, screaming at them to keep cover.

The figure was no longer on the roof of the Jeep. Falcone had no idea where he'd gone to. A black slug-like Porsche coupe was wheeling across the greasy cobbles, describing a fast arc in the space in front of the old church.

As he watched, it disappeared behind the group of police vehicles, and Leo Falcone found himself running again, with men by his side, good men, angry men, weapons in their hands, heat rising in their heads.

"Behind me!" he bellowed again, and forced them to fall back behind his extended arm.

A single raking line of repeat fire raged through the night air on the far side of the convoy of blue vehicles. He fell below the window line of the van in front, aware, as he did so, that thin metal was no protection against a modern shell.

It lasted a second, no more. They were going. This was a warning, not an act of intent. Falcone raised his weapon and pointed it across the open space of the Piazza di San Lorenzo in Lucina, back towards the Christmas lights still burning in the Corso, conscious that the men around him were doing the same.

"Do not fire," he said firmly. "Do *not* fire."

In the distance, walking down the road, struggling to get out of the way as the Porsche found the street and roared off towards the Piazza Venezia and the open roads of Rome, was a straggling group of revellers, with stupid Christmas hats on their heads, a bunch of happy young partygoers looking for the way home.

"Get the control room on this," he ordered, barking the license plate number of the black vehicle at them as he returned towards the door. "As if they won't know already."

He raced up the stairs and found the bedroom. The place was beginning to stink of gas.

"Find the source of that smell," he barked at the nearest officer. "The last thing we want in here is an explosion."

Nino Tomassoni lay on the floor of his squalid bedroom, openmouthed, eyes staring at the ceiling, his blood-soaked, shattered body strewn with broken glass.

"There goes the witness," Rossi observed with a degree of unhelpful frankness Falcone found quite unnecessary. "Do we have any more?"

"Just the one," Falcone murmured. "Franco Malaspina will not touch her, I swear."

# Part Eleven
## The Via Appia Antica

# One

$\mathcal{W}$HEN NIC COSTA OPENED HIS EYES, HE WAS somewhere that smelled familiar: the scent of flowers and pine needles.

People, too, in a room that wasn't meant for a crowd.

Christmas, Costa said to himself, waking with a start, then sitting upright in his own bed, in the house on the edge of the city, his head heavy, his mind too dulled by the hospital drugs to think of much at that moment.

He reached for the watch by the side of his bed, aware that his shoulder felt as if it had been run over by a truck, and saw that it was now almost four on the afternoon of December 23. He'd lost more than half a day to sleep and medication. Then his eyes wandered to the room and stayed fixed on the single point they found, the person there.

Franco Malaspina was wearing a grey, expensive business suit, perfectly cut, and sat, relaxed, on the bed-room chair where Emily used to leave her clothes at night. He stared back at Costa, legs crossed, hands on his chin, looking as if this were the most natural thing in the world.

"What in God's name . . ." Costa found himself muttering, wondering where a gun might be in this place that was so familiar, so private, yet at that moment so profoundly strange to him.

Malaspina unfolded his legs, then yawned, not moving another muscle. He had strong, broad, athletic shoulders, those of a powerful man. In the bright daylight streaming through the windows, his dark Sicilian features seemed remarkably like those of Agata Graziano.

"This was their choice, not mine," the man protested in his easy, patrician accent. "Take your anger out on them."

Costa's attention roamed to the others in the rooms. All eyes were on him. Some he knew. Some, mainly men in suits like Malaspina's, were strangers, as was a middle-aged woman with bright, close-cropped blonde hair who wore a black judicial gown over her dark blue business jacket and sat on a dining room seat in the midst of the others, as if she were the master of proceedings.

"What is this?" Costa asked.

"It is a judicial hearing, Officer," the woman said immediately. "Your superiors felt it so important, we came here and waited for you to wake up. This was their prerogative. My name is Silvia Tentori. I am a magistrate. These men here are lawyers representing Count Malaspina. The Questura has legal representation. . . ."

Toni Grimaldi stood next to Falcone, with Peroni on the other side. None of them looked happy.

"I thought he didn't like being called Count," Costa found himself saying immediately. His head hurt.

Agata Graziano sat next to Falcone, looking frail, bleary-eyed, and unusually upset.

"You know the judiciary," Malaspina observed. "Very well, I imagine. It's all formality, even these days. You can call me Franco."

"Get out of my house . . ."

He tried to move and couldn't, not easily, not quickly.

It was Agata Graziano who rose from her chair, picked it up, and came to sit by him. Costa couldn't help noticing the pain this caused Leo Falcone.

"Nic," she said quietly, "I'm sorry about this. It was never meant to happen." She glared at Malaspina. "His lawyers made it so. If there was some other way. If I could prevent this somehow—"

"You could just tell Signora Tentori the truth," Malaspina interrupted. "Then"—he purposefully looked at his watch—"I might be able to go about my business."

"The truth," Costa murmured.

"The truth?" Malaspina echoed in an amused, non-chalant voice. "Here it is. After the festivities I hosted on behalf of this ungrateful woman's gallery, I spent last night in my own home, until eleven, when I went out to meet a companion, who will vouch for me. After that, I received a call saying the police were making enquiries.

So"—he shrugged—"I did what any good citizen would. I went to the Questura. And sat there. From a little before one in the morning until five, when Inspector Falcone here finally managed to find the time to see me."

"I did not know——" Falcone butted in.

"That is not my fault," Malaspina responded.

"The others," Costa said. "Castagna. Tomassoni."

Malaspina's dark face flushed with sudden anger. "My friends, you mean? And Buccafusca too. They are dead, murdered, and you sit here pointing the finger at me when you should be out there looking for whoever did this. I wish to see their families. I wish to help them make arrangements. Yet all I hear are these stupid accusations. Again. I tell you . . . there is a limit to what one man will bear before he breaks, and you have crossed that limit now. To be told one is under suspicion in these circumstances. Of crimes committed when I am sitting in your own Questura, offering whatever assistance I can . . ."

Costa could read the look in their eyes. It was despair. He could only guess at what the night had brought them: death and disappointment. Malaspina believed he had won again, and this informal judicial hearing, with his rich-man's lawyers hanging on every word, was surely some formality he hoped to use to seal that fact. And to take pleasure from the act of entering the home of a man whose wife he had murdered. It was there, plain in his face.

Still, his timing was not perfect.

"Emilio Buccafusca was murdered...this painting was stolen...before you went to the Questura," Costa pointed out.

Malaspina leaned forward, like a schoolteacher making a point to a slow pupil. "While I was at a private dinner. With someone who can vouch for me."

One of the grey men in grey suits said, "It offends my client that you waste time on this nonsense when you could be looking for the real criminals in this case."

"It offends me that the man who shot my wife is sitting in my bedroom, smiling," Costa answered immediately. "Ask your questions, then get out of here. But this I tell you..." He pointed at Malaspina. "I am not done with this man yet."

The woman with the robes around her shoulders sighed and said, "After that I wonder if there is really any point in going on. From a serving police officer..."

"One who was shot in the course of duty last night," Peroni pointed out. "By this bast—"

A look from Falcone silenced him.

"The point of this proceeding," the woman went on, "is to discuss the police application for papers which will allow you to search the Palazzo Malaspina freely, and take specimens from Count Malaspina. Or is there something new you wish to add to that list now, Inspector?"

"That will suffice," Falcone replied. "It's all we need."

The woman picked up a briefcase and took out a substantial wad of papers.

"At a previous hearing, I established that you will not be allowed to ask Count Malaspina for specimens without firm and incontrovertible evidence linking him to these events, which you have so far failed to provide. There are rules about harassment. There are avenues open to an individual persecuted by the state."

"Four men died last night," Falcone pointed out. "One of them an innocent security guard. Sovrintendente Costa could have been killed. Sister Agata—"

"This is irrelevant to Count Malaspina unless you have proof," she declared with a peremptory brusqueness. "How many times do I have to say this?"

"I don't know," Falcone barked back. "Given that it always seems to be you who deals with these requests when they are made, possibly many, many more."

Grimaldi put a hand to his head and emitted a groan. The woman turned and glowered at him.

"Are you letting your officers accuse me now?"

"There is only one person in this room we accuse," Grimaldi answered. "Please address the point, Falcone."

"I merely note that," the inspector added icily, "I find it intriguing that whenever the subject of prosecuting Franco Malaspina comes before us, the name of Silvia Tentori invariably appears on the sheet. It is . . . illuminating to discover that the judiciary works so efficiently these days that it is able to supply us with magistrates who seem already to be familiar with the case we wish to bring before them."

"This will not take long," the woman muttered. "Sovrintendente?"

Costa nodded at her, taking in Falcone's bitter, resigned expression. "What do you want to know?"

"In spite of yet another application for discovery and specimens concerning Count Malaspina, your colleagues can supply no evidence linking him to these crimes. Nothing except this identification from you and Signora Graziano last night. Tell me. You are certain of this?"

Costa glanced at the seated aristocrat, who watched him, relaxed, waiting for an answer, a finger to his lips, something close to a smirk on his face.

"I am certain of it."

"How is that?" she asked. "The man was hooded."

"I recognised his voice. The tone of it. The way he spoke to Sister Agata."

The lawyer in the grey suit leaned forward. "You had not met the count until last night, and then spoke to him only briefly. We have witnesses for this."

"I spoke to him once before. When I followed him from the Vicolo del Divino Amore, the day he murdered my wife."

There was a chill in the room and an awkward silence. Then the lawyer added, "Another hooded man, in another hurried situation. Furthermore, if this was true, you would surely have reported the fact to the Questura immediately. Not returned to the Barberini studio to look at this painting. All the more so because of the personal nature of this so-called identification."

He was not going to pursue this. It was pointless.

"And what lying bastard was he supposedly dining with last night?" Costa asked. "When he stole that painting and killed Emilio Buccafusca?"

The lawyer sniffed. "The count dined with me, at home, just the two of us. My wife is away. We were together from eleven until twelve forty-five, when his household contacted us to say the police had enquired after him. After that I accompanied him to the Questura immediately in order to offer whatever assistance was required."

"Then," Costa replied, "after I am done with his lies, I will deal with yours."

Silvia Tentori glared at him, furious. "Thank you, Officer. That is enough. I reject this identification entirely. It is clearly based on nothing more than personal animosity."

"It is based on the truth," Costa insisted.

"I doubt that," the woman said. "This leaves one so-called identification alone. Signora Graziano."

"Sister . . ." Agata corrected her quietly. A surge of anger in Silvia Tentori's eyes indicated she did not appreciate this.

"You say you can identify Count Malaspina as the man you saw in the studio last night?"

All eyes in the room were on her.

"I believe so."

"You believe so?" the magistrate demanded. "What does that mean? We know you never saw his face. How is this possible?"

"I have known Franco for several years. I know his voice. I recognise the way he speaks to me."

Silvia Tentori nodded, listening. "And were you helped in this identification?" she asked. "Did one of these police officers suggest to you this man whose face you never saw, whose voice you only heard in the course of a violent robbery, was Count Malaspina?"

She shook her head. "No. I mean ... Nic and I ... talked."

"You talked. When? What was said? The details, please."

Agata looked so exhausted. Nic felt like screaming at them all to get out of the room.

"Sister Graziano was the victim of a violent attack herself," Costa pointed out. "You have to expect her to be hazy on some details."

He knew it was a stupid thing to say the moment the words were out of his mouth.

"Quite," the magistrate observed with visible pleasure, then openly, as if she didn't mind, glanced at Malaspina, who was studying his nails, and added, "but this is a very serious accusation to base upon a few barely heard words from a man whose face she never saw."

"I *know*," she insisted. "Say something for me, Franco."

Malaspina took his attention away from his fingers and stared at her.

"Say something?"

She didn't flinch. "Say, 'That bitch always had a sport in the blood.' "

He thought for a moment, then uttered the words in a precise, considered, aristocratic Roman accent, one both like and unlike the voice they had heard the previous night.

"Well?" Silvia Tentori asked. "Am I supposed to infer something from this?"

"It was him," she insisted. "I know it. He knows it. We all do."

Malaspina shook his head, then got up and walked to the window, with its view out onto a bleak grey winter's day and a field of slumbering vines. He placed his hands easily on the sill, looking at home, as if he owned the place.

"This is ridiculous, Agata," he said. "I know you have always resented me. You're not alone. Envy is everywhere. But to manufacture an accusation like this. Here . . . Let us see how far you will go with this mindless vendetta."

There was a bookshelf behind him. Half the titles in the bedroom were still Emily's, English and American literature, old books, about history and travel and classic stories she must have read time and time again. The rest were Costa's or the family's, a collection of texts that hadn't been looked at for years, Gramsci and *Pinocchio*, the hard-boiled 1940s thrillers his father loved, and more modern *gialli* by Italian writers.

One more book, too, its pages unopened for years.

Franco Malaspina pulled the ragged family Bible off the shelf. His father had insisted on having an edition in the house, in spite of his beliefs. He would refer to it from time to time, and not always to prove a point.

He threw the black, battered copy, with its dog-eared and torn pages, across the room. It landed on her lap. Reluctantly, she took hold of the thing to stop it falling to the floor.

"Look me in the eye, Agata, and swear on that precious object of yours that you know it was me last night."

She had her eyes closed, unable to speak. The faintest outline of a tear, almost invisible, like that of the Magdalene in the Doria Pamphilj, began to roll slowly down one cheek.

It was all lost. Costa knew it.

Painfully, he dragged himself out of the bed and sat on the edge, looking first at her, silent, remorseful, then at Malaspina.

"Get out of my home," he said again, and, with a glance at the magistrate and the lawyers, added, "and take your creatures with you. When I come for you, Malaspina, you will know it."

"That is a threat!" Silvia Tentori screeched. "A blatant, outright threat to a man against whom you have not the slightest evidence! I shall report this. I shall report *everything* here. We do not live in a police state where you people can go around terrorising any innocent citizen you choose."

There was a steady, dull ache at the back of his head, but Costa knew somehow this signalled the return of his faculties, not the failure of them. Life, his father had said from time to time, often depended upon the ability to drag oneself off the floor and learn to return to the fray anew.

"No, signora," he said quietly. "We live in a world where the law has become an instrument that protects the wicked, not the innocent."

A memory rose from the previous day, a single useful fact, prompted by Rosa Prabakaran, one he had filed, wondering if it would ever be of use.

"'Run quick, poor Simonetta!'" Costa recited. "'A sport in the blood.' You hate black women, Franco. Why is that? Would you care to tell us?"

It hit home, and that felt good. Malaspina's swarthy face turned a shade darker.

"I would guess," Costa pressed, "that it stems from something personal. Some experience. Some knowledge. Some grudge . . ."

Agata stirred with a sudden interest by his side. Smiling, she rose and walked towards Malaspina, placing her face close to his, examining his features with the same curious, microscopic interest she would normally reserve for a painting.

"Something personal? Why, Franco?" she asked. "The Malaspinas are cousins to the Medici, aren't they?

Is that the line? Oh! *Oh!*" She clapped her hands with glee. "I think I see it now. In Florence, in the Palazzo Vecchio, Giorgio Vasari has a wonderful full-length portrait of Alessandro de' Medici. The first son. A dark-skinned man, Franco. With his helmet and his armour and his lance. And a black slave, Simonetta, for a mother." She hesitated to emphasise what was coming. "Which gave him his hatred of anyone who reminded him of his bloodline. Is that you, too, Franco? Are you more a Medici at heart? Is the blood you hate most really your own?"

The effect was astonishing. Malaspina rose from his chair, livid, out of control, and began to bellow a stream of vicious threats and vile obscenities, so violent and extreme it was his own lawyers who raced to silence the man and drag him, still screaming from the room, down the stairs and out into the garden, where he stood for a good minute or more, yelling up at the window.

Every sentence seemed like a blow to her. Agata Graziano had surely never experienced words or threats like this, or expected that her idle taunt would generate such a response.

She listened, shocked, pale, glassy-eyed, until she could bear no more and placed her small, flawless hands over the wayward hair above her ears.

# Two

$\int$IVE MINUTES LATER, AFTER SILVIA TENTORI HAD left the bedroom issuing warnings and threats in all directions, Peroni brought coffee for them all provided by Bea and said, "We could arrest him for that performance. Threatening words and behaviour."

"For how long?" Costa asked. "You saw those lawyers."

Agata still looked shocked, and a little ashamed, at the effect her words had had on the man. The hearing was over. They had lost everything, in conventional judicial terms. And yet...

"You touched something," Falcone suggested. "But what?"

"I have no idea," Agata answered. "I was simply being mean and horrible. Taunting Franco. The Malaspina clan was related to the Medici. Everyone knows that. They survived when the Medici died out. He makes the odd racist comment from time to time. It always struck me as odd. There had to be the possibility of some distant link with Alessandro, and that meant he had some black blood himself. All the same. The idea he would respond so violently . . ."

She shook her head, thinking. "I should stick to paintings," she said. "This is all beyond me."

"You should," Costa agreed.

The idea raised a wan smile. "Good. Can I go home now, please? I'm tired and there are many duties I have missed. There's nothing more I can do for you."

Leo Falcone looked at her frankly. "I'm afraid that's impossible. Commissario Esposito will be here shortly with Dr. Lupo. We will review the case. Perhaps you should join us, for part of the conversation at least."

She laughed. "I'm a sister who agreed to help you identify a single painting, Leo. One you have lost, which means my work is done. I have more menial chores now. I do not belong here."

Falcone frowned, looking uncomfortable. "Agata, you're the only material witness in an investigation where every other one has been murdered. Those guards the commissario put in place last night were not temporary. They are outside now. They will remain there as long as I say. You cannot return to the convent until this is over. We cannot protect you there. You must be somewhere that is private, easily secured, and accessible."

"Then"—she threw her small arms open wide— "where?"

The old inspector said nothing and simply glanced guiltily at the floor.

"*Where?*" she asked again.

Costa tried to catch Falcone's eye. It proved impossible.

# Three

"No," HE SAID AGAIN AS THEY SAT TOGETHER AT the dining room table, after Bea had thrust more coffee and cakes at them, then taken Pepe out for a brief walk. "I won't allow it. This is a private home. Known to Malaspina. Also . . ."

The reason was personal in a way that made it difficult to share with these people. Perhaps it was the presence of Commissario Esposito. Perhaps the problem lay inside himself. It felt awkward having Bea in the house at times. Another woman . . .

"Nic," Falcone broke in, "in case you hadn't got the message by now, Franco Malaspina has many allies, and bottomless pockets. He could find anywhere we chose to keep Agata if it came to that. This place has a long drive, it's easily guarded, and we know it." He hesitated. "We've done this before. It worked. Until you broke the rules."

"Will you kindly stop talking about me as if I'm some

kind of invalid?" Agata broke in. "What am I supposed to do here for however long this sentence is meant to be?"

"What do you do normally?" Teresa asked out of interest.

"Sleep, pray, think, eat, write ..."

Teresa shrugged. "You can do those anywhere. There's Nic's housekeeper here, Bea. So you have a chaperone."

"A chaperone?" Agata asked, outraged. "Why would I need a chaperone?"

"I just thought ..." Teresa stuttered. "Perhaps it would make it easier with the mother superior or whoever it is you take orders from. I'm sorry. I'm not good around nuns."

"She is not a nun," Falcone interjected wearily. "Nor does she need a chaperone. But you do require somewhere safe and secure. And ..." He took a swig of Bea's strong coffee "... I hope this won't be for long. We have ... avenues."

None of them, not Teresa, Esposito, nor Falcone, looked much convinced of that.

"Your painting's gone, Leo," Agata pointed out again. "You've just been sent away with a flea in your ear by the magistrate you hoped would give you carte blanche to enter the Palazzo Malaspina and take whatever you want. Unless I have misread the situation, you have no scientific evidence in this case."

"We're drowning in scientific evidence!" Teresa cried, aghast. "Unfortunately, it now applies simply to dead people. Buccafusca, Castagna, and Tomassoni, who did things in that dreadful house in the Vicolo del Divino Amore a woman like you couldn't imagine."

"I am a sister in a holy order, Doctor," Agata said coldly, "not a child."

"Well, *Sister,*" Teresa retorted, "let me tell you this. I have had hardened police officers throwing up in that hell house these last few weeks. Don't play the heroine until you've been there. The plain fact is this. I have more than enough for what I would need in normal circumstances. But a fingerprint, a fibre, a DNA record . . . they don't mean a damn thing unless I am allowed to match them with something else, in a way that will stand up in court."

Agata folded her arms and looked at each of them in turn. "So I could be here for months."

It was Commissario Esposito who intervened. "We have plenty more possibilities to look at now. There were seventeen canvases in Nino Tomassoni's hovel in the Piazza di San Lorenzo in Lucina."

She blinked and asked, seemingly amazed, "Where?"

"In the man's house," the commissario replied. "Seventeen canvases. Eleven we have identified from the stolen art register. These are works that have been taken from museums as far away as Stockholm and Edinburgh. Tomassoni—and, by implication, one assumes Malaspina—was seemingly part of some illicit art-smuggling ring working on a massive scale. Perhaps this explains why our interesting count finds it so easy to gain access to the criminal fraternity when he has call for their talents. He is simply dealing with his own."

"Tomassoni's house? I didn't know where he lived. It was in the Piazza di San Lorenzo?"

She looked directly at Costa when she spoke. Once again, the name nagged at him.

"Yes," Falcone agreed. "Is this important?"

"I'm nothing but a humble sister, Leo. What would a little woman like me know?"

"The name means something," Costa said. "And I can't remember what."

They fell silent, all of them, and looked at Agata Graziano, waiting.

"You're asking me?" she said. "I thought I was just supposed to be the silent houseguest."

"Yes," Costa prompted her. "We are asking you."

"What a strange world you inhabit," Agata Graziano observed. "With your procedures and your science, your computers and your rigid modes of thought. Does it never occur to you that if an answer does not manifest itself in the present, that is, perhaps, because it prefers to do so in the past?"

She looked at Costa. "What did I tell you, Nic? When we were walking through those streets last night? Those ghosts are with us, always. Only a fool wouldn't listen to them."

"We're police officers," Falcone grumbled. "Not hunters of ghosts."

"Then perhaps I'll be here forever. This is not

acceptable to me, Leo. I shall allow you a week to bring Franco Malaspina to book. After that I return home, to some form of sanity. Or now, if you do not agree."

Falcone's thin, tanned face flared with shock. "No! That is impossible. You cannot set time limits on such things. Who do you think you are dealing with?"

"I've just watched Franco Malaspina tell me that. I'm a free woman. I may do as I wish. Best start working. Perhaps if you hammer those computers of yours a little harder. Or find some newer science for your games . . ."

"It's an old name," Costa interrupted, hoping to cool the temperature. "Tomassoni."

"It is an old name," she agreed. "Here is one more fact I doubt any of you know, for all your wonderful toys and resources. I would have told you, but it seemed irrelevant until today. Possibly it still is."

Agata got up and walked to the line of bookshelves by the fireplace. Volume after volume from the days of Costa's father sat in rows, gathering dust along the walls. She picked up two substantial editions, both bought years ago, books on art, then brought them back to the table, where she began to leaf through the pages as she spoke, looking, surely, for something she knew was there already.

"It is a known fact," she said, "that Caravaggio lived in the Vicolo del Divino Amore for some time. Not during the happier part of his life either. This was after he left the hedonistic paradise of Del Monte's Palazzo Madama. He had little money. He kept bad company.

Very bad. This was Ortaccio, remember. The Garden of Evil."

She found what she wanted in one of the books, placed it in front of them, and covered whatever lay there with a napkin from the table.

"I have walked every inch of Rome in that man's footsteps," Agata added. "I know where he lived and ate, where he whored and fought. No one can be sure of this precisely, but you must remember something, always. In Caravaggio's days, men kept records. They noted down details of crimes and property transactions, small civil disturbances and matters of money and debt. Many of those papers are with us still." She smiled at them. "Out of your reach, true, safe in archives in the Vatican, in a country where you people have no jurisdiction. But a small and curious sister of the Church, with a little interest in history..."

Costa found himself transfixed by her, and he wasn't alone.

"You looked up the records for the street?" he asked.

"Of course I did! When Leo first told me the painting had been found there. Who wouldn't?"

"Well...?" Teresa demanded.

"The house where Caravaggio lived was either that same property or one of the two to either side. I cannot be more specific. The street had a different name then, different numbering. But there is a record in the church register which names Caravaggio as a resident in 1605, with a young boy—a servant, a student, a lover, who knows? He was reduced to poverty. He was constantly in fights and brawls and arguments." She paused. "It was his home when he murdered the man whose death forced him to flee Rome."

They were silent and, Costa apart, dubious.

It was Peroni who spoke first.

"Agata," he pointed out, reasonably, "this was hundreds of years ago."

"Caravaggio took that man's life on May 28, 1606, while he was living in what we now know as the Vicolo del Divino Amore. Within days he was gone from Rome forever, travelling ceaselessly—Naples, Malta, Sicily— dependent on the help of allies and patrons to feed him and keep him from the executioner."

"A long time ago," Falcone repeated, staring at the book on the table, wondering, like the rest of them, what it contained.

"They fought in the street," she went on, ignoring him, "over what we don't know. When it was over, the man was dead. His name was Ranuccio Tomassoni. He died in the house where he and his family had lived for almost two centuries, and for all I know continued to live thereafter. It was in the Piazza di San Lorenzo di Lucina."

Costa closed his eyes and laughed. "How on earth did I forget that?"

"You forgot it," she said instantly, "because you regarded it as history and irrelevant to the present. As I may one day tire of telling you, it isn't. These are not the stories of people turned to dust. They are our stories, and in some curious way they became the stories of Franco Malaspina, Nino Tomassoni, and the rest." She shook her head. She looked exhausted, but immensely energised by her subject too. "Something has placed them alongside what happened then. Perhaps that painting that means so much. Perhaps ... I don't know. Look ..."

It wasn't the picture they were expecting, but another from the second book.

"Caravaggio painted this while he was in Malta."

It was a dark study of an elderly man, half naked on his bed, writing. Saint Jerome. Another of the canvases in Valletta that Costa knew, one day, he had to see.

"At this time of his life, Caravaggio chose what he did for a reason," she went on. "Money. Survival. The passing friendship of influential men. We know for a fact that this particular work was painted at the request of someone who helped him escape from mainland Italy and reach the temporary safety of the Knights Templar in Valletta. A few months later Michelangelo Merisi was fleeing once more after committing some other crime, which the Knights hid for fear it shamed them too. This patron continued to assist him. In Sicily. All the way to the end, when he returned to the mainland and sought to come back to Rome."

She took a sip of water from a glass on the table. "That man's name was Ippolito Malaspina. I have never raised this fact with Franco. But I know for sure that he must be a direct descendant. The man had many children. The castle Franco continues to own in Tuscany, from which he has lent the Barberini works for display from time to time, was the property where his ancestor lived with his family before leaving for Malta with Caravaggio."

Her dark eyes stared at them. "There was a connection between the Medici and the Malaspina clans. Perhaps Franco's fury stems from that. What more do I have to show you? Are these subjects you will pass on to some young police officer and hope they can comprehend? Even I don't understand them. Perhaps in time." She glanced at Costa. "With help and insight. But . . ."

She sat back, closed her eyes for a few seconds, then opened them and glared at Commissario Esposito. "You will provide the books I need. A computer. An officer who can carry out external research and fetch and carry when I require. Tomorrow I shall see this house of Tomassoni's. And the place in the Vicolo del Divino Amore . . ."

"It's not pretty," Teresa observed, shaking her head.

"As I keep telling you, I am not a child. You will do these things and I will help you. And if it's no use, then what's lost?"

They were silent, even Costa.

"Commissario," Agata declared. "I will not stay here and learn to knit. The choice is yours."

"Very well," Vincenzo Esposito snapped. "Indulge Sister Agata as she requires. You will organise security,

Falcone. Agente Prabakaran will act as go-between for anything the sister demands. The details of these visits outside will not leave this room. Franco Malaspina is a far more dangerous individual than any of us appreciated. If his talents run to taming magistrates and international art smuggling, then he will know men who are capable of anything. As is he."

"Good," Agata said, then removed the napkin from the page of the second book, an old biography of Caravaggio, one of Costa's favourites, and held it up for them all to see.

They found themselves looking at the black-and-white photograph of a portrait of a gentleman, round-faced with a pale complexion, a double chin, and large, very bulbous eyes. He sat on a velvet-covered chair and wore rich, sumptuous clothes, as if he were of some importance.

Agata ran a finger over the man's unattractive features. "You must excuse me in a moment. I'm tired. I need to rest. I expect some time on my own. This is by Caravaggio from his Malta period," she said. "It was in the Kaiser Friedrich Museum in Berlin from the early nineteenth century on. Unfortunately the work was destroyed when the city was retaken at the end of the Second World War. What you see is a portrait of Ippolito Malaspina painted by Caravaggio shortly before he fled Valletta."

Costa stared at the portly, bloodless individual in his faintly ridiculous court clothes. He had the face of a weak and lascivious civil servant. It was tempting to see some sarcasm or ridicule of the subject in the face; such sly, slight jokes were not unknown to Caravaggio.

"This pasty-faced idiot doesn't look anything like that pig we had here!" Teresa said, jabbing a finger at the portrait.

"Precisely," Agata replied quietly, then snapped the book shut.

# Four

AT EIGHT IN THE EVENING, BEA WAS STANDING AT the foot of the stairs, tapping her feet, looking mildly cross.

"A part of me wishes to say this is the worst girl you have ever brought back, Nic," she muttered, perhaps only half joking.

"I wouldn't call her 'girl' to her face," he said. "Nor do I think it accurate to say I brought her back."

"No," she grumbled. "More like putting her in prison really, isn't it? And I'm the warder."

Bea didn't like the men at the bottom of the drive. Some urge within her made it essential she take them coffee and water and panini from time to time. On the last occasion, she had encountered Peroni, who was singing a bawdy Tuscan song at the top of his voice. Costa understood this was as much to keep up morale as anything. It was Peroni's way to try to lighten the situation and keep a team going. He couldn't expect Bea to understand such an idea, and so there had been a chilly encounter between the two of them.

"Also . . . she hasn't yet had a bath. She may be a genius but to me the poor thing's positively feral in normal company."

"Normal company being us, naturally. Agata does not live the way we do. If you want to return to your apartment . . ."

"Don't be ridiculous. You can't expect a woman like her to be alone in a house with a man. It wouldn't be right. Also . . . someone shot you last night, in case you forgot."

"Buckshot," he answered. "Water off a duck's back, really. You know the Costa breed. We feel nothing. Seriously. It's uncomfortable. Nothing more."

"The arrogance of men . . ." she muttered. "There will be food on the table in five minutes. I would be grateful if someone turned up to eat it. I've called several times. Not a word in return. You speak with her. I give up."

With that she marched back to the kitchen, leaving Costa at the foot of the steps, wondering.

This was an awkward situation, but it was his house.

He went upstairs, along to the largest guest room, which had been hastily cleaned by Bea, with new sheets found for the double bed, and towels and soap for the bathroom. It was a beautiful room, his brother's when he was young, with the best view in the house, an undisturbed one back to the Via Appia Antica, and scarcely a sign of modern life, no roads, just the single telegraph pole leading to the property, visible in the very corner, beyond the vines and the cypresses lining the drive.

He knocked on the door and said, "There's food."

"I know."

Nothing more.

"Are you coming?"

"Yes."

He was about to go when she added, "Come in, Nic. Please. I want to ask you something."

With a sigh, he opened the door. Agata sat in front of the dresser staring at herself in the mirror, an expression of puzzlement and fear on her face. She was wearing a white cotton shirt and black slacks. Her hair was tied back tightly, drawing the rampant curly locks away from her face, which, now he saw more of it, was angular and striking. This was the head of some artist's model, not beautiful in a conventional sense, not even pretty necessarily, but one that was fated to be looked at, stared at even, because it contained such an intensity of life and thought and—the word did not seem inappropriate—grace.

"Look what they've done to me," she complained. "I asked for books and information. They bring me these clothes, too, and say I must wear them to look less conspicuous. Why?"

"Castagna, Buccafusca, and Nino Tomassoni are dead," he pointed out. "Like it or not, you're our only material witness. These precautions—"

"Franco simply hates anyone who's black. Even half black. We all saw that today." She couldn't stop looking at the image of herself in the glass. "We don't have these big mirrors at home," she murmured. "Or private rooms with beds large enough for four. And this house . . ."

She stood up and walked to the window. "I can't even see a light from here. Or hear a human voice or a car or bus."

"Most people would think that an advantage."

She turned and stared at him, astounded. "What? To be denied the sounds of humanity? I've lived my entire life in the city. I know it. Those are the sounds of its breathing. Why do people wish to run away from everything? What are you frightened of?"

"Tomorrow," he replied, shrugging. "Today sometimes too."

She laughed, just. "Well, thank you. That's one trick you've taught me. I never feared anything until you people came into my life. Now I see a man with a gun round every corner, and I look at a painting—a painting by Caravaggio—and wonder if it should shake my faith. Thank you very much indeed."

"This is the world, Agata," he replied meekly. "I'm sorry we dragged you into it. I'm sure, someday soon, you will be able to go back to where you came from. Just not now."

She was silent for a moment.

"And you?" she asked in the end.

"I will find my own way," he answered. "By some means or other. Provided I eat from time to time. Now, will you join us? Please?"

# Five

$\mathscr{A}$T NINE-FIFTEEN ROSA PRABAKARAN DELIVERED
the items Agata had demanded, then left for the night.
Costa watched Agata carefully unpack what had arrived,
taking immense care over several ancient academic
tomes and a notebook computer bearing the stamp of
the Barberini on the base, and very little notice indeed of
two plastic grocery bags with what she said were her personal items from the convent.

Bea stared at the paltry collection of cheap, well-worn
clothes and asked, "Is that it?"

"What more am I supposed to need?"

Bea walked out of the room and came back with her
arms full of soft towels, some so large and suspiciously
fresh Costa wondered if she'd bought them that afternoon, along with boxes of soap and other unidentifiable
cosmetics.

"The plumbing in this place can be difficult sometimes," she declared. "When you are ready, I will introduce you to the mysteries of the bathroom."

Then she went upstairs.

Agata watched her leave.

"What is Bea to you, Nic?"

"A family friend. She and my father were ... very good friends once upon a time. That died. The closeness remained."

"Does she think I'm odd?"

"Probably," he admitted.

"Do you?"

"You're not the normal houseguest."

"Who is?"

He groaned. Agata did not give up easily. She had insisted she wanted to retire to her bedroom to work. Yet now ...

"I have to speak to the men outside. You have your belongings. Is there anything else I can provide?"

"Yes. There is a room with some art materials in it. Along there ..." She pointed to the rear of the house and the place he hadn't entered, not since Emily's death. "What is it, please? I couldn't help but notice earlier. I may need something."

"Let me show you," he said, and led the way.

The studio was clean and tidy, though it smelled a little of damp, as it always did when the place went unused and unheated for any amount of time. Emily's work was everywhere: line drawings of buildings, sketches, studies, ideas, doodles.

"Your wife was an artist?" Agata asked.

"An architect. Or she was hoping to be one. When she finished her studies."

"You can't learn to build well overnight," she countered, picking up a sketch from the nearest pile. It was of the Uffizi in Florence, from the weekend in October when he'd found the time to take a break from work, the first since their wedding in the summer. He didn't find it easy to look at now.

"She could draw," Agata commented. "Very well. Art and architecture go hand in hand, but then, you know that. I'm sorry. I shouldn't treat you like an imbecile."

She looked around the room and shivered. It was cold. She was wearing just the cheap, thin white cotton shirt and the equally inexpensive slacks that came from the convent. The Questura budget hadn't run to clothes, though Rosa had told him quietly she intended to correct this in the morning. In some strange, subtle way, they were beginning to adopt Agata Graziano, form a protective, insular wall around her, and not simply as a way of keeping out Franco Malaspina and his thugs. A part of her seemed too delicate to be allowed to wander free in the world the rest of them inhabited. Costa wondered whether this was fair, or even an accurate reading of the facts.

"I shouldn't be in this place, prying. It's private. I'm sorry."

"It's just a room," he said, and smiled. "You're welcome to use it as much as you wish. Before Emily had it, my sister worked here. She is an artist too. It needs . . ."

The white walls were now a little grey and in need of paint. He remembered the sound of voices in the house when he was growing up, and how he would come in here for peace sometimes, watching his sister work at some strange, abstract canvas he would never understand.

"It needs company," he murmured, and found the thought began to bring a sharp, stinging sensation to his eyes.

She noticed and said quickly, "Good night, Nic. I must see what Bea has to teach me about this bathroom of yours."

# Six

$\mathcal{H}$E WAITED AT THE FOOT OF THE STAIRS, THINK-
ing, wondering whether he should stay nearby in case
there was some difficulty between the two. But after a
while he heard their voices from above, happy voices, followed by the running of water, then, drifting down the
steps, the smell of soap and shampoo.

If Bea had had a daughter, she would have been about
Agata's age. He had seen that glint in her eyes the moment this bright, dishevelled young woman had walked
through the door. *The poor thing's positively feral.*

Costa found himself amused by the description. It
was both apposite and somehow ridiculous. Agata was
an extraordinarily sophisticated woman. She simply
chose not to show it on the outside.

He found his coat, walked down the drive, and went
to the men in the marked car blocking the entrance. It
was a cold, clear night, full of stars, bright with the light
of a waxing moon.

Peroni was there with an officer Costa didn't recognise. They were listening to the radio—old, bad Italian jazz, the kind Gianni would force on anyone given half the chance—and drinking coffee from a thermos.

"Is there anything I can get you gentlemen?" he asked as they wound down the window.

"Some ladies, some wine, some food," Peroni responded instantly. "Actually, just the food will do. Got any?"

"You know where the kitchen is. I'm going to bed."

"How's the shoulder?" Peroni asked, suddenly serious.

"Aching. But it's not worth worrying about. Is everything OK here?"

"It's good," Peroni said, nodding, meaning it. "Better than it looked. You know, when that bastard stormed out of here all smug and knowing this afternoon, I didn't think so. I thought . . . there you go. Some rich jerk is going to walk all over us again. But I don't now. I have no idea why. It's probably the early onset of mental degeneration. I just think . . . we will nail him, Nic. We're here. There are a hundred good men and women or more on the case back at the Questura. This new commissario is on our side too. It will work out. Somehow or other. I promise."

He turned and stared out of the car window. "You know what makes me so certain? It's that awful detail Rosa got out of the hooker who went away. The idea that these animals photographed those women like that. You know. Just when . . ."

He did know. Costa thought he understood why too. It was the precise instant captured on the canvas. Agata described it exactly: *the moment of the fall.* In the cries of those women, however unreal, however they were brought about, by sex or violence or—and he had to countenance this—the imminence of death, lay some secret pleasure the Ekstasists craved to witness.

"I don't believe in God," Peroni went on, "but I'm damned sure that men like that will not walk away from us, not in the end. It's only Malaspina now, and we will have him."

Costa agreed. "We will," he said, then went back to the house, poured himself a small glass of the Verdicchio, which was barely touched, and found the chair by the fire, once his father's, always the most comfortable in the house.

The dog was there already, a small, stiff furry shape curled up in front of the burning logs, slumbering.

There was a photo on the mantel. He reached up and took it in his hands, wishing, in the futile way one did, that his father could have seen this before he died.

He and Emily stood where newly married couples often did on their wedding day in Rome, by the Arch of Constantine, next to the Colosseum, in their best clothes, Emily with a bouquet in her arms, smiling, happier than he had ever seen her, he in a suit Falcone had helped him buy, the best he'd ever owned, a perfect fit, now consigned to Teresa's evidence pile, torn apart by Malaspina's pellets, stained with Costa's own blood.

Lives were drawn together by invisible lines, unseen contours that joined waypoints one never noticed until they were already fading in the receding distance of memory. From the moment captured here to Emily's death was but a few brief months, and nothing could have told him that then, nothing could ease the ache he felt now, the pain, the regret over so many unspoken words, such a proliferation of deeds and kindnesses that never took place.

Time stole everything in the end. It had no need of an accomplice, some arrogant, deranged aristocrat hiding behind a mask and a gun.

From above him he heard a sound, one he struggled, for a moment, to recognise. Then it came...laughter. Bea and Agata, happy together, their amusement running like a river, almost giggling, the way that children did, or a mother and daughter, joined by some mutual amusement over something that would never, in a million years, reach his ears.

This was how it was supposed to be. This was how it should have been.

He closed his eyes and held the photograph in its frame close to him.

*God gave us tears for a reason.*

Perhaps, he thought. But something stood between him and Emily's pale, remembered face, still alive, still breathing in his memory. It was a figure in a hood, one who now possessed a voice and a face and a black, evil intent that was not yet sated.

Part Twelve

Fragments from the Past

# One

CHEY LEFT THE HOUSE AT MIDDAY, IN A CONVOY of three vehicles, Agata and Costa in the centre, with a specialist driver at the wheel, an arrangement Commissario Esposito said would be standard practise until Franco Malaspina was in jail.

Agata had risen early, spending most of the morning alone in the studio with her books and the computer, coming out only for glasses of water, saying nothing. Halfway through the morning, Rosa had arrived with fresh reference works...and new clothes. Agata had snatched at the former and scarcely even noticed the latter. When she emerged for the conference at the Questura, she had, it seemed to Costa, no conscious knowledge of the fact that she was now wearing, probably for the first time in her life, the kind of apparel most Roman women would regard as standard, half-elegant office wear: smart black slacks and a matching jacket, with a cream shirt. With Bea's help, her hair now seemed relatively under control, snatched back in a band. The dark, angular lines of her face made her look a little older, a little more businesslike perhaps, though the effect was somewhat ruined by her insistence on wearing her old shoes, a pair of worn, black, deeply scuffed half-boots that looked as if they had marched over most of Rome several times over. She continued to carry two overstuffed plastic bags, one so heavy it gave her a marked tilt.

Agata said nothing in the car, and walked through the Questura, catching curious, occasionally admiring looks along the way, as if heading for some routine academic conference, not a desperate convocation of law enforcement officers struggling to find some way back into a case of multiple murder, one in which she might be the only worthwhile witness.

Finally, at one o'clock, as sandwiches were passed around the table, the meeting began, with a summary of the case from Falcone and the forensic from Teresa Lupo. Costa, with Agata on one side and Rosa Prabakaran on the other, listened avidly, hoping there would be some lacuna in the exposition of what he knew by heart, some gap or flaw in what they had done which would give them some new foothold that would lead into the Palazzo Malaspina.

He heard none. Falcone described at length the extended Questura investigation into the murders in the Vicolo del Divino Amore and Emily's. Rarely had such resources been brought to bear on a single investigation in recent history, in part because of the continuing media and public outcry over the case. There was shock that such dreadful events could be uncovered in Rome. The newspapers were outraged at the lack of progress and ran editorials daily, lamenting the seeming impotence of the police. At the same time, they were—with the lack of logic allowed to the journalistic profession at times—beginning to question the expense of the operation, with its thousands of officer hours and overseas trips, which now included Angola, Nigeria, and Sudan, all without the least sign of progress.

Nor was the usually productive route of forensic making much of a contribution. The new rules brought into force following Malaspina's legal applications made most of the conventional processes—the accidental, covert, and deliberate sampling of DNA in particular—unusable. The deaths of Castagna, Buccafusca, and Nino Tomassoni two nights ago had left Teresa Lupo's team swamped with work, and would doubtless provide a sea of evidence which might one day prove useful. But neither she nor Falcone had any fresh material which linked Malaspina directly with the case outside the forbidden area of genetic identification.

Malaspina's lawyers had dispatched the Questura back to the age of intellectual deduction, with little recourse to science. Castagna's suicide would, Teresa felt sure, soon prove to be fake. There was, however, no calling card from Malaspina, not a phone call or a speck of physical evidence that could connect him with the man's death. The two were acquaintances, perhaps even friends. This was only to be expected among two leading members of Rome's younger glitterati. A magistrate like Silvia Tentori would not give a moment's consideration to a name in a contact book or a few bland emails on a computer. They were, for the moment, entirely reliant on the relationship Malaspina had had with the reclusive Nino Tomassoni, and there, Falcone said, something different surely existed.

In the way of Italian law enforcement, it had only that morning come to light that both men's names were on Interpol's list of art-smuggling suspects, which had been handed to the Carabinieri's specialist team in the field. That same list, Falcone had gleaned from his contacts within the Carabinieri, also identified Véronique Gillet as a suspect, to the extent that there was active discussion about whether to question her shortly, an act which would inevitably have led to her suspension from the Louvre.

"Sick, out of work, and on the verge of getting busted," the pathologist interjected. "No wonder she was feeling a touch suicidal."

"Isn't that enough to get us a warrant for Malaspina on its own?" Rosa asked.

It was Esposito who intervened. "Not at all. If Gillet or Tomassoni had named him, of course. But since they are dead . . . Malaspina is simply one name on a long list, the result of anonymous information. Rich men attract this kind of gossip all the time. On its own it's worthless. We need more than tittle-tattle."

They stared at one another, and Agata Graziano eyed them in turn, waiting.

"So?" she asked. "Is that it?"

"There may still be some room for opportunity here," Falcone suggested. "We know he was obsessed with that painting in the Vicolo del Divino Amore. If we can prove some connection there . . . We don't need evidence of the other crimes. It's a stolen artwork like the rest, even if it's not on the list. We can proceed on that basis alone."

She glanced at Costa and he knew, immediately, why.

"That painting wasn't stolen, sir," he said.

"What are you talking about?" Esposito snapped. "Of course it was stolen. We have seventeen like it from Tomassoni's house. Positive identification for fifteen of them now. Every one taken from some European art institution over the past decade. You're telling me this one is different?"

Agata's small hand banged the table. "Of course it's different."

Teresa Lupo wore a sly smile. "It was in a different place, gentlemen," she said. "It was on a stand, out there to be viewed. Those others were items of trade, in storage, awaiting a buyer. I believe our sister here is right."

"Thank you," Agata murmured, with the briefest of glances at Teresa as she spoke. "I am. This painting cannot have been stolen, not in the same way, for one very simple reason. As far as any of us knew, it didn't even exist. Explain that to me, Leo. I am listening."

"So what did happen?" Esposito asked, looking prickly when Falcone stayed silent.

"I have no idea," she replied, shrugging her small shoulders. "I'm simply telling you what didn't happen. Isn't that important too?"

Teresa nodded. "Very. But if it wasn't stolen, where the hell has it been for these past four hundred years?"

"Here," Agata cried. "In Rome. Where it belongs. Where else? If it had been sold or gone abroad, we would have known. Who could have kept quiet about a work like that? An unknown Caravaggio, with a secret no one might guess at?"

"A secret?" Falcone asked.

Costa sketched out the details of the hidden signature and the alternative title. They looked baffled. This was beyond conventional police work.

"All of which means what exactly?" Peroni asked in the end.

Agata sighed and looked at Costa hopefully.

"I'm not sure," he admitted.

"It means," she said brusquely, "this was a private work of art for a gentleman's bedroom. One that had a certain moral ambiguity that came from the artist, and was not, I suspect, part of the original commission, or indeed noticed by the men who owned it. For them, it was a kind of pornography. For Caravaggio, it was a discourse on the nature of love, a question for the viewer, asking him or her to define an attitude towards the origin of passion. Did it come from earthly flesh or was there some divine intent, some holy, sacred plan there, daring you to find it?"

"And this is important?" Peroni asked.

"For Franco Malaspina," she said quietly, "this painting is the most important thing in the world. Why else would he risk so much to regain possession of the work? He needs it. So did Véronique Gillet. Castagna. Buccafusca. Everyone except Nino Tomassoni, who was a quiet, sad little thing, I think."

"He said something," Falcone pointed out. "Tomassoni. Before he died. 'The Caravaggio is mine. Ours. It's the only one that is.'"

"Then Franco took it from him," Agata responded. "To enjoy what it brought. Which was . . . you tell me."

They were looking at each other, wondering who would be the first to say it.

"I cannot assist you if I don't know the facts," Agata complained. "You are all very bad liars, by the way. So kindly stop."

Costa took the leap. "We have evidence that the Ekstasists took photos of women while they were having sex. That they tried to capture the instant of passion, not that it was passion, of course, but that doesn't seem to have mattered."

She took a deep breath and asked, "You have the photos?"

"We have a few," Teresa replied. "Some of the victims are among those who died in the studio. Others . . . they don't seem traceable."

"What do they show?" Agata asked.

Costa intervened. "They show women in the throes of sexual ecstasy or some kind of torture, or perhaps even a fatal spasm. There's no way of knowing."

Agata took a sip of water from the glass in front of her.

"They wish to experience the moment of the fall," she said quietly. "The transformation Caravaggio's painting describes. The very second the world turns from Paradise into what we know now. If they do that, they become part of that moment, something witnessed only by God. They celebrate their own power over everyone, over these poor women. Over you and me. This was Franco's doing, not the others'."

The slight, dark woman ran her fingers through her hair, exasperated. "You should surely realise this for yourselves by now. He is an obsessive human being. This is not just a painting for him. It is a hunger. An object of worship. A need. Something that acts as a catalyst to deliver what he wants."

Costa looked at her. He had an objection. "They didn't know about the other title," he pointed out. "Or the signature beneath the paint."

"They must have known. Perhaps Tomassoni had passed it on as some family history. Perhaps they simply read it in the canvas itself. This is art of the highest order. That painting was designed to be some cunning kind of mirror. It gave back to the viewer what he himself sought in it. For someone like Franco that would be the equivalent of turning the key in some dreadful lock. He found what he sought. Caravaggio painted it that way deliberately. Were I writing some dry academic paper, I'd be tempted to hypothesise that this was his revenge on the commissioner, if you like, since he clearly wasn't in the habit of painting this kind of material, and probably didn't enjoy it. He was paid to produce pornography. In return, he created something infinitely more subtle. Crude and lascivious to those who wished to see that. Subtle and spiritual and didactic—a warning against lasciviousness and decadence—for those who sought that. And perhaps..." She stopped in mid-thought, looking lost for a moment. "...a little of both for those who deem themselves 'normal.' Do you understand what I am saying now? Or do I have to spell it out?"

No one spoke.

Agata groaned. "Franco and his friends needed to see this voluptuous Eve because what they did became more important, magnified, by her presence. I know nothing of these things, but I know what ecstasy means. Is it possible that this work would so infect a man that, in its absence, he was unable to achieve that state? And perhaps Véronique Gillet too? I am asking you this because I cannot know. Is that possible?"

They were all silent, until Teresa Lupo wrinkled her nose and said, "One thing you learn in this job, Sister, is that it's amazing what pushes some people's buttons. I think you just put your finger on our man. Not that it helps. In fact, it makes him scarier than ever."

Agata smiled. "Does it? I thought it made him more human. Now I would like to go to the Vicolo del Divino Amore, please." She waited, staring at Commissario Esposito. "Unless someone has a better idea . . ."

"You have helped us enormously," Falcone interrupted. "We're very grateful. Now, please, return to the farmhouse. You will be safe there. We will provide what you want."

"What I want," she said bitterly, "is to help. How can I do that if you treat me like a prisoner?"

"Agata . . ." Falcone began.

Esposito waved him down. "She's right," he conceded. "We need all the help we can get. Costa, you take her with your team, since you all seem to know each other. Falcone and I will stay here and go through what little we have so far."

He stared at Agata Graziano. "There is a condition, though."

She listened, arms folded.

"You will do as you're told, Sister. In particular what Agente Prabakaran advises, since she will be by your side throughout."

Agata nodded and said simply, "I know a little of obedience, Commissario. You have my word."

# Two

C HIRTY MINUTES LATER AGATA SAT IN THE BACK of the car with Costa, sorting through the contents of a plastic grocery bag: books, notepads, pens, and pencils.

She didn't say much until the vehicle rounded the Piazza Borghese and came to a halt at the top of the little alley, some twenty metres short of the small crowd of spectators and a couple of photographers who stood, bored and stationary, outside the yellow barrier of tape now beginning to look old from the rain and mud.

"This city seems different from a car," Agata mused. "I prefer walking. Don't you?"

"No sane person drives in Rome," he replied with feeling.

"In that case this is a city of lunatics," Rosa Prabakaran cut in from the front seat. "Sister Agata, do you mind if I make a suggestion?"

The car had stopped. The two guard vehicles were either side, front and back. Officers were getting out, checking the area, as was Rosa, with a professional, calm intent Costa liked.

"You can't drag your life around with you in a grocery bag," Rosa said suddenly, then passed something over from the front seat. It was a smart new satchel in black leather with a shiny silver buckle. "Please take this. A gift from the Questura."

Costa caught her eye. This was surely not from the police fund. The thing had all the hallmarks of the cheap yet serviceable goods Rosa's father sold to tourists from his stall near the Trevi Fountain.

"I'm worried you will lose something from one of those bags," she added. "This is purely practical..."

Agata took it from her and stared at the shiny leather, sniffing it for a moment and wrinkling her dark nose at the smell.

"Grocery bags have served me well for a very long time," she noted.

"You're not walking from convent to work and back, a few minutes each day. Not anymore." Rosa was adamant. "Please."

Agata shrugged and took the thing, flipped up the buckle, then prepared to empty the entire contents of one bag by the simple act of turning it upside down over the satchel's open mouth.

She stopped, staring inside, then reached in and delicately removed a black metal object there. It was a small police-issue handgun.

"What is this?" she asked. "No. That was a stupid

thing to say. I know what this is. Why do you want me to have it? That's impossible."

"Guns are not useful in the hands of people who don't know how to use them," Costa remarked. "What on earth are you thinking, Agente?"

"Commissario Esposito spoke to me before we left, sir," she replied. "He wants Sister Agata to have this and for me to give her instructions on how to use it if necessary. It won't come to that. Nevertheless . . ."

Agata held the gun in front of her, touching the black metal gingerly, as if it were something poisonous.

"Those are your orders, Rosa, not mine," she muttered.

"Why did Commissario Esposito suggest this?" Costa asked, furious the man had never raised the subject directly.

"Operational reasons."

The duty guard officers were beginning to mill around the car door, anxious to move. Costa persisted.

"What operational reasons?"

Rosa frowned. "Sister, do you have any idea what the Camorra is?"

She shook her head. The hair didn't move anymore. The crucifix around her neck, lying on the cream business shirt, and the bulky, scruffy boots apart, Agata Graziano no longer looked the woman she still felt herself to be.

"Should I?" she asked.

"There is no reason whatsoever," Costa snapped,

angry that Esposito, for some reason, had not used him to approach Agata on such a sensitive matter. "The Camorra are criminals."

Agata stared at him, wide-eyed, curious. "Just 'criminals'?"

"They're a criminal fraternity based in Naples, though they have arms, tentacles, everywhere in Italy, and in Europe and America too," he went on. "Imagine a kindred organisation to the Sicilians, the mafiosi. I imagine you've heard of them."

"As I told you once before, I am not a monk."

"Quite," he answered. "What on earth has this to do with us?"

Rosa wasn't taking the proffered gun from her.

"They're good Catholics, too, mainly," she said. "At least they think of themselves that way. We heard from Naples this morning that one of them, a man who is occasionally friendly with the police there, wanted to warn us of something he'd heard. That a Roman, one unidentified, at least someone he was unwilling to name, was seeking someone to carry out an attack, and looking to pay well for assistance." She gazed at Agata, a mournful look in her brown eyes. "He said the target was to be a Catholic nun."

"I am not—"

Rosa put her hand on Agata's tightly clenched fingers. "We know. But the name he had was yours. This is good news, Sister, trust me. At least we are forewarned. We also know that no one accepted the commission. The man was appalled by the very idea and believed those in the Camorra would feel the same. But they are just a few criminals among many. Franco Malaspina knows more and he has money that shouts very loudly. So please . . ." The policewoman pushed the weapon back over the seat. "Do this for me," she added. "I will show you how to handle a gun safely should the need arise. But it won't. We will protect you. Nic and I and"—she indicated the officers beyond the door—"all of us. This will not be necessary. It's simply a precaution."

Agata uttered a small, slight curse and, with pointed disdain, placed the weapon back where it came from.

"I like the bag, Agente," she conceded with a curt brusqueness. "Thank you for that."

# Three

$\mathcal{T}$HE LAST PIECE OF PHYSICAL EVIDENCE HAD BEEN removed from the studio in the Vicolo del Divino Amore. But the smell of death—sweet, noxious, sickly—remained. Agata feigned not to notice. Rosa Prabakaran and Peroni, on the other hand, both made excuses to stand outside. Costa understood why. Something—perhaps the work in lifting the floors or the exposure of so much dull, dark earth itself—made the stench worse than it had been at the moment the first body was found.

There was, surely, nothing left of interest to be removed from the charnel house that had been the lair of the Ekstasists. Nevertheless, Teresa Lupo, as she guided her visitors around its interior, explaining its grim, dark secrets, insisted each of them wear the standard white forensic suit and move within the tapes while she went through each and every victim with painstaking care and in exact detail.

Agata listened, asking questions only rarely, eyes wide open in wonder mostly, occasionally misted with shock and dismay.

"What do you know about these women?" she asked when Teresa had finished her main exposition. "Who they were. Where they came from."

"Not much," Teresa said sadly. "Not real names. Not history. They worked the streets, probably in the rougher parts of town. That much we know. Not a lot more." She hesitated. "You understand what AIDS is?"

"Of course," Agata answered with a sigh.

"Four of them were HIV-positive. One possibly was developing AIDS itself."

Agata shook her head. She looked oddly young in the white bunny suit. "Poor things . . ."

"They weren't alone in that," Costa pointed out. "Véronique Gillet suffered from AIDS too."

"What a world you inhabit," Agata murmured. "And you think that of Caravaggio was primitive by comparison. Did you find any artist's materials that didn't seem to be modern?"

This was a subject that clearly didn't interest the pathologist.

"There was some paint and a small number of brushes that were a few years old. They hadn't been used in a while." Teresa glanced around her. "This was a studio, though, wasn't it? You can see how it would be suitable for that purpose? Tell me I'm correct, Agata."

"I think so," she answered.

"Caravaggio's studio?" Costa asked.

Agata gave him a stern look. "You can't give me firm answers about events that happened here in the past few months. Yet you expect me to illuminate you on matters that may or may not have occurred four hundred years ago?"

Teresa folded her strong arms. "Yes, Sister, we do. Otherwise why are you here?"

Agata laughed. "Very well. Let me tell you what I read about last night, in the deadly quiet of Nic's lonely farmhouse. Caravaggio did live in this street, right up until the moment he fled Rome after killing Ranuccio Tomassoni in a brawl, involving several others on both sides, and knives. It's difficult to be more precise than that. In those days this street had a different name. It was the Vicolo dei Santi Cecilia e Biagio—don't ask me why it changed, I have no idea."

She turned and stared around the room. "When Caravaggio fled, the authorities made an inventory of his home. Most of the possessions, one assumes, were his, not those of his boyfriend or servant." A look of brief dejection crossed her face. "Reading the list of his belongings, you wonder what he had come to. It was pathetic. A guitar. Some very old and poor furniture. Some weapons, of course, among them a pair of duelling swords in an ebony case, possibly the most valuable things he owned."

She stared at them. "That was the man. He saw everything, lived everything. Good and evil. The touch of grace, the absence of it. He simply wished to paint it all, every last detail. But here?" Agata Graziano held out her arms in empty despair. "I don't know. Perhaps he lived and worked in the same room. Many did when they were poor. The street name has changed. The numbers have changed. I have no idea. Did you find nothing?"

"We were looking for evidence from now," Teresa answered. "We're forensic scientists, not archaeologists. Of course we found other material. We were digging up bare earth."

"Old brushes? Papers? Anything with writing on it?"

Teresa brightened a little and said, "Let me show you what we have."

They followed the pathologist over to a set of bright red plastic boxes stacked four deep. They were positioned next to the rear exit to the yard behind, a sight that brought back too many memories for Costa, so that he turned and looked away for a while, wondering if it was really possible to feel the past, to detect the presence of an extraordinary human being through some odd sixth sense that defied explanation.

When he turned, Agata was rummaging forcefully through the boxes, turning over broken crockery and trash and piece after piece of unidentifiable rubbish accrued across the centuries in the black Roman dirt.

"A brush," she said, and threw something on the floor at his feet. "It's probably of the period. But it could be anyone's. This is a waste of time. There's nothing . . ."

She stopped. Costa and Teresa watched in silence as she withdrew an object from the box and put it to one side. Then she tore into the second box with flailing hands, raked through the contents for a minute or more before finding something else and removing it.

They scarcely had a chance to see what she had found before both items went into her bright new shiny black satchel.

Agata Graziano gazed at her small, silent audience.

"I don't care to remember things that happened months ago," she declared. "It seems to me a waste of my time to dwell too much on the immediate past. But..." There was a sharp glint of excitement in her eyes. "I do recall a conversation I had with Véronique Gillet one night when they were opening that exhibition at the Palazzo Ruspoli, the one that had so much Caravaggio material from abroad."

Costa closed his eyes. He had worked security for that event. He and Emily had decided, at its close, to marry.

"I teased Véronique. She was French, for pity's sake, and the French demand it. Besides, they have stolen so much of ours, and do not even deign to share it either. This was"—she pointed at them to emphasise the matter—"the subject of our little playful argument. There was a painting that ought to have been there. *The Death of the Virgin.* The Louvre wouldn't allow it out of their grasping hands. Some excuse about security or preservation or whatever. It should have been in Rome, not sitting in Paris, gawked at by tourists who haven't the slightest understanding of what they see. Listen to me now. Caravaggio painted from life. Always."

"I'll try," Teresa replied. "And the point you're making...?"

"There was an outcry when he delivered that painting of the Virgin. The Madonna was swollen and lifeless. She was dead, after all. Very obviously human, not some goddess awaiting the call to divinity. Worse, there was a widespread belief that he painted her from the corpse of a common Roman whore recovered from the Tiber. I believe this too. It's there for the world to see. In the way she looks. In the sympathy with which she is regarded by the figures around her—a common sympathy. *Disegno.* He sought the sign of God in all of us."

She stared into space, not seeing anything, intent only on the questions racing through her head. "We know precisely when that work was executed, because it was a Church commission. There are records. If this was Caravaggio's studio, that corpse must have lain here," Agata said finally, staring at Costa with eyes that brimmed with both shock and a terrible knowledge. Her fingers pointed to the ground. "*Here.* Four hundred years before your poor black street women . . ."

"If . . ." Teresa murmured.

Agata shook her head free of the forensic suit's hood and started to struggle out of the white plastic. "I wish to go to the Doria Pamphilj immediately," she declared, then, still fighting with the bunny suit, swept through them, marching for the door. No one moved.

"I can phone Commissario Esposito if you like!" she shouted, turning to face them, beckoning with her short, skinny arms.

"So you could," Costa groaned, and followed.

# Four

$\mathcal{T}$HEY STOOD IN THE PIAZZA DEL COLLEGIO RO-
mano, in mild winter drizzle, six police officers crowding
around the small figure of Agata Graziano, who was huddled inside a raincoat Rosa Prabakaran had spirited from
nowhere. The gallery was closed for the afternoon. Costa
took it upon himself to phone to the Doria Pamphilj internal office, but by the time he'd finished the call the
door was open and a beaming attendant was waving
them in. Agata had spoken a few words into the inter-
com; that was all it required.

"Sister, Sister!" the middle-aged man in the anti-
quated uniform bleated. "Come in! Please! Out of this
awful weather." He stared at the army of police officers
and Teresa Lupo stamping her big feet on the doorstep.
"And your . . . friends too."

"Thank you, Michele," she answered, and stomped
into the dark hallway, then marched directly up the
grand flight of stairs, to the second-floor gallery.

It was hard to keep up. By the time they got to the top

of the stairs, Agata had gone through the public entrance, walked quickly through the Poussin Room and the Velvet, and was passing the ballroom, seemingly picking up speed with every step. Then she almost ran through the closed bookshop and turned right, towards the series of chambers that included, in its midst, the sixteenth-century room and the two Caravaggios they had come to visit just a couple of days before.

She was standing rigid, fascinated, in front of the smaller canvas, the penitent Magdalene, when they arrived, her shoulders moving, some unexpected emotion gripping her small, taut body.

Costa felt concerned. Then he realised what was happening. She was laughing quietly, to herself, not minding what anyone thought at all.

"Agata . . ." he said gently.

"What?" Her sparkling eyes turned on him. Her mouth broke in a bright, white smile.

"Is everything all right?"

"Everything is wonderful. And I am an idiot. We are all idiots. Here. Take a look at this . . ."

She reached into the black leather satchel and took out the first object he saw her retrieve from the red box in the Vicolo del Divino Amore. Surreptitiously, she must have been working at it in the car on the way to the gallery. It was no longer a dusty, unrecognisable shape. What Agata held in her hands was a glass carafe of the kind used for water or wine, one with such gentle curves it could only be handmade and very old.

Agata rubbed the sleeve of her raincoat hard against the edge.

"Tell me that's not evidence," Teresa said, alarmed.

"It's wonderful evidence. The best I could ask for. Not for you, though. For me."

They watched as she held the flask next to the slumbering Magdalene in the painting. An identical glass object sat close to the figure's feet, next to some discarded jewellery, evidence of some regretted tryst or a life that was in the process of being abandoned.

"It's the same jug," Agata said firmly.

"It's *a* jug," Teresa pointed out.

"No. He painted from life. He had no money most of the time. Perhaps he was sentimental too. Throughout his life the same objects reappear—props and models. He used what he was familiar with. The items he loved . . ." She glanced at the painting with the deepest of affection. ". . . he tried to keep. Caravaggio painted this work while he was in the Palazzo Madama under the patronage of Del Monte, alongside bohemians and alchemists, geniuses like Galileo, and vagabonds and quacks from the street. In the seven years between the Magdalene here and that squalid pit in the Vicolo del Divino Amore, he rose and fell, to become the most acclaimed artist in Rome and then a hunted criminal, wanted for murder. Why? *Why?*"

"It's a jug," Teresa said again.

"A poor man growing poorer sells what's of value to others and attempts to hold on to what is of value to him-

self," she declared. "This is the flask. It was like everything else. He used it more than once. I can show you the
paintings if you still doubt me. *Bacchus* in the Uffizi. *Boy
Bitten by a Lizard* in London. Nothing later. Nothing after he fled Rome." She stared at them and her eyes didn't
brook any argument. "Because he didn't have it."

She held up the glass for them to see. There was a distinct stain, like old blood, in the base.

"Wine, I imagine," Agata added. "There's another
reason to keep it. He could paint it. He could drink from
it too."

She noted the scepticism in their faces.

"If Caravaggio lived in that house," she went on,
"Franco Malaspina must have known. He said it himself.
It's part of the Malaspina estate, the poorer part, in
Ortaccio, but property all the same. These families keep
records for everything. Most of what we know about
painting in the sixteenth and seventeenth centuries
comes from the bookkeeping of either the Church or the
aristocracy."

"Even for me," Teresa remarked quietly, "this is
stretching things."

"Nic! Tell them what we discovered on that painting
before Franco stole it from us. *Tell them!*"

"We saw a signature," he said. "Caravaggio's. It
said . . ."

He paused. All the paintings they'd seen, all the same
faces, the same objects . . . these were alive in his head
and intermingled, one with the other.

"It said," Agata interjected, "*fra. michel l'ekstasista.* Michelangelo Merisi, the Ekstasist. Franco did not pluck the name of his murderous, thuggish gang out of the ether. He picked it out from history. Or it picked him. What he and Buccafusca and Castagna and poor, stupid Nino Tomassoni did came from that act, and it destroyed them in the end. Look . . ."

She pointed at the beautiful slumbering woman with the tear shining on her cheek like a transparent pearl.

"We know her name. Fillide Melandroni. A prostitute, a violent one, too, a woman who had been to court for marking her rivals by slashing their faces with a knife to make them less saleable. Here she is the Magdalene. Elsewhere Judith slaying Holofernes, Catherine leaning on a wall before her martyrdom. *Here!*"

She indicated the adjoining painting and the figure of Mary, with the infant Jesus in her arms, on the flight to Egypt.

"A holy whore," she said quietly. "And note the dress." She pointed at the rich olive fleur-de-lis brocade of the sleeping Magdalene's flowing halter gown. "This was the costume of a moneyed Roman prostitute, the kind of woman who slept with cardinals, then talked art and philosophy with them afterwards, before going out onto the streets of Ortaccio at night and . . . what? Making mayhem with Caravaggio and his friends."

To Costa's astonishment, Agata reached out and touched, very briefly, the soft, pale skin of the sleeping woman on the wall.

"Both good and evil, and each to excess," she said quietly. "*Nec spe, nec metu*. Without hope or fear. She was surely with them. Franco Malaspina did not invent the Ekstasists. He merely revived them, brought back from the dead the ugly gang that included Caravaggio and Fillide before everything fell apart so terribly."

Agata took her attention away from the wall. "Here is a word I thought I would never utter," she said again. "I read what records there were of the case against Caravaggio last night. They disclosed that one possible reason for the fight was that Ranuccio Tomassoni was Fillide's pimp. The man who sold her to others. Is that right?"

She closed her eyes for a moment. "No, no. I know it is. This is all part of your world, not mine, but yours intrudes, I can't avoid it. Tell me also. Is it possible this was Véronique Gillet's relationship to Franco Malaspina too? Accomplice. Lover. Muse. Fellow criminal. Could that be true?"

Costa was lost for words. Watching Agata struggle with these ideas—ones that seemed to make so much sense to him—he could see the mix of excitement and distress they caused.

"They re-created something we still don't understand," Agata went on. "Something to do with that painting. With Tomassoni, perhaps, or some link with Franco's own lineage."

Her eyes scanned each of them. "This much I do know from what I've read. Ranuccio Tomassoni was the *caporione* of his quarter. The boss of it. The man who ran the gangs, who ruled the streets, and handed out vengeance and a kind of justice as he saw fit. Just as Franco is today. For a while Caravaggio was with him, alongside Fillide. Somehow..." She squeezed her eyes tight shut again, trying to concentrate. "Franco and Nino Tomassoni found out about this, and re-created it around that painting. Then, with Véronique's assistance, they made everything so much worse. How? Why? I have no idea."

Teresa shook her head and sighed. "If this is true, it still doesn't give us enough evidence to put Franco Malaspina in front of a magistrate. Even if we could find one who wasn't tame. They'd look at us as if we were crazy."

"It's a question of time," Costa insisted. "And work. The more we know, the closer we get to this man. Sooner or later..."

"Nic," Teresa objected, "it's a piece of very old glass and a lot of interesting connections that may or may not add up."

"No, it's not," Agata said, and reached into her bag again.

She took out something else and rubbed it hard against her sleeve. Dust and dirt fell from it onto the Doria Pamphilj's polished floor. Then she held the object next to the painting on the wall for all to see.

It was a fragment of fabric, a square, deliberately cut, about the size of a hand.

Agata kept it there and no one said a word.

"A memento," she suggested, "of love at a time when Michelangelo Merisi was happy, inhabiting a world full of light. And later, an item of comfort, a reminder of that abandoned past, when he himself lived in permanent darkness and violence and blood. *Look!*"

It bore the same fleur-de-lis pattern as the fabric on the dress of Fillide Melandroni, sleeping as the penitent Mary Magdalene. Costa reached out and touched it with his fingers. The cloth felt thick and expensive.

If one imagined away the dust and the dirt of centuries, it would surely exhibit the same olive colour too.

# Part Thirteen
## The Ekstasists' Lair

# One

N INO TOMASSONI CAN WAIT. SHOW ME THIS statue you looked at," she requested as they left the Doria Pamphilj. "It's not far."

"It isn't," Teresa agreed from the front seat. "But don't hold out your hopes. We've scraped everything we can off these damned things, looking for something that might link us back to Malaspina. Paper. Ink. Spit. You name it."

The pathologist sighed. She looked exhausted too. There was a nervous tension about them all, one that spoke of desperation and failure.

When they were about to get back into the car, Costa had taken a call from Falcone in the Questura. The legal department was getting restless. Toni Grimaldi, never the most forthcoming of colleagues, was suddenly saying nothing at all.

"We've tried the other statues too," Teresa added. "We could spend months working on that material. Perhaps we will. I don't know... We would need something extraordinary, something direct. Plain DNA won't help us. We still run up against the same brick wall. We can't get a thing to corroborate it with."

They waited for the other cars to stop and the officers to crowd round Agata's exit. Then they got out and stood in front of the crude, worn statue of Pasquino underneath a grey winter sky. Dusk was descending over the city, and black clouds full of rain, their bellies dotted by the slow-moving starling flocks that circled endlessly high above them.

"This is ridiculous," Agata hissed under her breath. "Why would anyone wish to kill me? The magistrate has already thrown out my evidence."

"If we find more evidence, we can reintroduce you as a witness," Costa argued. "Also . . ."

He didn't want to say it now, but she was staring at him intently.

"Perhaps he thinks you're the person who might see something the rest of us will miss. That would worry him deeply."

"He's wrong there, isn't he?" she grumbled. "I can't even uncover the truth of what happened to Caravaggio and I've been studying him for years."

Like her, he'd read so many books, so many biographies. None of them gave any good answers about what happened the day Ranuccio Tomassoni died, or why.

"Why don't we know?" he asked, with a genuine curiosity. "It was a criminal case. There were records, surely."

"Nothing reliable. Caravaggio fled. Most of the others, too, and when they returned, everything was hushed up, damages paid, reputations mended. I simply don't know. What information we have comes from contemporary accounts by partial bystanders. Caravaggio's friends. Or his enemies. By rights there should be something in the Vatican archives. I have contacts there. I've looked. The cupboard's bare. Perhaps they incriminated someone important. Del Monte himself even. What's the point in speculating?"

She took one step forward towards the statue, then reached out and touched the stone. It had been scraped clean recently by the forensic team. Even so, the posters had returned, with their customary vehemence. There were five messages there, all in the curious scrawl of a computer printer, artificial letters posing as handwriting. Three seemed to be nonsense. One castigated a senior politician as a criminal. The final poster was a foul-mouthed rant, calling the Pope any number of names and comparing him to Hitler.

"So much hate in the world," Agata said quietly. She stared at the statue's battered face, barely recognisable as a man. "Why do the police spend their time looking at things like this?"

"Because sometimes it's worth it," Rosa cut in. "It was here, in the end. Though normally"—she shrugged—"it's just racist or political material. We need to keep tabs on that kind of information. Where else would you find something that . . . frank?"

"Where else?" Agata echoed, not taking her eyes off Pasquino for a moment. "Where were the others?"

Rosa told her. Then the slight woman in black pushed her way back through the huddle of officers, finding the middle car, only to sit there, waiting, engulfed by her own private thoughts.

When he got in, Costa found her staring at him.

"Tell me about these statues, Nic," she asked. "I must have walked past them a million times. I'd like to know."

It was good to discuss something that was not to do with paintings or Caravaggio or, directly, Franco Malaspina.

So Costa told her about Pasquino, Abate Luigi, and Il Facchino, and some of the other lesser-known statues he'd discovered in his recent research, the curious encrusted figure of Il Babuino beyond the Spanish Steps, Madama Lucrezia in the Piazza San Marco, and Marforio, once Pasquino's partner, until the displeased authorities of the Vatican moved the recumbent figure of a sea god to the Campidoglio.

She laughed at his stories, a little anyway, and then, in a few short minutes, they were in the Piazza di San Lorenzo in Lucina, where she ceased to laugh at all.

# Two

*C*HE TOMASSONI HOUSE WAS WREATHED IN BARRI-
ers and yellow tape. A lone press photographer hung
around outside. For no obvious reason he pulled out an
SLR and began firing it the moment the three-car convoy
arrived. The officers from the front car leapt out and were
around him in an instant. Costa ordered Rosa to take
Agata straight to the house. While she was doing that, as
quickly and efficiently as her charge would allow, he
walked over to confront the individual with the camera.

"What the hell do you think you're doing?" Costa
asked the man, who was struggling and swearing in the
arms of two plainclothes officers.

"Earning a living," the photographer barked back in a
southern accent. "Or trying to. What do you bastards
think you're doing? This is a public street. I can do what
I like."

"ID," Taccone, the sovrintendente in charge of the
first car, said, and it wasn't a request. He was pulling the
card out of the man's wallet already.

"All you had to do was ask," he moaned. "This is persecution. We've got rights."

Costa took the wallet and looked at the photograph and the bare details there.

"Carmine Aprea," Costa read off the state identity card. "Well, Carmine . . . where are your press credentials?"

"I don't work inside the system, man," Aprea answered.

"Then how do I know you do what you say?"

"You call any of the papers. Give them my name. They know me. Maybe they don't like me, but what the hell? So long as they're buying . . ." He nodded at the house. "Normally I take pictures of the living. But all these dead people you've got around here. It's been a while since I took a few stiffs. A man needs a change from time to time."

"Paparazzo," Taccone muttered, and spat on the ground. "There are no bodies for you in this place. Go find some cheap little actress to pester."

"How much are you making, moron?" Aprea retorted, looking Taccone up and down. The old sovrintendente never was one much for sartorial elegance. It was almost a joke in the Questura. "I could buy you with one picture, man. . . ."

At that point Peroni intervened and his big, scarred, ugly features made the small, pinched-faced individual with the camera go very quiet.

Peroni snatched the bulky black Nikon from Aprea's hands and held it in front of the man's face, lens uppermost, fat metal barrel just a couple of fingers from his swarthy nose.

"Do you know what an endoscope is, Carmine?" he asked.

Aprea screwed up his swarthy features, baffled. "Kind of, it's—"

"Wrong. This," Peroni barked, pushing the Nikon right into Aprea's face, "is an endoscope. If I see your plug-ugly face again, I'll shove the thing so far up your ass you'll be taking pictures of your own throat. Now get the hell out of here."

It didn't take another word. Aprea snatched the camera and was walking quickly away, muttering, just loud enough for them to hear, "Big guys. Big guys. So really big . . ."

"Get out of here . . . Hey!" Peroni yelled.

The photographer had turned and was firing away at them as he walked backwards. Except the lens wasn't aimed in their direction. It was going to the door of Nino Tomassoni's house.

Agata was there, looking at the exterior and the cobbled street, as if trying to re-create some scene in her imagination.

"Inside!" he yelled at Rosa. "Like I said."

Peroni started to move. Aprea stopped shooting, just long enough to call out to the two women by the door, "*Grazie, grazie!* I will make you both look beautiful tomorrow."

Then he turned on his heels and ran, faster than a

man of his age ought to, a bulging black shape disappearing into the web of lanes that fed towards the river.

"Leave it," Costa barked at Peroni.

"We didn't even check——" the big man began.

"I said . . ."

He stopped. There was a bigger argument going on and it was coming from the door of Nino Tomassoni's home.

THE TALL, SKINNY WOMAN FROM THE CITY COUNCIL waved some kind of card in his face, yelling, "You will not touch a thing in this house or I'll call my superiors and have you in court for cultural terrorism before dinner."

Costa looked at her ID. She was from the city heritage department and seemed quite senior.

"Signora . . ." he said calmly. "We are in the course of a very serious investigation. One that involves multiple murders. Please . . ."

"You are not allowed to knock down protected buildings," she shrieked.

"For Christ's sake, I keep telling you! I don't want to knock it down."

Silvio Di Capua was in a white bunny suit that didn't look very white anymore. It was covered in mortar and dust. He was holding a sledgehammer in his hands. It looked as if it had been used.

"What do you want to do?" Costa asked.

"Just rip it apart," Di Capua pleaded. "A little bit. Not much."

"You cannot . . ." the woman began.

Agata Graziano had placed her small body between Di Capua and the councilwoman. There was clearly some recognition there.

"Signora Barducci! Please. You know me. This is important. Listen to these men."

"You're that nun from the Barberini," she said. "What are you doing here?"

"Helping," Agata replied, and not bothering to correct her. "Making sure there is as little disruption as possible. This house . . ."

The downstairs hall was covered in the detritus of a police forensic team. Even so, the place was remarkable, like the faded set from some historical movie, with battered furniture and paintings, and a musty, damp smell that spoke of age and solitary occupation.

"Are those gas lamps?" Agata asked.

"The very thing," said a voice coming down the stairs. It was Teresa Lupo, and she appeared to be covered in even more brick dust than her deputy.

She shook some of the muck off herself, then smiled.

"And that," she said, "is why we have to take down the wall."

The woman waved her long arms in the air. "No, no, no! I will not permit it."

"Show me," Costa ordered, and they followed Teresa up the winding staircase.

# Three

$\mathcal{I}$T WAS A SIMPLE CONUNDRUM: THERE WERE GAS-
lights on the ground floor and the top. On the landing of
the middle floor the lights were electric, though very old
indeed.

"This means?" Costa asked.

Teresa glanced at Di Capua. "He's the building freak.
You tell him."

"It means there's something wrong," he explained.
"This landing abuts the house next door. This place is
such a mess it's hard to tell whether you're up or down
half the time. There are no building plans we can refer to.
Nothing formal at all..." He cast a vicious look at the
woman from the council. "Not even among the preservation people."

"It's preserved!" she said. "The place is sixteenth century, for God's sake."

"It's preserved," Costa agreed. "What's wrong?"

Di Capua picked up the sledgehammer and, ignoring

Signora Barducci's shrieks, tapped it lightly on the wall to the left, then to the right.

"That."

They all heard it. A distinct, resonant tone came from the right wall, one that had to indicate some space behind.

"The gas line runs up the original right-hand wall," Di Capua explained. "There are so many twists and turns on this narrow staircase, it's hard to make out what's happening here. But this isn't the same wall, and that's why it doesn't have it. The mains goes straight up from the ground to the top floor, and into that room over there . . ." He pointed to the single door across the landing. "But not here."

Agata walked up and tapped the wall with her knuckles.

"It's still brick," she said. "If you're right, this predates gas surely. These houses are from ancient and difficult times. The *caporione* lived here. A man who might have been involved in crime. It would not be unusual to have some private, secret storage place. Most houses of this kind would."

"Precisely," Di Capua agreed, and lifted up the sledgehammer again.

Costa tried to think this through, aware that he felt tired and his shoulder was beginning to ache again.

"But . . ."

Di Capua was getting ready to strike a blow.

"If it's a hidden compartment," Costa pointed out, voice rising, "there has to be a way in."

The hammer stopped in midair. He was aware they were all staring at him, as if expecting an answer.

"Maybe," Di Capua suggested, "there used to be a door."

Teresa swiped him around the head. "In that case, idiot, it wouldn't have been much of a secret, would it?"

Signora Barducci pushed her way to the front, then stood in front of Di Capua, between his hammer and the wall.

"This is another reason why you can't start knocking things down. This and ..."

She began to reel off a seemingly endless string of statutes and orders, laws and conventions, all to do with her own city department, each demanding prior written permission before a single brick of a protected building in the *centro storico* could be touched.

"Also ..." she added happily, "does it possibly occur to you for one moment that this wall might be structural? That by removing its support you could bring this whole house down around our heads? It's happened. I've seen it."

Di Capua blinked and shook his bald head from side to side. He was wearing his remaining hair long again these days, and the locks deposited dust everywhere as they moved.

"Structural?" he asked. "Structural? Of course it's not structural. If it was, don't you think—"

He stopped. They all went quiet, even the Barducci woman. There was a sound, a new sound, at that moment, and it took a few long seconds for Nic Costa to appreciate its source.

Someone was behind the wall, making scrabbling noises, like some gigantic rat rummaging around in the dark.

"What the hell—" Teresa began to say.

And then stopped. There was a human being behind the brick and she was screaming.

"Agata," Costa murmured.

He looked upstairs, closed his eyes for a moment, swore, and then took the steps to the upper floor three at a time.

THERE WERE TWO FORENSIC OFFICERS IN THE BIG OPEN room and they retreated behind a couple of paintings when he stormed in.

"Where is she?" Costa shouted.

"Went in there," said the first one, who looked like a student fresh from college, with bright yellow hair and a terrified expression.

"Where?"

The woman was pointing at a large, long, fitted wardrobe running almost the entire length of the wall. It wasn't difficult to work out this had to stand over the suspect area on the floor below.

"We gave her a flashlight," the other forensic monkey added plaintively, as if that were an excuse.

Costa was at the door by then, staring into a Stygian pool of inky darkness.

"Wonderful. Do you have a spare one for me?"

They shrugged.

He stepped through into the wardrobe and almost immediately found himself struggling to stay upright.

"Agata? *Agata?*"

It was like yelling into a black hole that lurked somewhere beneath him. Costa stumbled, and managed to hold on to something made of old, dry wood. The hatch, he guessed, and it was up.

"Where are you?"

His right leg found whatever chasm led down to the floor below, and he began half testing, half lunging for some kind of step.

"Nic?" said a small, frightened voice from below him.

Then a yellow beam of light worked its way back towards him and he saw, for the first time, what she'd found. There was a trapdoor, and steep, almost vertical steps, virtually a stepladder made of worn old wood, though there was little in the way of dust, as if this place was used regularly.

"It's all right," he said, reaching the bottom of the stairs. "I'm here. Walk towards me. Bring the flashlight."

The light turned further towards him. She kept it low to the ground always. He couldn't see her face, but soon she was close enough for him to sense her presence. Her hands found his and thrust the flashlight into his fingers. That brief touch told him she was shaking like a leaf.

"It's all right," he said again automatically.

"No," she whispered into his ear. "It's not."

Voices began to clamour from behind and above. Teresa had found the entrance too. Costa called up for them to await orders.

The place was a narrow rectangle, perhaps two metres wide and longer than he expected, a good eight metres or so. Big enough to be a child's bedroom, but that wasn't the purpose. She had understood what this was for from the beginning, understood too that there had to be some way in that wasn't obvious, and it could only be from above or below.

At first glance there seemed to be nothing there but battered cardboard boxes that looked many years old and, at the very end, some kind of tall cabinet reaching up two metres.

"I thought the painting might be here. I don't know why. I dreamed . . ."

That she would be the one to find it. He understood that urge on her part. In some way she felt responsible for its loss.

She pulled away from him. He felt, briefly, the touch of her cheek. It was damp with tears, and she must have realised he'd noticed, since she was soon wiping them away with her sleeve, as she'd wiped away the dust on the glass jug in the Doria Pamphilj.

"It was here," she insisted. "Look!"

Her firm, determined fingers forced the beam to the left wall. Costa looked and found his breath locking tight in his lungs.

It was the same shape, surely. The same size. Dust stood around the paler wall where the canvas had hung, undisturbed, for years, centuries perhaps. Above the missing frame, scribbled in pencil, in a hand that looked ancient, someone had written *Evathia in Ekstasis.*

Costa looked at it and thought, *That was how they knew.* A line of pencil, scribbled God knows how long before, gave Tomassoni the insight into the true nature of the painting, one he passed on to Malaspina with such terrible consequences, ones that were now visible and very real.

Something had taken the place of Caravaggio's work.

Knowing she wouldn't look too closely, Costa walked forward and peered at the items that were stuck there. They were the same kind of photos they had found in the studio in the Vicolo del Divino Amore, colour shots from a computer printer, of poor quality, as if snapped by a phone or the cheapest of digital cameras.

There were perhaps ten in all, stuck there with drawing pins. Each depicted a close-up of a woman, all apparently foreign, all seemingly in the throes of ecstasy or pain or the onset of death. Tomassoni may have been reluctant to take part, but he clearly liked to watch, then spill out his fears in anonymous emails to the police afterwards.

"The canvas was here all those centuries," Agata said,

with a cold, sad certainty in her voice. "Then Franco found out and took her. He heard what she said to him. He wanted to. That was Caravaggio's point."

"We mustn't touch anything," he insisted. "This place will soon be crawling with forensic. Teresa . . ."

"I'm waiting," said an enthusiastic voice from above.

Agata took the flashlight from him. Then she strode to the back of the chamber and the cabinet there. The black wooden door was ajar. She'd looked already. It was this, Costa understood, from the way she steeled herself, that had made her scream, not the shocking photographs in the space that had once held the painting.

She stopped, her wary eyes urging him to go on.

"Please. I have seen and wish to see no more."

Costa walked past her and opened the door.

There was a figure there dressed in an archaic tattered and rat-gnawed velvet jacket, an ancient shirt the colour of ochre visible at the point that had once been a human neck. It was merely a skeleton now, dusty bones and the familiar rictus of death set in a crooked skull.

Costa paused for a moment, thinking. Some kind of notice sat on the bony chest, held there by dusty string tied around the back of his head.

He picked it up and read out loud the archaic, awkward words, knowing they sounded familiar.

"*Noi repetiam Pigmalïon allotta,*
*cui traditore e ladro e paricida*
*fece la voglia sua de l'oro ghiotta.*"

"I know that," he said, not expecting a reply. "Almost. It's familiar . . . and strange too."

"Everyone's favourite poet," she murmured. "Around here anyway. Dante. From *Purgatorio*, if I remember correctly. You probably read the modern translation. Most schoolchildren do.

> *Then we tell of Pygmalion,*
> *Of whom a traitor and thief and parricide*
> *Made his greedy lust for gold."*

Agata reached out and touched the notice, seeing, with her historian's eye, something that had been lost on him.

"There are two lines through the word *paricida*," she pointed out. "What do you think that means?"

He looked. She was right. It had been crossed out the way a teacher would mark a mistaken word in a piece of homework.

"Perhaps that part at least is untrue. They regarded him only as a traitor and a thief."

"Good," she said, nodding. "I would see it that way too. They were like Franco. They enjoyed showing off their so-called learning, even when it was in part inappropriate."

She had recited the words with the perfect precision of a poet herself. He recalled what Malaspina had said in the palazzo that night: *She sees herself as Beatrice. Beautiful, chaste, alluring. And dead.*

"I'm sorry. I thought I would be some use to you. All I do is make everything murkier. I bring you more puzzles when you need more light. It's a waste of time. Put me somewhere safe if that's what Leo wants. I won't complain."

"I will," he said, shifting the sign to one side, looking at what lay beneath it, resting on the grey bones of the rib cage that was visible through the ripped fabric of the shirt. "We need you."

"Why?" she asked softly. "So that you can bury your wife, finally? Is that what I'm supposed to do for you?"

Costa turned and looked at her. In the yellow half-light of the flashlight, she seemed, for the first time, he thought, a woman, much like any other. Not part of some different life he couldn't begin to comprehend.

"No," he replied simply. "I'll do that myself, when I'm ready."

"Then what?"

The heat rose in her eyes.

Costa put a finger to his lips. This once, she obeyed him and became silent. He walked to the steps, barked a few questions at Teresa Lupo and Silvio Di Capua, then had them throw down a couple of clear plastic evidence bags.

"You may not want to watch this," he said when he got back to the cabinet.

"Why not?" she demanded. "What have you seen? Tell me!"

"This . . ."

He moved the sign to one side and indicated an area on the left of the corpse's chest. There was an object there, some kind of round medallion, dull dark metal on a similarly coloured chain, but with the outline of the emblem at its centre still visible, still comprehensible.

Three dragons, limbs thrashing, talons wrapped around the figure of a woman who writhed in their grip, screaming, eyes rolling wildly.

"This is the same symbol we found on the notes the Ekstasists placed on the statues," he said. "Now we know where that came from. It's a link. A tentative one, but I'll take whatever I can get."

"A link," she grumbled, and folded her arms.

"And this . . ."

He pushed aside completely the yellowing paper bearing Dante's words and shone the flashlight directly on the portion of the velvet jacket next to the dull black medallion. At first it had seemed a wild guess. Now, under the fierce beam, it was unmistakable.

"You don't recognise it, do you?" he asked.

It was a heraldic badge: a shield divided into two halves, with a skeletal tree bearing three short horizontal branches on one side and two on the other, dotted with spines.

"I don't notice much except paintings," Agata replied with a frown. "Usually."

"It's all over Franco's beautiful palace. It's his family crest. The bad thorn."

In this small, stuffy room that was cold and damp, Agata Graziano laughed. "That's impossible!"

"Take a look."

She did and shook her head. "Who on earth is this? What does it mean?"

"Finally," he said, "you're asking me a question."

"Yes."

"Then, as a police officer, I would guess this is a murder victim."

"I know that . . ."

"Given the identification, one who was once known as Ippolito Malaspina."

"That's impossible! How could you know?" She put her fingers to her mouth with shock, then stopped, thinking, eyes glittering.

*Everything connects in Rome,* he reminded himself. Past and present. And in this case the crimes of four centuries before.

"I can't. But I can guess," he said emphatically. "You showed us the portrait that was supposed to be Ippolito in Malta, several years after he left Rome. You said yourself, it was nothing like the description of the man in all the reference books you found . . ."

"That doesn't mean . . ."

"He had a family," Costa interrupted. "Was that before he left the city with Caravaggio or after?"

"Before. Afterwards he travelled constantly and never . . ." She stopped and stared at him. "He never returned home. Never went anywhere he had been before as far as I recall. They inherited everything when he died. And . . ."

He watched her turn this over in her bright, constantly active mind.

"Is it possible," he asked, "that they inherited everything without ever seeing him again? That Franco Malaspina is descended from the real Malaspina, but the man who went to Malta with Caravaggio was an impostor?"

"Yes," she answered in a low, firm voice. "From what I've read . . ."

"Good," Costa said, then took out the plastic envelope and stared at the grey, dusty skull in front of him.

"What are you going to do?" she asked.

"Find the evidence to put Franco in jail."

"From a corpse that's four hundred years old?"

"Why not? We can't go near him. But he is an aristocrat. His lineage is there, set down in the state archives. If the DNA of this corpse is related to that we have from the Vicolo del Divino Amore, all we have to prove is that this gentleman"—he prodded the velvet jacket with his forefinger—"is Ippolito Malaspina. It won't put his descendant in the dock. But it would make it damned hard for a court to refuse a few tests to prove the truth one way or another, and that's all we need."

She didn't look scared anymore. She looked fascinated.

"You can do that?" she asked. "Take a sample from a skeleton that's nothing but . . . bone?"

"No!"

The loud female voice made them both jump. Costa couldn't work out how Teresa Lupo had found her way down the stepladder without their noticing. She barged her way in front of him and stared at the skeleton. Then she snatched the envelope out of his hands.

"But I can," she said with a grin that was wide and friendly in the yellow light of the flashlight.

The pathologist leaned forward. In her gloved hand was an implement very like a small set of pliers. She gazed at the skull's open mouth. The left-hand front tooth was missing already. Teresa fastened the pliers to the remaining one, then, in a swift, twisting movement, snapped it free and dropped the object into the bag.

"You're coming home with Mummy," she added, greatly pleased with herself. "Right now."

She stared at the pair of them. "And you two should go home as well. You've done enough for one day."

Teresa held up the bag. "There is a time for happy conjecture and a time for science, children. Tomorrow is Christmas. Come back and see what La Befana and her little elves have for you."

Part Fourteen
The Night Before Christmas

# One

*L*A VIGILIA WAS ALREADY STEALING OVER ROME: Christmas Eve, a pause from the rush and chaos of everyday life. The convoy drove back to the farmhouse through streets that were dark and deserted. There was no need for the fairy lights anymore, no cause to be anywhere but home, in the company of family and friends. Teresa and her team might relish the idea of spending the night poring over the contents of Nino Tomassoni's secret lair, trying to decode the genetic fingerprint hidden inside the tooth of a skull of an unknown man who just might—Costa knew this was a stretch—turn out to be Ippolito Malaspina. But for the rest of the city, this was a time for reflection and enjoyment.

And food: *seven fishes.* No real Roman ate meat at La Vigilia. It was always fish, by tradition seven types, one, his father used to say, for every Catholic sacrament. Even in the Costa household, which, during his childhood, was more solidly communist, and atheist, than any he knew in Lazio, it was impossible to separate La Vigilia from the custom of the seven fishes.

The godless needed rituals, too, from time to time.

As they reached the drive and the two guard cars peeled off to block the entrance behind them, Costa wondered why this memory had returned at such a time. Then, dog-tired and ready for bed, just as Agata clearly was, too, he opened the door for her to enter, and a succession of aromas and fragrances wafted out from the kitchen beyond, ones that took him back twenty years in an instant and sent a strong sense of urgent hunger rumbling through his stomach.

Bea stood there in her best evening dress, wearing a huge white, perfectly ironed apron. By her side, Pepe the terrier sat upright, a red ribbon round his neck.

"Happy Christmas," Bea said, welcoming them with a bow, then making to take their coats.

Agata's face lit up. She sniffed at the rich and exotic aromas drifting from the kitchen.

"What *is* this?" she asked.

"And you a Christian," Bea scolded her. "It's La Vigilia. Christmas Eve. And I am a spinster with much time on my hands and a fondness for the old ways. So you will sit down and dine with me. Do not try to play the vegetarian here, young man. I've seen you eat fish."

"Seven?" he asked.

"Of course," she replied, as if it were an idiotic question. "Now go upstairs and change. This is a special occasion. If the dog can dress for it, so can you."

Agata ran her slim fingers over the black hand-me-down coat. "I am fine like this, Bea. I have nothing . . ."

Bea wiped her hands on her apron, then helped Agata out of the coat, holding it away from her, as if it were a thing of no value.

"Sometimes La Befana comes early. Even for those who come home late. Now go upstairs! Shoo! Shoo!"

The dog barked.

"La Befana?" Agata gasped, eyes glittering.

Bea watched her ascend the stairs quickly, like a child.

"See," she said quietly, "she is only human after all."


THEY SAT AROUND THE LONG TABLE IN THE DINING room, Bea at the head, guiding them through the spread of food, which seemed to grow with every passing minute: cold seafood salad, salt cod, mussels, clams, shrimps, a small lobster, then, finally, the delicacy his father always insisted on, however much it cost, *capitone,* a large female eel, split into pieces and roasted in the oven, wreathed in bay leaves.

Agata sat there, astonished, eating greedily. Somehow, during the shopping, Bea had found time to buy her a new white shirt and plain blue trousers. She wore them with the customary battered crucifix around her neck, and within minutes had sauce and debris spattered everywhere, on her clothes and on the table. Bea gave up staring in the end. It was of no consequence.

"This is obscene," Agata cried when the eel finally appeared.

"Compared with what we've seen . . ." Costa observed quietly.

"No work," Bea snapped. "I didn't sweat in that kitchen for hours to listen to you two moan about your day. That is the rule. La Vigilia! Eat! And then . . ."

She went to the kitchen and came back with a plate of sweet cakes and a bowl full of small presents wrapped in gold paper.

"Then what?" Agata asked.

"Then we choose from the bowl," Bea responded. "What do you normally do at Christmas, for pity's sake?"

Agata shrugged, then picked up a large piece of eel, stuffed it in her mouth, and said, while chewing, "Pray. Sing. Think. Read."

"And?" Bea asked, ignoring the warning glance Costa hoped he was sending her way.

"And . . . take a little wine before midnight mass." She cocked her head towards the window. Her hair was now so different. She was different. Costa wondered whether he ought to feel guilty for that change.

"Can you hear the cannon from the Castel Sant'Angelo when they fire it?" she asked brightly.

"No," he answered. "Sorry. We could find it on the television perhaps."

"It wouldn't be the same."

Bea carefully refilled their glasses with *prosecco*.

"Is a cannon important?" she asked.

"It means midnight mass is not far away," Agata responded immediately. "I love midnight mass. More than anything. I love the little shows the churches have, with their manger and their infant, Mary and the shepherds. I love the way people look at one another. Another year navigated. Another year to come."

She put down her knife and fork, then wiped her hands with her napkin.

"There are churches nearby," Agata said hopefully. "Beautiful ones in the Appian Way. Do you think I could go? How many people would be there in a desert like this? You could come with me." She glanced at Bea. "Both of you, I mean, naturally. I would not hope to evangelize. You've shown me your world. Can I not show you a little of mine?"

Bea coughed into her fist and stared at her plate.

"Do you think Leo Falcone would allow that?" Costa asked. "A church is . . . a very open place."

"It's supposed to be," she said quietly.

There was silence. Then, after a while, she added, somewhat downcast, "I've never missed midnight mass. Not in my whole life. Or the sound of that cannon for as long as I can remember."

"I'm sorry."

She smiled at him. "But you would do it if you could."

"Certainly."

Agata was watching him in a way he found vaguely unsettling.

"What would you have done?" she asked. "Before. With Emily."

He had to think. "Last year we had a meal with Leo and his friend, and Teresa and Gianni," he said, when he finally managed to recover the memories. "In the city." He nodded at Bea over the table. "It wasn't a patch on this food."

But this Christmas it would have been different, more private, spent at home, just the two of them. Emily was his wife, finally. Had they not lost the child she was carrying in the spring . . .

This thought—another of those painful, hypothetical leaps of a cruel imagination—assaulted him. Had Emily kept the child, she would have given up college by now. There would have been no reason for her to have been lurking near the Mausoleum of Augustus on a dull December day, no energy left to be wasted following a fleeing fugitive the way her old skills from the FBI had taught her.

There would have been two new lives in the old farmhouse at that moment. *If . . .*

Costa blinked back something in his eyes. The two women were watching him. He wondered whether to make an excuse and leave the table.

"I'm sorry," Agata murmured. "I should never have asked that."

"No," he replied emphatically. "You can't undo the past by ignoring it. What has happened has happened. I don't want anyone"—he glanced at Bea—"to let me pretend it can be undone somehow."

The two women exchanged a brief look. He could see they hoped he hadn't noticed.

"It's the silence," Agata said, changing the subject rapidly. "To me it shouts. Is that strange? That I miss the noise of the traffic? The buses? The people outside my window who've had a little too much to drink and sing so loudly, so badly, I have to laugh beneath my sheets?"

"Of course not," he answered. "You miss what you're familiar with. It's only natural. You miss the background of the world you know. You miss what you love."

"Just like you," she said quickly, without thinking, glass in hand, her eyes bright with life and interest now. "I'm sorry. Just like . . ."

Her fingers flew to her face. She had drunk the wine too quickly, too freely. Something in her firm reserve, which had been so resolute ever since he first met her in the Barberini's studio at the back of the Palazzo Malaspina, was now crumbling visibly.

"I didn't mean that," she stuttered. "It's the food, the drink. It's me. Oh . . . *Oh* . . ."

Agata ran from the room, tears welling in her eyes, and raced into the corridor beyond.

Costa blinked. "What did I say?"

Bea sighed and declared, "Nothing."

"Then . . . what?"

"Oh, try to think, Nic. The poor child's not seen anything like this. She's not used to family. Or the idea two people can talk honestly with each other. Damn the Church for doing that to someone. I doubt she's had that much decent food and *prosecco* in her entire life. That and God knows what you've shown her. It's my fault. I'm sorry. This meal was an idiotic idea."

"You cannot judge her like that," he said, with a sudden brief burst of anger.

Bea put out her hand and touched his cheek. "I don't. Believe me. I was trying to help. To show her what it's like outside that prison of hers."

"She doesn't see it that way. It's none of your business. Or mine either."

"Isn't it?"

The day had been too long. There was a surfeit of ideas and images and possibilities running round his exhausted head. His shoulder hurt. His mind felt bruised from overactivity.

"You really don't have the faintest idea, do you?" she asked tartly.

"No . . ." he answered softly, a vague, disturbing thought rising from somewhere he wished it had remained.

Bea held out the bowl with the tiny presents in it. "You might as well take one anyway."

He did. It was what had always happened, even when he was a child. The rules, the laws that governed this game, demanded one small box be empty, and as usual it was his.

"This is not your day," Bea declared. "Go to bed now, and leave everything—including our young friend Agata—to me."

# Two

$\mathcal{H}$E KNEW THE HOUSE SO WELL HE FELT HE COULD hear the old stones breathing as they slept. When he awoke, the clock by the bed said 3 a.m. and someone, elsewhere, was awake.

Costa pulled on a dressing gown and went downstairs. She was where he least expected, in the studio, and it didn't look anything like he remembered.

From somewhere—Rosa had brought them, he guessed—she had found a series of photographs of the missing painting. Caravaggio's sensual, fleshy image of Venus—or Eve, he was unsure which anymore—stood on several of Emily's easels, in full frame, close-up, and very fine detail in several of the shots too. Agata was perched on the single artist's stool by the desk, staring at the biggest photo, a finger on her cheek, brooding, seemingly as alert as ever, a large pile of documents and what appeared to be an old book by her side.

"It doesn't really look like that now, though," he said.

She jumped, surprised, perhaps a little embarrassed,

by his appearance. She still wore the clothes Bea had found for her, the shirt spattered with food. She hadn't been to bed at all.

"How do you mean?" she asked, placing her elbow over the papers, as if she didn't want him to see.

"You found the signature. And the real name."

She frowned. "*You* found the name. Besides, now I've had the chance to think about it, I'm not sure it's as important as all that. Caravaggio was playing a game with them. Painting something they thought they could keep to themselves because it was so shocking . . ."

She pointed to the face of the satyr, the artist's own. "He was part of it too. One of the Ekstasists. The man had a sense of humour, you know. He was laughing at them, and perhaps at himself as well."

Costa came and stood next to her. The photograph did not do the painting justice. The work seemed distant somehow, lacking in the force and meaning that were so powerful, so unavoidable, when the canvas was in front of one's face. It possessed something that could not be conveyed through the modern medium of a camera.

"It doesn't mean he was a part of whatever they did. Perhaps he simply knew them and accepted the commission."

"Oh, don't talk such rubbish." She gave him a withering look. The teacher in her had returned. "Remember the way he signed it? Why would he describe himself as an Ekstasist if he was outside the club? How would he even know the name? Don't blind yourself to the truth,

Nic. Michelangelo Merisi was part angel, part devil. Like most men, only more so. We know he was involved in cruel and criminal acts. In the end it cost him everything. He was with them. I can feel it. Nothing else makes sense. I just wish..." She stopped and scratched her head.

"Why are you still awake?" he asked.

"How can I sleep?" she complained, still unable to take her attention away from the photographs. "I miss everything about my home. The noises. The female company. The routine. The fact I'm safe there. I don't have to worry about all these troubles that bother you..."

"You will return," he assured her. "As soon as possible."

"I hope so," Agata replied, but not with much conviction. She stared at him. "Tell me. If there was some way I could find out why it all went wrong that first time round, with Caravaggio and Tomassoni. Why some stupid, juvenile band of thugs degenerated into murder and bloody hatred. Just as it did with Franco. Would that help?"

"You still don't understand this, do you?" he declared, almost exasperated. "What it is that we do."

"You establish facts and then act on them. Of course I understand that."

Costa shook his head. "No, you don't. Sometimes the facts lead nowhere. You have to fill them out with guesswork, imagination."

"That idea offends me. It's not scholarly. Not scientific."

"Is the Bible?"

"It's scholarly."

"As is Teresa's laboratory, but Franco Malaspina has denied us that. We don't have those luxuries anymore. Emily and those women are dead. Franco Malaspina and his accomplices were responsible somehow. What we need are plain, ordinary, unassailable facts that link him to them. We can't find any. So instead . . ."

"Guesswork," she grumbled. "But would it help if you understood about the Ekstasists?"

"I have absolutely no way of knowing. Why?"

She hesitated and eyed him nervously. "I was just curious. I'm sorry about tonight," she said in a low, nervy voice. "Sometimes I speak too freely."

"Too much wine."

"That was an excuse. I hardly touched the wine. I simply . . ." Still she wouldn't look at him. "I don't belong in a place like this. It's mundane and close and personal in a way that's beyond me. I know that's selfish. I'm sorry."

"It doesn't matter."

"Don't say that. It does. All that beautiful food. The care Bea took." She shrugged her slender shoulders and wrapped her arms around the stained white shirt. "I never expected to be a part of such an evening. I didn't even know anything like it ever existed really . . ."

Agata walked rapidly over to the desk, which was still

littered with Emily's drawings. "Do you think I'm wasting my life?" she asked him from across the room. "Be honest."

"Do you?"

"It's very unfair to answer a question with another question. Answer me, please. Look at what your wife did. She drew, she thought, she tried to create things. One day I imagine you would have had a family. And I . . ." She scowled, an expression of moody dissatisfaction spreading across her face. "I stare at paintings and try to find life in them. Why? For myself. Because I daren't face the real thing. It's egotistical, obsessive, unnatural."

"I can't give you an answer," he said.

"Why not?"

"Because I don't know you well enough. And even if I did, it would be presumptuous. To ask another human being whether there's value in your own existence . . . that's for you to judge."

She thought about this.

"But you placed a value on Emily's life," she pointed out. "You still do. I see her in your eyes, like a mist that's always there. Her memory drives you, more than anything I have ever seen in another person. I can't imagine what you'll feel if this need you have to bring Franco Malaspina to justice isn't satisfied."

"That won't happen."

"It might."

She walked over and stood in front of him again.

"You're trawling through grey dust and old bones for an answer now. How desperate does a man need to be to do that?"

"I prefer to think of it as determined."

Agata laughed. Not in the way she did when they first met. This was open and happy and carefree.

"You know," she murmured, "I used to stare at people in your world and pity you all. So much pain. So much to worry about." She grimaced. "And so much *life* too." Her hands came away from the silver cross on the chain. Nervously, she tucked a stray strand of hair behind her ear, then looked him straight in the eye and said, "I had to ask myself tonight whether I really wanted to go back to the convent. Whether this life—your kind of life— wasn't a more honest one. I've never really faced that question before. But it's been there. Before any of this happened. I recognise that now."

"Agata . . ."

Her dark eyes burned with the keen curiosity that was never far away.

"It's very late, Nic. I think I should go to bed."

His head felt heavy. He was unsure what to do, what to think.

Then the lights came on in the corridor, and he heard the sound of feet on the old wooden floor, and not long after the yapping of the dog.

Bea appeared at the door and turned on the big bright floods Emily had installed in the ceiling of the studio for her work. Costa stood there, blinking in the glare.

"I . . . I'm sorry," Bea stuttered, embarrassed. "I heard voices. I didn't know—"

"No matter," Agata cut in swiftly. "We had business to discuss, Nic and I. Now that's done I shall sleep. Good night."

She walked away from him, kissed Bea on the cheek, and left the room.

"Good night," Costa said to the small, slight figure disappearing towards the stairs.

Part Fifteen

A Sport in the Blood

# One

CHRISTMAS DAY WAS GREY AND WET, THE CLOUDS so low they almost touched the tops of the jagged monuments littering the horizon of the Appian Way. Costa woke late, his shoulder hurting. The women were downstairs already, dressed and ready for whatever the day would bring. Peroni was with them, looking thoroughly miserable.

"Coffee," Agata ordered, raising her cup. "*Buon Natale!*"

The smell of Bea's cappuccino could wake the dead. He gulped it down gratefully with some fruit and pastries. Then Bea went through the ceremony that had been interrupted the night before: the bowl and the little gifts.

This time round he got a tiepin. Peroni picked out a cheap keyring with a tiny flashlight attached to the chain and managed to look extraordinarily pleased with it. Bea grabbed one of the remaining two boxes—and didn't open it—then pressed the final one on Agata.

"This seems like a fix," she murmured, but took it anyway.

There was a small silver crucifix inside.

"It's beautiful," Agata said gratefully. "I will wear it on special occasions. It's too good"—she wrinkled her nose—"for anything else."

"Whenever suits you," Bea said easily, and opened her own box. It held something similar, doubtless from the same collection: a brooch in the shape of a butterfly. She looked at the two men. "Now go away, you two, and have the conversation you want to have. We don't wish to hear."

"Conversation," Costa began, and found Peroni dragging him off to the sitting room, his face like stone.

They sat down. Peroni pointed back towards the kitchen.

"That is the most stubborn, pigheaded woman I have ever met in my life. She makes Teresa look like a saint, for God's sake. I can't believe——"

"Bea?"

"Not Bea."

"I've been sleeping, Gianni," he said quickly. "And you speak in riddles. Please . . ."

Costa listened, and wished, deeply, he didn't have to.

EVEN MAFIOSI CELEBRATED CHRISTMAS. THE TENTATIVE tip-off from the informer in Naples had been superseded. The previous evening one of the most senior capos in the same city had taken an equally senior police officer into his home for a traditional La Vigilia supper. In the course of the meal, the crime boss had told his acquaintance that a contract on the life of Agata Graziano was now in place, in the hands of the 'Ndrangheta from Calabria, secretive men, rarely penetrated by the police, professional criminals who took on commissions from outsiders only rarely, and usually saw them through.

"You told her?" Costa asked.

"Of course I told her," Peroni answered. "How can you keep something like that secret? Falcone has made all the arrangements. We have a safe house in Piedmont she can use. If necessary we could come up with some kind of new identity, a place in the witness protection scheme . . ."

"Agata won't agree to that. Not for an instant."

"Why not?" Peroni demanded. "These are serious people. Malaspina wants her dead. We can't protect her properly here. Falcone has decided. She must go. Today. Now." He folded his arms. "Tell her. I have. She refuses. She says if we keep on nagging she'll take a cab back to that convent of hers and send us the bill."

"You could try making her," Costa suggested.

"Don't play the smart-ass with me, sir. We can't make her. If she wants to walk straight out of here and wander round Rome till she's dead, there's nothing we can do to prevent it. She's a free woman."

"I'm not sure that's really true," Costa found himself saying.

"We can't stop her. She's adamant she wants to be part of the next conference we have. Teresa has called one at the Tomassoni place for two. After that we have to go to the morgue. Like an idiot, Falcone told her."

"She's helped us, Gianni," Costa pointed out. "We'd still be arguing with Toni Grimaldi if it weren't for her."

"She won't be able to help us much if she's dead. Besides . . ."

Costa stared at the damaged, miserable face of the man who'd come to be one of his closest friends over the past few years. There was more to Peroni's sorrowful state than the steadfast refusal of Agata Graziano to disappear from Rome.

"Besides what?"

"We are still arguing with Grimaldi. There are bad noises coming from above. The kind people make when they are facing nasty decisions." Peroni's big farmer's face, scarred in ways Costa barely noticed anymore these days, fell into a deep, miserable scowl.

"Such as?" Costa asked.

"I don't know, but I have a rotten feeling we're about to find out. Malaspina is starting to affect us in all kinds of ways. Other forces are starting to become involved. The Carabinieri are on the line constantly. I imagine that is just what he wants. There are investigations everywhere crawling to a halt because of evidence problems. The word is getting out there, Nic. These hoodlums understand all they have to do is cross their arms and say no to a swab or a fingerprint and everything goes into the queue with the lawyers."

"How the hell do they know?"

Peroni looked at him as if he were an idiot. "Because we're in Rome. Because people are human. There's talk.

What's new? Everyone's starting to realise what the problem is. If we can't corroborate what we have, Malaspina will simply prance up and down in front of us, waving his fingers in the air, and there's not a thing we can do about it." Peroni's sharp, piercing eyes didn't blink. "Those men from Calabria will get their chance and then they'll be gone, without a single footprint back to the Palazzo Malaspina. We've lost enough people already. Let's not lose any more."

Costa got up and walked into the kitchen to find Agata sitting on a stool, her attention deep inside the pages of one of Bea's women's magazines. She looked bemused.

"I think there's something important we need to discuss—" he began.

"The answer's no," she cut in. "I called Leo and told him again while you were talking. He is . . . acquiescent. This meeting with Teresa is at two. I would like to visit my sisters briefly along the way, if that is permissible."

She looked up at him and smiled: a different woman? The same? He wasn't sure. There was something in Agata Graziano's face at that moment he didn't recognise, though in another woman he would have called it guile.

"So, shall we go?" she asked, picking up the black leather bag Rosa Prabakaran had provided the day before, one that looked as much at home on her now as it would have done on any young woman in Rome.

# Two

SHE SPENT AN HOUR IN THE CONVENT, AN ANONY-mous grey building close to the river and the bridge to the Castel Sant'Angelo. No men were allowed past the high wooden door, so Rosa Prabakaran and two other female officers accompanied her, and came out none the wiser. Agata had simply gone to her room and the chapel, spoken to some other sisters, entered the library to consult some books, then returned in just enough time for them to make the meeting with the forensic team.

The terraced house in the Piazza di San Lorenzo in Lucina was unrecognisable. Half the square was now blocked off to allow forensic officers clear access. The ancient, moth-eaten furniture from the ground floor had been removed. A sanitized plastic tunnel now ran through the front door for visitors. In the space between plastic and wall, men and women in white suits were on hands and knees performing a fingertip search of every last crack in the ancient floor, every mote of dust in the corners. The route led through the entire central, twisting staircase, a sterile cocoon through which they would pass until, Teresa said, they got to the top floor, where the work was essentially done and there was enough room for a meeting.

Halfway up, Agata stopped and stared at the area where, the day before, she had found herself face-to-face with the skull of the corpse Costa prayed would turn out to be Ippolito Malaspina. This section of the building was unrecognisable. Silvio Di Capua had clearly won his battle with the city planning authorities. Gigantic iron supports had been brought in to run from floor to ceiling, and workmen had removed the wall brick by brick, revealing the rectangular hidden room behind. Open to view, it seemed much smaller. The cabinet was still there, now empty. The boxes of documents that he had seen lining the far wall had disappeared too.

He knew Teresa's methods well. She was a woman who was directed, always, by priorities, and possessed an instinctive grasp of what was worth seizing first. Forensic on the strange skeleton Agata had found would surely be uppermost in her mind. But she understood, as well as any, that this was no straightforward case, no hunt for incriminating evidence. They had that already. What they needed was a link—a connection that placed Franco Malaspina in this dingy, rotting building, and made him a part of the Ekstasists, in such a firm and undeniable way that even the most sceptical or malleable of magistrates could not ignore it.

Whatever hopes he had in that direction faded the moment they entered the top floor, where the canvases were now stacked neatly to one side. Toni Grimaldi stood close by in a grey suit, a short cigar in his hand and a sour expression on his face.

"Oh, wonderful," Peroni murmured, rather too loudly for comfort.

"Merry Christmas, gentlemen," Grimaldi announced with a yawn before lifting the sackcloth on one of the canvases, squinting at what he saw, and adding, "They say this stuff is worth millions."

Agata strode over and threw the sackcloth off entirely.

"Poussin," she declared, with the briefest of scowls. "At least it's supposed to be. Leo?"

Falcone came away from the window, where he'd been staring idly into the piazza.

"Poussin it is," he agreed. "If you think it's a fake, best tell the people in Stockholm now, because they have other ideas."

"It's their painting," she replied, then stared at the newcomer.

"How goes your case, Sister?" Grimaldi asked under the heat of her glare.

"I don't have a case."

He shrugged. "Maybe you're not the only one. Let me make my position clear. Today . . . Christmas Day . . . I listen to what they have to say. Then I decide whether to allow you to put it in front of a magistrate. Once again.

Think of me as that man or woman of the judiciary. Before you can convince them, you must convince me. Should you fail . . ."

He bestowed a humourless smile on all of them. Grimaldi almost always wore the expression Costa associated with Questura lawyers, the one that said, *I will stop you doing anything stupid because I know I can.* He was also one of the smartest and most assiduous men they had, a decent, dedicated police official who would work every minute of the day to get a conviction when he thought there was a chance of one.

"Franco stole all these paintings, didn't he?" Agata asked, raking her slender arm around the room. "Isn't that enough?"

"Prove it," Grimaldi replied.

Falcone's long, lean face wrinkled with displeasure. "You know we can't. Yet. But look at the circumstantial evidence."

"I've looked at little else for weeks," the lawyer answered. "Let me summarise. Nino Tomassoni was involved in an art theft ring. So, the French would have it, was this Véronique Gillet. Malaspina knew both of them socially, and perhaps, in the case of the woman, intimately."

"He slept with her," Costa said. "He told me so."

"Sleeping with a suspected criminal is an offence?" Grimaldi threw his big arms open in a theatrical gesture.

Peroni spoke up. "Toni, we have known each other for many years. I understand your caution—"

"This is not caution. This is plain common sense and good practise. You have nothing. Even those dreadful photographs you found here. Have you one single woman to interview as a result?"

The colour rose in Falcone's face. "They're either dead or back in Africa. Give us a chance, man. A little time."

"You don't have time, Leo. This investigation has cost the Questura a fortune in legal fees alone. And how far have you gotten? Malaspina has all of us tied up in knots. You can't ask him to take the most basic of scientific tests because he's used your ham-fisted investigations against you—"

"Not ours," Falcone cut in.

"The law does not distinguish between competent police officers and incompetent ones. You're all the same in the eyes of the magistrate. That is why you cannot use your swabs on this man. Or anyone else who is unwilling if they know about this loophole. Please, you have made us enough work already. Do you know what *our* priority is at this moment?"

"To put this murderous bastard in jail?" Peroni snapped, as livid as Falcone now.

"Live in the real world, Gianni," the lawyer retorted. "In the absence of an impending arrest, our priority must be to overturn this judgment in principle that Malaspina obtained against you."

Falcone turned and looked at him. " 'In principle'?" he repeated.

"In principle. Must I spell this out for you?"

Agata, clearly baffled, said, "For me you must."

"Very well," Grimaldi agreed. "If I try to attack the individual ruling that Malaspina won, then I open up every nasty black bag of worms you people have provided him with. The harassment. The unproven and unprovable allegations. The use of evidence that does not meet the most basic of legal rules. The very personal nature in which you pursued this investigation."

"Malaspina is a crook and a murderer," Falcone snarled.

"And an aristocrat with more money and connections than most of us could dream of in several lifetimes," Grimaldi said, unimpressed. "Think about it. See this through our eyes."

Costa was starting to get a sick feeling in his stomach. "Through your eyes?" he asked.

The lawyer hesitated. He didn't appear to enjoy his position any more than the rest of them.

"We may have to make choices. Unless you can come up with something very soon. Such as today. Or tomorrow at the latest . . ." He coughed into his big fist, embarrassed by what he was going to say. "Without that I'm going to have to recommend to the commissario that we scale down this investigation, take the heat off this man, and hope we can come to some kind of arrangement."

"What the hell does that mean?" Peroni bellowed.

"It means . . ." Grimaldi looked deeply unhappy. "I have to be practical about this. If you can't nail him, I must ask myself a broader question. Shouldn't I be thinking of the future instead? Of all those men like him who'll get away using the same trick? If I can cut a deal with Malaspina so that he leaves us alone to close that loophole, and we don't make it retroactive, which might be hard anyway . . ."

There was silence in the room. Even the handful of scene-of-crime officers had stopped work and turned to stare at the large lawyer in the grey suit, astonished, appalled.

"It's not as if Franco Malaspina is going to go out there and start his tricks again, is he?" Grimaldi looked like a man at bay. "You people tell me what the right thing to do is. Fail to imprison some murdering bastard who's finished killing? Or find a way to try to hit the sons of bitches out there who are about to start?"

The man appealed to Teresa Lupo. "You're forensic. You tell me. What would you rather have? Him on the streets, not daring to touch another woman in his life, and the way it all was before? Or him on the streets and you still trying to do the job with your hands tied behind your back. Well?"

It was Agata who spoke.

"I'm just a sister," she said, staring at him. "But I think you can only judge a man on what he's done, not what he might do. These crimes . . ." She caught Costa's eye. "If one turns a blind eye to them, what sense of justice is there anywhere?"

"Fine!" the lawyer yelled. "I deal in the law, Sister. I

leave justice to priests and nuns like you." He stabbed a finger at Teresa Lupo. "Tell me, do you want your toys back or not?"

The pathologist just stared at him and shook her head. "You know," she said quietly, "just when I think I'm working my way out of the habit of wanting to hit people, someone like you comes along. Will you shut up and listen for a moment? I'm greedy. I want both. Let's run through the small business here quickly, then go to the morgue and stare at some bones. And if that fails—"

"Then I go home to my family," Grimaldi cut in. "So do you have anything that links Malaspina with this place? Anything at all?"

The two forensic scientists stared at one another, anxious and, for once, silent.

THERE WAS, IN TRUTH, VERY LITTLE TO TIE ANY OF IT to Malaspina. A set of stolen paintings worth tens of millions of euros, looted from a variety of public institutions throughout Europe over a period of seven years. Some documents, found in the boxes in the hidden room, indicating that Nino Tomassoni acted as a kind of warehouseman for whatever gang was involved in the thefts. The photographs from the gap in the wall where the Caravaggio had once stood. One single piece of paper that linked the late Véronique Gillet to the loop: an email sent from her Louvre address, revealing the movement of a Miró canvas from Barcelona to Madrid, a journey during which it had been stolen. Finally the clear evidence that it was Tomassoni who had been sending messages to the Questura in an anonymous effort to draw the police's attention to the crimes.

"This is it?" Grimaldi asked. "Not a trace of Malaspina in the house. Not a fingerprint. Not a single document..."

"The emails Tomassoni sent to the Questura name Malaspina," Teresa pointed out.

"Uncorroborated gossip from a dead man," the lawyer observed.

"Give us time," Falcone pleaded. "We're inundated with material. We can't cope with what we have. It could be weeks. Months."

"You don't have months, Leo," Grimaldi replied with marked impatience. "I wish I could say you did. This happens to be my professional opinion. But it's more than that. It's a political issue, too, these days. The Justice people are calling. Everyone is calling. The wheels are starting to come off everywhere, not just with us, with the Carabinieri, the local police, the customs people... Everyone is affected by this and I'm the one who gets the phone call. The criminal fraternity *know*. Very soon every last one of them will understand they can, in the absence of other hard evidence, duck a fingerprint or a swab. Fifteen years ago we didn't even have these things and we put people in jail all the time. Now it seems that, without them, we're screwed."

Costa thought he could hear Esposito's voice in all

this. The new commissario was a pragmatic man, one who would not wish to be tied by the mistakes of others.

"We've a wealth of material," Teresa said confidently. "We're working as quickly as we can. There are reams of documents downstairs . . ."

"You said they were historical," the lawyer retorted.

"They are," she answered, uncertain of herself.

"So what use is that?" Grimaldi flung his hands in the air. "This is here. This is now. If you want me to prosecute Franco Malaspina, I need evidence from this century, not the scribbles of a few ghosts."

"And if a ghost could talk?" Agata asked quietly.

"I'd look even more of an idiot trying to sell this farrago of loose ends to a magistrate."

Agata took the black bag off her shoulder and Costa realised, at that moment, what was wrong. The thing was heavier, and had been since sometime the previous day.

She retrieved a large, thick book from its interior, one bound in dark leather cracked with age. Agata opened it and they all saw what was on the page: line after line of scribbled script, broken into paragraphs with dated headings. A journal. A diary from another time.

"You took this from that room?" Costa asked her. "Without my seeing? You stole it before I even got there?"

She'd been reading it, too, when he'd walked into Emily's studio the previous night. He recognised the book. It had been by her side.

Grimaldi groaned. "There goes any possibility of

introducing it as evidence. Not that I believe for one moment—"

"You have the evidence," Agata interrupted. "You've told me that. Time and time again. What you want is the link, isn't it?"

Teresa walked over and placed her gloved fingers on the cover. "Prints," she said. "Silvio. Arrange it. God knows..." She glanced at Agata. "We'll have to take yours to exclude them from anything we get."

She held up her hands. They bore white forensic gloves just like Teresa's. They must have been in the bag as well, and she had slipped them on as she withdrew the volume.

"I stole these from your forensic officers," she said. "Now, do you wish to prosecute me for petty theft? Or would you like to know what I found?"

# Three

ℐT WAS A DIARY, ONE THAT COVERED A PERIOD OF nine years, from June 13, 1597, to May 29, 1606, the day after Ranuccio Tomassoni's murder. She had spent much of the previous night reading it, but parts had still, Agata said, only been skimmed. She had focused on those that appeared to contain the most activity. Then, when she had made the excuse to visit the convent, she had consulted with another sister there, one skilled in documents of that period and capable of translating some of the words and terms with which she was unfamiliar.

There were many. Agata Graziano's dark complexion hid her blushes, mostly. The front page of the book bore the title, in ornate gilt lettering, *Gli Ekstasisti e Evathia*, "The Ekstasists and Eve." It concealed the private chronicle of the Ekstasists themselves, a week-by-week account of a secret male brotherhood that began as a prank of wild young men and developed over the years into something darker, more malevolent. The contents were, to begin with, frank and boastful, the record of a private gang of talented and often moneyed men who spent their days in the bright, chattering intellectual society of Renaissance Rome and their nights in the bleak, hard, physical violence of the Ortaccio underclass. There were wild tales of sexual adventures with society women and prostitutes, and practises among the members themselves that could have attracted a quick death sentence had the truth become known to the Vatican. There were sketches, pornographic cartoons, and ribald, obscene poems. And the pages recorded rituals, too: ceremonies only hinted at, but, Agata said, with pagan and alchemical antecedents.

Among the ancient scribbles were preliminary drawings for paintings, at least some of which were the work of Caravaggio.

"Here," she said, indicating the strange rough outline of three naked muscular figures seen from below, set around a globe. "This is a sketch for his only fresco, commissioned by Del Monte for the casino of the Villa Ludovisi. It's still there today. Jupiter, Neptune, and Pluto, although in truth these are allegories for the triad of Paracelsus, and alchemical conceit . . . sulphur and air, mercury and water, salt and earth. The casino was used by Del Monte for dabbling in pursuits the Vatican would have regarded as heretical. Possibly with Galileo at his side."

She turned to the beginning of the book and another sketch, one occupying two full pages as the frontispiece.

"*Evathia in Ekstasis. Eve in Ecstasy*. The moment those worldly sins they worshipped in secret entered our lives."

They all crowded round to see. Even this sketch, in crude ink, took Costa's breath away. It possessed the finished work's subtle play upon the mind, the ability to shift in perspective and daring, depending on how the viewer gazed on the rapturous woman's tense and highly physical moment of bliss.

"She," Agata said quietly, "was the goddess of them all. Mother and wife. Whore and slave. Bringer of both joy and damnation. This was what they worshipped. *This*"—her fingers traced the sensuous outline of the female nude on the page—"is what Franco Malaspina worships today. Like his ancestor."

There were, she said, seven of them, never referred to by name, only by trade or position: the Painter, the *Caporione,* the Merchant, the Servant, the Poet, the Priest, and, more often than any, *il Conte Nero*, the Black Count. This was Ippolito Malaspina, she believed, while Ranuccio Tomassoni was the *Caporione,* Caravaggio the Painter, and the Priest someone in the service of Cardinal Del Monte, the artist's landlord at the turn of the century.

"How do you know about the Priest?" Falcone demanded.

"It was"—a sly smile flickered in Costa's direction—"guesswork. I was in luck. The records of Del Monte's household still exist. In these days of modern miracles, I can even examine them in the Vatican repository on

Christmas Day, at two in the morning, on someone else's computer. There was a name there... Father Antonio L'Indaco, son of an artist recorded in the annals of Vasari, one who had worked with Michelangelo. This was a bohemian household."

"And it was him...because?" Costa asked, half knowing the answer.

"Because at the end of May 1606, Antonio L'Indaco disappeared and was never seen again. Why?"

They waited, listening, all of them, the police officers and the lawyer, and scene-of-crime people in their suits.

"He is the one who went to Malta with Caravaggio and pretended to be Ippolito Malaspina, while the man himself was dead, inside this house, murdered in the violence that also brought about the death of Ranuccio Tomassoni."

Costa touched the pages. The paper was thick and felt a little damp. It was not hard for him to imagine Caravaggio and the other Ekstasists standing over this book, scribbling down the details of their exploits, and small sketches, almost doodles, in the margins.

"Why did he die?" he asked. "Do you know?"

"I can guess," she answered with a marked, quiet reluctance. "This book covers nine years. A substantial part of many a man's life in those days. In the beginning"—she frowned—"it's nothing more than a game. Drinking and fighting and women. The way it began for Franco, I think. Until something—the 'sport in the blood'—took hold of him. Then..."

She flicked to a page with a yellow bookmark, towards the end of the book. They crowded round and gazed at what was there: an ink drawing of a terrified woman naked on her back, surrounded by grinning, laughing men. . . .

He followed the line of her extended finger. In the margin of the page was written, *God forgive me, for I know not what I do . . .*

The flowing, easy writing, sloping, somehow almost regretful in its very nature, was the same as that on the missing painting, the same as that of Caravaggio himself.

# Four

$\mathcal{Y}$OU CAN SEE THEM FALL APART," SHE WENT ON. "over the final two years. I am certain that it is Antonio L'Indaco who writes most of these entries. There are phrases and terms he uses that would be natural to a priest and to no one else. Here . . ."

She turned to a page dated November 16, 1604. There was no illustration this time. The entry described the abduction of an Ortaccio prostitute and her removal to a private place, "in front of the Goddess," where she was subjected to a humiliating series of sexual acts, each described in precise detail though in a fashion that led the reader to believe the author of the account did not approve—or perhaps witness—what had happened.

"It became worse, and it was Ippolito Malaspina and Ranuccio Tomassoni who led this throughout. Time and time again. It is here in these pages. A steady downward cycle of despair and abasement until . . ."

Another yellow bookmark flagged the place. Agata

opened the page. It was dated May 27, 1606, one day before the murder of Tomassoni.

"Read it," she ordered.

The hand of the writer must have been shaking, with
fury or terror or both. In large, uncharacteristically inel-
egant letters, he shrieked:

> *The Count is mad! He and Ranuccio run to the Pope
> and blame us! And believe they may win over some
> corrupt and crooked officer of the "law" by giving him
> the Goddess! There is no justice in Rome. No hope. No
> life. We flee for our lives. We pray for God's forgiveness
> and his eternal damnation on the Black Count, who
> has forced this shame and humiliation upon us. Hear
> me now, O Lord! With your hand I defend myself!*

Agata glanced towards the window. "The following
day, out there, Ranuccio Tomassoni was slain by
Caravaggio and the others. In here, I believe, Ippolito
Malaspina died. The two of them were about to betray
their brothers, using that painting they all adored as a
bribe to shift the blame from themselves. This is how the
Ekstasists disintegrated, in blood and hate and murder.
Remember the sign around the corpse's neck?"

"A traitor and a thief," Costa said, recalling every
word.

"Lines from Dante," she added. "Who better than a
priest to remember them? These were ordinary men in
the main. Ranuccio had brothers, good, honest citizens,

who were not involved with the Ekstasists as far as I can see. The records show that they fled Rome a few days after these events, but were allowed to return and remained here, handing their property on to their heirs. As it has been ever since, until poor, weak Nino Tomassoni. I suspect the brothers were ashamed of what had been done in the family's name. I believe they gave assistance to Caravaggio too. They kept the painting. They stored the body of Ippolito as respectfully as they could. Meanwhile, Antonio L'Indaco assumed the guise of the dead count, escaped alongside Michelangelo Merisi, then wrote letters, copious letters—we have some still—from Malta and the other parts of Italy where he lived thereafter." She slapped her finger hard on the page. "It is here. It is all here!"

Grimaldi sniffed, then looked at his watch. "I don't doubt that, Sister. You may have solved a crime that is four hundred years old. Unfortunately, that is outside my jurisdiction. Now—"

"Nino Tomassoni knew that room," she cried. "It was a secret, handed on from generation to generation. One he shared when he began this second career as an accomplice to Franco's art thefts! Here! Look!"

She turned to the final page of the book. There, in what looked like modern ink, scrawled with the casual ease of graffiti, stood four names, each in a different hand: *The Pornographer, The Merchant, The Servant,* and *The Black Count.*

The word *Black* was underlined in Malaspina's entry.

"Four hundred years on, they saw that painting and decided to revive the brotherhood. They read this book. They followed in the footsteps of Ranuccio Tomassoni and Ippolito Malaspina." She hesitated. "And sad, lost Michelangelo Merisi too."

Something bothered Costa. "Franco had this obsession with black prostitutes," he pointed out. "Did they before?"

"No," she replied, a little hesitantly. "Not at all. The street women of the time, those who lived in Ortaccio, were primarily white. We see that from their portraits, from the records we have. Simonetta was a kitchen maid in Florence, almost a century earlier. A slave, effectively. I suspect the real Ippolito Malaspina would have thought it beneath him to mix with a woman of colour. He must have been like Alessandro de Medici. Ashamed of his heritage. Like Franco too . . ."

Teresa Lupo looked the lawyer in the face. "There. Something modern. Something that goes from there to here."

"Which means what?" Grimaldi asked. "Tell me."

"It means," Agata suggested, "that something happened to light a fire in Franco Malaspina's head. Something that turned this idea into an obsession. Though what?" She uttered a long, despairing sigh. "This defeats me. It was always a joke in company. That he had a touch of the African in him. I remember . . ."

She stared at the page in the book, trying to think. "I remember perhaps a year or so ago that it became a joke one no longer made. Franco's sense of humour had disappeared on this subject." Her slender, dusky fingers stroked the page. "Yet I can see nothing here that would have proved this connection at all."

Teresa Lupo glanced at her assistant. "It's in the blood, you know," she said quietly. "I just might be able to help."

# Five

$\mathcal{T}$HIRTY MINUTES LATER THEY WERE IN THE QUES-
tura morgue, with Grimaldi glancing constantly at his
watch, still looking as if he didn't understand why he was
listening to history when he could have been home with
his family. Teresa stood over the skeleton that lay on the
shining table at the centre of the room, a collection of
grey bones now covered with labels and brightened in areas by obvious examination.

"The first thing to say," Teresa began, indicating the
skull, "is that everything I see here supports Agata's interpretation of events. This man was murdered sav-
agely."

She indicated a gaping, shattered rent in the skull
above the right temple. "It's a pretty typical sword
wound and would have been deep and serious. But"—
her gloved fingers ran over the arms—"there are any
number of defensive injuries here, on both limbs. Stab
wounds to the rib cage. A broken femur. He was attacked
and murdered, probably by more than one person."

"Could this have been a fight?" Falcone asked.

Teresa shook her head. "No. He was fighting them off with his arms. The balance of possibilities is that he was struck down by several men. And also—"

Peroni was staring at the skeleton with a gloomy expression on his long, pale face. "They did that," he cut in, and stabbed a long, fleshy finger at the largest obvious wound, one a good hand's length long that ran down the left side of the chest and tore open several ribs.

"Someone did," she observed with a long sigh. "But not in the way you think. This happened after he was dead. Technically it's what's called a postmortem ablation of the heart. It was a known, though not common, funerary practice in some medieval communities. The heart was removed for"—she shrugged—"worship usually. You know the kind of thing you get in churches? 'Here are the saint's remains. Pray for his soul . . . and yours.' This is how it was done."

"He wasn't a saint," Agata pointed out.

"No," she agreed. "I think that much is clear. But it was done for famous men, too, sometimes. Kings. Lords. Dukes."

"Where would they put the heart afterwards?" Costa asked.

"I can tell you where it was meant to be," she replied immediately. "Silvio?"

Her assistant came over with a series of large blown-up photos. They showed in detail the cabinet in which the skeleton had been found.

"This was specially made," Teresa said. "When they killed him, they meant to preserve him. The skeleton didn't get this way by natural decay either. It was boiled. Sister Agata isn't the only one who's been looking at the Tomassoni family. Do you know what the brothers did for a living?"

Di Capua flung a few more photos on the table next to the bones. They were medieval prints depicting some kind of charnel house, men working hard to dismember a corpse.

"They were undertakers," he revealed. "Specialist knowledge would have been around in a profession like that. They would have boiled the body in a mixture of water and vinegar. We can still detect traces of it. It must have taken a couple of days. There would have been some evisceration too. It's nothing compared with what the Egyptians did, but still pretty impressive."

"And the heart," Teresa interjected, "surely sat here." She indicated a hole in the base of the cabinet, one that looked as if it had been purpose-made for some kind of box. "Whatever was in there has gone missing. And recently," she added. "We can tell that from the lie of the dust. It must have disappeared around the same time as whatever stood on the wall where Nino stuck up his dirty pictures."

"Franco took it," Agata said straightaway. "This was his ancestor."

"That's one explanation," Teresa said hesitantly.

"Can you make the connection?" Falcone asked simply.

"I think we know the answer to that already," Grimaldi moaned. "Otherwise we wouldn't be listening to this rambling dissertation."

"I can make some connections," she answered quickly. "Whether our friend here thinks they're enough..."

"I..." Grimaldi looked around at them. He knew when he was outnumbered. "I will listen a little more."

"Excellent," Teresa replied, and didn't take her beady eyes off him. "I have four separate examples of male DNA from that hellhole in the Vicolo del Divino Amore. Three of them come from semen, on the corpses of those women, on the floor, that sofa they used. One has no sexual connotation at all. It is primary physical contact of an everyday nature. Fingerprints and sweat, the kind of evidence anyone would leave walking around a place and touching things."

"Nino," Agata intervened. "That was him."

Teresa nodded. "Good guess."

"I knew these men," she objected. "Not well, but I saw them quite often. Franco was their leader. Castagna and Buccafusca were his henchmen. Nino was subservient to all of them. This nonsense Franco believes in, about the life of the knight, his right to behave as he wishes... Nino was a frightened little man. He couldn't have felt that way for a moment."

"We have no evidence Nino Tomassoni took part in

any of the sexual acts or the murders," Teresa confirmed. "It's undeniable from the pictures we found in that house he was there. Maybe he was a bystander."

"And the rest?" Falcone asked.

Silvio Di Capua picked up a couple of folders of reports from the nearest desk and waved them in front of him.

"We have Castagna and Buccafusca identified without a shadow of doubt."

"Two dead people," Grimaldi moaned. "Thanks . . ."

Silvio Di Capua clenched his small fists and let out a brief scream, then said, "For Christ's sake, man. Use your imagination. We have one sample that remains unidentified. It has to be Franco Malaspina. All we need is a chance . . ."

"Imagination?" Grimaldi shrieked. "We're on the brink of getting sued for harassment as it is and you want me to go in front of a magistrate and talk of history and imagination? When will you people learn? We can't screw around with this individual anymore."

"We should know our place," Costa said quietly.

"I didn't say that!" the lawyer objected. "Do you think I like this? Do you think I want to defend this monster? He's a murderer and a crook and I'd give my right arm to see him languishing in a cell for the rest of his life. The only way we can do this is through the law. What else do we have?"

Agata looked at him and smiled, a quizzical expression on her face. "The law is an ass. Who said that?"

"Every last stupid cop who thinks I should be able to close a case he can't," Grimaldi snapped. "Give me something to work with. Something that isn't several hundred years old."

"Like most lawyers, Toni, you have a very closed mind," Teresa Lupo observed in a censorious tone. "Silvio? Let us talk genealogy."

# Six

$D$I CAPUA WALKED OVER TO THE MAIN DESK. THEY followed and watched him unroll three long family charts, two of them clearly printed and official, the third scribbled in the tight, clear hand Costa had come to recognise as the forensic scientist's own. Di Capua was the department magpie; if an avenue of research existed that didn't interest him, Costa had yet to see it.

"Alessandro de' Medici. The Moor," Di Capua said, and threw a photograph on the table. It was the portrait of a pale-faced scholarly individual dressed in black. He appeared to be drawing, unconvincingly, the face of a woman on parchment with a metal stylus. The man might have been a cleric or a philosopher. His young face was solemn and plain, with a skimpy beard. His skin . . .

Costa leaned down and looked more closely. Agata was there with him instantly, smiling, pleased, it seemed to him, that someone else had been looking at paintings for a change.

"Do you know this?" he asked her.

"Am I supposed to be familiar with every work of art there has ever been? No ..."

"It's in Philadelphia," Di Capua explained. "You're the expert. What do you think of the pose?"

Agata frowned. "It's a joke. This man was the capo of the Medici dynasty, as ruthless and venal as any. Here he is pretending he can draw, as if any of these great people could do that. Their talent lay in sponsorship, if at all."

Di Capua produced another photograph: it was of a painting depicting the same man, seated this time in a suit of armour, with a lance on his lap, his face only half seen, turned away from the artist and the viewer, his skin again oddly underpainted, as if the artist had refrained from finishing the final tone.

"A sport in the blood," she said firmly. "This is the one I know. Giorgio Vasari. It's in the Uffizi. Vasari's timidity is even more obvious in the flesh. They wouldn't dare admit it, would they? You know the story. We all know the story."

"Yes," Grimaldi agreed. "It's a story. His old man had an affair with a black kitchen maid and the bastard got to inherit the family silver."

Agata scowled at the lawyer. "His old man was Giulio de' Medici, who became Pope Clement VII. Not that Giulio admitted it. He got his cousin to put his name to the child. It was inconvenient for a Pope to take his off-spring to Rome. We know this for sure."

"How?" Costa asked.

"Someone like me can go places police officers can't,"

she said, smiling. "The Vatican keeps records." The body of the crucifix played in her fingers for a moment. "This all happened just sixty years before Caravaggio came to Rome. It's my job to know. If this cadaver is Ippolito Malaspina..." She reached out and touched the curving line of the rib cage, close to the point where it had been torn apart. "He is the grandson of Alessandro de' Medici, the great-grandson of Lorenzo, the Duke of Urbino. He comes from a line that produced three Popes and two Queens of France. Do you wonder they took out his heart, even though they killed him for a traitor and a thief?"

"Can we use any of this?" Falcone asked.

"It's fact," Agata insisted. "I can give you the names of any number of historians who will swear to it in court. Alessandro was the son of a future Pope and a black kitchen maid. But the idea that the Malaspinas were in part the Medicis' illegitimate line... It was just rumour. Gossip among the nobility. Centuries old."

"No," Di Capua insisted, and pointed to the second family tree, that of the Malaspinas, running from the 1400s and ending three centuries later. "It wasn't rumour. See this woman..."

He pointed to a name: *Taddea Malaspina.*

"She was Alessandro's mistress. It's documented in the Medici archive. Gifts. Love letters. Alessandro wasn't the most faithful of men. But he loved Taddea. This painting"—he pointed to the Philadelphia portrait—"was given to her as a gift."

Agata looked impressed. "That must have meant something. Alessandro was murdered, if I recall correctly."

Teresa stepped in. "He was slaughtered by his own cousin, supposedly on the way to some bedtime appointment. They smuggled out his body in a carpet and even I can't give you DNA from that. But . . ."

Agata laughed and clapped her hands. "They opened the tombs a few years ago," she declared. "I read about it in the papers."

"Correct," Teresa answered. "In 2003 the Florence authorities began a methodical examination of the Medici tombs in order to check the structural state of the building. At the same time, they let in a few friendly scientists to look at the bones." She stared at them all. "The remains of Alessandro are lost. His father, Lorenzo, is buried in the chapels, in a tomb by Michelangelo. There can be no mistake about his identity."

She gave a set of papers on the side table a sly glance. "It took a little persuasion with those damned Florentines. However, I now have their reports, and preliminary tests back on the DNA from the remains we recovered here yesterday. They need confirmation before we can put them into a form that is good enough for a court. But what I can tell you is this . . ."

She paused, for obvious effect, then ran her finger along the skull of the skeleton in front of them. "This dead man was a descendant of the duke in the Medici chapels. The unidentified DNA found in the semen on

all of these murdered women is a part of the same line."
Her fingers rattled on the cadaver's ribs as if they were a
child's musical instrument. "These bones belong to the
line of Alessandro de' Medici. That semen comes from
the same recognisable dynasty, ten, fifteen, twenty, who
knows how many generations on . . . Who cares?"

Grimaldi smiled for one brief second, then gave a
brief nod, as if to say "Well done." This was, Costa
thought, the most enthusiastic sign he had displayed
all day.

"And there's more," the pathologist added. "Silvio?"

"Do you see this?" The assistant was pointing at the
open jaw. "Both front incisors are missing. We only took
one. We only need one. Someone else snatched out that
other tooth, and they did it recently. You can see that
from the socket."

"Why on earth would someone steal a dead man's
tooth?" Grimaldi asked, bemused.

"For the same reason we did," Teresa butted in. "The
same reason the heart was removed. To find out whether
the rumours were true. Look . . ."

Di Capua produced a printed report bearing the
name and crest of an American medical institute in
Boston. "If you want to find out about black heritage
from DNA, there is only one place to go," he went on.
"This lab specialises in tracing African ancestry from the
most minute of samples, however difficult it might seem.
They've built up a database over the years, tracking down

slave movements from all over Africa to the rest of the world."

Agata rolled her eyes in amazement. "So they could even find my father?" she asked.

Di Capua nodded. "With a match. With two samples. Even from just yours they could look at the DNA and tell you whereabouts in Africa he came from. We contacted these people yesterday and sent them the preliminary results of our own tests. They looked them up for us. This is still early. As Teresa said, we need to work on the confirmation. But this corpse and the semen sample from the Vicolo del Divino Amore show clear connections with female DNA from the Bamileke tribe in what we now call Cameroon, an area plundered regularly for slavery for centuries."

He threw an indecipherable scientific graph, covered in lines and numbers, on the examination table next to the bones there.

"This is the mark of Simonetta, the kitchen maid some Tuscan aristocrat impregnated in Florence in the autumn of 1509."

"I told you," Agata sighed, her eyes full of wonder and elation. "They are us. We are them."

"It's in this skeleton," Di Capua went on, regardless. "It's in the semen on those dead women. The reason we got to know that so quickly..." He flashed a covetous glance at Teresa.

"It was your call, Silvio," she said gently.

"He was there before us. Franco Malaspina first sent

the heart, hoping they could work with that. It was too old. The man knew nothing about forensic pathology and what was required of remains this old. So later he took that tooth, on the direct instructions of the only laboratory in the world you'd go to if you wanted to trace some black ancestry from a sample of ancient DNA. They already had the work done. They could fingerprint the black strand and come up with some rough geographical location too. It was just a matter of looking up the records."

No one said a word.

Di Capua made a *faux*-modest little bow, then took out one more sheet from his folder and placed it next to the skull.

"One final thing. I found this in the archives of the Art Institute of Chicago. It's by an artist called Pontormo."

Agata was poring over the image in an instant, holding it in her shaking hands.

"Jacopo Carrucci . . ." she murmured.

"Pontormo," Di Capua corrected her.

"It's the same man," she said, smiling, and placed the object in front of them. "I have never seen this before."

"It's certified that it was painted in 1534 or 1535," Di Capua went on. "The work is recorded in the Medici archives. This is a genuine representation of Alessandro de' Medici, the only one that ever acknowledged who he really was."

They began to crowd around the image. It was a full-face portrait of a young and apparently sensitive man, clearly the Alessandro of the two earlier images, but this time seen at close quarters, where there was a baleful, almost malevolent look in his eyes, and some militaristic metal brooch at his neck. His skin was almost the colour of Agata's, darker than any native Tuscan, and his lips were full and fleshy.

"It's Franco," Agata whispered. "It is *him*."

Costa stared at the painted face of this long-dead aristocrat and felt an icy shiver grip his body. The hair was different and the skin had been lightened a little, even in this frank depiction of the man. But the resemblance was obvious and disturbing.

Falcone turned on the lawyer. "Is this not enough for you?" he demanded.

Grimaldi shrugged. "A picture? Some old books? And many, many circumstantial connections? Of course it's not enough."

Teresa swore.

"All the same," the lawyer added quickly, "this business in Boston. It's here. It's *now*. If I can prove he was in contact with them, that he dispatched first the heart, then the tooth on their instructions . . ." Toni Grimaldi burst into a broad grin that changed his countenance entirely and made him look like a grey-suited Santa shorn of his beard. "If we have that, then we are home. It places Malaspina in the Tomassoni house, at the centre of everything, with undeniable knowledge of those stolen paintings. I will push the swab into his mouth myself.

After which we will throw so many charges at the bastard he will never walk free again."

"The swab is mine," Teresa said softly.

"So," Grimaldi added, beaming, "these people in Boston will provide an affidavit. A statement. We can take such things by email these days. If I have that tomorrow, I go before a magistrate immediately."

The two pathologists stared at each other.

"When I say it came from Malaspina," Teresa continued carefully, "what I mean is we know it came from Rome. A year ago. It was a very expensive business. Not something one would do lightly."

The lawyer's smile disappeared. "Did they give you his name?" he asked.

"The lab said it came from Rome. Who the hell else could it be?" she pleaded. "How many other people here had the motive, the money, and the opportunity?"

"I need his name," Grimaldi emphasised. "On a piece of paper."

"This is medical research! There are ethical issues! Of course they won't give me a name."

The man in the grey suit swore. "Ever?" he asked.

"Show a little faith," Teresa pleaded.

"This is not about faith. Or justice. Or anything other than the law."

"The law is an ass," Agata repeated quietly, staring at the bones on the table.

"The law is all you have," Grimaldi muttered. "I have wasted Christmas Day. As have you. Excuse me. I will leave you to your bones and your books and your fantasies."

"Sir," Agata said, and stood in his way.

She had the photo of the portrait from Chicago in her hands.

"Look at him," she implored. "We all know this face. We all know what he's done. There is a man here"—she glanced at Costa—"who lost his wife to this creature, and I am only here thanks to this same man's courage. Do not abandon us."

Grimaldi's face contorted with a cold, helpless anger. "I abandon no one. Give me a case and I will work day and night to put Franco Malaspina in the dock. But you have none, and these officers know it. I have a duty to those who will be harmed in the future by this paralysis he has created in our investigative procedures. It cannot be allowed to continue."

He turned and looked at them all. "In the morning I must tell Commissario Esposito the truth. I have no confidence we can bring this man to book. We should . . . sue for some kind of peace that lets us go back to catching fresh criminals the way we wish. We draw the line with Malaspina. In return we negotiate to be allowed to bring back the old evidence rules he has removed from us, with no retroactive clause applied to him. I am sorry. Genuinely. That is my decision."

"Toni . . ." Peroni began.

"No. Enough. We do not have the resources or the evidence to defeat this man's money and position. There comes a time when one must admit defeat. I see it in the eyes of all of you, yet you refuse to let it enter your heads. This is your problem. Not mine. Good day."

Teresa Lupo watched him walk out the door, then muttered something caustic under her breath.

"No." Falcone was holding the photograph of Alessandro de' Medici and spoke in a quiet, dejected voice. "He's a decent man who has the courage to tell us the truth. We've done what we can and we've failed. Malaspina has defeated me as surely as he defeated Susanna Placidi. Money . . ."

"Tomorrow—" Costa said firmly.

"Tomorrow this all becomes history too," Falcone interrupted him. He pointed a long bony finger at Agata Graziano. "Tomorrow you will go to that safe house in Piedmont. Until we have concluded these discussions with the man. I will make your safety a precondition, naturally."

"You will not negotiate with this evil creature on my behalf, Leo," she shouted. "How can you even think of such a thing? *How?*"

He waited for her fury to subside.

"If we cannot prosecute this man, then negotiating something quietly, through a third party, is the best we can achieve." He cast a brief glance in Costa's direction. "I'm sorry, Nic. Truly. That is the way it must be. Now, go home all of you, please. It's Christmas. We should not spend it in a place like this."

Part Sixteen
The Madonna's Touch

# One

TWO YEARS BEFORE, THEY HAD DINED TOGETHER
on Christmas Day: Falcone, Peroni, Teresa, he and
Emily, all of them at the farmhouse on the edge of Rome,
watching a rescued Iraqi orphan build a snowman
among the vines outside the back door in the fields that
led to the tombs and churches and monuments of
the old road into the city.

It seemed a memory from a different lifetime. The
streets were deserted by the time they climbed into the
cars of the convoy, and a steady drizzle fell on the cobblestones of the *centro storico*. A chill wind was now beginning to build from the north. There would be no snow,
not even a little. Costa felt sure of that, and a part of him
regretted the thought, because he would have liked to
show Agata Graziano the Pantheon in that kind of
weather, would have enjoyed the look of wonder on her
face at the line of soft flakes swirling through the oculus.

He felt tired. His wounded shoulder hurt. It wasn't
mending as quickly as he'd hoped. Over the past few

weeks Costa had become conscious of some rising interior knowledge within himself; he was getting older, now a widower, one who would be unable to put Emily's memory to rest for a long time.

It may have been the doubt and distance on his face that prompted her remark. As they fell into the back of the centre car, Agata Graziano looked him in the eye and asked, "Do all policemen give up this easily?"

He closed his eyes and tried to laugh. "I don't think anyone would call this easy," he replied. "We've worked for weeks. Susanna Placidi was there before us. All told, we've spent months trying to bring this man to justice, and we've failed. Leo is right. As usual."

"The arrogance of men."

"We have nothing to put in front of a magistrate, Agata. That's the truth. Accept it."

The car began to move. Her eyes turned from him. She stared out the window, at the rain and the gleaming, empty cobbled streets.

"I do," she sighed. "And I shall go to Piedmont as Leo dictates." She looked at him, a quizzical frown on her dusky face. "Will you really negotiate with a man such as Franco? After all this?"

"We negotiate with terrorists and kidnappers in Iraq if it saves a life sometimes. In the end, if you want peace, you talk to your enemies. Who else is there?"

"And then they kidnap someone else because they know they have you."

"Perhaps," he answered with a shrug. "But would you

like to explain that to the relative of someone in their custody? That the life of a man or woman they love should be sacrificed in order to save other, unknown human beings in the future?"

"No," she said instantly. "I would not like that responsibility."

The car turned into the Corso. There was not a single Christmas light in the shop windows, not a soul on the street.

"Why do you do this?" she asked. "Why do you take on the pain of others?"

The question puzzled him.

"We don't, do we? It's just a question of ..."

He remembered his father, and the routine round of charity, money to men and women without homes, without hope, quiet donations, often to Church institutions a good communist was supposed to avoid.

"The point is ... we don't walk away. We don't stop. We don't give up. Not until ..." He thought of Teresa and her forensic people working through the night; Falcone bending the rules, agonising over what might work and what might make the situation with Malaspina worse. "Not until it's hopeless."

"And then?"

"Then I go home, open a good bottle of wine, and drink myself stupid."

"Nic!" Her small hand dashed across his knee. "That is shocking," she cried. "You will not do this tonight. Bea will have cooked another wonderful meal for us. Then tomorrow I expect a personal escort to this hovel in Piedmont Leo has in mind for me, and that will be no pleasure at all if you have a thick head."

"Sir," he said, with a mock salute.

She reached into her bag. He wondered, for a moment, what other surprises might lurk there. All that came out was a small, very modern mobile phone.

"That looks like a possession to me," he pointed out.

"One more gift from Rosa. It's better than a gun, isn't it?"

He listened to her make a single short call to the convent and wish someone well. Then, as they were turning onto the Lungotevere by the river, she said, "Please turn round. This is important."

"What is?" he asked.

Her bright eyes held him, pleading. "I can't go through this entire day without entering a church, Nic. Please. Sant'Agostino would be suitable. It is open. I know."

She watched him, waiting.

"We'd allow in an atheist, you know."

He spoke to the two guard cars on the radio and ordered them to turn round. It didn't take long. There was scarcely another vehicle on the damp, shining roads.

"As long as you're under our protection," he answered, "you'll have to let in more than one."

# Two

$\mathcal{T}$HE CHURCH WAS DESERTED EXCEPT FOR A LONE priest extinguishing candles and tidying chairs. He didn't look pleased to see seven men in winter coats march into his church at that moment.

"We're closing," the man said, scurrying towards them in his long black robes, causing them to halt. "Please, please. Even a priest deserves some time at Christmas."

Then he stopped, seeing Agata Graziano, and put a hand to his mouth.

"Sister Agata," he murmured. "Are you . . . well? I hear all these stories. About you. And the police."

"The police," she said, and waved a hand at Costa and his colleagues. "See, I am on business. Perhaps it touches them too."

"Oh," the priest answered hesitantly, then added, "You won't be long, will you? I'm hungry. It's been a tiring day."

"We won't be long," Costa interjected. "Will we?"

"No," she murmured, and immediately went towards

the altar, small feet making light, echoing steps in the vast, empty belly of the nave.

On his orders four of the men followed discreetly, in the dark shadows of the aisles on both sides. Agata stopped, crossed herself, and fell slowly to her knees. Costa stayed with the priest, his eyes straying, as always, to Caravaggio's Madonna, the child in her arms, the simple peasants in front of her. The pencil-thin halo above the Virgin's head seemed brighter, more obvious than he'd noticed before.

"The painting's about her," he noted quietly. "I never realised before."

The priest laughed. "It is called *The Madonna of Loreto*. You should always read the name on the frame."

"I should," he agreed. "This whole church"—something, some revelation, hovered out of reach—"is about women somehow, isn't it?"

"Primarily," the man observed, "I would have said it was about God. But then, I'm biased."

She was done. Agata was walking back towards him again, head down, face serious. She couldn't have prayed for more than a minute.

Costa thought of Fillide Melandroni taking much the same steps on the selfsame flagstones four hundred years before. Making some compact with the Church, then striding out into Rome in the company of Caravaggio and Ranuccio Tomassoni and Ippolito Malaspina for a different life, one of surfeit in the name of the Ekstasists, one in which she would take a knife to the cheeks of her rivals simply to earn a little more money for her favours. Men and women enduring lives steeped in the cruel reality of everyday existence, still seeking spirituality wherever, whenever, they could find it. Watching her slim, dark shadow slip towards him through the nave, Costa understood, at the moment, that Agata Graziano was their diametric opposite: a bright, engaged mind that had never, until late, considered anything of the earthly world at all.

He glanced at the Caravaggio, wondering what to say.

She didn't arrive. The priest next to him uttered a short, shocked sigh. Costa turned.

Sister Agata Graziano stood in front of the milky-white statue of the Virgin in the scallop-shell alcove, triumphant beneath her starry halo, a silver circlet beneath her breast, the child standing on her knee, loins girt with metal like a tiny warrior from some distant Greek myth.

Tentatively, with an expression on her face that was part anticipation, part fear, she reached out and touched the lustrous argent cap on the Madonna's foot, placing her fingers on the shiny worn object as untold numbers of Roman women—Fillide Melandroni among them—must have done before.

"Now that is something new," the priest whispered.

It only took a moment. Soon she was walking towards the door.

"Please excuse the rudeness," Costa said, preceding her. The rain had halted. The long sweep of steps in front of the church gleamed like yellowing dirt-stained ivory. The three cars were at the foot. He went ahead, Agata behind, with the men at her back.

When he got to the bottom, he found Taccone there, fuming.

"Dammit!" the tall, broad-shouldered sovrinten-dente yelled out into the piazza, apparently at no one.

They stopped by the middle car. Costa was conscious of the large, familiar shape of Peroni by his right side, standing in front of Agata, trying to guide her towards the rear door.

"That stupid photographer we saw yesterday," Taccone grumbled. "The one outside Tomassoni's house. He was here too. I swear. He went past on a scooter. Looking."

The sovrintendente turned to face them. "Don't scum like that ever take a day off?"

Peroni's eyes caught Costa's. "What the hell would a photographer be doing out here on a night like this?" the big man retorted. "Where is he? What—"

"Let's get inside . . ." Costa started saying, then heard his words drowned out by the roaring, whining sound of a two-stroke engine, coming somewhere from the right.

He caught Agata by her slight shoulders, gripped her hard, and dragged her down to the damp, dirty stones be-hind the rear doors. From the corner of his eye, fast ap-proaching the three vehicles, lined up together, locked in formation, he could see the scooter roaring into the piazza.

There were two men on it, both hooded. The passen-ger sat backwards on the pillion, one hand tight on the rail by the seat. In his other sat a weapon, black, with a long barrel and a long magazine.

# Three

OOSTA TORE AT THE DOOR, FORCED IT OPEN, AND managed to bundle her inside, ordering her to keep low on the floor of the big police sedan. Then his words disappeared beneath the chatter of a machine pistol, barking repeatedly into the black night, its metallic voice echoing off the old stone façade of the church.

As Costa looked up, Taccone caught a shot to his upper torso and fell back screaming onto the steps. Peroni was yelling at the others to get down behind the vehicles. There were seven men there. Enough, surely. But it was night. It was Christmas. They weren't expecting any of this. This was Rome. Not some gangster town on the Ionian Sea in Calabria, where Malaspina had surely hired his deadly 'Ndrangheta thugs.

*Hide or fight.*

It was that choice again. The only choice.

He looked at the stricken Taccone, crawling across the steps to try to find some safety from the constant horizontal rain of machine-pistol fire raking the piazza.

For a brief second, he found his attention straying to another figure at the head of the stairs: the priest, upright, hands to his face again.

Peroni had the man in view already and was yelling at him, a long angry sentence filled with the kind of curses a Roman priest rarely heard, and a final threat that if the man didn't get indoors soon a police officer would likely shoot him instead.

"Gianni!" he barked over the noise, and then found himself catching his breath.

The piazza had gone quiet. All he could hear were the pained groans of the wounded sovrintendente, the anxious breathing of Peroni by his side, and, like a distant echo, the faint reverberation of remembered gunfire rattling around his head.

Peroni peered hurriedly around the car for a second, then got back to safety and shook his head.

"He's changing magazines, Nic. We have to—"

Costa didn't wait. He lunged over to the wounded Taccone and snatched the weapon from the man's hand. Then, with both his own and the borrowed gun firm in his grip, he stood up, walked out from behind the long, dark shape of the unmarked police Lancia, and pointed both barrels at the two figures on the bike, the gunman struggling with the machine pistol, the rider looking anxiously around, jerking at the throttle.

He didn't waste time with procedure, with a warning. They were five, eight metres away at most. Costa walked forward, firing loosely at both men, intent on getting as close as he could, and aware that others were beginning to follow him. His own body surely blocked their shots. At that moment, he really didn't care. There was nothing else that mattered on the planet but these two men, in the familiar black hoods he'd come to associate with Franco Malaspina and his works.

A cry of pain broke the brief silence between two shots. The figure in black on the pillion jerked, threw his hands in the air, and began to fall sideways. The machine pistol rolled out of his hands and clattered on the wet cobblestones. The engine whined madly and the scooter's front wheel jerked towards the black coverlet of the sky before the vehicle shot forward, leaving its wounded passenger behind, racing for the web of streets beyond the Piazza Navona, cutting a fast, direct path into the confusion of lanes and dead ends and alleys that was Ortaccio.

He kept firing, one gun after the other, until every shell was gone and he found himself pulling hard on dead triggers. He flung the spent weapons to either side and kept walking. Across the square the figure on the scooter got smaller and was gone.

Peroni appeared at his side. All the others were soon there, too, even, barely able to stand, Taccone, who was shivering, teeth chattering with cold and fear and pain.

Costa took one look at the injured man.

"Get him an ambulance," he ordered.

He watched them take the sovrintendente back towards the broad steps of Sant'Agostino. Peroni walked over to stand by the bent, broken body on the ground, still staring in the direction of the disappeared scooter.

"You know," he said, when Costa got there, "you always told me you were a lousy shot."

The man on the shiny cobblestones lay on his back, eyes wide to the sky, mouth gaping open to show two lines of badly cared-for teeth. There was a wound in his left temple the size of an espresso cup, bone and gore around the edges.

"I guess," Peroni added, "our friend Aprea here might not agree."

"We could have used a witness," Costa grumbled. "That bastard gets all the breaks."

Peroni was going through the dead man's clothes, pulling out nothing but money and ammunition.

"We could have used a real name too," he replied. "It certainly won't be Aprea. If he's one of our Calabrian friends, I doubt we'll ever get to know."

"Damn," Costa muttered. Then louder, "Damn, *damn!*"

He strode back to the car. The men stood in a huddle around Taccone, who, to Costa's amazement, was clutching his wounded shoulder with one hand and sucking on a cigarette with the other.

"I like the first aid treatment," he said to them caustically. "What is the point of all this training exactly?"

They didn't answer. They had the expression junior officers wore sometimes, the one he'd come to recognise since promotion, one that, at this instant, filled him with dread. The look was furtive and it spelled guilt.

"Where is she?" he asked.

He stormed over to the centre vehicle and threw open the rear doors. The back seats were empty.

"Where is she? Where in Christ's name . . . ?"

"She's gone, boss," Lippi, the youngest of the officers, said. "She must have run off while we were trying to help you out there."

Furious, Costa scanned the piazza.

"She could be anywhere by now," the agente added unhelpfully.

Costa spun round on the slippery marble pavement and found himself roaring her name into the darkness.

"Agata! *Agata! AGATA!*"

All that came back in the night was the echo of his voice off the marble façade of the church and the clatter of unseen pigeons, invisible wings rising into the black, enveloping sky.

Part Seventeen
The Company of Ghosts

# One

$\mathcal{H}$OURS LATER COSTA WAS SITTING IN FALCONE'S office in the Questura, dog-tired, head fuzzy from the painkillers the medic had given him to take away the hurt from his throbbing shoulder. They'd pulled in men and women from everywhere, once again dragged officers from the warmth of a family Christmas, and sent them out onto the damp, cold streets of Rome, looking for a lone woman of the Church who had disappeared into the dark.

It was almost as if she had never existed. There were no relatives to visit, no friends to check out. The city was deserted. The stream of officers dispatched into the *centro storico* by Falcone could find scarcely a soul to question, and anyone they did come across had no recollection of a slight young woman in black making her way through the rain to someplace Costa could not even begin to guess at. Falcone had stationed a team at the house on the Via Appia Antica, and further officers were scouring the roads leading to it, looking for some lead. Rosa

Prabakaran had visited Agata's convent and talked to the women there, pleading for help, getting nothing but sympathy and bewilderment. Agata had vanished into the heart of a city that was empty for the holiday. Finding a missing person in the overcrowded metropolis of a normal day was difficult enough. Locating her in this strange, deserted labyrinth of ancient streets, alleys, and dead ends was even worse. She had surely gone to ground somewhere or been taken by a different set of Malaspina's men, seeing their advantage when Costa led the response to the armed attack by the man who had called himself Aprea.

That idea—the thought that his own willfulness had left Agata exposed—tore at his conscience. When he closed his eyes, he saw another incident, another time. On the feeble winter grass and mud of Augustus's mausoleum, where a hooded man with a shotgun had his arm round Emily's neck, her voice in his ear, then, now, always . . .

*Don't beg, Nic . . . You never beg. It's the worst thing. You can do. The worst . . .*

But begging was what a man resorted to when the stakes were high, when he was desperate and there was no other option left. He would have begged for Emily's life, given his own in exchange. And the same for Agata. Instead . . .

He screwed his eyes tight shut and tried to force these thoughts from his head. A firm hand on his shoulder brought him back to the real world and shook him awake.

It was Peroni, his broad, ugly face creased with concern.

"Why don't you go home?"

"Yes," Falcone added from across the desk. "Go home. You look terrible."

"She was my responsibility," Costa shot back at both of them furiously. "I go home when we find her."

Falcone flicked through some papers in front of him on the desk. "The truth is this. Agata walked away from that church of her own volition. It's not possible she was snatched. That priest would have noticed."

"The priest didn't notice a thing," Costa pointed out.

Falcone scowled. "That's what he said. These Church people stick together like glue. You'd think we were the enemy sometimes. Agata did this for a reason. Perhaps she just can't take any more. When she wants us to know, we will."

"That's comforting," he grumbled.

"In a way," Peroni said thoughtfully, "it is. Better than some of the alternatives anyway. Now go home. You're no damned use to us here. Besides, nothing's going to happen tonight now, is it? This is something we're going to have to pick up in the morning. It would help us all if you were halfway awake by then."

"In the morning," Costa pointed out, "Grimaldi plans to offer Franco Malaspina a pardon."

"Then Agata will have nothing to fear at all," Falcone pointed out without emotion.

"Do you think she'll be happy with that idea?" he asked.

"Since when was this job about happiness?" Peroni grumbled. "Get out of here. You're starting to become tedious."

He nodded. Peroni was right. "True," Costa agreed, and walked out of the Questura, out into a bleak and empty Rome.

# Two

$\mathcal{H}$E DIDN'T WANT TO GO HOME. HE WANTED TO think, not sleep. Costa walked from the back street in which the Questura stood out into the broad, open Piazza Venezia and, this once, strode straight across the cobbles without seeing a single vehicle tearing maniacally from one side to the other. From the ugly white wedding-cake monstrosity of the Vittorio Emanuele monument, he went on to the Via dei Fori Imperiali, Mussolini's flat, broad highway through the heart of ancient Rome, with the Palatine and the jagged ruins of the old forums on the right, and the terraced ranks of Trajan's Market, red-brick walls leading up to the Quirinal Hill, rising in a semicircle to the left. Even close to midnight on Christmas Day, the lights set amid the monuments were burning brightly, cutting out soft yellow silhouettes of a different city from a different time. Rome looked beautiful. He knew, at times like this, he could never live anywhere else. This was home. It was a part of him, and he a part of it. Weary, he strode on to find the low bench seats by the side of Caesar's Forum, a place he had often visited as a child with his father, listening to all those tales from history, building in his own imagination a picture of the solemn night that saw the cremation of the dictator there. He could name without thinking the buildings that sat in the space beyond, a collection of wrecked columns and porticoes bearing such grandiose names they seemed eternal, the temples of Castor and Pollux, of Saturn and Vesta, the forums of Augustus and Nerva, the great Arch of Titus . . . relics of a race of men and women with whom he still felt some kind of affinity. In their struggles against their own dark nature, their endless striving to attain goodness, justice, in a world that seemed, at times, hopelessly fallen, Costa sought some kind of comfort, some distant sign of grace.

He had sat here sometimes with Emily, talking, listening, and wondering in silence. All those moments were equally precious to him now. Yet the vista that stretched before him was simply old stone, as Caravaggio's paintings were in essence nothing but ageing pigment on ancient canvas. Without the presence of humanity, without imagination and the gentle touch of another—a gesture that said *I see, I feel, I hurt, I love too*—they were nothing. That was what the artist was saying in the painting that had come to obsess Ippolito Malaspina and, four centuries on, his descendant too. Beyond the mundane and the physical lay another experience, one that could be reached only through the selfless route of compassion and surrender.

It must have been the night. Stray dust in the wind. Something pricked at his eye. Costa wiped it away, a single, stinging tear, from the corner. Then he saw he was not alone. By the low, feeble bushes at the edge of the pavement overlooking the small, once-holy place where a famous man had been turned to ashes, a woman sat on the ground with a child on her lap. She wore the heavy clothes of an immigrant: bulky yet exotic once, with a patterned headscarf that might have been colourful years ago, and a flowing, grubby dress beneath a man's winter parka.

The child could have been no more than five or six, so tightly wrapped against the cold or rain it might have been a boy or a girl, there was no telling. In front of them lay all the usual signs of the lost and destitute, the illegal and starving, carried around the city. *We are hungry. I look for work. Have pity.*

And a cardboard box full of small objects, barely visible, glittering under the bright illumination of the Forum.

He got up, walked over, and retrieved one of the items. It was fashioned from rubbish: foil and silver paper tightly wrapped together to make something that approximated a piece of jewellery, a brooch perhaps. This was how they spent their day, he guessed. Trawling through litter bins, trying to turn the detritus of the city into a handful of small change, enough to buy a little bread.

Costa put the thing back in the box. The woman was

staring at him, silent. Afraid, he thought. It was late at night. They were on their own. Sometimes, rarely, but it happened, a band of racist thugs might emerge from the suburbs and beat up people like these, just for the hell of it.

He took out his wallet, leaned down, and gave the woman a fifty-euro note.

"Happy Christmas," Costa said, and some dimly remembered line from a song repeated in his memory with a cruel insistent irony . . . *War is over*.

"Thank you, sir," the woman said in a heavy Middle Eastern accent.

The child's eyes stared at him, shining, puzzled, fearful.

"You don't need to be out in this kind of weather," he said, reaching for something else in his wallet. "There are places . . . the church . . ." His voice seemed to wobble. "Nuns . . . sisters . . ."

He threw down the card he'd kept for years, the one he hadn't handed out to anyone for a while because the old routine, the one he had inherited from his father—a gift a day, always to a stranger—had disappeared from his world altogether somehow.

"Please . . ." he croaked.

The woman looked up at him, a shadow of a smile on her wide face, which was, he suspected, both tanned and dirty, and said, "I am Muslim, sir."

"It doesn't matter to them," he snapped. "Does it to you?"

The tone in his voice alarmed them. He could see it on their faces. They were frightened, of him, of what he stood for.

"I'm sorry..." he stuttered. "I didn't mean to sound like that. The point is...there's help. Please. Go. Tomorrow. Please..."

He took out the wallet again, opened the flap, turned the thing upside down, let all he had—notes and cards and scraps of paper that no longer meant a thing—fall out, mumbling incomprehensibly as he did this, not even knowing himself what the words were.

Everything tumbled down to lie in the grimy fabric between her knees, so much, so loose in the wind, it spilled over onto the pavement and began to scatter on the breeze.

They were more frightened this time.

"Too much, sir," the woman said.

"It's not too much. It's nothing. It's...meaningless."

It wasn't the night. Or dust on the breeze. Costa was crying, his eyes so full of tears he could scarcely see. Everything was a blur—the lights on the ragged lines of ruins, the white wedding cake of the Vittorio Emanuele monument.

He staggered back to the stone bench and sat, head high, staring through these tears, choking, sobbing, feeling, at that moment, as if the world had ceased to matter.

\*       \*       \*

*HE DIDN'T KNOW HOW LONG THIS WENT ON. IT CAME* to an end when the child walked over and tapped his arm. It was a boy, with a face as innocent as an infant in one of the paintings Costa loved so much. In his hands he carried the cash that had fallen from the wallet— most of it—and the cards and the notes. And a small brooch made of tinfoil and the lining of a cigarette packet.

"*Grazie.*"

"*Prego,*" Costa mumbled, and looked at it, unable to raise a smile however hard he tried.

At that moment his phone rang. The boy retreated, back to his mother. The living world returned.

"*Pronto . . .*" Costa said in a voice he didn't recognise.

"*NIC? ARE YOU ALL RIGHT? YOU SOUND—*"

"Where are you?" he asked. Just hearing her voice made his throat well up with emotion once more.

"It doesn't matter. I'm safe. Listen to me. This is important."

He did listen. He wasn't sure he heard the words correctly. He wasn't sure he understood anything much at that moment.

Besides, there was something he had to say, something so important it couldn't wait, whatever Agata thought.

"No—" he interrupted her in mid-sentence.

"You must listen to me," she insisted, "carefully."

"Where are you?"

There was a quiet, impatient silence on the line. Then...

"I told you this before," she said with a clipped, angry precision. "There are places I may go where you cannot."

"What kind of an answer is that?"

"It's the best I can do."

"*No!*"

He was getting to his feet, screaming like a madman on Mussolini's deserted highway under the silhouetted skeletons from another time.

Out of the corner of his eye he saw the woman get up, grab her son, and bundle the child away, stumbling down the broad pavement, carrying their belongings, the cardboard box, some plastic bags—the sight of them ripped at his feelings—and a huge roll of grubby bedding.

"Where I come from," he said as calmly as he could, tears rolling down his face again, warm and salty, welcome in some strange way too, "you do not run away. You do not abandon people as if they mean nothing whatsoever. In my world there is nothing worse."

That silence again, and he wondered how it was possible to interpret nothingness, to sense in this absence of sound that she was listening, shocked, baffled, wondering what to say.

"In my world," Sister Agata Graziano replied eventually, "I have never had to think of things like that. You must do as I ask. Please. Alone. That is the only way. I will call."

She said no more. The line was dead. Costa was utterly alone, wishing, more than anything at that moment, that there was something he could say to the woman on the street and her frightened child, fleeing into the night, afraid of what he had become.

But, all too swiftly, they were gone, out towards the Piazza Venezia, and the places where the homeless gathered together for safety when winter closed in: the Pantheon and the Campo dei Fiori, the riverside haunts by the Tiber where he and Emily had once helped save one—just one—young foreigner from the night.

The tears still pricked at his eyes.

Costa wiped them away with the sleeve of his jacket. Then he limped across the empty roadway of the Via dei Fori Imperiali, found one of the cheap flophouses off the Via Cavour, and rented a hard, cold single bed for the night.

# Part Eighteen
# The Garden of Evil

# One

At 8 a.m., when the noise from the neighbouring room woke him, Costa walked out into the street and found stallholders in white jackets firing up charcoal braziers for hot chestnuts, panini stands getting ready for the day. A lone tree, sprinkled with artificial snow, stood erect at the entrance to the square. Next to it was some kind of musical stage at the foot of the Vittorio Emanuele monument, complete with a gaggle of bored-looking musicians and a troupe of skimpily dressed girl dancers shivering, clutching at their bare arms, trying to find some protection against the weather. A bright winter sun did nothing to dispel the bitter, dry, bone-chilling cold. A trickle of people wrapped in heavy clothing meandered past the moody entertainers on to the broad pavements of the Via dei Fori Imperiali, spilling out into the traffic lanes now closed to all but pedestrians, as they were every Sunday.

It was still Christmas in Rome, just. The place felt unreal, expectant somehow. Costa walked down the middle of the road, where a thousand cars and vans normally fought each other daily, thinking, praying for his phone to ring. Then, when he got near the foot of the tree, close enough to see the low illumination of the fairy lights still lit even in the brightness of the day, a familiar unmarked blue Fiat worked through the barriers and came to a halt next to him. Peroni was behind the wheel. He looked bemused. But not unhappy.

The big man pushed open the passenger door and said, not quite angry, "You left your ID card in that crummy hotel. Amazingly they phoned to tell us. You'd better get in."

Two minutes later—far more quickly than he could ever have expected on a normal day—they were parked in the Piazza Navona, the place empty save for the pigeons. Peroni said little along the way, except for murmuring a couple of cautious remarks about his looks. Costa ignored them. He felt distanced from everything, as if this were all part of a waking dream. As if . . .

They got out and walked round the corner towards the statue of Pasquino.

Costa's heart skipped a beat. There was a slender figure in black there, back to him, facing the battered, misshapen statue, staring at some fresh sheet of white paper stuck on the base.

He ran, ignoring Peroni's anxious calls from behind.

A sister, a nun. He didn't know the difference. He no longer cared.

When he got there, he placed a hand gently on her

shoulder. The figure turned, smiled at him, then stepped backwards, primly removing herself from his touch.

She was a woman in her forties, with a very pale and beautiful face, light grey eyes, and silver hair just visible.

"I'm sorry," he muttered. "I thought . . ."

His attention was divided between her and the poster on the statue. A poster she'd fixed there the moment before. There were other figures in black nearby too. They had pieces of paper in their hands and rolls of tape. They were placing the sheets everywhere, on walls, on shop windows, carefully aligning each at eye level to make them as visible as possible.

"They're all over the city," Peroni said, catching up with him. "On the other statues. In the Piazza Venezia. This lady asked for you in particular." He glared at the woman in black. "Which is all she'd say."

"Not true," the sister objected. "I wished you a good morning and happy Christmas too. You should be flattered. Normally I would say nothing at all."

"Sister," Peroni replied, "Agata Graziano is missing. We would very much like to find her. There is no time for these antics."

She shrugged and responded with nothing more than an upturned smile, a worldly gesture and very Roman. Much the kind of response Agata would have given if she'd wished to avoid the conversation.

He read the poster, a new message for the talking statues, one they were determined to post everywhere, as Falcone had posted his, though this was very different.

"It was Agata's idea?" he asked quietly. "Sister . . ."

The woman's grey eyes returned his gaze, unwavering, interested, and, he thought, marked by an inner concern she was reluctant to reveal.

"You're Nic?"

"I am."

"This is true," she replied. "You are as she described."

The woman looked at Peroni and began to motion with her hands, saying, "Shoo, shoo, *shoo!* This is for him. No one else."

Under the fierceness of her stare, the big man backed off, towards the large public square behind.

She waited, then retrieved an envelope from the folds of her black cloak.

"Sister Agata sends this. For you and you alone."

He ripped it open and read the contents: a single sheet in a spidery academic hand. Unsigned.

"God go with you," the woman said quietly.

He took one more look at the words on the poster beneath the malformed, crumbling statue. His childhood studies, literature and art, had never really left him. The quotation was recognisable. Given the book, he could have found it. The words were an adaptation from Dante again, with a message, direct and personal, tagged on the front.

Costa read the words out loud, listening to their cadence, hearing her voice in each syllable.

" 'Franco, Count of Malaspina. Do you not know that, for all your black deeds and black blood, you are

like all of us "worms born to form the angelic butterfly"?
For Emily Costa and all those murdered women whose
lives were taken by your sad anger, God offers forgive-
ness. Take it.'"

The sister watched him impassively as he spoke, her
head tilted to pay attention to the words.

"He's not looking for salvation," Costa noted, stuff-
ing the letter into his jacket pocket, then taking out his
gun, checking the magazine was full, and thinking
ahead of what might lie in wait.

Agata was attempting to force Malaspina's hand,
both by revealing his guilt and by what she believed to be
the secret he hated most: his ancestry. It was ... Costa
wished his head were functioning better. It was wrong,
he felt, though he was unable to be precise about his reasons.

The woman in the black robes eyed the weapon with
a baleful expression.

"Everyone is looking for salvation," she murmured
with a quiet, simple conviction. "Whether they know it
or not."

He wasn't in the mood for distractions. Peroni came
over, looking hopeful.

"I have to do this on my own, Gianni," Costa said, ignoring the woman.

"But—"

"But nothing. That's how it is."

The sister's smug smile was becoming annoying.

"Arrest these women for flyer-posting," he ordered.

"Keep them inside under lock and key until this evening."

She began to protest, and her colleague across the way too.

"Sister," Peroni interrupted, "you have the right to remain silent. Or call the Pope. But he might be busy today."

"You've no idea how many women there are in Rome like us," the senior one hissed at him. "None at all."

He didn't. Nor was it important. There was only one thing that mattered.

Costa started running north, back into narrow streets and lanes beyond the Piazza Navona, back into the streets of Ortaccio, letting the long-forgotten rhythm of his movement across the cobbled streets of Renaissance Rome remind him of a time before this pain, a time when he was nothing more than a single, insignificant agente in a city full of wonders.

# Two

BY NINE-THIRTY GIANNI PERONI WAS SICK OF SEE-ing nuns and sisters. It seemed as if an army had assem-bled on the streets of Rome, every last woman in a religious order who could walk, flocks of them, no longer scampering through the streets quickly, discreetly, like skittish blackbirds brought to earth, but instead throw-ing off their shy invisibility to stomp around the de-serted city with one idea only: putting up Agata Graziano's curious message in places even the most ad-venturous flyer-posters would never dare to venture. Her adaptation of Dante, with Franco Malaspina's name and crimes now attached, was plastered on some of the most famous and visible buildings in the city.

Copies ran like a line of confetti across the roadside perimeter of the Colosseum, to the fury of the architec-tural authorities, who had interrupted the peace of their holiday break to call the Questura in a rage. All the other talking statues were now covered in them, too, as was the statue of Giordano Bruno in the Campo dei Fiori and the stone sides of the Ponte Sant'Angelo, the pedestrian pilgrims' bridge across the Tiber on the way to the Vatican. A handful of sisters had even managed to attach several to the front of the Palazzo Madama, the Senate building where Caravaggio once lived under the patronage of Del Monte, an act that had brought down the tardy wrath of the Carabinieri, who now, the TV stations said, had fifteen sisters and nuns in custody, for vandalism against public, though never church, buildings throughout Rome.

The Questura, Peroni was alarmed to discover on his return with the two silent, smug women from the Piazza Pasquino, was in possession of no fewer than twenty-three, which was why Prinzivalli, the duty uniform sovrintendente at the front desk, threw up his hands in horror at the sight of Peroni leading two more through the door and wailed, "What are we doing, man? Collecting them?"

Peroni turned and looked behind him. The quieter of the two women he had apprehended was patiently taping a poster to the notice board in the public waiting room. She seemed to have an entire roll of them stuffed inside the voluminous dark folds of her gown. He found himself wondering at the idea that a community of sisters should have a photocopying machine, then cursed his own ignorance. All along, Nic had understood something that had eluded the rest of them. These women were not shy and weak and unworldly. Some, perhaps. But not all. Many had a determination and a conviction that escaped the daily population of the city who nodded at them on buses and in the street, never thinking for a moment there was much life or interest beneath that drab uniform. Yet they possessed a certain kind of courage, needed it to withdraw from conventional humanity in the first place.

When that resolution was tested ... Peroni checked himself. They were still women on their own, and Agata Graziano a defenceless sister, seemingly alone in a city where at least one 'Ndrangheta thug remained on the loose and looking to take her life.

Falcone bustled in. The inspector looked bright-eyed, full of vigour ... and damned angry.

"What is this?" he demanded, ripping the sheet from the wall, staring at the words as if they were in a language he couldn't understand. "Well?"

"Don't ask me," Peroni answered. He nodded at the two by his side. "Ask them."

"I've been asking their kind all morning. All they do is stare back at me, smile sweetly, and say nothing. Well?"

The two women smiled at him, sweetly, and said not a word.

"Dammit! Where's Costa?"

"He had a message," Peroni replied, fully expecting the storm to break, and utterly without a care about its arrival. "Sister Agata passed it on through this lady here."

Falcone asked tentatively, "And ...?"

"He's gone. He didn't say where. She—"

"I don't know," the older sister interrupted. "So please do not be unpleasant. You will only make yourself more choleric."

Falcone's eyebrows rose high on his bald, tanned forehead. The door opened and two uniformed officers walked in with four more women in long, flowing winter robes.

"Arrest no more nuns," Falcone ordered. "Put that out on the radio, Prinzivalli."

The sovrintendente nodded with a smile, made some remark about this being one of the more unusual orders he'd had to pass to the control room of late, and disappeared.

"Sister," Falcone went on, standing in front of the woman who had delivered the message to Costa, "you must tell me where Agata Graziano is. Where our officer is too. I don't understand what she's doing, but it is a distraction, perhaps a dangerous one, in a case of the utmost seriousness. I cannot allow her to be dragged in any further. I regret bitterly that I allowed this involvement at all."

The woman's grey eyes lit up with surprise and anger. "You arranged it in the first place, Falcone."

The inspector's cheeks flushed. "You know my name?"

"Naturally. Sister Agata spoke to us at length last night. We broke our own rules. We were awake long past the due time." She smiled at Peroni. "We know about you all. And more." Her face became serious. "We know you have no case, *Ispettore*. This man . . . Malaspina. He has defeated you. He has money and the law on his side. He is one of those nasty, thuggish Renaissance knights Sister Agata told us of, a man who has"—to Peroni's astonishment she stabbed Falcone in the chest with a long, hard finger—"bested you entirely. For all your power. All your"—this time her eyes flashed in Peroni's direction—"men."

"That is an interesting observation, Sister," Falcone barked. "Now, where the hell are they?"

"You think God has nothing to do with justice?" the woman asked, seemingly out of nowhere.

"If he has," Falcone answered immediately, "he's been doing a damned poor job of it lately. If . . ."

The tall, lean figure in the slick grey suit went quiet. Peroni hummed a little tune and rocked on his heels. It was a remarkably stupid—and quite uncharacteristic— comment for such an intelligent man to make.

The long, bony finger poked at Falcone's tie again.

"God works through us," she said. "Or not, as may be the case."

"Where are they?" he asked again.

She took his wrist and turned it so that she could see his watch. "All in good time."

Then the woman took one step back and exchanged glances with the others there, all of whom had listened to this exchange in silence. She was, it seemed to Peroni, the senior among them, and they knew it.

"There is one thing," she said with visible trepidation.

"What?" Falcone snapped, but not without some eagerness.

"Sister Agata told us your coffee isn't like our coffee. From powder. In big urns. She said . . . your coffee was . . . different. May we try some? It is Christmas."

Falcone closed his eyes for a moment then took out his wallet.

"The Questura coffee is not fit for animals," he declared. "Take these women out of my sight, Agente. If you can find them somewhere that's open, buy them whatever they want."

# Three

*T*EN MINUTES LATER THEY WERE IN THE NEAREST cafe that was open, a place famed for both the quality of its coffee and cakes and its foul-mouthed owner, Totti, a middle-aged bachelor now stiff with outrage behind his counter, like a cock whose territory had been invaded by an alien species.

"It's not right," he confided to Peroni behind his hand as they stood at the end of the bar, a little way away from the gaggle of black-clad women sipping at their cups of cappuccino and tasting cornetti and other cakes as if this everyday event were entirely new to them, as it probably was. "It's bad enough when there are more women here than men. But these women."

"They are just women," Peroni grumbled.

He didn't like Totti. The man was a misanthrope. If there had been anywhere else within walking distance that was open . . . But the coffee was good. From the expressions on the women's faces, it was a revelation.

"A waste of a life," Totti replied. "What good does

that do any of them? A couple would look decent scrubbed up and in a dress too."

Peroni gave him the stare, a good one. There were, he reflected, decided advantages to being an ugly brute at times. Totti's toothbrush moustache bristled, and without a word, the man walked off to polish, halfheartedly, some beer glasses by the sink.

Each of the sisters now possessed a half-brown, half-white cappuccino moustache above her top lip. Oblivious to something they seemed not to notice even on one another, they were gossiping, the way all Roman women did, but quietly.

He walked over, trying to make sense of the thought that kept bugging him.

"Ladies!" he said cheerily, picking up one of the empty coffee cups. "So, how was it?"

"Very rich," the senior one said immediately, for all of them, that was clear. "Enjoyable but a luxury. Perhaps once a year. No more."

"Once a year is better than once a lifetime, Sister," Peroni observed.

"Before Rome, I worked in Africa," she answered tartly. "They would have been happy with once a lifetime there."

"Happy?" Peroni echoed. "I doubt it, don't you?"

"I never realised a police officer would be so precise about words. Sister Agata said you were remarkable. The three of you. So what now?"

He beamed at them. "Now you clear your debts. You tell me something."

"Falcone paid," she said. "He's not here."

"It's a small thing and, being sisters, you believe in charity. It is this." He had checked with Prinzivalli while Falcone was berating them in the Questura. It had seemed, to him if not to Leo Falcone, an obvious question to ask. "You've performed Sister Agata's bidding on most of the prominent buildings in the *centro storico*. It's an impressive feat. You must have been very busy."

"Thank you," she said, bowing her head gracefully.

"Yet there is not a scrap of paper on the walls of the Palazzo Malaspina, even though it would be an obvious place for your attention, with or without the connection you suppose."

They became very still and stared at him.

"I believe Count Malaspina will know what has happened," the vocal one said eventually. "It's everywhere. One would have to be blind, surely . . ."

"One would," Peroni agreed. "All the same, I don't see why you should leave that building untouched, almost alone of any of some importance." He paused. "Unless . . ."

"Unless what?"

"Unless that is precisely where you do not wish us to be."

She fell silent. Peroni leaned forward.

"Sister," he said quietly, "I don't know how much you comprehend of the game you are playing. But understand this. If your colleague and my friend are in that place, there is nothing we can do to help them. Nothing. Without cause. Without evidence. Without a reason so compelling we feel able to drag away a magistrate from his lunch to beg for the right papers. The Palazzo Malaspina is inviolate in Rome, beyond our powers, outside our jurisdiction. We can't go there under any circumstances at the moment. It might as well be the Vatican for all we can do."

"I can go to the Vatican anytime I like," she said, and laughed. It occurred to Gianni Peroni that he might not, in everyday life, like this woman very much at all.

# Four

$\mathcal{I}$T WAS A BRIEF PHONE CALL. FALCONE LISTENED TO his request. Then he said no.

"You didn't hear me correctly, Leo," Peroni insisted. "I know we can't go inside. I am simply telling you. These witches in wimples are up to something and it involves Malaspina's place. They think they can handle this on their own. We know differently. I want five good men and an unmarked van. No one will see us. No one will know."

Falcone's voice went up a couple of notes. He was furious; he was flustered.

"I don't have five good men to spare, sitting in some van, waiting for God knows what. Everyone we have is out there, looking for Agata Graziano and Costa. What else do you expect me to do?"

"Something that isn't obvious," Peroni replied. "Something that's you, not an order handed down from upstairs."

The line went silent. Peroni could imagine the flush

of rage racing up Falcone's tanned cheeks at that moment.

"Listen to me," he went on hastily. "You know you won't find them. They don't want to be found. That's the point."

"What is?"

"The boss sister you just met told us. We've failed. The law's failed. All the ways we have of dealing with situations like this . . . they're done with, busted, and Agata knows it. The best we can hope to come out with at the moment is a green light from Grimaldi to start using Teresa and her magic DNA machine again on anyone except Malaspina. That's the payoff . . . and your cunning little sister thinks she has another way."

He didn't hear an instant explosion. That was good.

"Five good men," he added hopefully. "An unmarked van. An hour or two. No more. I don't think we'll need it."

"I don't have—"

"If she's in there, she will surely need our help before long. Whether she—or they—know it or not. Do you want to leave that to a phone call and the off chance we might have a spare car to send round from the Questura? Would that make you happy?"

Falcone uttered a quiet, bitter curse, then added, "For a mere agente you have a lot to say."

"Nic's there. I rather like Agata too. What do you expect?"

"Wait outside," he ordered. "And don't let anyone know what you're doing."

# Five

$S$HE HAD SPECIFIED THE PLACE, AND THE LOCATION
filled him with dread. It was the area behind the studio in
the Vicolo del Divino Amore, the dank cobbled yard full
of junk and stray weeds where he had first encountered
Malaspina, hooded, armed, and deadly, before chasing
him out into the open streets, towards the Mausoleum of
Augustus.

Towards Emily.

Costa stopped for a moment as he entered the narrow
brick corridor from the street, the place where Malaspina
had turned and made that perfect O shape behind the fabric, murmured "boom," and then dodged his fire in return. After that . . .

He didn't want to think about it. There wasn't time. He
retraced his steps down the alley, wondering where she
might be, whether he was too late already. The place
seemed different. Smaller. Even more squalid. Looking
everywhere, half running, close to the wall, trying to move

532   David Hewson

with as little noise and visibility as possible, he went on until he got to the small enclosed yard at the end.

The sight of the junk, and the vicious, clear memory of Malaspina hidden behind it, brought back such bitter recollections. For one fleeting moment he could see Emily's face rising in his imagination, staring at him, angry, determined, the way she always was when danger threatened.

Then a sound, thankfully, sent her ghost scattering from his head.

Agata emerged in the far corner of the yard, creeping out from behind some discarded mattresses leaning against the blackened stones of the grimy terrace that had once been the home of Caravaggio. She was trying to smile. There was something in her hand he couldn't see.

Her clothes were ordinary: a simple black nylon anorak and plain jeans. The kind the convent probably gave out to the poor, he thought. She looked like many a young woman in Rome at that moment, except for the expression on her face, which was excited, with a fixed resolve that worried him.

He walked over and stood in front of her.

"You will come with me now," Costa said forcefully. "You will leave this place and go to the Questura. Even if I have to carry you."

"Do that, Nic, and you lose forever. Franco Malaspina will walk free. He will negotiate with that lawyer of yours. His guilt will be forgotten in return for allowing you to establish that of others. Do you wish to bargain with the devil? Is that who you are?"

"Agata—"

"Is it?" she demanded, her dark eyes shining.

"I lost my wife to that man," he said quietly, hearing the crack in his own voice. "I don't wish to see another life wasted."

"Don't fear on my account. That's my responsibility. How did he come here for those women?" she asked. "Did you think about that? He's a well-known man. He wouldn't walk in the front door. It was too obvious. Nor . . ." She turned her head briefly to the brick corridor. ". . . would he have risked that. It opens out into the Piazza Borghese. He would have been seen there too. People notice. You hardly ever meet Franco out in the open, in the street. It's beneath him."

"This is all too late."

She leaned forward, smiling, her pert, smart face animated as always. "He owns everything. Every square metre. Every last brick and stone. He came through his own house." She glanced towards a shadowy alcove half hidden behind some discarded chests. "You never looked. It never seemed important. After all, you couldn't enter his palace anyway."

Costa struggled to find the words to make her understand.

"Malaspina wants you dead."

"No." She shook her head. Her dark curly hair flew wildly around her with the violence of the gesture. "That's only a part of it. What he wants is to forget what he is, where he came from. All those black women. Women like me. 'The sport in the blood.' He's ashamed of his lineage, as were Ippolito Malaspina and Alessandro de' Medici before him. There is your resolution, if only you knew it. Franco Malaspina is at war with himself and flails at everything in order to hide that simple fact."

He sighed. "I don't think so," he said.

"So what, then?"

Something still didn't ring true, however hard she tried.

"This is all conjecture," he answered. "Useless and dangerous."

"No," she insisted. "It's not."

"Did you ever stop to think for a moment how we all felt when you ran away?"

"Nic," she whispered, black eyes sparkling, her mouth taut with emotion and something close to fear, "this is not about me."

"I lost my wife . . ."

"I'm sorry. I didn't mean to hurt you. I never meant that."

"You don't know what hurt is. You're too afraid to feel it. You're terrified something real might penetrate the cocoon you have built for yourself."

"That's not fair . . ."

"I don't care about fair anymore. I just want you to live. Please. Let me take you out of here."

He held out his hand for her. She looked up at him, scared, resolute too.

"You really think I can go back into my shell now?" she asked, amazed, perhaps resentful too. "As easily as that?"

"I think—" he began.

"It's impossible," she cut in, shaking her head. "You made it so. You and Falcone." She hesitated. "You more than any."

He took a step forward. She shrank back against the wall, put a hand out in front of her. He saw now what she'd brought. Another large plastic bag with the name of an economy supermarket on the front lay at her feet. An object he couldn't quite make out protruded from the top.

"Wait . . ." Costa ordered.

Before he could go on, she had ducked away from his grasping arms and was running behind the discarded chests into the shadowy alcove.

He followed. When he got there, she had the crowbar in the bottom half of a small, battered wooden door, black with soot and grime. The top had been splintered already. Agata had found a way into the Palazzo Malaspina earlier, before his arrival. She was, as always, prepared.

"This is madness," he muttered. "I should call the Questura now. Why take such risks when you have your sisters all over Rome putting up that poster about the man?"

She leaned hard on the crossbar. The lower half of the door refused to budge.

"Because of what Falcone says," she answered. "You pile on the pressure, you see what happens. Franco will not walk out of this place for you, will he? But with a little force here . . . a little force there . . ."

She had known Leo Falcone longer than he had. It was, he thought, only natural that she should pick up his ways.

"The question is," she went on, "will you come with me? Or do I go into his palace on my own? There are"—she leaned hard on the crowbar again, to no effect—"no other alternatives. Can't you see that? Your law won't help you. Nor your grief."

Agata gave up on the door and looked at him. Her face shone in a stray shaft of winter sun. "All we need is the painting," she insisted. "Where else can it be?"

He muttered a quiet curse, walked over, and took the metal bar from her. It was a strong door, in spite of appearances. But after the third attempt the old wood cracked and they could see beyond, into the interior of this distant wing of the Palazzo Malaspina. There was darkness there, nothing else. It was prescient of her to bring along the flashlight in the plastic bag. It now sat in her hand, extending a long beam of yellow light into the gloom.

"I go first," Costa said. "What are you doing?"

She was pressing the keys of the mobile phone Rosa

had given her, dispatching a text message with the speed and enthusiasm of someone who did this every single day.

"Talking to my sisters," Agata replied cryptically, then pushed past him, flashlight blazing, into the black maw behind the door.

Costa followed quickly. Ahead, high on the wall to their left, a red light blinked persistently. He reached forward, took her hand to guide the beam towards it. There was a security camera there, a single glass eye, blinking. There had to be hundreds in a place like this. He turned round and looked back at the door. There was no entry detection device that he could see. Costa knew how difficult such large and sprawling buildings were to monitor. There was no way of knowing whether they had been seen or not; the probability was that no one had yet been alerted to their presence.

All the same he picked up the crowbar off the floor and dashed the forked end hard into the lens of the camera, stabbing at it until the glass broke and he was able to lever the unit off the wall.

She watched in silence. In the half-light she looked afraid.

He took the flashlight from her hand. There was no protest.

"Stay behind me," he ordered, and strode forward into the gloom.

# Six

$\mathcal{I}$T WAS BITTERLY COLD INSIDE WHATEVER REMOTE, deserted wing of Franco Malaspina's palace now enclosed them. They walked in single file down a long, straight, narrow corridor, then came directly to a plain grey wall, windowless, nothing but old stone and mortar.

"This must be the rear wall of the palace proper," she whispered. "That was how they built in those days. The master's part would be erected on its own. The rest—the quarters in the Vicolo del Divino Amore, everything that wasn't integral to the palace itself—would be added later. We must be in some kind of access corridor between the buildings. It's—"

"Quiet," he whispered, placing a finger to his lips.

Agata stopped speaking instantly. Her eyes, whiter than usual in the bright, unforgiving beam of the flashlight, betrayed her fear.

She can hear it too, Costa thought.

Footsteps. Heavy and echoing, with a loud, insistent rhythm.

He flashed the beam around both sides of the junction. They were trapped in a slender stone vein deep within the bulky mass of the palace. The sound danced around them deceptively. There was nowhere to hide, no easy way to discern the source.

Before he could think this through, Agata tugged on his arm and then did something so strange, yet so obvious.

She placed one hand on her left ear, then one on her right, dividing the echo from its origin, measuring which was stronger. Quickly, decisively, she pointed to the left. Then she arced her arm over to indicate the opposite direction.

Costa looked behind her, at the corridor they had already traversed. A way back to freedom. She cast him one brief, withering look, then snatched the flashlight from his fingers and was moving, down the right-hand side, in the lead, brushing vigorously through thick grey cobwebs with her arms, away from whoever was on their trail, or so she hoped.

He kept pace behind, continually glancing backwards, seeing nothing. There were no alternatives, no other route to follow, and very soon they found themselves in another constricted stone channel, this time wide enough only for a single human body, one that curved with a regular, geometric precision, as if tracing a circular room beyond the wall. He had no idea what the interior plan of the Palazzo Malaspina looked like. Costa had only seen the first public rooms, which covered a tiny proportion of the total site. Great Roman palaces often contained many surprises: private chapels, baths, even a secret place for alchemical experiments, like the private casino of the Villa Ludovisi, where Caravaggio had painted for Cardinal Del Monte. It was impossible to judge in which direction they were headed, impossible to see anything except the grimy walls of uniform stones laid almost five centuries before.

The other sound quickened, became louder, and was now identifiably behind them. And closer.

Costa caught up with Agata, felt for his gun to make sure it was safe to hand, and found himself brushing against her, accidentally, inevitably, before realising why.

The corridor was narrowing. In the space of a few steps it became so slender his shoulders rubbed against the walls as they moved, half running. Then the change in dimensions stopped. It would, he thought, stay this way for a while. He caught her arm, stopped her, and mouthed, *Go ahead*.

Her sharp eyes flared with anger and she whispered, "No!"

All the same, when she resumed her pace he managed to drop behind, just a little, enough to stay inside the penumbra of the flashlight beam that was trapped like them in this confined, enclosing space.

Whoever was following was near. He was sure of that.

Costa took out his gun, held it tight, trying to work out some strategy. He blundered on in the semidarkness, weapon in hand, wondering what the possibilities were in the belly of this stone leviathan, where the chances of anything—a scream, a forlorn message on the police radio—reaching the world outside were infinitesimal.

No easy answers came. None at all. Then, abruptly, with a force that made him apologise automatically, he found himself barging into her small, taut body, which was locked in an upright position, hard against stone.

She had stopped. Her breathing was so rapid and so shallow he felt he could hear and feel every gasp she made. The corridor had come to a dead end. It led nowhere, which seemed impossible. The only way was back.

"Stay still," he murmured.

She wasn't listening. She was turned to one side, as stationary as the stone that trapped them, and when his eyes adjusted to what he now realised was a new kind of light, he understood why.

The corridor ended in a bare stone wall, but down one side stood a long, musty drape that flapped into his face as the hand she had wrapped tightly in its folds began to shake. This was an entrance into another room, one that, as he began to look, was huge: a circular chamber, bathed, incredibly, in light so bright that even this side view made his head hurt.

In the centre, beneath a domed glass roof that let in the piercing rays of a low winter sun, stood the painting. *Evathia in Ekstasis.* It shone under the incandescent illumination pouring down from above, the central fleshy figure, frozen in Caravaggio's pigment, seemingly alive, energised, almost exultant, as she opened her throat to release that primal scream.

In front was a couch, a chaise longue much like the one they had found in the squalid studio of the Vicolo del Divino Amore. On it Franco Malaspina, still in a business suit, his trousers hitched halfway down, heaved and groaned over a naked African woman, her skin the colour of damp coal, her eyes wild with terror.

Malaspina's long, strong body strained over her. They could hear his panting, whimpering, grunting, and the obvious desperation behind the pained sighs. When Costa looked more closely, he could see the man's eyes flickering between the floor and the figure in the painting, never to the woman beneath him.

"Sweet Jesus," Agata moaned. "What's wrong, Nic?"

He didn't answer. He was thinking of the footsteps behind. Or trying to.

"What's wrong?" she demanded. Then, when he remained silent, she answered her own question. "Even with the painting he finds no . . . gratification. That's it, isn't it? Even now?"

They were watching the man who had murdered Costa's wife struggling to reach some kind of satisfaction with another woman snatched from the street, another pawn in his desperate, pitiless manoeuvres.

Agata shook her head. Her face seemed full of self-doubt, self-hatred even.

"We have to get out of here," he insisted, casting a glance through the small gap created by the portion of curtain she was holding.

As they looked on, Malaspina let out a long, pained

bellow of misery, then stood up from the couch, clutching his trousers to himself, refastening them. Costa's fingers tightened on the gun, but the woman was quick. While Malaspina remained absorbed in his own misery, scarcely noticing her presence, she fled, as many must have done before, scampering from him in fright, snatching some clothes off the floor, and then leaving, Costa noticed, by an open door that lay almost exactly opposite from where they now stood.

It was an opportunity. If the two of them could escape alive, he'd be happy, he thought, and wondered how many 'Ndrangheta men Malaspina had in his service. One was dead already. If luck was on their side, perhaps that left no more than a single hired thug to guard the Palazzo Malaspina on this quiet, lazy day after Christmas.

"I pity him," Agata murmured, taken aback by her own surprise. "I . . ."

He heard the metallic sound echo down the corridor and recognised immediately what it was. The checking of a magazine. One last prerequisite before violence.

"Get out! Get down!" Costa ordered, pushing her rapidly, roughly, through the drape, into the sea of light beyond and, he knew, the presence of Franco Malaspina.

A deafening burst of automatic fire burst deep within the stone vein back along the route they had stumbled. Sparks flew off the walls around him. Costa rolled forward to follow Agata, loosing off a wild succession of shots back into the gloom as he fell.

# Seven

$G$IANNI PERONI SAT IN THE PASSENGER SEAT OF A white Fiat van bearing the name of a drain-clearing company on the side. It was parked a hundred metres from the main entrance to the Palazzo Malaspina. The place looked dead. The double doors at the top of the front staircase were closed. Not a soul had come or gone in the twenty minutes since they'd arrived. The four other officers with him—men he didn't know, men who were deeply unhappy about having their holiday leave interrupted and didn't seem too keen to accept his assumed authority over them—were starting to grumble the ways cops did when boredom took hold.

"I sat outside some place on the Gianicolo for four days once," the one behind the wheel, a skinny, tall individual with a Florentine accent, complained. "Turned out it was the wrong house. Belonged to a big—and I mean *big*—woman opera singer and we thought we were staking out the capo of some Sicilian family. Four days. You take that with you to the grave."

"Did you hear her sing?" asked a voice from behind.

"Yes. . . ." The driver answered in a petulant whine.

"So why didn't you check?" another one demanded. "I mean . . . a capo doesn't normally have opera singers around, does he?"

"Hindsight," the driver moaned. "Every smart-ass I ever met has it running through his veins."

"It's a fair question," another voice from the back piped up.

"We checked! It was someone else's fault."

"It usually is," Peroni observed. "May I make a request, gentlemen?"

They went quiet and listened.

"Shut up and watch, will you?"

"Watch what?" the driver asked. "And why? You're just an agente now, Peroni. You're not the boss."

Gianni Peroni muttered something obscene under his breath, then caught the dark figure in the distance, slowly making her way down the cobbled street towards the palazzo.

"Watch that," he ordered.

And they did.

IT WAS A NUN—OR A SISTER, PERONI HAD NO WAY OF telling which—on the oldest motorcycle he had ever seen, one that belonged in a museum, not on the road, since it was probably illegal: rust everywhere, bald tires, a cracked exhaust that, even from this distance, sounded like a flatulent pigeon recovering from the night before.

"What the hell is this?" wondered a puzzled voice from the back.

"Watch," Peroni ordered again.

She made her way slowly down the street. Then, outside the palazzo, she stopped. The woman wore black flowing robes, so long and billowing he wondered whether they might catch in the spokes. If she'd ridden a two-wheeled vehicle before, she didn't show much sign of it. She was perhaps sixty, tall, skinny, awkward. A bright red cyclist's helmet sat over the black-and-white headgear he had come to associate with the uniform of a nun in Rome.

"It's Evel Knievel's grandma," the driver joked, and the rest of them snickered, until they caught sight of the displeasure on Peroni's ugly face.

The woman struggled to flip down the stand, got there eventually, then dismounted. After that she reached into the flapping folds of her robe and withdrew a large kitchen knife.

They watched as the woman looked around to check no one was watching, then bent down and started stabbing at the front tire with the kitchen knife. It deflated in a matter of seconds; the wall must have been paper thin.

After that she walked up the broad, semicircular stone staircase of the Palazzo Malaspina, found the bell by the shining wooden double doors, put her finger on the button, and kept it there.

"Next time I go undercover, I go as a nun," one of the voices behind muttered, and there was more than a modicum of admiration in it too.

Finally the door swung open. Peroni squinted to get a good look at the man there. He was relieved by what he saw. Sister Knievel might have pulled one of Malaspina's 'Ndrangheta thugs. Instead she got a flunky, a tired-looking middle-aged individual of less than average height, one who didn't look too smart and had probably been called away from cleaning the silver.

He didn't seem much interested in helping a stray sister whose ancient motorbike had developed a flat tire. The way the woman was talking at him, she plainly meant to ensure he didn't have much choice. At one point she took hold of the collar of his white cotton servant's jacket and dragged him out onto the steps. Peroni watched, impressed. He could almost hear the conversation.

*Sir, I am in a hurry for mass. I am only a nun. You must help.*

*Yes, but . . .*

*SIR!*

Reluctantly, with a very Roman shrug of his hunched shoulders, the servant gave in and walked down the broad steps, followed her to the rusty machine, bent down, and started looking at the flat. Naturally, he left the door ajar. This was a rich man's residence. No one expected opportunistic thieves. Nor could the servant see what the woman was doing as she stood over him—

namely, beckoning to someone around the corner, half hidden at the top of the street.

The five police officers in the drain-clearing van watched what happened next in total silence. Peroni couldn't even find the space in his head to raise a laugh. It was so... extraordinary. And also so obvious. What the police needed, they clearly knew, was an excuse to enter the Palazzo Malaspina. They had spent weeks trying to find that through myriad means: forensic and scientific investigation, detective work, and an exploration of Franco Malaspina's ancestry.

They hadn't counted on the cunning of a bunch of scheming nuns who, doubtless under Agata Graziano's tuition, had spent the night preparing to penetrate Malaspina's fortress in a way no law enforcement officer could possibly have imagined, let alone entertained. They would bring in the police by the very simplest of expedients: committing the small crime of trespass themselves.

They flooded round the corner, an entire flock, black wings flapping, running with the short, straitened gait their robes forced on them. Perhaps twenty. Perhaps more. A giggling, excited mass of sisterhood raced down the street and poured onto the steps of the Palazzo Malaspina, scampering upwards, to the door, not stopping to heed the cries of the servant, who was no longer staring at the flat tire on the crippled motorbike because its owner had swiftly departed to join her fellows, leading them exactly where Peroni expected.

Through both doors, now the intruders had thrown the second one open, the black tide flooded happily into the interior of the Palazzo Malaspina, as if this were some schoolgirl jape, the most amusing event to have occurred in their quiet, enclosed lives for years.

Peroni gave each of the men a look that said *Stay here.*

Then he slid out of the passenger door and strode down the street.

The servant was starting to flap and squawk, his pasty face red with outrage, lost for words, unsure what to do. He looked scared too. Peroni didn't need much imagination to guess that Franco Malaspina wasn't the nicest of bosses.

The man didn't take a single step towards the black mass of figures pushing into the palace on the steps above either. Peroni understood why. They seemed a little scary too.

"Sir," Peroni said, pulling out his police ID card, "I'm from the Questura. Is there a problem?"

"A problem?" the man squawked. "What the hell do you think?"

Peroni glanced at the pool of women. It was diminishing. Most of them were in the palace by now. He could see their silhouettes moving alongside the windows on both sides of the entrance as they ran in all directions.

"You know," Peroni observed, "this has been a bad day for nuns. It's shocking."

"What the . . . ?"

"This is why you pay for a police force. To create

order from chaos. To save ordinary citizens from . . ." He glanced at the steps. The last black-clad figure was struggling through the doors. ". . . the unexpected."

"Oh, crap," the man moaned. "Malaspina will go crazy."

Peroni leaned down and put on his most sympathetic face.

"Would you like me to go inside and deal with this for you?" he asked in a noncommittal fashion. "Discreetly of course."

"Yes . . . but . . . *but . . .*"

Peroni wasn't listening. He had what he wanted: a legitimate invitation to enter the Palazzo Malaspina, one prompted by a bunch of nuns and sisters who would surely impress any court.

He turned and beckoned to the men in the van. Four burly police officers jumped out, looking ready and eager for action.

The servant groaned, put his hands to his head, and started to mumble a low series of obscene curses.

"You can leave it to us now," Peroni shouted cheerfully down the street as he walked towards the staircase, wondering what a private Roman palace looked like from the inside, and where on earth, within its many rambling corridors, he might find Nic Costa and Agata Graziano.

He paused on the threshold. This really was not his kind of place. Then, out of politeness more than anything—since he had no intention of waiting—he placed a call to Falcone, explaining, in one sentence, what had happened.

There was a silence, pregnant with excitement.

"We're in, Leo, and I am not leaving until I have them," Peroni added, walking through the door, almost blinded by the expanse of shining marble that glittered at him from every direction. "Send me all the troops you have."

# Eight

$\mathcal{I}$T WAS LIKE THE PANTHEON IN MINIATURE, AND that brought memories crashing back. Costa rolled on the hard stone floor, hurting already, worked out where Agata was, and dragged himself in front of her. They were right up against the wall of a room that formed a perfect circle marked by ribbed columns, each framing a fresco, each fronted by a plinth with a statue. The ceiling was glass held by delicate stone ribs, incandescent with dazzling sunlight. The floor seemed to be sunken, and above it, no more than the height of two men, ran a balustraded gallery, like a viewing platform for some contest that would take place on the stage below.

It took a second or two for him to adapt. The gun was still in his hand. That was some consolation. He got to his knees, then stood up, glancing at Agata, understanding the shocked expression on her face, guarding her with his body as much as he could.

She had reason to be silent, to be shaking with fear behind him. This was Franco Malaspina's most private of sanctuaries, and it was dedicated to a kind of classical pornography that defied the imagination. Behind the still-confident figure of Malaspina stood a marble Pan, larger than life and so beautiful he might have been carved by Bernini, laughing as he raped a young girl, every crude physical detail of the ravishment laid bare for the beholder. To their left stood a warrior in silver armour, painted to resemble Carpaccio's Saint George, savaging the maiden at the stake as the dragon lay bloodily at his feet. Equidistant around the circular chamber stood figures that were semi-human, beasts and men, half-real creatures and, everywhere, naked, vulnerable women, young, virginal, portrayed as if they were on the precipice of some revelation, afraid yet desperate for knowledge, too, lips open, ready to utter the primal scream of joy and release that Caravaggio had placed in the throat of Eve in the painting at the heart of the room.

These were all plays on known works of art, paintings and statues he recognised, transformed by an obscene imagination, and they were old, as old as the Palazzo Malaspina itself, perhaps even more ancient, since Costa believed he could see some that must have preceded Caravaggio's enticing goddess, the original Eve, in the ecstatic throes of the original sin, taunting them with a conundrum—carnal love or divine?—that was lost, surely, on most of those who saw it.

Franco Malaspina stood next to the canvas, watching them, unconcerned, amused.

As Costa struggled to consolidate his position—

Agata behind him, protected, silent, astonished by what she saw—the count strode forward. He was unarmed but Costa could see where his eyes had drifted before he took that first step. Around the room at intervals—there surely to enforce the impression that this was a knight's secret lair, a chamber of the Round Table, dedicated to the sexual power of men—were collections of armour and weapons: swords and daggers, gleaming, clean, ready for use.

"Do you like my little temple?" Malaspina asked, stopping a short distance in front of them, smiling, bowing.

"Consider yourself under arrest," Costa retorted, his voice hoarse from the dust in the corridors. "The painting's evidence enough for me."

The man laughed and took one more step forward.

"You can't arrest me here. No one can. This place belongs to me. To us. To my line. To my ancestors. You two are merely insects in the walls. Nothing. Does it not interest you, my little sister? Did you see me well enough from your little peephole?"

"What is this, Franco?" she asked softly.

"This?" Malaspina replied, still moving slowly forward. "This is the world. The real world. As they created it. Those who came before. My ancestors and their friends. Artists. Poets. And lords to rule over them all." His face turned dark. "The world has need of lords, Agata. Even your Popes understood that."

"Raping black women from the streets is scarcely a sign of class," Costa observed, casting a nervous glance at the curtain to the hidden corridor, wondering what had happened to their pursuer, praying that one of his shots—how many remained in the magazine he'd no idea—had hit home.

Malaspina stopped and looked at them, his cruel, dark, aristocratic face full of contempt.

"Be honest with yourself, Costa. Given half the chance, you would have stayed and watched, too, then said nothing. That small, dark demon is in us all. Only the few have courage to embrace it. The Ekstasists have been here always, in this place, in this city. My father was one. His before him. When I have a son . . ."

It was clear. Costa understood the truth implicitly, and it horrified him, the idea that such a cruel and vicious decadence might be passed on through generations, though surely not with such savagery.

"Your father didn't kill people, did he?" he asked, trying to work out a safe way to reach the door by which the woman had left earlier. "He didn't murder some penniless immigrant on a whim." He nodded towards the canvas on the easel in front of the couch, its cushions still indented with the weight of Malaspina's body and that of the woman they had seen. "He didn't need to place that painting in some squalid little room to hide the blood and the bones."

"Black blood, black bones," Agata murmured behind him.

"It was just a sick game before," Costa went on. "A rite of passage for rich, bored thugs. Then Nino showed you that painting. And it became something worse." He clutched the gun more tightly. There was a noise from near the curtain. "Why was that?"

He backed her more tightly against the wall. The thunder in Malaspina's face scared him. The man didn't care.

"I will kill you first," he said without emotion, then nodded towards Agata, who was still cowering behind Costa's shoulder. "Then I will have her. This is my domain, little policeman. I own everything. I control everything. When I am done, what is left of you will disappear forever, just like those black whores. This . . ."

He strode over to the wall and took a long, slender sword, a warrior's weapon, real and deadly, from one of the displays there, tucking a short stiletto into his belt for good measure.

". . . is why I exist."

Costa held the gun straight out in front of him. He didn't care about the consequences anymore, or whether some bent lawyer or magistrate would one day accuse him of murder. He had the man's cold, angular face on the bead and that was all that counted.

Then Agata was screaming again, slipping from beneath him. Costa's attention shifted abruptly to the drape and a figure crawling through it, bloodied, wounded, dying maybe.

It was Malaspina's man and in his gory hands he clutched a gun, clinging to the cold black metal as if it were the most precious object in his life.

The 'Ndrangheta never gave up, never stopped till the job was done.

One brief rake of fire ran low against the circular boundary wall. Costa could feel Agata's small body quaking behind him. Before the man could find energy for a second run, Costa directed his gun away from Malaspina and released a single shot straight at the bloodied figure wrapped in the curtain, struggling to get upright. The shock of the impact jerked the stricken figure back into the drape, back into the dark chasm at the corridor's mouth. He didn't move again.

Grinning, Malaspina took two steps forward, slashing the blade through the air in an easy, practised fashion.

"This is for my wife, you bastard," Costa murmured, and drew the short black barrel of the Beretta level with the arrogant face in front of him, keeping it as straight and level as any weapon he had ever held, with a steady hand and not the slightest doubt or hesitation.

He pulled the trigger. The weapon clicked on empty.

# Nine

GIANNI PERONI HAD NEVER BEEN IN A BUILDING like it before. There were women in black robes, nuns and sisters, wandering everywhere, lost once they had gained entrance, puzzled about what to do. And there were so many rooms: chamber after chamber, some grand, some small and functional, many looking little used in this sprawling palace that was home to a single human being detached from the reality beyond his domain.

Any servants around clearly had no desire to make themselves known. Perhaps they realised the Malaspina empire was crumbling under this strange invasion and knew what that meant. As he raced through the building, screaming out that they were police and demanding attention, Peroni became aware he was simply becoming more and more lost in some glorious Minotaur's maze, a travertine prison in which Franco Malaspina lived as solitary ruler of an empire of stiff, frozen grandeur. It was like hunting for life in a museum, like seeking the answer to a riddle from yet another riddle, a journey that wound in on itself, circling the same vistas, the same monuments and paintings and galleries.

The men from the Questura followed him, just as bemused. Twice they met sisters and nuns they had encountered before, and got nothing from them except a shake of the head and equal puzzlement. The women's brief, it seemed to Peroni, was simple: find a way into the Palazzo Malaspina and breach its invisible defences, in such numbers that the police would surely be summoned. Once that had been achieved . . . Peroni tried to imagine the extent of Franco Malaspina's home. It covered a huge area, extending by second-floor bridges beyond neighbouring streets, as far as the studio in the Vicolo del Divino Amore, where this tragedy, one that had such powerful, continuing personal dimensions for them all, had begun.

It was impossible to guess where to start looking. Then they turned a corner, one that looked much like any other—gleaming stone, carved heads on plinths, sterile splendour everywhere—and saw her. Peroni stopped, breathless. Just one look at the woman on the floor, terrified, clutching her clothes to her, made him realise exactly what they were seeking. Somewhere within this vast private empire was Franco Malaspina's clandestine lair, the sanctum where he felt free to do whatever he liked. This cowed and frightened woman in front of him understood where it lay. He could see that in her terrified features.

One of the other officers got there first, dragged her

roughly to her feet, and started to throw a series of loud, aggressive questions into her frightened face.

"Shut up," Peroni barked at the man and pushed him out of the way, found a chair—all ornate gilt and spindly legs—by the window, brought it for her, and let her sit down. Then he kneeled in front, making sure he didn't touch her, even by accident, and said, "Please, signora. We need your help. We must find Franco Malaspina, the master of this palace, now. There are people in danger here, just as you were. We must know where he is."

"Yeah," the officer who got there first butted in. "Start talking or we start asking for papers."

Peroni glowered at him and pointed at the broad glass panes next to them. "If you utter one more moronic word," he said quietly, "I will, I swear, throw you straight out of that window." He looked at the woman. In truth she was little more than a girl, a slim, pretty creature, with scars on her cheeks and short hair caught and braided in beads, now dishevelled. She was terrified still, but perhaps not as much as before. "Please," he repeated. "I am begging you. This is important. This man has hurt people in the past." He hesitated, then thought, Why not? "He's killed people. Women like you. Perhaps you've heard..."

Her eyes were astonishingly white and broad, fearful but not without knowledge and some strength too. Her body, which was lithe and athletic, shook like a leaf as she clutched her cheap, skimpy hooker's clothes more tightly as he spoke those words.

"He's a rich man," she muttered in a strong African accent.

"You heard about those women who were murdered," Peroni replied immediately. "You must have done. We've had officers out on the streets telling everyone."

She nodded, the gesture barely perceptible.

"Rich and powerful he may be," Peroni continued, "but he killed those women and a good friend of mine too. Where is he?"

Her eyes grew bright with anger. "I show you," she told him, and led the way, down a set of stairs at the end of the hallway, down a long, dark, narrow corridor, over a footbridge, with the bright chilly December morning visible through the stone slats, like emplacements for imaginary archers, open to the air, then on into a distant sector of the palace they would never have found so quickly on their own.

# Ten

COSTA EDGED BACK TOWARDS THE DRAPE AND THE corpse of the 'Ndrangheta thug, making sure Agata stayed out of range by forcing his right hand down behind and guiding her along the wall. When they were close enough—he could feel the man's body hard against his foot, he could smell the rank odour of the wound—he turned and caught her gleaming eye.

"Go down the corridor as fast as you can and make your way outside. Keep running," he whispered. "Leave this to me."

She didn't move.

"Not now," he insisted, beginning to feel desperate.

Malaspina was taking his time. He was no more than a few steps away, playing with the sword, watching them, an athletic, powerful figure in a place where he felt confident, secure.

"What do you take me for?" she murmured softly, her breath warm in his ear. "I didn't come here to run away."

"Agata . . ."

She was moving, slipping out from beneath him in a way he couldn't prevent. With a couple of short, deliberate steps, Agata Graziano worked herself free, then paced into the circular hall to set herself between him and Malaspina.

The gleaming blade ceased moving in the man's hands. He looked . . . interested.

"How many years have you known me, Franco?" she asked. "Will you kill me? Will you kill me now?"

He shrugged, amused, in control. "After . . ." he said, half laughing. "Sorry. Needs must."

"Why?"

He blinked as if it were a stupid question. "Because I can."

She took one more short stride to stand in front of him, thrust her slender, dusky arm in front of his face, pinched her own skin on her wrist.

"Not because of this? Because of the shade of someone's skin? A sport in the blood? Some small thing inside you've come to hate and a painting that obsesses you?"

Malaspina's eyes strayed to the canvas in the centre of the room. "You're a fool, Agata," he murmured. "You understand *nothing*."

"I understand everything! My father was an African. My mother was a Sicilian whore. I am a little more black than you, Franco. But not much. Does it matter that Ippolito Malaspina shared my race? *Our* race?"

Costa couldn't take his eyes off the man's face. There

was nothing there. No recognition. No emotion whatsoever.

The machine pistol lay in the dead thug's arms, no more than one step away.

"No," Malaspina answered Agata, almost with sadness. "It doesn't."

"Caravaggio—" she began.

"We were here before Caravaggio," he interrupted. "We were here before Christ, before Caesar. We are what Man was meant to be, before you and yours came to poison us."

She shook her head. Agata was lost, her eyes flying around the chamber with its sunken floor, its obscene statues and paintings, the paean to brutality that was everywhere.

"You hate them," she insisted. "You hate me. You hate yourself."

Malaspina stared at her and there was contempt in his eyes. "Not for that," he murmured. "So much wisdom, Agata, and so little knowledge..."

"I forgive you everything," she said, trembling like a leaf in the wind. "Those poor women. Everyone." She glanced in Costa's direction for a moment. "Even Nic can forgive you. He's a good man. Everything can be atoned for if you wish it. Accept who you are, what you have done. Ask for justice and it is yours."

He shook his head and cut the knife through the air in front of her, unmoved by a single word.

*   *   *

COSTA ROLLED LEFT, EYES NEVER LEAVING THE WEAPON that lay in the dead man's bloodied hands. He turned as quickly as he could, snatched the metal stock up, rose to a crouch, felt for the trigger, gripped it, played once with the metal stub, heard a single shot burst from the barrel and exit through the drape behind. Then he rolled sideways once again, trying to avoid any attack that was coming, landing on his knee, a firm position, one that would take him out of Agata's way and give him a direct line to Malaspina, an opportunity he would take on the instant, without a second thought.

It was all too late. By the time Costa wheeled round with the weapon in his hands, Agata was in the man's grasp, his strong arm around her throat, the stiletto tight to her neck. Her eyes shone with terror.

"Drop it," Malaspina ordered.

Agata screamed. Malaspina had curled the blade into her flesh in one short, cruel flick, fetching up a line of blood.

"Drop it or I will slit her like a pig," he declared with no emotion, then turned the knife further into her neck as she struggled helplessly in his arms.

The weapon slipped from Costa's hands. To drive home the point, he kicked it away, watching, listening, as the black metal screeched across the shiny marble, fetching up near the circular boundary wall opposite, well out of reach.

He could hear something from above. Footsteps, short and feminine, and the rushing of long robes. It was the sound Agata made across the polished tiles of the Doria Pamphilj.

Then something louder. The heavy approach of men. And another noise he recognised, and welcomed.

"Nic!" Peroni bellowed down from above.

Costa looked upwards, to the gallery that circled this strange Pantheon in miniature. They were gathering there, police officers and nuns, a crowd of witnesses, an audience which spelled a certain end for the last of the Ekstasists.

"The lawyers won't get you out of this, Franco," the big man bellowed from above, scanning the gallery, trying to work out some way down to the ground floor. "We're in this place now. Legally. There are more officers on the way. Even you can't walk away now."

There was fury on Malaspina's face. Nothing more. Not fear, not an acceptance that this was the end, which was what Costa wanted. The knife was still hard on Agata's neck. The blood there welled like a river ready to burst its banks.

"Little men, little women," Malaspina shouted, head jerking from side to side, taking in the flood of visitors now racing onto the balcony. "All of you. No idea of your place. No idea of the ..." The count's face contorted until there was nothing there but hatred, a black, dead loathing for everything. "... impudence."

The knife moved again. Agata yelled, more faintly. A second wound line started to appear beneath her ear. The balance had shifted, Costa sensed. In Malaspina's mind, the dark, savage place where he imagined himself to live supreme, this was the endgame, the rich knight's final hour, the moment of death and dissolution, the final opportunity to place a bloody mark against a world he detested.

She was, to him, as good as dead already.

Costa strode forward to confront him, stopping within reach of the sharp, deadly stiletto that never strayed from her neck, tempting the blade away from her dusky skin towards his own.

The idea had been buzzing in his head now for days. He had never discussed it with anyone, with Agata least of all, and it was her opinion, more than any, that he had come to value about Franco Malaspina.

Yet Agata Graziano was wrong. Costa understood this instinctively and he believed he knew why. He and Malaspina shared the same pain.

He leaned forward until his own features were so close to Malaspina's he could see the wild, crazed determination in his eyes, smell the sweat of anticipation on him, and feel the sense that there was no going back now, not for any of them.

"What about Véronique Gillet?" he asked quietly, eye-to-eye with the man, close enough for him to switch his attention away from Agata if he wanted, if this taunting did its work.

"Véronique is dead." Malaspina's black eyes burned with fury.

"Would this have been part of the game too? If she were still alive?"

There were more sounds from above. More men. He

thought he heard Falcone's voice. Malaspina's features were locked in bleak determination.

"Do not come near," Costa ordered in a loud, commanding voice. "Count Malaspina has a hostage and a weapon."

Falcone's voice began to object.

"No!" Costa shouted.

There was quiet.

"They listen to you," Malaspina murmured. "That's good. There'll be many people at your funeral. There was a crowd for your wife, wasn't there? I read it in the papers. I sent a man to take photographs. They amused me."

"Did they comfort you, Franco?" he asked.

"You speak in riddles."

"I don't think so," he disagreed. "Will there be many mourners for Véronique?"

"I have no idea."

Costa could see the interest in Agata's eyes, detect, perhaps, a loosening of Malaspina's grip on her neck.

"Her body is in the morgue still. Autopsies . . ." Costa shrugged. "It's not a pretty event. We cannot release her for a burial, naturally. Not with the case open. She must stay stiff in that cabinet, perhaps for years."

The point of the stiletto twitched in his direction.

"I may kill you first," Malaspina murmured. "Just for the pleasure."

"It's all in the blood," Costa said, wondering.

"You bore me. You both bore me, and that is dangerous."

"It wasn't the black gene at all, was it?" Costa

demanded. "You checked your ancestry too. That was merely curiosity. The arrogance of proving you are what you are."

He watched the point of the knife, tried to measure how Malaspina might move if he managed to goad him enough for Agata to get free.

The man said nothing. The circular chamber was silent, save for the breathing of Malaspina and the captive Agata Graziano.

Costa pointed to the painting: the naked goddess, the eternal sigh, the moment the world became real.

"What took her was all much more simple, much more human, which is why you hate it so," he continued. "Your game. Véronique's game. The game of Castagna, Buccafusca, and Nino Tomassoni when you drew them into it."

He took one step back and traced a finger along the outline of the naked figure's fleshy thigh. Malaspina stiffened, infuriated.

"Was that your idea? Or Véronique's?" There were so many questions, so many possible answers. He didn't care what Malaspina replied. He only cared that soon, very soon, he might get Agata away from the knife.

"You're guessing," Malaspina growled.

"I'm guessing it was yours. She was a weak, difficult woman. Beautiful, I think. Not unwilling to play as you dictated." He stepped back to them, close again. "The whores. The violence, sham perhaps at first, all part of the price to be paid. Then..."

In the distance, above the shining floor and the bright painting that seemed so alive, he could see Falcone watching from the gallery, listening to every word.

Costa moved yet closer to him. "Something changed. An obvious thing. But something you believed could never happen to you and your kind. This game caught up with you." He leaned forward. "It came with a price."

"Shut up," Malaspina muttered.

"You have sex with poor, miserable street whores. *And* one day you catch a disease. The disease. It's not some black gene that gets passed down from generation to generation. You don't care about that. You like to fool yourself you care about nothing at all. Then the sickness comes and it's the worst sort, the sort that can kill you. HIV. AIDS, in Véronique's case. A disease that's not supposed to affect people like you. Aristocrats, lords with money and power, little gods in your own private world. And when it does . . ."

He reached for the man's jacket, watching the blade all the time. There was a shape behind the breast pocket. One he had noticed before, in the farmhouse. A shape that could be one thing only.

Costa dipped his fingers quickly into the pocket and withdrew a small silver case, popped it open, revealed the pills inside.

"Véronique had something like this," he went on. "Drugs. Expensive drugs, I imagine. Not ones they give to street whores because they can't afford them and they're just animals in any case. Special drugs. Ones that work. Mostly."

The man's face was stiff and ugly with strain and hate. Costa looked into those black, dead eyes and knew this was the truth.

"You paid for them for yourself, naturally. And for the others too. I imagine you paid for them for Véronique but"—he smiled, deliberately, as he continued—"even the richest man in the world cannot buy a cure for death. With Véronique, they didn't work. She was ill already. The drugs made her worse. They shortened a life that was in jeopardy to begin with. In the end they killed her—"

"Shut up, shut up, shut up," Malaspina repeated through clenched teeth.

Costa caught Agata's attention. Her eyes were glassy with tears. She stared at him in horror. This was an explanation from a world she had never known, one that would never have made sense if she had stayed where she thought she belonged, quiet and safe inside a sister's plain, coarse uniform.

"All your money, all the drugs and treatment... they weren't enough for Véronique, were they? She'd left it too late," Costa said simply. "You could save yourself and the others. But you couldn't save her, the very woman you wished to keep alive. And what was worse, so much worse, was that, as she began to die... as you *killed her*... a part of you thought this might be love. Some stray strand of humanity inside of you looked at her wasting away and regretted that fact." He watched the man's reaction, prayed he saw some dim sign of recognition in his eyes. "But this being you, that small part spoke to the larger part and all it could think of was blood and murder and hate. To take some cruel vengeance on the innocent that should, by rights, have been directed at yourself."

"You will die," Malaspina murmured, his voice low and lifeless.

"How did you work the others into your scheme?" Costa asked. "Did you murder some poor black hooker who failed all of you one night, then tell them they were a part of it anyway? Did you promise them lawyers, too, the way you promised them drugs?"

The knife flashed back and forth in Malaspina's clenched fist, cutting through thin air a finger's length from Costa's eyes.

"Most of all, Franco," Costa asked lightly, "I would like to know what you told her. When Véronique knew she would surely die. Did you offer her one last chance to indulge you, in front of your painted goddess, as a . . . reward somehow? Was that supposed to be some kind of comfort? Do you really believe this passes as love?"

He folded his arms, waiting for the explosion. "I know what love is, Franco. Most people do. But not you. Never you. She was simply an obsession. Something you owned. Like this palace. Like the painting you forced Nino Tomassoni to give you. One more beautiful object you've torn apart as if it were worthless . . ."

He was screaming, moving, releasing Agata Graziano, throwing her to one side in his fury. Costa backed up, watching the stiletto flash through the air, feeling it make one arc in front of his chest, just close enough to cut a scything line through the fabric of his jacket.

Another sweep, another blow. There was nothing he could do, no weapon, no physical manoeuvre he knew that would offer any defence against a man like this.

Then the growing hubbub from the gallery above, the sound of racing footsteps, shouts, screams, disappeared beneath a deafening, cataclysmic clamour.

The blade swept through nothing and fell from view. The rage was gone from Franco Malaspina's face. In its place was shock and surprise . . . and fear.

Costa looked beyond the figure stumbling towards him and saw her now. Agata Graziano had withdrawn something from the pocket of the cheap office-girl's jacket. It was the gun Rosa Prabakaran had given her, a weapon Costa had never expected to see again. Grey smoke curled from the short snub barrel. As he watched, Agata raised the pistol again and fired one more shot at the falling figure between them, then a third.

Malaspina jerked with pain and the physical blow of the impacts. Blood rose in his mouth. His eyes turned glassy. The knife fell to the floor with a hollow echoing ring, followed by the stricken man, who clutched at the legs of the stand on which Caravaggio's naked goddess rested, watching the scene, unmoved, her throat locked in a cry that was lost in the clamour of Franco Malaspina's death.

A pebble-sized hole, surrounded by broken shards of skull, gaped above Malaspina's ear. The dun, viscous matter Costa could see beneath the man's hairline matched that which now ran in a spraying line, mixed with blood, across the naked figure of Eve like the splash of a murderous graffiti artist seeking something beautiful to defile.

Agata was shouting, screeching; was not herself; was quite unlike the woman he knew.

He watched in dismay as she emptied every last shell from Rosa's gun into the still, frozen form on the canvas, painted by the artist she had come, in her own fashion, to love, watched as the mouth and its inaudible eternal sigh disappeared beneath the blast of a shell.

When the bullets ran out, she began to tear at the canvas with her bare hands, ripping into four-hundred-year-old pigment with her nails, weeping, screaming.

He strode over and pulled her away.

Her face stole into his neck, damp with tears. His hand fell on her rough, tangled hair and held her small, slim body close.

Agata Graziano looked up and the power of her gaze was unmistakable. She was staring at him and there was something in her expression—a kind of dislike, bordering on hatred—that was reminiscent, for a moment, of Franco Malaspina.

"This is done now," Costa said, and wondered, seeing the look persist in her eyes, what it was that she saw.

Part Nineteen

Fresh Beginnings

# One

$f$IUMICINO WAS ALWAYS BUSY JUST AFTER THE NEW year. Families on the move, businesses returning to life. Part of the daily round of modern life. They were together at a small table in the cafe drinking coffee, an awkward silence between them, one he was desperate to break.

It was the mother superior of the convent who had called and asked if it was possible for him to give Agata a lift to the airport. The sisters were, she said, too upset about her decision to be trusted. He didn't have to think twice before saying yes.

Now they sat, she with two plastic grocery bags bulging with personal detritus on the floor after checking in a small, cheap canvas tote for the flight. Costa with . . . nothing but regrets and thoughts he found difficult to turn into words. He wished she weren't leaving so soon and was determined not to burden her with that knowledge. Agata had enough to carry now.

"What's the order like there?" he asked finally, unable

to bear the thought that they could part in a few minutes without having exchanged more than a few perfunctory words. "Is that the right word, 'order'?"

She smiled weakly. Her face seemed to have aged over these past few weeks. She now looked like the person he would have met had she never worn the black robes of a nun: a beautiful woman just turning thirty, with flawless dark skin, high cheekbones, and eyes that shone with intelligence, and a new sense of sadness that had never been there before.

"There is no 'right word,'" she said. "I left. Didn't they tell you that?"

"No . . . I mean, I assumed you wanted to move to a convent somewhere else. Away from Rome."

"I'm not just going somewhere different," she replied emphatically.

"Oh . . ."

She reached over and touched his wrist. Automatically—he knew this gesture so well by now he never thought about it—he turned it so she could see his watch.

"I only have a few minutes before I need to go. I can't explain everything. I don't want to. Talk about something else."

"I don't want to," he objected. "You spent your entire life in that place. I don't understand."

Her eyes widened with outrage. "I killed a man, Nic. How can I be a sister after that? It's impossible." She looked at her hands, as if remembering the moment Rosa

Prabakaran's weapon sat in her fingers. "I feel no guilt either. That's the worst thing." She stared at him. "He would have killed you. Instead of me, because your friends, Gianni, Leo, would have been there in time to stop that. But why do I tell you this? You know already. This is what you do, isn't it? Put yourself in the way instead."

He tried to pull a wry smile. "It seems to work most of the time."

"No, it doesn't. Not really."

He stirred the sugar in the grounds of his coffee a little harder, hearing that.

"What will you do?" Costa asked.

She seemed relieved to be able to shift the focus of the conversation. "There are many illegal immigrants coming to Malta each month. Mostly from Africa. They want to come to Italy. One way or another most of them will. The Church has a program trying to help them. I will teach. Children, young men and women. These are people who need me. They're desperate. As my father must have been once. I can't sit by and ignore them. It's unthinkable."

He had no difficulty imagining her excelling at that kind of work. Or being in Malta.

"Will you go to Valletta? And the co-cathedral? You said you always wanted to see those paintings." An image of the Caravaggio flashed through his own mind. "John the Baptist. And Saint Jerome, of course."

The laugh returned, and it was still light, still mostly untroubled.

"I'm there to try to help people in difficulty. Why would I walk away from that to see a painting? I spent too long in that daydream. I was like Franco Malaspina, obsessed with something that was unreal. Trapped in a world that had nothing to do with the way people actually live."

He shook his head firmly. "Caravaggio's real, Agata. Those people he portrayed . . . You said it yourself. They came from the streets. They're you and me."

"Oh, Nic." Her hand crossed the table and almost fell briefly on his before returning to the plastic bag by her side. "I have work to do." The amusement in her face vanished. "Sins to atone for . . ."

"What you did was self-defence," he replied instantly. "Not a sin."

"That's not for you to decide. Or me. It's a question of faith."

"Faith," he snapped without thinking, his voice rising so that the woman at the next table raised an eyebrow in their direction.

"Yes," she went on. "Faith. You think I lost it? No. Not for a moment." Her eyes stayed on him, clear, insistent, knowing. "I found more. I found real faith was awkward and uncomfortable. It asked questions I didn't want to hear. Demanded sacrifices I didn't want to make." She shook her head. The stray black curls flew around her neck in a way that mesmerised him. "I discovered it existed for my salvation, not my enjoyment. That it was awkward and uncomfortable and occasionally"—she peered at the empty coffee cup on the table, her eyes misty—"that it meant I had to avoid . . . forgo things I might come to want for myself."

"And I don't have that?" he asked.

"Not in the same way," she answered carefully. "I've watched you. Your faith lies in others. Not in politics. Not in religion. Not even in the law or justice, I think, anymore. It's rooted in the people you love." Her voice caught with emotion. "More than that. I envy it. I look at you and think, 'I wish I could feel that way too.' But I can't."

"Love isn't something you can control or call up on demand. None of us knows when it might happen. I didn't with Emily. I had no idea and nor did she."

Her slender lips curled in a deprecating smile. "You're not listening. This isn't about that kind of love. I'm trying to stay away from my beliefs for a while in the hope I might find some answers to my doubts. You're making the same journey, but in reverse. We're moving in opposite directions. It's not Emily you're looking for, it's God, and since you think he doesn't exist that makes it all the worse for you." Her shining eyes held him. "Also, people die. Everyone in the end. Does this small, plain faith of yours die with them?" Her fingers reached out and touched his hand, for the briefest of moments. "Did it?"

"For a while," he answered honestly.

He felt so inadequate, so tongue-tied, and had no idea whether he believed what she said, about him or about herself.

Over the hubbub of the busy airport, they were calling the plane. He could see from her face she had heard the announcement.

"If I came to visit in Malta . . ."

"I don't think that would be a good idea."

Costa sighed and said nothing.

"I have to go," she murmured. "There's no need to see me to the plane. I have a little time, I think. I would like to spend it on my own."

She was standing, picking up her two plastic bags, an independent young woman entering a world she barely understood, alone, determined to explore its dark corners and intricacies without the help of another.

"Here," he said, getting up too. "You'll need one of these at some stage."

He took off his watch and passed it to her. She tried to put it on. The leather strap was too large and needed another hole. She'd no clue how to make one, no idea that a man would simply push the spike hard through the old soft leather and find some new purchase that way.

"Let me . . ."

Gently, he wound the strap around her soft, warm wrist, worked out the size, removed it, forced through the hole, and wound it back around her dusky skin again, fastening the strap, making sure it fitted well.

They stood there, so close.

Nervously, Costa extended his right hand and waited.

Agata Graziano closed her eyes and there was a single line of moisture beneath each dark lid.

"Oh my, oh my," she whispered, laughing, crying, he wasn't sure quite which. "For God's sake, Nic. My hand?"

She opened her arms and walked forward, enclosing him, waiting as his own arms fell hesitantly around her slender shoulders.

Outside the dead, half-forgotten nightmare of the funeral, it was the first time he had embraced anyone since Emily had died. He was crying now, he knew that, not much, but enough to feel some tight interior knot inside him relax, release, then, if not disappear, begin to dissipate somehow.

Costa held her, tightly, his face against her dark hair, acutely aware that she was unlike any woman he had ever known, simple, pure, innocent. There was no fragrance about her, nothing but fresh soap and her skin against his, as young and smooth and perfect as that of a child.

"Enough of this," she said, her voice breaking a little, pushing him away. "Farewells are something new to me also, and clearly I am as terrible at them as you."

They looked at each other, lost for words. Then, very quickly, she came close again, reached up, and kissed him once, tenderly, on the cheek, with a swift, embarrassed affection.

"Goodbye, Nic," she murmured, then, without looking back, scooped up her bags and scurried off down the corridor towards the gate.

# Two

TWO HOURS LATER COSTA WAS SITTING IN THE kitchen. It was a chill, bright afternoon. Through the window, he could see planes high in an eggshell sky leaving vapour trails in their wake. Beyond the lines of black, dormant vines, crows bickered in the trees by the road. Bea had returned to her apartment with the little dog. The house was empty. He was alone again, back in the sprawling farmhouse his late father had built with his own hands, a place where every brick and tile was familiar, every angle and corner carried a cherished memory.

Grief was a journey, a transition through opposing phases, of knowledge and ignorance, togetherness and solitude, pain and consolation. What counted was the passage, the recognition that at the heart of life lay motion. Without that there was nothing but stasis, a premature quietus that rendered everything and everyone it touched meaningless.

Here, surrounded by Emily's lingering fragrance, the shelves with the food and drink only she would eat, her music by the hi-fi system, her jars and bottles still lurking in cupboards in the bathroom, it was to his dead wife that his thoughts turned constantly, and would for years to come. Her presence was everywhere, a benevolent ghost forever active in his conscience. He had lost her, but not entirely. When he closed his eyes, he could hear her voice. When he called up those precious memories of their time together, he could sense the soft grip of her fingers in his, the warmth of her breath as she whispered in his ear.

As she whispered now, calling, *Live, Nic, live.*

He felt the shiny marble urn in his fingers, its smooth surface as cold as a statue's skin, the way it was the day he'd taken it home from the crematorium.

Costa got up from the table and went outside into the cold, walking on until he was among the rows of vines they had tended together, so carefully, and with such rudimentary skill. As he reached that point he began to let her go, to let the stream of dust and ashes tumble from the vessel's grey marble neck, out into the air, to scatter among the slumbering black trunks, across the dun, chill earth. He walked on and on, the horizon rising and falling with his steps, blurred by the tears that flooded his eyes in a way they never had before. It took no more than a minute. Then he threw the empty container as far as he could, out towards the road and the distant outline of the tomb of Cecilia Metella.

In the field, shaking with fierce emotion, lost, blind, choking, he found himself consumed by a swirling plume of grey dust raised from the earth by a sudden fierce squall. It clung to his head. Like a sandstorm in miniature, a miasmic cloud of pale particles, it swirled around his head, danced in his eyes, his mouth, his nostrils, clung briefly to his fingers like a second, shedding skin.

Then a fresh blast arose and it was gone.

# Author's Note

*C*HIS IS A WORK OF FICTION CONSTRUCTED AROUND some certain facts, so I feel it is important to give a few guidelines on where this division is drawn. There is no painting entitled *Evathia in Ekstasis,* by Caravaggio or any other artist of the same period. Canvases close to its subject matter certainly did exist, however, among them Annibale Carracci's *Venus with a Satyr and Cupids,* which remains in the possession of the Uffizi today. Erotic paintings, some by well-known artists, others pure graphic pornography, were popular throughout sixteenth- and seventeenth-century Rome among the richer classes and with influential men of the Church. The more risqué works would be kept in private rooms, covered by a curtain, and shown only to close and discreet friends. This penchant for private interests bordering on vice was not uncommon. Cardinal Francisco Maria Del Monte, Caravaggio's patron and landlord for a while, did indeed tinker with the forbidden art of alchemy in the privacy of the casino of the Villa Ludovisi, and paid the artist to produce a unique fresco associated with his experiments there.

Caravaggio lived in turbulent and hypocritical times, variously fêted as the new saviour of the coming generation of Roman artists and vilified as a dissolute sinner who used prostitutes as the models for saints. His output while he lived in Rome—from 1592 until he fled a sentence of death for murder in 1606—was prolific but is in part uncharted. Like many of his colleagues and rivals, he veered between pious works commissioned by the Church and smaller, often more daring, canvases paid for by private collectors seeking something for their galleries and intimate chambers, where visitors were allowed only by invitation.

The reputation of Caravaggio today stands, to a great extent, upon his religious paintings, some of which, such as *The Martyrdom of Saint Matthew* (San Luigi dei Francesi, Rome), *The Beheading of Saint John the Baptist* (Oratory of the Co-cathedral of Saint John, Valletta, Malta), and *The Crucifixion of Saint Peter* (Santa Maria del Popolo, Rome), remain on the very walls for which they were first painted. But the artist accepted private commissions as well. There is no doubt that he embraced a wider range of work when the money and the job interested him. The poet Giambattista Marino certainly owned a painting entitled *Susannah* by Caravaggio, now lost, which is assumed to have been a rare female nude. Caravaggio was prolific and temperamental, a difficult and violent man, willing to walk away from valuable projects simply because they failed to interest him. At the height of his career he was celebrated as the most famous artist in Rome, and hailed by poets as the defining spirit of a new age of painting. Within the space of a few years, however, he was impoverished, living in simple conditions with a single servant in the alley now known as the Vicolo del Divino Amore.

The Palazzo Malaspina depicted here is entirely fictional, though sprawling palaces similar to it do exist in Rome today. One of the most famous still in original hands is the Palazzo Doria Pamphilj, which contains the canvases mentioned in the book and is, in part, open to the public. A palace more reminiscent of the imaginary home of Franco Malaspina is the Palazzo Altemps in the Piazza San Apollinare. The residence of a powerful cardinal related to the papacy by marriage, this ornate and glorious property is on the edge of the area once known as Ortaccio, a red-light district created by the Vatican to be a zone for the city's prostitutes. In the sixteenth and seventeenth centuries the inns and lodgings of Ortaccio came to be popular with artists and writers, and were the scene of many brawls and arguments, feuds and vendettas.

Long-running enmities were common in this volatile community, and gangs such as the fictional Ekstasists depicted here certainly existed, taking their cue from the real-life knight's handbook written by Domenico Mora, which argued for a violent, arrogant attitude towards others. It was a street fight that cost Caravaggio his career in Rome when, in 1606, he killed Ranuccio Tomassoni close to the Piazza di San Lorenzo in Lucina. The circumstances remain a mystery. Contemporary accounts are coloured by bias and riddled with lacunae, though the popular modern theory that the brawl stemmed from a dispute over a game of tennis is probably a myth. Tomassoni was indeed the *caporione* of his district and closely involved, sometimes intimately, with several of the women Caravaggio knew, among them the notorious Fillide Melandroni.

Alessandro de' Medici ruled Florence briefly from 1532 until his assassination in 1537. It is generally accepted that he was the son of a black kitchen maid named Simonetta and the seventeen-year-old Giulio de' Medici, who was to become Pope Clement VII. His lineage was carefully hidden in most portraits, though his enemies frequently referred to him as *il Moro,* the Moor. Ippolito Malaspina was a real figure and a genuine patron of Caravaggio in Malta; his coat of arms can be seen on the artist's *Saint Jerome,* which remains in the co-cathedral in Valletta, for which Malaspina commissioned it. The Malaspina family was at one time powerful in Tuscan politics; an ancestor of Ippolito receives a mention in both Dante's *Purgatorio* and Boccaccio's *Decameron.* The aristocratic Malaspina dynasty disappeared in the eighteenth century. In the time of the Medici, however, the Malaspina clan had a visible and important presence in Florence. The favourite mistress of Alessandro de' Medici was Taddea Malaspina. The depiction of Alessandro by Pontormo, which is now in the Philadelphia Museum of Art, was originally his gift to her. In turn, she bore Alessandro's only children.

Apart from the canvas of *Evathia* and the imagined lost portrait of the man pretending to be Ippolito Malaspina in Malta, all the paintings mentioned in this book are real and mostly on public view.

DAVID HEWSON

*Rome, Kent, and San Francisco, October 2005–November 2006*

# About the Author

A former staff writer on *The Times,* David Hewson lives in Kent, where he is at work on the eighth Nic Costa crime novel, *The Blue Demon*.

*The Garden of Evil* is the sixth novel in a crime series that began with the acclaimed *A Season for the Dead,* set in Rome and featuring Detective Nic Costa. The seventh novel, *Dante's Numbers,* is available in hardcover from Delacorte Press.

If you enjoyed *The Garden of Evil,*
you won't want to miss any of the thrillers in the
electrifying Nic Costa series. Look for them at your
favorite bookseller.

And don't miss the newest thriller from David
Hewson, coming from Delacorte in April 2009.

DAVID HEWSON

*Dante's*
NUMBERS

A NOVEL